THE SUPERMODEL'S BEST FRIEND

Resort to Love 1

GRETCHEN GALWAY

Eton Field

Chapter 1

This was not in the plan, Lucy thought, staring at the handsome face on her phone. Her fiancé was supposed to be standing by her side, pen in hand, not using video smartphone technology to dump her from another state. *I don't love you enough to let you ruin the plan.*

"You must've known I had some doubts," Dan said, his voice as small as he was.

Lucy looked around the empty living room of the spacious three-bedroom California bungalow with original plank hardwoods and walnut built-ins. "You said you'd kill to have this house," she said, wondering if the real estate agent, laying out the pages for their revised offer on the granite breakfast counter in the kitchen, could hear them.

"It's a great house," he said, sighing. "A perfect house. But now I see that it would just tie us down, drag out the inevitable."

She blinked, not sure what she was hearing. "We've been planning this for almost five years."

He hesitated. "I met someone."

"When? This morning?"

Licking his lips, he said, "Why don't we talk later, after you've had a chance to calm down."

She frowned. "I'm hardly hysterical, Dan."

"Yeah, I noticed."

"You'd like me to be hysterical?"

"Forget it. Of course not. It makes everything easier."

She nodded, belatedly piecing together some clues he'd dropped over the past few months. "Your six-month assignment in Seattle wasn't the opportunity of a lifetime, then."

"Well…"

"Ah. A personal opportunity, you meant."

"I wanted to be sure. For both—for all of us."

"Very considerate of you," she said.

"Damn it, you don't have to be sarcastic."

"You're hardly in a position to tell me what to do. I'm the wounded party here, wouldn't you agree?"

"I think we'll both need some healing."

Lucy dropped the phone to her side and noticed that Robin, the real estate agent, had come up behind her. Her face was pale.

This was really going to screw over the older lady, the two of them walking away from the deal now. Robin needed a sale badly. Typical of Dan to think the world revolved around him.

Lucy lifted the phone. "We'll have to call the mortgage broker."

He jutted out his chin. "I already have."

"You told Inez the mortgage broker before you told me?"

"She kept after me to sign the latest thing. It didn't feel right to string her along anymore—" He stopped and cleared his throat. "Look, you're getting digitized. I think the connection is breaking up…"

"It didn't feel right to string *her* along?"

He sighed. "So much of our lives together is what you wanted. Not me. I felt… superfluous a lot of the time." He

tilted the screen of his laptop so she was staring out the window of his suite at the Extended Stay America. It wasn't supposed to be sunny in Seattle. It looked sunny. She wondered if the new girlfriend was there, listening off-camera. Dan came back into view with a coffee cup at his lips.

In Berkeley, outside the house she wasn't going to have, the sky was as gray as lint. "Our relationship was always shaped by what you wanted. We talked about marriage years ago. I hoped to have my first child before I turned thirty. But you wanted to save up for the house first, so we did, even though that was third on my list."

"You and your lists. That's one thing I've learned from Brittany—how to trust my heart."

"Ah, so she's one of those." She took a deep breath and peered into the phone for a glimpse of her. "What else did the little ho say?"

Dan's mouth dropped open in shock.

"You wanted hysterical. This is my version."

He looked away, then back at the screen, his lips popping up and down like a broken garage door. "Brittany is not—" He shook his head and stared off to the side, made an apologetic face, then jerked his head.

So she had been there. "Thanks for making this such a private moment."

"I can't believe Brittany had to hear *you* call *her* a—a—I can't even say it."

"What? She's been sleeping with my boyfriend. For months, apparently."

"Brittany has nothing to be ashamed of."

"Does she know about me?"

"Of course. She knows everything."

Lucy snorted. Her college advisor would've broken out in a rash to hear her insult a woman for exercising her sexual liberties, but to hell with it. She was under a lot of stress. "Ho."

Dan's eyes went wide as he leaned into his laptop camera. "She is completely innocent. Brittany's not in such a hurry to take her clothes off. Unlike *you*."

Lucy felt an odd snapping inside her, her last grip on reality disengaging from Dan's voice. "We lived together for five years. You think we should have waited until we were, what, forty?"

"It's not how long we waited, it's how *often* you wanted it. And how much you wanted to do it. I'm a man, Lucy, and I didn't need half as much sex as you did." Then he ran his hand over his eyes and said, "I'm sorry. I never intended to talk to you about this."

Her throat suddenly felt tight. She realized Robin the real estate agent was hanging on every word. "Did you talk to her about this? Brittany?"

His sheepish look grew sheepier; he leaned away from the camera. Faintly, she heard him say, "That's how we… how we knew we were perfect for each other. She was avoiding her boyfriend, and I… I was taking a break, too."

"And where was this? Her convent?"

"Lucy," Dan said, shaking his head, looking so *disappointed* in her.

Humiliation didn't feel right, so she tapped into the rage, breathed it like oxygen. "I'm just trying to get the full picture here. I deserve to know the details."

"Information isn't knowledge, Lucy," Dan said. "Knowing everything doesn't make you wise."

"And having a penis doesn't make you a man," Lucy said.

Robin snorted and patted her hard on the back. Lucy closed her eyes. *He didn't like having sex with me*, she thought. It's not like she had a he-harem of previous boyfriends to call up for rebuttals. She was thirty-four, but she'd started late.

Damn. It took him five years to propose. She didn't have another eight to work on someone new. There were houses to buy, retirement accounts to fund, ovaries to harvest.

She frowned at him. "You've really messed up my plans."

"Sometimes I think that's all I was to you, Lucy. Just part of your plans." He leaned back and put his hand over his heart. "I've learned that I need a partner who acts without analyzing everything to death. Someone more flexible."

Lucy glanced at Robin, but it was far too late for any privacy. Holding the phone up to her mouth, she said, enunciating each word, "One of my plans was for decent sex. I was flexible about giving up on that."

She drew back to see his reaction, but the window had gone black.

Robin peered over her shoulder. "He hung up?"

Teeth clenched, Lucy shoved her phone in her bag. "He never could handle a fight."

"Or much of anything, from the sound of it."

Lucy looked at her.

"Sorry," Robin said.

"It's true." Lucy thought of what he said—*unlike you*—and crossed her arms over her chest. She didn't know what to say. She was angry and embarrassed. Too upset to think clearly, an unfamiliar experience for her.

Robin touched her shoulder lightly. "Maybe you can explain to Inez—"

"No. Half the income now—less than half, since his big wanking Y chromosome gets him a higher salary. There's no way I can afford it now." She closed her eyes. *He didn't need sex half as much as you did.* An old pain flared to life, like bumping a bruise you didn't know you had.

"I'm sorry," Robin said, moving away into the kitchen to give her some space.

Lucy leaned against the window and stared out blindly at the overcast sky. To her annoyance, her heart beat too fast and her hands shook.

Just like that, he'd ended eight years together. Over the *phone*.

She needed another few minutes to calm herself down before she could follow Robin into the kitchen.

"I'm really sorry," Lucy finally said to her, putting her hands on the counter next to the now-useless paperwork. All that personal information, numbers and accounts and addresses. She'd have to make sure every page was shredded.

Such a waste of… everything.

"Oh, honey," Robin said, reaching out to squeeze her hand.

"I know how much you needed this sale." Robin's ex-husband was eager to see her fail at her new life away from him.

"Not *your* fault." Robin swept the pages together on the counter, her hands heavily veined, the long fingernails painted pale pink. Every time Lucy had seen her, she'd been wearing the same black pantsuit—high-quality but at least a decade old.

Lucy took a deep breath. "I just want you to know, if Dan calls you back, wanting to buy it without me, go ahead and do it."

"No! I could never—"

"Any other agent would. You should too. You found this place before it was listed, you should get the commission."

"Do you think he'd do that? Just go buy the house without you? After what he did to you?"

Two weeks earlier, the moment he'd heard about the house, even though it was after midnight, he'd insisted they get in the car and do a drive-by. They'd been waiting at the door at eight the next morning for the broker's tour. With their pre-approval loan package. He made an online photo album of the pictures he took, emailed them to everyone he knew.

"I've never seen him so excited about anything in his life.

Yes, if the nun is willing"—Lucy snorted—"and even if she isn't. Yes, I think he'll contact you about buying it alone."

"Yes, but..." Robin shook her head. "It's so heartless of him."

"Apparently he does have a heart." Looking at her phone to check the time, Lucy sighed. "What a surprise."

EVEN AMONG ADULTS, Miles was used to looking over people's heads. Coaching his kindergarten volleyball clinic, he was a California redwood in a patch of sorrel. An ent among hobbits. A frickin' giant.

Man, he loved Saturday mornings.

"Got it!" A five-year-old girl with long black hair ran right under the net (without having to duck) and plowed into him. Before he could react, she bounced off his legs and fell to the gym floor, her glittering purple Twinkle Toes sneakers up in the air. The white volleyball she'd been chasing rolled into the cluster of kids behind him.

Miles bent down and offered a hand. "Way to go after the ball, Caitlin!" He helped her up and guided her back to her side of the court. "Next time you gotta stay on your side, okay sport? But way to move those feet."

Grinning, he looked over into the stands to see if Felicia was enjoying the game, but her glossy blond head was bent over her iPhone. He shrugged it off and got the kids to rotate positions for the next serve. Or roll, since the little ones couldn't usually get it over the net.

"Everett, your serve, sport. Get closer to the net, that's it." Everett swung his arm like Tiger Woods at tee-off; the ball slipped out of his fingers and bounced past the stationary feet of three small children frozen in the ready-squat position. Miles had another ball ready in his hand and tossed it over.

"Here you go, Everett. Now try again from right up here, dude. That's a lot of power you've got in that swing."

Everett stepped forward, swung, and the ball tripped and rolled over the top of the net into Caitlin's waiting arms.

Miles clapped. "Way to pay attention, Caitlin!" Beaming, Caitlin hugged the ball to her chest. "Next time you go ahead and swing your arms. No need to hold on to it."

After another five minutes attempting a game, Miles called a water break, sending off a dozen squealing kids to the fountain or to their parents. Miles strode over to Felicia, who was flinching at the noise and wore a skin-tight black and red track-suit that showed off her long, lean body. Though she liked to meet him in Berkeley on Saturday mornings, she usually went for a run instead of sitting around the clubhouse.

"Morning, honey," he said, stealing the Starbucks cup from her hand and taking a sip. "Didn't expect you until ten."

She frowned. "I'd rather you let me buy you one of your own."

He swallowed another mouthful of coffee, handed the cup back to her. "I only wanted a sip."

"You always say that."

He leaned down to her ear, lightly touched her thigh. "Afraid of getting my germs?"

Her leg jerked away and he drew back to study her face. She looked cool and put-together, her straight hair sleek along the sides of her narrow face, her soft brown eyes carefully made up with mascara and something faintly shimmery. She must have skipped her run altogether, not just finished early.

"What's the matter?" he asked.

"Nothing."

Stifling his annoyance, he scanned the gym for aimless balls and children just as his watch beeped. "Got to get back."

"Miles, we have to talk."

The kids were starting to go wild. They liked to run up and

down the bleachers to make them rattle, usually knocking over the adults' assorted coffee containers in the process. "Sure, soon as I'm done here." He jumped down and jogged over to the net, calling the kids back for the second half hour of almost-volleyball.

Arms folded over her chest, Felicia scowled at him. The coffee cup sat abandoned at her feet.

He shook off his dread and got back to work. He only had to remind Caitlin six times to stop running under the net, which was progress, and by the time they were in the end-of-clinic huddle for a go-team shout, he'd almost forgotten his angry girlfriend was watching.

No, not watching. Back to her phone.

The kids scattered to their parents and grandparents and he went around the gym to collect the stray balls. Fourth through sixth grade boys' basketball was at noon, but he had Ronnie coaching that group. He was off until Monday morning, just like corporate types, which was probably what was annoying Felicia again—how he wasn't one.

When the last ball was locked up and the net put away, Miles stood in the middle of the gym with his hands on his hips and regarded the classic profile of the brooding blonde staring at the neon exit sign.

Marriage. Another birthday had come and gone; she was still single; it was all his fault.

He climbed up the bleachers two at a time to reach her. He sat down beside her and didn't touch the coffee, though he was dying for it. "I'll marry you this weekend," he said, kissing her sweet-smelling hair, "if you agree to move into my place." She hated his two-bedroom condo in the Mission District of San Francisco, calling the neighborhood a ghetto. He'd sunk all his savings and years of sweat equity into it and really didn't want to give it up. He knew she'd learn to love it if she gave it a chance.

She twisted around, tilting her head back to look down her nose at him. "Excuse me?"

He raised his eyebrows. Managed a grin. "Kidding?"

She stood up and he had to lurch forward to grab the Starbucks cup before it tipped over. He got tired of mopping up spilled coffee under his bleachers.

"I can't stand talking to you here." She tromped down the stairs to the floor. "You're so childish."

He didn't get up. "What's your problem now?"

"Oh, *now*. As if I'm the one."

"Aren't you?"

She closed her eyes and shook her head at the ceiling. "I should have waited until we got back to the city, but I thought it might be easier for you here. See? I'm still putting you first, thinking of your needs, ignoring what would be best for me." She pointed at her chest, drawing his attention to the swell of her breasts, the shadow of her erect nipples under the thin jacket. She moved her pointer finger higher, to her face. "Up here, buddy. This is me, not my tits."

He got up, jumped down to the floor to close the doors and drop her coffee in the trash. The last thing his club needed was some paranoid Berkeley mother walking in on an intimate conversation. And Felicia could go from G to Mature Audiences Only in a matter of seconds—one of the things he liked about her. "You're right. This isn't the place," he said.

"Fine. I'll meet you at your hovel. I drove over."

He moved to stand in front of the door, his six-five, two-hundred-forty frame easily blocking her exit. "No. You started this, let's finish it."

She glared up at him, hands on her hips. "Yes, let's."

He waited, but she kept fuming in silence, and he felt the anger seep out of him. He wasn't the one who was pissed off, after all. He was having a perfectly nice day. And it probably was a mistake to joke about getting married. "What is it, Felicia?" He softened his expression and stepped toward her. "Let's grab breakfast somewhere. I'll buy you another coffee. Promise I won't touch it."

To his horror, the tough, independent woman he was starting to think about maybe someday spending the rest of his life with began to cry. Her glossy lower lip trembling, her forehead wrinkling in pain, she sank to the floor.

For a long, stunned moment, all he could do was stare at her hunched over with her face in her hands. What was wrong with her? In all their three years together, the only time he'd seen her cry was during a sad movie or after too many glasses of wine.

"Have you been drinking?"

With a screech, she reached forward and pounded him on the shins. "You big oaf! Of course I haven't been drinking! But if I married you I'd have to!"

Well, that wasn't what he expected to hear. He went over to the bottom seat of the bleachers and sat down. "This isn't about the coffee, is it?"

She buried her face in her hands and rocked back and forth.

"Is there anything I can do?"

She shook her head but didn't look up.

"I'll just wait here, then, until you can talk."

Her head popped up, her eyes wide with rage. "That's all you can say?"

"What should I say?"

She rolled her eyes in disgust, swiped away her tears with her sleeve. "Forget it." She got to her feet. "I should know better than to expect you to be serious."

"Felicia…"

"No, it's hopeless. You're never serious."

"I'm at work, Felicia."

"Work! You call this work?" She flung her hand out dismissively. "Come to the firm sometime, I'll show you work."

He stood up. "That's what's bothering you again? My job?"

She sniffed, walked to the exit. "No," she said sadly, shoving the door open. "You could change your job."

Miles looked around the gym one more time before flicking off the lights and following her into the clubhouse lounge. Past the foosball table, through the glass window of their tiny office, he could see the back of Ronnie's shiny head as he bent over the desk. Felicia circled the pool table, dragging her fingers along the felt. He flinched, having intimate knowledge of just how sharp her nails were.

The lounge was empty now but it would be filled with eleven-year-old boys in about thirty minutes. Whatever she wanted to hash out, it'd better be quick.

He bent over and picked up a ping-pong ball. "So, not just my job. What else?"

"This isn't going to work."

"Fine. We'll talk on the way home. I'll tell Ronnie—"

"No, I mean us." She scowled at him through her tears. "I can't marry you, Miles."

Whatever he'd expected her to say, that hadn't been it. She'd been nagging him to get married for... ever. "All right, we won't." He placed the ping-pong ball on the edge of the pool table. "I was just kidding about eloping anyway."

Her rage flared again. "See? Oh my God! I can't believe you!"

"What's the matter with me?"

"That's what I want to know!" She lowered her voice, slackened her jaw, and slurred her words. "'I was just *kidding* about eloping. What's the *problem*?'"

He picked up the ball and squeezed it in his fist. "That's a great impersonation of me, Felicia. You must have spent a long time practicing that."

"You knew from the start I wanted a family. You *knew* that."

"And you knew I was afraid of screwing one up. I didn't have the rosy home life you did. Of course I'm more cautious."

"But three *years*, Miles? I'm going to be thirty-three this month. When I was twenty-nine, I thought I had time to wait for you. But now…"

"You'd risk having children without knowing for sure we'd last? You refused to move in with me——"

"Yes! And you refused to move in with me!"

"You have a studio apartment in Pacific Heights. I barely fit in the door."

"Which is why I wanted to look for another—oh, forget it!" She threw her hands up. "I was stupid for thinking a nice guy who seemed to care about kids would be in a hurry to have some of his own."

"'Seem' to care?" The ping-pong ball in his palm was now a curved lump of broken plastic. He took a deep breath and studied the frayed felt of his clubhouse's fourth-hand pool table. "I see so many kids whose parents should've waited. Who divorced, or never got married, or work all the time. I can't be that kind of parent. I promised myself——"

She made a rude noise. "Excuses, excuses. You like the kids here because they grow up and move on. You don't really want to commit to anybody. Not them, not me. You're immature. Emotionally stunted. Willfully obtuse."

He squeezed the broken plastic harder, but he kept his voice soft. "Gee, if that's true, why were you so eager to marry me?"

She let out a scream through gritted teeth and jammed her hand into the pool table's pockets as though looking for something to hurl at him. Luckily the balls were locked up in the office with a sign-out sheet.

"Don't you smirk at me, you giant idiot!" She snatched up

an empty Dr. Pepper bottle out of the recycling bin and hurled it at his head.

He crossed his arms and let it bounce off his shoulder. He was starting to get seriously pissed.

She hurled another one, a can of Red Bull, and he had to turn his head so it only clipped him. This enraged her, like he knew it would, and she reached into the bin with both hands and started throwing wildly until Ronnie opened the office door.

"Dude, you going to clean that up when she's done?"

Without taking his eyes off of Felicia, Miles said, "I'll handle it."

Their manly conversation seemed to pierce the last of her temper. She sank to a striped yellow couch, its stuffing seeping out of the cushions, and started sobbing again.

If he hadn't been so angry he would have gone over to touch her, try to soothe her, but he wasn't a saint. He held himself still, watching her, feeling his heart pound in his chest and finding some comfort in the fact that he wasn't driving to Nevada this weekend.

He shoved the broken ping-pong ball into his pocket, vaguely aware of pain in his palm. "So, this is the end of everything between us?"

Swiping her hair out of her face, she got up and marched out of the building without looking at him again. He watched her tight ass swing out of sight. A minute later he doubled over the surface of the pool table to ease his throbbing skull.

Maybe she was right. He hadn't really let her in, hadn't tried hard enough. Three years was a long time, long enough that he should be feeling more than relief—

But damn, she'd really confirmed his worst fears. He'd been stupid to even consider marriage, however theoretical that consideration had been. The only happy marriages he'd ever seen were on TV. His father had been married four times,

and not once to his own mother. And his current stepmother…
His thoughts skated away from Heather in disgust.

No, he didn't have a clue about women or happily ever after. He was a product of his genes and his environment, nature and nurture, and he wouldn't forget it.

Thank God he'd found out in time.

He stood up, wiped some Dr. Pepper off his jaw, and began cleaning up the mess.

Chapter 2

"I never liked him," Fawn told Lucy in the middle of their Sunday morning water aerobics class.

Lucy kicked her right leg behind her and smiled at her best friend. The water was chest-high, just enough to support her breasts while she jogged up and down the lanes with the dozen other women in the pool.

"Yes, you did." Following the instructor's lead, Lucy leapt out of the water as though she was shooting hoops, took a deep breath, jumped again. "You thought he was hot."

Six feet tall, Fawn could jump high enough to flash the bikini line she'd displayed on the pages of *Sport's Illustrated* when she was nineteen. The other women, some in their eighties and barely able to raise their arms above the surface, watched her with awe and affection. "I still didn't like him."

"You could've said something."

Fawn snorted. "As if you would've listened."

Lucy started to protest then caught the look in Fawn's eye. She turned and jogged after her neighbor, a sixty-something woman in a red tankini with biceps like Michelle Obama. "Well, I wish I would have."

The class began punching the air over their heads again and Lucy and Fawn joined them. They were younger than most of the other women by several decades, but they liked the plus-sized instructor and the friendly atmosphere.

"That's okay, Lucy. Nobody can take advice about their love life. Look at me, do I ever listen to you?"

"You dumped Craig McPherson in seventh grade when I told you he'd called me Little Orphan Annie." Lucy's hair was bobbed, curly, and on the reddish side, so it wasn't the first time she'd heard that name.

"That wasn't advice, that was information."

Lucy kicked at the water—one, two, one, two—like a slow, buoyant chorus girl. "Well, I wish you'd had information for me about Dan early on. I feel like I've wasted eight years of my life. Who knew he was sappy and impulsive? Would you have ever guessed?"

"No way. He was about as sappy and impulsive as you are."

"Exactly! At least, he seemed to be." Lucy punched the water. "He has a calendar with appointments extending ten years into the future. Mine only goes two."

"And he really loved that house."

Lucy snorted. Obviously, there had been some problems between her and Dan she hadn't been willing to acknowledge. "Nevertheless, he's not willing to marry me to get it."

"I didn't mean it that way. Obviously, I thought he loved you too. I hoped he did, anyway."

"I don't. It would make me think even less of him to think he could do that to somebody he cared about."

Fawn floated closer. "I'm so sorry."

"Pffft. The main problem here is biological." She waited for a buoyant old lady in a daisy swim cap to jog past. "Once I turn thirty-five, my womb is pretty much elderly. Getting through a pregnancy brings on more interventions. I hear it all the time from women at work."

"Elderly! You're in your early thirties!"

Lucy grabbed Fawn's slender arm and pulled her over to the edge of the pool. "Quiet, please. I was speaking from a gynecological perspective."

"Your hoo-ha isn't elderly either. I'm sure it's lovely."

Lucy snorted into the water. "Thanks. Right back at you."

"You've got plenty of time to have children. We both do."

"You do. You've got your sperm donor all lined up. Mine just shacked up with a nun named Brittany."

Fawn wiped wet hair out of her eyes. "Don't call Huntley that, please. He's sensitive about being objectified."

"He can't hear me unless his servants swim at the Berkeley Y," Lucy said. "Besides, if he's that touchy he should be in therapy. Hell, with his family's loot he could afford a full-time shrink." She grinned. "Dr. Minion."

"It's not all in his head. Women have been after his money his whole life. It's important that he knows I'm not like that."

"I didn't say you wanted his money, just his DNA."

"It's all the same to some women."

Lucy made a rude noise. "I don't know any women like that. Sounds like sexist bullshit."

"They're really out there. Women are always throwing themselves at him because he's rich, just like men chase me because I'm a model." Fawn hugged her arms to her chest, looking chilled. "It's horrible the way people use each other."

"That's life. Everybody uses someone else in one way or another. We're just biological organisms, dependent upon one another, mortal and insignificant." Lucy rested her arms on the edge and let her legs float up behind her. "No point getting upset about it."

Fawn braced her hands on the edge of the pool and lifted herself with effortless grace. "Either you're lying to yourself or you didn't love him." She got to her feet and walked to the spa.

Lucy watched her long-legged runway stride for a moment,

unhappy with her accusation but not entirely disagreeing with it. She knew her feelings for Dan had been, well, somewhat tepid.

But her feelings for the life they almost had together, the family they'd planned, ran deep and fierce. Her relationship with Dan had been—or she thought it had been—based on respect, friendship, and psychological compatibility. It should've been just fine for living together, buying a house, raising children, growing older together.

But sexual compatibility was more important than she had realized. She'd ignored the fatal flaw in her relationship with Dan, their boring sex life, thinking it was just a small negative in her calculations of their total compatibility—like, say, five percent. Nothing close to a deal-breaker. And really, what did *he* have to complain about? He got more than he wanted, poor baby. Then had the nerve to feel sorry for himself and find solace elsewhere.

Lucy really should've asked Fawn what she'd thought of him a long time ago, saved herself a lot of wasted time, effort, and embarrassment.

She crawled out of the pool and staggered to her feet. She needed to find someone new. Soon. Given that her child-bearing years were limited, and she admitted that biological drive was mighty strong, she might have to settle for a man who was eighty percent compatible, or even seventy-five. If they were motivated and mature, that was more than enough to live together in peace for a few decades.

A few? Not even. Just until the children were in college, though if they wanted help paying for graduate school, it would help if their parents weren't estranged. Surely there was a man out there who was as practical as she was.

She just needed to find one before her "lovely hoo-ha" was as old as her fellow water aerobics classmates.

Slipping into her Old Navy flip-flops, Lucy wrapped a

small white towel around her hips and glanced over at the spa, noticing her two other best friends were there with Fawn. They kept glancing over at her. Betty and Krista only came into the pool to recover from their Flirty Girl Fitness class. Putting on a one-piece black Speedo was flirty enough for Lucy.

She joined them with a sharp look at Fawn, noticing that their conversation came to a halt when she slipped into the water.

"Fawn told us everything," Betty said, her plump arms stretched out to either side. She wore a skimpy lime-green bikini in the exact same color as the streaks of color in her chin-length bob. "Sucks to be you."

Krista, who was sitting rigidly upright so the water didn't touch her hearing aids, reached forward and pinched Betty's arm. "Don't be that way."

"Yow!" Betty glared at Krista. "What the hell!"

Krista scooted away from Betty's under-the-surface kicking, her white halter swimsuit exaggerating her broad, light brown shoulders. "Show a little sensitivity, Betty Hsu."

Stepping into the spa next to Fawn, Lucy gasped at the thrill of the hot water and sank down to the seat. "She said the same thing when I told her I was marrying him."

"Show some sensitivity?" Fawn asked.

"No. 'Sucks to be you.'"

Eyes twinkling, Betty shook her head. "Except then I really meant it. I never did like him."

"Neither did I," Krista said.

Lucy sighed with feeling. "I really could've used this information earlier."

Fawn caught the others' skeptical gaze. "As if she would have listened."

"If you'd all said it, I might have. I might not have done anything differently, but I always want to have as much information as possible when I'm making decisions, especially major ones."

Fawn, Betty, and Krista laughed, avoiding her eyes.

"What?" Lucy demanded.

Fawn put an arm around her. "You wouldn't have considered my stupid little opinion to be information. More like—what did you call it when I told you my multivitamin was totally making me have more energy?"

Lucy sank a few inches into the water. "Confirmation bias."

Betty nodded, pointing at her. "Like when I told her that hairdo made her look like a middle-aged man and she said that was just because I knew she'd had it done at QuickieSnip. As though its utter horror had no objective reality."

"So says the Chinese girl with green hair," Krista said.

"As if the Hippie of Color would ever go to QuickieSnip," Betty replied.

Krista, who had one German and one African American parent, patted the halo of dark curls she'd pulled up with a tie-dyed bandanna. "It's beside the point. People don't listen to trash about their significant other. You love who you love, no matter how stupid."

Lucy sighed. "You still should have told me how you felt. You're my best friends and you've known me forever. I don't have a mom or a sister or whatever to tell me, so I rely on you guys." Her father, an associate professor at Berkeley, was way too self-absorbed to think she might need anything from him. What little social skills he had were exhausted with his new wife.

Fawn pulled her closer and squeezed. "I'll remind you of that next time you're dating a loser."

"*I* never hid how I felt about him," Betty said.

"Yeah, but you're gay," Lucy pointed out.

Betty rolled her eyes. "That is so prejudiced. I can love

men." She jerked her thumb in Fawn's direction. "I love Huntley."

"He bought her an island for her birthday," Lucy said.

Betty lifted her chin. "I loved him before that."

Fawn sighed. "Me, too."

The three mortals turned their attention to the super-model. "So, you set a date yet?" Betty asked.

"Let's not talk about my life today. Lucy's having a crisis," Fawn said.

Lucy pushed Fawn's narrow hips aside and stole the best jet. "Nope. Not anymore. No thanks to any of my *friends*."

Krista, staring at Fawn, had moved on. "It's like a movie. Everything's happening so fast. I mean, to propose after only two months!"

"Good thing he accepted," Lucy said.

Fawn's sharp fingernails poked her Lycra-clad ribs. "We're so happy we're having a fabulous destination wedding. As soon as all of you can take a week off at the same time."

Krista adjusted a hearing aid. "A week? To get married? Is that some East Coast blue-blood thing?"

"As soon as gay people start creeping in on the action, straight people go crazy," Betty said.

"There's no way I can take a whole week off, Fawn," Lucy said. "I'd never be able to catch up on the paperwork when I got back." She was a process analyst for a biotech company, and the labs worked 24/7.

Fawn sat up tall and gave them the haughty stare she used for couture. "This will be the only time in our lives that I know the three of you will let me cover all the expenses for a real vacation. Lucy's idea of getting away is playing poker in some dive in Silicon Valley—"

"Those guys down there are fucking brilliant. Some of them—"

Fawn slapped her bony hand over Lucy's mouth. "And Krista never takes any time off because she's a workaholic who lets evil, stupid people walk all over her."

"I happen to like my job."

"And finally, Betty," Fawn continued. "You've put every dime you make in some stupid bank account that you probably plan on giving to your parents, even though they never wanted you to be the awesome, successful blogger you have grown up to be, not to mention a gay one."

"I haven't given it to them *yet*," Betty said quietly. "They have a few decades to evolve."

"In conclusion, the three of you are going to take an all-expense-paid vacation for an entire week, exact date to be determined, culminating with the ceremony uniting me and Huntley Bernard Sterling III in holy matrimony."

They stared at her and let the bubbles rise up around their nearly naked bodies while her declaration sunk in. The determination in Fawn's voice was obvious and Lucy, for one, was rather mesmerized by the words "all-expense-paid."

"What kind of vacation spot are we talking here?" Lucy asked. "Or does he get to choose that?"

"Your island sounds pretty cool," Betty said.

Fawn leaned back into the steaming water and stretched out her arms, a smile growing on her face. "My mom won't get on an airplane, so it has to be within driving distance. I'm looking at an eco-resort in Mendocino that specializes in restorative, unpretentious, transformative ceremonies. It would be totally relaxing, spiritual, rejuvenating, wonderful." She glanced around. "What do you think?"

They saw the desperate eagerness on Fawn's face. None of them was evil enough to disappoint her. "It sounds wonderful, Fawn," Krista said. "Any time between the second week of June and the third week of August is great for me."

"Is there wireless there?" Betty asked. "Because if so, I could stay longer. Like, a few months if you need me. A year, if necessary." She grinned, twisting the stud in her lip between her thumb and forefinger.

Fawn turned to Lucy. "Well?"

She did like the idea of free, that was true. And Mendocino was beautiful—if the pot growers didn't shoot you. Lucy imagined what their week-long wedding would be like. Huge, probably, given how many people they knew. Huntley was a sociable guy in his thirties with a rich, powerful family and tons of connections. Fawn had friends all over the world.

It would be a buffet of eligible partners she might never have access to again. But while a week was a long time to be at a wedding, it wasn't a lot of time to pick out a spouse. Not enough time to talk to each one, get a sense of temperament, of goals. And, as her friends had pointed out, her own judgment in men was flawed.

The Erasure song suddenly stopped blaring on the other side of the pool; the water aerobics class was finishing, the other women climbing out on the ladder and making their way to the spa.

Lucy turned to Fawn. "I'll do it on one condition."

"You'll have to wear the bridesmaid dress I pick out for the ceremony. That's non-negotiable."

"I suppose I can live with that. It might even help. You see —" Lucy bit her lip and looked into Fawn's shining, heat-flushed face. "You've convinced me that I misjudged Dan. For a really long time. And since I didn't really date a lot of guys before him—"

Fawn snorted. "I was about to set you up with Betty."

"Please," Betty said. "One bad haircut doesn't make her a lesbian."

Her friends doubled over laughing but Lucy couldn't stop now. She put a hand on Fawn's arm and squeezed. "Since I didn't date much, and you know me better than anyone else in the world"—she took a deep breath—"I want *you* to pick out the next one. My new guy."

Laughter fading to smiles, her friends looked at each other.

"And whoever he is," Lucy went on, "I'll marry him."

Chapter 3

The last week of July, when the rest of the country wore tank tops or sweltered in business clothes, when the national media ran daily news features on how to stay cool and which sunscreens lived up to their SPF claims, San Franciscans zipped up their North Face parkas and laughed at the teeth-chattering, shorts-wearing tourists standing in line for the cable cars.

It was freezing. The sun hadn't pierced the ceiling of fog since Memorial Day, and though he loved the cold nights for sleeping, Miles was starting to resent the lack of vitamin D.

Riding his motorcycle over to Berkeley to his clubhouse brought a little relief; the East Bay had sun in the afternoons, though the wind was fierce, and only teenage girls wore summer clothes, because when else could they wear them? But a little sun was better than nothing and Miles was glad he'd invited Huntley to meet him at work instead of in the city.

Since Felicia had dumped him, Miles had become a little defensive about his humble lifestyle. Huntley had earned more from investments by his first birthday than Miles would earn in a lifetime. Maybe his rich best friend would agree with his ex that a two-bedroom condo in the Mission was unsuitable for a thirty-four-year-old man who'd once attended Stanford.

Even if that attendance had been rather brief.

No, better to meet him at the clubhouse, his pride and joy, something he really cared about.

And it would give Miles the opportunity to hit him up for a donation. While he would never ask for anything for himself, he'd happily prostrate himself to beg for his kids. Not as if Huntley would miss a million bucks. Hell, he probably had that much in change under the seats of his Porsche.

Miles parked his bike in the narrow spot he'd had painted just for him, right at the front door of the small yellow cinder-block building in a semi-industrial neighborhood near the bay. Lots of his kids lived in the neighborhood, though many got a ride from all over Berkeley and Emeryville, Albany and El Cerrito—kids with protective parents who wouldn't let them play outside, kids with parents who worked late, or kids without anyone at all. The schools sent home flyers, the word got out, and they came.

The Porsche Huntley kept in the Bay Area (one in every port) was already there, parked in the red with a man—not Huntley—in the passenger seat staring at his phone. Only a rich guy would have a chauffeur who rode shotgun. Miles tucked the helmet under his arm and strode into the clubhouse, rehearsing his speech about self-esteem and physical fitness, male role models and the devastating effect of the recession on charity coffers, but before he could say anything, Huntley jumped out from behind the door and dumped a bucket of ping-pong balls on his head.

"Heads up, coach!" his friend cried, running past the foosball table into the gym.

Miles paused and took a deep breath. Stepping carefully over the rolling balls, he made his way to the office while he unzipped his motorcycle suit.

Ronnie turned from his computer and raised an eyebrow, his forehead wrinkles cascading up his bald head. "What's with your friends throwing things at you?"

Miles pulled open his desk drawer and locked his helmet inside. "I wish I knew."

"He like kids? We could use him on Wednesday night basketball. All that energy."

"Peter Pan has a big trust fund," Miles said, stepping out of the suit. "I don't think he's ever had a job."

"Some woman's going to marry a guy who's never had a job?"

Miles snorted. "She's never had one either. Some kind of model. And once she marries Huntley, she's set for life. Whether she sticks with him or not."

Ronnie leaned back in the old desk chair, arched his back, scratched his generous belly. "Not too romantic, are you buddy? That blonde did a real number on you."

"She did me a favor." Miles hung up his armored suit and slapped Ronnie on the shoulder. "I'm going to see if I can do the same for my best friend."

"Turn him into a bitter old man?"

"Takes one to know one," Miles retorted. He looked out the glass wall of the office into the lounge where Huntley stood, hands on his hips, grinning at him and waiting for retribution. Blond, glossy, and expensive, he looked like a male version of Paris Hilton—not a comparison Huntley relished, but it was made so often he had to put up with it.

He was a numbnuts, but Miles loved him. "I'm going to open his eyes before it's too late."

Ronnie swung back to his computer. "Well, keep me out of it. And clean up when the party's over."

The old grouch worked for him, but Miles said, "Yes, boss," and sauntered out to Huntley. "You looking for trouble, little man?"

Huntley whipped a ping-pong ball at him and ran back into the gym. Miles waited two seconds before he grabbed a basketball and strode after him.

But just as he stepped into the gym, another ball nailed him in the forehead. Miles froze, weighed the heavy basketball in his palm. "You are dead meat, rich boy."

Huntley hooted and ran down the court. "Just try and catch me." He jogged in place and gave him come-hither motions with his fingers.

Miles sighed, bounced the basketball on the ground, regarded the ceiling. "Does your girlfriend know you're a total dipshit?"

"Not yet. That's why I have to marry her before she catches on." He pitched another ping-pong ball and Miles ducked, wishing he hadn't bought them in bulk the week before. He strode toward his friend and dribbled the ball like a sledgehammer.

Eyes dancing, Huntley dropped into a defensive stance. "Hey, I love it when you wear green. You look like the Jolly Green Giant."

"Ho ho ho." Miles lurched forward with the ball as though he was going to attack, then drew back at the last second. Huntley flinched and drew up his hands to his face. Miles grinned, faked him out again. "What's the matter, little fella? Afraid I'm going to *kick your ass*?" He lunged forward, only inches away, but this time Huntley held himself still. So instead of pulling back, Miles bopped him on the head with the ball and laughed at Huntley's shocked expression.

Unfortunately, Huntley had a black belt in judo. He deftly grabbed handfuls of Miles's green sweatshirt and threw him down to the ground.

As pain shot through Miles's hip, he thought he heard one of his shoulders dislocate.

He stared at the metal pipes and exposed ducts of the gym

ceiling and wondered when Huntley would outgrow this annoying compulsion of his to knock him over. It was hardly reasonable, considering how often Miles had protected him when they were growing up. Miles guessed it was like therapy to be able to bring down the biggest guy around after having the shit knocked out of you so often as a kid.

Huntley's face came into view, grinning down at him. "Timber!"

"One of these days I'll actually fight back."

"You're getting old, big guy." He squatted down, lifted Miles's sweatshirt, and poked him in the stomach. "And look at this flab! Soft in the middle."

Miles slapped his hand away and growled, "Watch it, Huntley."

He tsked, jumped out of reach, and pulled his T-shirt up. "Check this out." He slapped his abdomen. "Fuck six-packs. I've got a goddamn case."

"I'm sure the other boys love to look at you, honey." Miles got up to his feet. "The rest of us work for a living."

"Excuses, excuses. I've been working for years. I have a desk and everything."

"How's it going, working for Daddy?"

"It sucks, thank you very much. But it keeps Puritanical assholes like yourself from giving me a hard time." Huntley grinned. "You're just pissed I dropped you again."

"Damn right. One of these days I'm going to break something. It's a long way down for some of us." Eyes on the floor, Miles stepped closer to his friend.

"Poor Jolly," Huntley said, poking him in the belly again.

Which gave Miles the excuse he needed to haul his pretty ass into the air and hold him upside down by the ankles.

"Aiiieeee, shit!" Huntley flailed around like a fish on a hook and tried to grab Miles's legs.

Miles just lifted him higher, shook him a little bit. "You got any change in those pockets? Fancy-ass cell phone?" He shook him harder. "Damn, your sissy jeans are too tight."

Laughing and swearing at the same time, Huntley arched his back and lashed out with his arms. "You can't—last—forever!" he gasped. "Then—you're—toast!"

A large voice boomed from the doorway. "You need help, Mr. Sterling?"

"No—Eric—I'm—fine," Huntley managed.

"If you're sure," the man said, and left.

Shoulders burning, Miles let Huntley down just far enough for his hands to reach the ground, then pushed forward so Huntley was forced to walk on his hands. Miles wheelbarrowed him for ten feet, dropped him, and jumped away, feeling a triumphant grin stretching across his face. "Truce."

Huntley started to get up, then sank back onto the floor. "Oh sure, now it's a truce." But he was smiling as he flopped onto his back.

Glad for the chance to catch his breath, Miles sat down on the ground and gazed at his oldest friend. "Since when do you have a babysitter?"

"Not my idea."

"I guessed that. Your mother's or father's?"

He snorted. "Please. Dad thinks it's ridiculous but lets her get her way. Doesn't like to argue." Still flat on his back, Huntley turned his head to gaze seriously at Miles. "Guess I take after him in some ways."

"What does your model friend think of them?"

Huntley's smile faded. "Don't call her that. It's bad enough I have to put up with that shit from my parents."

"Maybe they see something you don't. They just want the best for you."

"My parents only see what they want to see." Huntley jumped to his feet. "Which is usually money and other people named Sterling."

Wincing at the sudden pain in his shoulder, Miles got up and went over to pick up the basketball. "Maybe they're afraid that's all she sees, too," he said softly.

"No. Not you too."

"How long have you known this girl? Two months?"

"Half a year next week."

"Not even six months. Not nearly enough time. What's the hurry? Fine, she wants to get engaged. Get engaged, then—I know how that is. But couldn't you put things off a bit?" Miles dribbled the ball. "God knows you've got the charm to convince women of anything."

All the playfulness gone, Huntley said, "It was my idea to get married."

"Yours?" Miles made a long shot for the basket, missed. "You sure about that?"

Huntley looked like he wanted to knock him down again. Normally he wouldn't attack when he was angry, but he looked like he wanted to. "Watch it. You want me to choose between you and Fawn and it's no contest." He gave him a hard stare, ran after the ball. "No fucking contest at all."

"None at all. Great." Miles had a sudden flashback to a can of Red Bull hitting him on the forehead. This hurt worse.

"Damn it. I don't mean that. I mean, I do, but—shit. How'd we get in this hole? I came here to ask you to be my best man." He jumped and put the ball through the net.

Best man. Miles shouldn't have been surprised, but he was. Years of living on opposite coasts, wildly different lifestyles—and Miles still hadn't gotten used to the idea of him being engaged. "I haven't even met her yet."

"That's the problem right there. Once you meet her you'll understand." Huntley grinned. "Why do you think I kept her to myself for so long? I know how chicks get one look at you and start thinking about mountain climbing."

"Oh yeah, I'm a real ladies' man."

"Now that I'm pretty sure she loves me, I'm willing to take the risk," Huntley said. "And you're too slow to make any moves in time."

"*Pretty* sure? And you're marrying her?"

"Damn right. Though I'm keeping my parents away from her until the wedding. I'm not an idiot."

Miles shook his head. "I was with Felicia for three years—three—and it turned out we needed every single one of them to find out we weren't compatible. You keep her away from your friends and family, run off to marry her like her daddy's got a shotgun and you're just some poor slob like the rest of us—"

"I am just a poor slob like the rest of you. You were the first to understand that."

"Under the six-pack and the private jet."

"Exactly!" Huntley picked up the basketball and bounced it to him. "Don't let me down now. There's nobody else I'd rather have at my side."

Touched but unconvinced, Miles didn't say anything, just shot a few hoops and worried about his friend. "I'd be honored to be your best man—"

Huntley whooped and ran for the ball. "Excellent!"

"—but you have to promise me to do a prenup. And be real clear with this girl—"

"Her name is Fawn. Use it."

"—be real clear with *Fawn* about the terms of the agreement. Don't let your heart push you into something stupid. Have your mother write the contract herself, see if this—if Fawn—loves you enough to sign on without the hopes of big cash prize at the end."

"Did Felicia do this to you? I'm supposed to be the paranoid one. You didn't even get engaged. Or is this all about your dad again?"

"Will you do it? The prenup?"

Huntley slapped him on the shoulder. "You wasted your leverage, dude. You think my mother would let me have her grandmother's wedding ring without a prenup? The Ballbuster of Connecticut?"

Relieved, Miles nodded. "Of course. Right. Look, I'm sorry to be the practical one here. It's just, you need somebody to look out for you, and ever since my own experience with this I've—"

"Become a sad, bitter loser. I know. Don't piss on my parade."

"I'll piss wherever I want."

Huntley laughed. "Good thing we'll be roughing it for the ceremony. We're going Full Granola—barefoot on the beach, improvisational vows, New Age bullshit. It'll be awesome."

Only half-serious, he said, "Why didn't you say so? I wouldn't miss seeing your mother having to swallow Full Granola for the world."

"Excellent. The wedding is in two weeks."

Miles froze. "Are you shitting me? That's—"

"Any longer than that and my parents will find a way to cause trouble. And by the way, I'll need you for the whole week. It's a vacation thing Fawn has set up."

"A whole week? Right before school starts? There is no way I can get away from the clubhouse on such short notice for so long. I'm sorry, but—"

"I set it up with Ronnie months ago. He'll take over when you're gone. He's bringing in a young guy from the Boys and Girls Club to back him up."

"You little shit. You did this behind my back?" Miles stared at him in wonder. "Months ago? That must have been right after you met."

"I really love her, Miles."

Huh. Miles ran his hand through his hair. "How did you get Ronnie to agree to it?"

Huntley's grin faded a little. "He made me write your club a check for two million dollars."

Miles was only going to ask for one. Slinging an arm over Huntley's shoulder, Miles guided him to the clubhouse lounge, wondering if he was a sentimental fool or a greedy bastard to suddenly feel better about the whole thing.

"Guess now I have to give Ronnie a raise."

THE NARROW, winding drive through the redwoods was making Lucy sick. Between the slow, sideways lurching of the limo on each turn and the quart of champagne in her stomach, Lucy had never been so miserable in her life. She should have gone in the Honda with Krista and Betty. No bubbly in the Civic.

"I can't believe you're not even going to tell me the guy's name," Lucy said, trying to distract herself from the nausea.

Fawn didn't look so great herself. She'd stopped talking about her fantastic Huntley about forty minutes earlier to grip the door handle and stare straight ahead with her lips in an unusually thin, tight line. "If it's meant to be, you'll know it in your heart."

"But I'm going to be eyeing every man remotely my age like—I don't know—like my dad shopping for a new recliner."

Fawn sipped a bottle of water. "Better that than you sitting in the cabin doing paperwork."

"If he doesn't know me, either..." Lucy sank down into the limo's leather seat. "I don't see how this is going to work. Men don't usually... go for me right away. This wasn't our deal."

"We found the perfect guy for you. He'll be at the spa all week. If it's meant to be..."

"Cut it out with this meant-to-be crap. That's why I asked you guys to set me up. To eliminate the guesswork."

"I thought the point was to find a compatible life partner."

"With your help. How do I know you've really found someone for me? What if he's not interested?"

"He will if it's—"

"Don't say it." Lucy closed her eyes. She should have known Fawn would try to inject some touchy-feeliness into it. She sighed. Ah, well, no harm in keeping her eyes open. She'd been a little crazy to ask her friends to interfere, anyway.

She glanced at the GPS screen mounted on the glass behind the driver: estimated arrival time, 9:27. "One more minute."

"I hope I don't look as shitty as I feel," Fawn said. "I'll probably barf on his mother."

"It'll be her first test. Any good mother-in-law would forgive you. A great one would clean it up."

Fawn laughed weakly. "Rosalind Sterling was even richer than Huntley growing up. From what I've heard, she's never had to clean anything in her life."

"Not even her own butt?"

"Stop it. If I laugh, I'll hurl." Fawn got up onto her knees, sticking her head out the open window on her side. "God! It smells so good here!"

Lucy leaned her head out on her side and inhaled the scent of cedar and redwood. July days were long, but it was past nine, and the huge trees blocked the last of the daylight. They'd have to wait until the morning to see what the remote property really looked like. The slicing glow of the headlights lit up lots of trees with ferny undergrowth and not much else. No buildings, no farms, no vineyards, no people.

She felt a bug slap her in the cheek and drew her head back in, frowning at the GPS. 9:28. "We should be there by now."

"I think we are. I saw a little sign back there." Fawn came back into the car looking wind-blown and refreshed, her tangled blond hair flying around her head like a Barbie that had been stuck under the couch cushions for a while. "Oh my

God, I've got to clean myself up." She lurched across the seat to grab her bag, pulled out a square box shaped like a miniature suitcase—chrome and studded, like in a movie about jewel thieves—and popped it open. Shelves of makeup and brushes slid apart under a mirror. Fawn propped it on her lap and got to work while Lucy watched in fascinated disgust.

"Don't," Fawn said without looking over at her. "You have your ways, I have mine."

"I didn't say anything."

"I could hear your thoughts pouring out of your ears, like in a cartoon." Fawn made a face into the mirror and brushed on her mascara. Her large eyes became impossibly enormous, her lips lush and pouty, her skin a delicate porcelain.

The transformation always amazed Lucy. The supermodel of today had never been popular or pretty like some of the other girls while they were in grade school. Fawn was awkward and kind of funny-looking, like Lucy, until that day in seventh grade she'd come to school with some contraband makeup she'd scored from a cousin. Something about her face, with a forehead as big as a man's hand and the wide mouth, made her look like a magazine model as soon as she put makeup on it. Which is where she ended up within a few years.

"I don't suppose you have an extra brush in there," Lucy said. "Mine is packed in the suitcase."

"Sure, here." Fawn flipped open a travel brush that looked like sterling silver. It was engraved—with the initials Fawn would have next week if she changed her name—and had little crystals around the rim.

Lucy peered more closely. Not crystals. *Holy Moses.*

Afraid to touch it, Lucy ignored the treasure Fawn was waving at her and ran her fingers through her short hair, tugged out the tangles. "Never mind, this is fine." Nobody would see her and it was dark. She had plenty of time to doll up for her potential marriage partner tomorrow.

Fawn was smiling at her. "Your hair always looks great. I'm so jealous."

She would have snorted at anyone else, but she knew Fawn meant it. "Thank you," Lucy said. "For what it's worth, I'm grateful to be beautiful with so little effort."

The car slowed to a stop in the middle of a dark clearing; the driver got out and opened Fawn's door. Lucy got out by on the other side by herself and sucked in the fresh, conifer-scented air, happy for the solid gravel under her feet. They were in a parking lot with no buildings in sight, just trees.

"We have to take an electric golf cart to the spa from here," Fawn said, grabbing her arm. "Isn't that cool? It's like going into another world!"

"Or a country club."

"It keeps it pristine. Prehistoric. Totally eco. Back to earth."

Lucy sighed, knowing the cheapest rate at the earthy prehistoric spa was over nine hundred dollars a night. She couldn't imagine what the exclusive use of the complete resort cost for a billionaire's wedding party for a whole week.

A trio of four-seater golf carts appeared out of the dark-ness, their electric motors quietly humming, and three men in white uniforms got out and helped the driver move their luggage. The young men were solemn and polite and said little other than "hello" and "over there." They were more like ushers at a funeral than waitstaff at a wedding. Lucy caught one of the guy's eyes, the oldest one with black plugs in his ear lobes and a Groucho Marx mustache.

"How do you drive around in the dark without hitting anything?" she asked as she climbed into his cart. "Sonar?"

He flashed her a grin, his mustache unfurling like a fan. "Hold on tight."

They thanked everyone and went off into the quiet night, Fawn and Lucy in the back of Groucho's cart, their luggage—and the driver—coming on the other two carts.

Lucy bent around and watched the third cart pull behind them. "Why is the limo driver coming?"

Fawn shrugged. "Making sure we get there okay?"

"Maybe somebody has to sign for you. I bet he has one of those electronic clipboards, like a UPS guy."

Fawn didn't laugh. "Yeah, probably."

The cart bounced over a rut in the dirt road, covering up Lucy's pained groan to think her friend was marrying somebody who would put a tracking number on her, have her in the grasp of his minions at all times.

But she had to admit he had great taste in vacation spots. In spite of the cold and the fog and her limited nighttime view, the Soul of Muir Resort was clearly paradise. Already Lucy was thinking it might be worth a month's salary to come back again. She'd scoffed at the golf carts, but having them slide through the trees so quietly drew her attention to the cathedral canopy above. She never would have noticed it if she'd been in the limo.

Groucho pulled up in front of an unassuming little cabin that blended into the forest. She got out, enjoying the sound of her footsteps, muffled and peaceful, on the damp earth. For the first time that day, she let a genuine sense of peace wash over her.

And then, like an explosion, a thundering motor roared behind them, the sound rising as it grew closer, much too fast. All five of them froze in surprise to stare back into the darkness at the single headlight that flared to life between the trees.

The Groucho staffer pulled out a walkie-talkie. "I'll get Linda out here," he said to one of the other guys, moving to head off the motorcycle in the road.

Annoyed with the disruption of her moment of peace, Lucy looked at Fawn. To her surprise, Fawn was grinning, her hands clasped together near her heart. "Oh, this is awesome! He came!"

"That's your prince?"

Fawn gave her a funny look out of the corner of her eye, her lips pressed together in a smile she couldn't read. "No, it must be Huntley's friend. His best man. He was afraid he wouldn't be here until later."

"Well, the wedding isn't until Saturday."

Fawn exhaled loudly. "We reserved the whole week and want you guys to enjoy it."

Lucy frowned at the man in black leather as he cut the engine and straddled the bike. A mechanical popping continued, echoing into the disturbed peace of the clearing. "I don't think he's supposed to drive that here."

Fawn gave her another look, the kind she gave Lucy in junior high about not wanting to wear blue eyeliner, the one that said *loosen up*. She hurried over to the bike, one hand lifted in a girly wave. "You must be Miles! I'm Fawn! Huntley told me all about you and I'm so happy so see you, he wasn't sure if you'd be here, so I'm really glad—"

Miles held up a gloved finger, shook his helmeted head, and turned away from her. Taking all the time in the world, as though a crowd of people weren't staring at him, he dismounted, put down the kickstand, and straightened.

Chapter 4

*L*ucy took an instinctive step back. The man was
ginormous. She had to tilt her head back to see the
top of him.

He took off his helmet, pulled some neon orange foam out
of his ears, and fixed his gaze on the staffer with the walkie-
talkie. "Excuse me, am I in the right place for the Sterling
wedding?"

He had a deep voice, soft but carrying, and looked just like
the type of guy you'd want to hide behind in battle. His move-
ments were slow and deliberate, graceful, no energy wasted.

Groucho, walkie-talkie at his ear, stepped close to him. "I'm
sorry, sir, but no motorized vehicles are permitted past the
Greeting Lot."

"Oh, I'm sure he just didn't realize," Fawn said, slipping
between them, flashing her trademark smile that, even lit only
by the subtle glow of the cabin's porch light, instantly captured
both men's attention. "You are Miles, right?" she asked,
turning the beam of enchantment directly on him.

"I am," he said, then put his helmet back on, remounted

the bike, and kicked it back to life. Ignoring his best friend's future wife and the rest of them, he started to drive on.

Lucy jogged over and stood in front of the bike. "Hey!"

He waited, then hung his head, lifted it, and killed the engine again. "Yes?" His voice was muffled through the visor.

Lucy pointed at Groucho, who had moved a few feet away to talk on his walkie-talkie, and at Fawn, who was biting her lips and staring at Miles like a kicked puppy. "Did you hear what they said?"

He pushed up the visor and stared at Lucy with rather nice gray eyes. "And who are you?" His gaze slid down to her feet and back up to her face.

She felt the hairs on the back of her neck stand on end. "I'm a guest here, unlike these guys, who are just trying to do their job. If you drive past them they'll get in trouble."

He glanced at the three young men in their white tunics and baggy pants. "I can't park my bike back there."

"I'm sure they can work something out," Fawn said, though her smile was beginning to slip. She would never be happy if her husband's best friend didn't like her, and as far as Lucy was concerned, nobody had any reason not to like Fawn. He'd barely even glanced at her, and everyone glanced at Fawn. Sometimes right before driving into a telephone pole.

"Look, it's been a long drive and my ass is asleep," Miles said. "Please get out of my way."

Lucy stepped closer to the bike. "After you promise—"

Fingers wrapped around Lucy's upper arm, Fawn yanked her away into the darkness and hissed in her ear, "Do you want him to hate me?"

"But—"

"Let the resort people handle it!"

Lucy stopped struggling. She was ten inches shorter than Fawn but twenty pounds heavier; she could have broken free if she'd wanted to, but Fawn had a point. She went with her up a handful of wooden steps to the door of the cabin marked "Ceanothus" in metal script. The doorknob was wrapped with a large blue satin bow, and it opened without a key.

She glanced back at the small crowd around the bike and decided she really should mind her own business. They stepped inside and flicked on the lights, illuminating a cozy interior decorated in creams and blues. A pair of four-poster beds, heavy with pillows in all shapes and sizes, were lined up in parallel. Though Fawn had spent every night with Huntley for months, she wanted to share a cabin with Lucy before the wedding—for appearances and for luck, she'd said.

Looked like she would need all the luck she could get. "I didn't like the way he ignored you," Lucy said, dropping her purse on a loveseat near the front bay window. Someone tapped on the door, and Fawn let in one of the guys who was carrying their bags.

When he left, Fawn said, "It was a hard drive on us, and we were in the limo. Miles was probably feeling even worse."

"You can't get carsick on a motorcycle."

"Lucy—"

"Sorry. Not my business."

"It is your business," Fawn said. "You guys are paired up for the ceremony."

Lucy had a sick feeling. "Don't tell me he's the... the..."

Carrying her makeup case into the bathroom, Fawn paused in the doorway. "The what?"

"You know. The one you're setting me up with."

Fawn's mouth fell open. "*Miles?*" She stared at Lucy. "Do you like men that big?"

"God, no. I just thought you might be tempted. Maid of honor, best man, you know."

Fawn sighed, rolling her eyes. "No, no, no. Can you imagine the two of you trying to get it on? You barely reach his belly button." Laughing, she began unloading her inventory of cosmetics, lotions, brushes, and perfumes. "Can you imagine?"

Lucy smiled, grateful her friend had some sense, and left her to unpack her own things.

But she could imagine.

Oh, yeah.

MILES WATCHED the two women walk away, his eyes following the round, jean-clad bottom of the curly-headed, angry one. She was cute in a miniature tomboy kind of way, but he was too tired and sore to flirt with anyone right now.

He took his helmet off again to rub his eyes. What the hell just happened, anyway? He'd been driving through the woods, trying not to impale his skull on a tree or a deer after the GPS and the lights gave out, thinking that when he'd finally seen the faint glow of moving cars ahead he could find out where he was going.

Then the beautiful blonde and her spunky elf friend accosted him just as his bike started making a sound it wasn't supposed to make, and his back told him what it thought of riding a motorcycle for five hours after playing flag football with prematurely strong (and sadistic) twelve-year-olds all afternoon.

Huntley had told him to drive past the lot and a series of cabins until he came to the main building, but apparently this was not so cool. Typical rich man's son, Huntley, not thinking any rules applied to him and his people.

"Sorry to make trouble," Miles told the guys in the white pajamas, "but I didn't realize I was supposed to stop back there. And my ears are still ringing."

The one with bushy black mustache put down his walkie-talkie and smiled, the officiousness forgotten. "No need, Mr. Girard. Just found out you need a special spot for your wheels."

Ah, no doubt the other person on the walkie-talkie knew how much money was being thrown around here. "Nothing too fancy," Miles said. "Something with a roof would be nice. I have to do a little maintenance."

"No problem. Just follow me in the cart." He held out his hand. "I'm Shawn. Technically my title is Lead Greeter, but everyone calls me Golf Cart Guy."

Miles took his hand. "How about I call you Shawn?"

His face broke out in a toothy grin. "I'd like that, Mister—"

"Miles. Just Miles."

Shawn smiled more widely, eyes darting to the bike. "How fast can it go?"

"A lot faster than I drive it."

"Not into speed?"

"I'm an old man who values his life too much."

Shawn directed the other staffers to deliver the women's luggage into the cabin, then stuck the walkie-talkie on his belt and lowered his voice. "I'm saving up for a Ducati, myself."

"Nice. Lot fancier than my wheels," Miles said.

"No, no, yours are excellent."

"It's pissed at me right now. Needs some TLC." He rubbed his back. So did he.

Within ten minutes, Shawn had his motorcycle parked inside a private garage behind a long, squat building made out of rough timbers, stucco, and tile—a cross between a Spanish mission and a ski lodge. Many of the cabins at the spa appeared to be covered with solar panels; Miles wondered how well that could work in a forest blanketed in fog much of the year. No doubt it looked good on the brochures.

Huntley wasn't expected until early the next morning, so Miles found his own cabin—on foot, his pack on his back—

and slept off as much of his soreness and annoyance as he could.

Which, when he woke up after ten the next morning, wasn't nearly enough.

"Oh my God," he said, rolling to one side, amazed at the soreness all over his body. His legs, his butt, his back, even his arms ached. "I'm getting old," he mumbled, moving his feet off the edge of the organic, hand-made mattress to the bamboo floor. Thirty-four, and he couldn't play pretend football and go for a little ride without falling apart. If Huntley wanted to flip him to the ground today, Miles wouldn't be able to put up much of a fight.

Ignoring the private hot tub out the cabin's back door, he got dressed and walked through the forest to the lodge, willing his body to do his bidding without any coddling. He would enjoy a soak later.

The lodge wasn't arranged like a hotel, but like a school, with a wide open space when you walked in and an office to the side. No front desk, no command center, no focal point of authority, just couches and little tables with bowls of fruit too pretty to be real.

He picked up a geometrically precise pear and took a bite, relieved it was juice, and not wax or plastic, that dribbled down his chin.

"Miles! My man!"

Miles swung around, legs braced for impact. "Huntley the Third." When he was sure he wasn't going to be jumped, he held out his hand. "This place creeps me out."

Huntley pulled him close and slapped his back. "Shut up and enjoy it."

"Is that what you tell your women?"

Looking over his shoulder, Huntley gave him another whack, this one harder. "Keep your jokes to yourself until Saturday, will you? Emotions are flying high."

Miles glanced around the lobby, looking for coffee and finding it on an antique stove near a white slip-covered sofa. "Still can't talk you out of it, I suppose." He poured a cup and sipped, steam rising up into his nostrils, not caring if it burned.

"Wait until you meet her. She's perfect. In absolute terms, not just for me. I haven't even seen her yet this morning. We're in separate cabins for good luck or something—I'm not sure, but who am I to argue?" Huntley poured himself a glass of something that looked like water with leaves floating in it.

"Actually, I met her last night," Miles said.

"You did?" He put his glass down. "Well?"

"She's beautiful, obviously."

Huntley grinned. "See?"

"That's just the problem. I do see."

"I thought we'd settled this."

"I thought you'd come to your senses. She's a model. Of course she looks good. I'm sure she's been *really* nice to you, too." Miles took another scalding sip. "Admit it, Huntley, you're thinking with your dick again. "

Huntley grabbed the mug so fast it spilled the coffee, scalding Miles's hands and dripping on his favorite sneakers.

Looking over his shoulder, his voice rough, Huntley said, "If she hears you say anything like that, *ever*, I'll probably try to kill you, so prepare yourself."

Miles took a step back, found a napkin, and wiped his hands. The edge of his right hand was bright red and throbbing, but it was his own damn fault. He was an idiot. The man was up shit creek in love. "I shouldn't have said that."

Huntley shifted his shoulders uneasily. Miles could see he was trying not to apologize. It had been decades since Huntley idolized him, but the residue of the boy's feelings were there in the grown man. "You're burned," Huntley said.

"My fault. Though I'd probably rather you'd knocked me down instead. After I'd put the cup down."

"Are your shoes okay?" Huntley frowned at the dark stain spreading over Miles's old gray sneakers. Then frowned more deeply when he saw the old gray sneakers more clearly. "What the hell are you wearing on your feet?"

"Don't disrespect my sneakers. Insult to injury." Miles bent down and wiped coffee off the rubber toe, which had the ironic effect of cleaning off some of the grime. "I'm a teacher, Huntley the Third. I can't afford the pretty shoes you rich people wear."

"Stop calling me that."

"Rich?"

Huntley laughed. "No, that's a fact."

"So is your father going to pay—"

"I invited your parents," Huntley said suddenly.

Miles froze in place, feeling the blood drain out of his face. He balled up the soggy napkin in his fist. "What?"

"Actually, it was my father who invited them. I couldn't stop him."

"I assume you mean my father and stepmother." His biological mother died in a car accident when he was three. A few days later, he was dumped on his father, an executive where his mother had worked as a secretary, a man who was already married (to wife number two) with a son. That stepmother was a really nice lady, and she still sent him cards on his birthday, even though that marriage ended soon after. His current stepmother was wife number four.

Huntley squeezed his eyes shut. "Sorry. Yes." He opened them and leveled the baby blues on Miles with genuine agony shining forth. "Maybe they won't come."

Miles looked down at the napkin in his hand. He'd wrung all the liquid out of it, and coffee dripped between his fingers. "He knows you asked me to be your best man."

Huntley hesitated. "Yes."

"Well. That's too bad." Miles threw the napkin across the

floor toward a green bin labeled COMPOST. "I'm really sorry, but you'd better notify your runner-up. Alex is coming, didn't you say?"

Huntley reached out to grab his arm, but Miles was already moving toward the door. "Your father won't be here until Friday," Huntley said, jogging after him, "and I've stuck them in a cabin that the manager promised me is halfway to the Pacific." He dug his fingers into Miles's forearm. "Damn it, Miles! You're my best friend. You have to be here. This is it for me, Miles. Fawn is it."

Miles may have been sore from the ride up, and his back still tweaked at a forty-degree angle, but nothing was going to stop him from getting back on his bike and riding the hell out of there. Except for distant glaring at his half-brother's wedding, he hadn't seen his father in sixteen years. He was going for a few more—like, forever. Forever would do it.

"If I believed in this marriage, Huntley, I might stay. Given she's just another model who's done something special to the little man in your pants—no. Absolutely not."

He flung open the door of the lodge, not surprised, given his luck, to see the beautiful girl in question and her little redheaded friend standing there.

Chapter 5

"Fawn!" Huntley cried, leaping past him and taking the tall blonde in his arms. He spun her around to face Miles. "Help me convince him to stay. He's trying to make a run for it."

The girl smiled at Miles, all gorgeous and toothy.

Huntley stood off to the side looking smug, as though one glance at the genetic miracle of his girlfriend would stop him dead.

"Hello and goodbye." Miles brushed past her and strode into the woods. He'd found a shortcut through the trees that went straight from the lodge to his cabin. Huntley said his father was coming Friday, but that may have been wishful thinking. Alan Girard wouldn't pass up a free week's vacation at an exclusive spa, especially if he could watch his old rival, Huntley's father, bleed a fortune. Even with a prenup, Alan would be rubbing his hands together anticipating an extracted divorce with lots and lots of lingering financial pain.

"Damn it, Miles!" Huntley caught up to him and grabbed his arm. "You're the do-gooder, always trying to save the criminals of tomorrow. How about you lavish a little of it on me?"

"'Criminals of tomorrow.' Nice."

Huntley jogged alongside him over the ferny undergrowth, his blue eyes perking up with hope. "Who else do I have in my life to look out for me like you do?"

"You're a billionaire. Put someone on salary."

"Underlings only tell you what you want to hear, like stop buying so much useless shit, do fifty squats, invest in Google. The important stuff, never."

Miles stopped walking, aware the women behind them were watching. The short spunky one, Lucy, wore all black, setting off the brightness of her hair. Tight jeans, tight sweater, tight leather knee-high boots. Next to Fawn, who wore something girly and transparent in pink, she looked like a redheaded Catwoman.

Blinking away that enticing thought, Miles turned back to Huntley and lowered his voice. "I told you what I thought and you bribed my employee."

"You didn't really mean it. You just have a bad attitude about all marriage right now."

"Do you really want that in a best man? When your parents are fighting you too?"

"You'll back me up. You're too decent not to."

"It's better I go. I won't be polite to my father, your parents will see I'm not happy here—and let's face it, I'm no good at pretending to like people when I don't." Kids he could manage. Adults, not so much. "I've already hurt your bride's feelings."

"You haven't even talked to her. Listen—you agree to give Fawn a chance and I'll keep your father and stepmother away from the wedding."

"How? You'd tell your father to disinvite one of his oldest connections? One with almost as much money as he has?"

Huntley's gaze fell to the ground.

"Thought so," Miles said, the corner of his mouth twitching. "You don't have a lot of practice defying him."

"Are you calling me a coward?"

Sighing, Miles squeezed his shoulder. "You're going ahead with the wedding, aren't you? When even your best friend is giving you a hard time?"

"But that's the exception, that's what you're saying. That I'm the chickenshit." Huntley moved up closer, chest to chest, and stared up at him. "This from a guy who can't even be in the same state as his own father because of something that happened over fifteen years ago. *Almost* happened. You're still running away from one little come-on—"

"Watch it, Huntley."

"Maybe it's not your father you're afraid of. Maybe it's his horny little wife."

Miles's body went rigid. He glanced at the women, still watching them, and let out a long breath. "I'm leaving now," he said, stepping back.

"You don't think you can fight off a woman? Big guy like you?"

"Shut up."

"I could teach you a few defensive moves." Huntley jumped in front of him and grabbed the lapels of his leather jacket. "Come on, we'll go practice in the Yoga Yurt."

"Let go of my jacket." Even though Huntley was holding on to him, he leaned his chest back and kept walking, dragging his friend alongside.

"Oh, *Miles*," Huntley cooed in a high voice, "you're so big and strong, so big and handsome, so big and, oh, so *big*—"

Refusing to laugh, Miles gave him an icy stare and dragged him another step. Really getting into the spirit of things, Huntley lifted his foot and rubbed it up and down his calf through his jeans. "Such big muscles," he chirped, and when his foot went a little too high, Miles grabbed him and flipped him over onto the ground.

Flat on his back, Huntley didn't try to get up. "Then again, she might like it if you got rough. Think it's foreplay." He shifted, trying to roll over, then flinched and gave up. "Whoops. I think I'm hurt."

Miles looked down at him. "Good."

"Tweaked my back. I don't think I can get up." He closed his eyes and grinned. "Here comes the bride," he said, just as Fawn came running up and flung herself onto her knees in front of him.

"Baby, are you okay?" She cupped Huntley's face with her hands, then looked up at Miles in angry confusion. "Why did you attack him?"

"I'll be fine." Huntley smiled into her eyes. "I'm used to Miles beating me up. He's just so big, you know?"

Miles snorted and moved to finish what he'd started when Catwoman jumped in front of him, poking his chest with a pointy fingernail. "I think it's time for you to go."

He looked down at her finger. She couldn't have been much over five feet tall and didn't look very muscular, either—more bunny rabbit than pit bull. Goth bunny. "You going to make me?"

She jabbed him again, this time in the belly. "I'll give it a shot."

Huntley groaned and got into a sitting position with Fawn's help. Pressing his face into her chest, he groaned louder. "I need him to—help get me to the cabin. Then he can—go. I'll ask—Alex—to be my—best man. He's a—nice guy."

Miles looked down at Huntley's petite bodyguard. She had green eyes, as green as the oxalis growing under the redwoods. She acted as if her finger, still pointed at his heart, carried magical powers.

Maybe it did. He found it mesmerizing.

"You're bleeding!" Fawn cried.

Huntley stared at a red smear on his hand. "So I am." He turned an overly mournful gaze up to Miles.

"Oh, for God's sake." Miles gently pushed Lucy's hypnotic finger out of his way and squatted down to his friend. He put an arm around Huntley's ribs and hauled him to his feet, not immune to his genuine gasp of pain. Huntley sagged against him, unable to straighten completely. "Where's your cabin, you big baby?" Miles asked softly.

Fawn put an arm around Huntley's other side, her face twisted with worry. Good thing she was tall. "We'll get you a doctor." Eyes shining, she frowned at Miles over Huntley's golden head. "Be gentle with him."

Huntley grinned, then flinched. "It really—wasn't—his fault," he gasped.

Rather touched by Fawn's attitude, Miles took more of Huntley's weight and wiped a floppy chunk hair out of his eyes with his free hand. "Sorry, buddy. Sometimes I don't know my own strength."

They stumbled down the dirt path until they came to the paved walkway leading away from the lodge. "It's the Live Oak cabin," Huntley said. "Number seven."

"Lucky seven," Miles said.

"Asked for it—on—p-purpose."

Miles caught Fawn's eye and managed a smile. Her concern wasn't faked, that was obvious. "Maybe you are lucky, Huntley." He stopped, nodded at the cabin next to them, and bent his knees. "I'll try to carry him from here. That's cabin four already."

"Thanks, Jolly," Huntley said, rigid in his arms. "Fawn—sweetie—would you tell Eric to get Rita for me?"

"Don't you want a doctor?" Fawn asked.

"No, Rita can massage it out of me. It's just a little tweak." She frowned. "But—"

"Leave Lucy with us. She'll keep an eye on Miles," Huntley said, smiling faintly.

Fawn kissed him tenderly before throwing Miles a warning look and departing.

Sweat building on his forehead, Miles shifted his load and hurried through the trees to the distant cabin. Huntley wasn't very tall, but he was loaded with high-maintenance muscles and weighed more than he'd expected.

"I'm getting old," Miles muttered, staggering past cabin six.

"*You* are," Huntley said. "Look at me."

They both laughed until Miles stumbled over a tree root and Huntley swore. "Easy, Jolly."

"Call me that again and I'm dropping you right here."

Lucy jogged ahead of them, her round bottom a welcome distraction. "I'll get the door," she said, hurrying up the stairs.

Pausing to gather his strength, Miles took a deep breath and hauled his friend up the stairs and inside. It was like his cabin, but all brown and mossy green and the bed was bigger. He gently lay Huntley down on top of the covers.

He was more concerned about his friend than he wanted to admit. "You sure about the doctor? You seem pretty screwed up for one little fall."

Sinking back into the pillows, Huntley closed his eyes. "No doctor."

Miles leaned over him on the bed. "Not like you have to worry about paying for it." He made a move toward the end of the bed to take off Huntley's shoes but Lucy was already there, her pale fingers working apart the laces.

"Nice boots," she said.

"New," Huntley said, opening his eyes. "Miles?"

"Yeah, buddy?"

Huntley was gazing at him, his face serious. After a long moment he said, "Please stay."

"Of course. But if you can't get up soon, I'm bringing you to a hospital."

"I mean for the wedding. The week. I need you, Miles." He closed his eyes, opened them again. When he spoke, his voice was so soft Miles had to lean down to hear him. "You were right. I don't think I can stand up to my parents without you here."

Miles glanced back at Lucy, saw by the shock on her face that she'd heard. No help for it. He cleared his throat. "If you really love her, you will."

"Not if I'm too weak. You know how I am around them."

"You've just never been sufficiently motivated." Miles squeezed his shoulder. "Just do it."

"Easy for you to say. You know you can, being on your own so long. Maybe it's too late for me, like that part of my brain just didn't develop at the critical time."

"Huntley." Miles sat down on the bed, careful not to jostle his friend. "You're a good guy. You love your parents. They're devoted to you and you're devoted to them. It's usually a good thing. Just sometimes, you need to push back a little more, take a stand. Like now. There's nothing wrong with your brain." He flicked the guy's forehead. "At least, not in that way."

Huntley glanced at Lucy, who had politely turned away to pour a glass of water from the bar, and gestured Miles closer. "They *really* don't want me to get married," he whispered. "I'm afraid of what they might do."

"They can't keep you apart if you don't let them."

"Please, Miles. Stay. We'll back each other up."

Miles took the glass of water from Lucy and set it on the bedside table. Her expression was thoughtful, unreadable. He wondered what she was thinking, if she'd tell Fawn about her groom's confession, and realized he couldn't leave Huntley alone in that mess. That he never really had any choice.

"I'll stay," Miles said, just as a knock sounded on the door.

The worry lines in Huntley's face eased into a broad smile. "I knew it! You big softie."

Miles got up. "You're welcome." Lucy was already opening the door to Eric, Huntley's driver-bodyguard, who had a large, padded rectangular object slung over his shoulder. Behind him was an older woman in a purple velour sweatsuit.

"Rita, thank God!" Huntley cried. "It's that tweaky thing in my back. It just snapped."

"We'll have you fixed up in a jiffy. Everyone out!" Rita waved her arms.

Fawn slipped in past the others and knelt at Huntley's bed. "How are you feeling, honey?"

Rita scowled at her. "That means everyone."

"I'm not going anywhere," Fawn said, her voice steely.

"I'll be in our cabin," Lucy told her, and Miles followed her out the door into the foggy morning.

He looked at his watch. Not even eleven yet, and it was only Monday. He dreaded the week ahead, wondering if he'd been stupid to give in.

For a short person, Lucy had a quick walk, and he found it easy to match his stride to hers. He thought about the impending reunion with his father and stepmother, the terrified look in Huntley's eyes, and made himself focus on how the air was humid and fresh and felt good against his face. There were worse places to be stuck for a week.

He looked over at his companion.

Less cute people to spend it with.

"She loves him," he said after walking next to her for a few minutes. "Your friend. Fawn."

About time he figured that out, she thought. "You assumed she was a gold digger."

"Most of them are."

"Most of whom?"

"Relax. The women who chase after Huntley."

"If there was any chasing, it was the other way around," she said.

He sighed. "That doesn't make me feel any better."

"Don't worry about Fawn. She's the real deal. She's beautiful, smart, funny… and strong. Independent." She shot him a glance. "Unlike her groom."

"Not thrilled for them to get hitched?"

"I was okay with it until a few minutes ago. Now I'm worried."

"He'll come through."

"She deserves more."

Miles smiled. "More than Huntley the Third?"

"Kind of a mama's boy, isn't he? And they haven't even been together a year."

"He owns most of New England."

"His family does. Huntley is more of a lapdog than a tycoon, from what I can see."

Miles studied her, looking more amused than offended. His gaze dropped down over her body, and she almost wished she'd put on one of her new marry-me outfits instead of her basic black. "What do you do for a living?" he asked.

"I'm a process analyst in the pharmaceutical industry," she said. "How about you?"

"What the heck is a process analyst?"

"Well, most days I analyze the process," she said. "Then, to shake things up a little bit, I process the analysis."

He smiled. "I see. Sounds exciting."

"It is to me."

"I'm glad." He bowed his head. "I'm the founder and director of a non-profit after-school facility. Though Huntley will tell you I'm a gym teacher, and that's about right."

"Now *that* sounds exciting," she said.

"It is. I love it." He sucked in a deep breath and let it out in a slow whoosh. "I wish I were there right now."

"Stop worrying. Fawn is no gold digger. She made her first million before she was twenty."

"Big difference between a million and a billion."

"She's not—"

"Sorry, forget I said that. I believe you. Maybe it's not her devotion I'm worried about."

Lucy looked down and kicked a pine cone with her boot, sighing. "I'm going to have to tell her."

"You really shouldn't."

"What kind of friend would I be if I didn't? She's tough enough to handle the truth. She'll have a better idea of what she's up against."

He put his hands, warm and heavy, on her upper arms. "It would be cruel to both of them. He was just laying it on thick to get to me. You wouldn't want to worry her for nothing."

"He's that sneaky?"

He released her, shrugged his massive shoulders. "Maybe. If he were desperate. He's a bit immature sometimes."

"Jesus." Lucy ran her hand through her hair and looked back at Huntley's cabin, relieved he wasn't touching her anymore. Too distracting. "I'm really going to have to tell her. She's back there thinking he's dying. If he's just putting on a big show—"

"I think he's in some pain, just exaggerating it. Like how he insists he can't stand up to his parents without my help."

"This is not the kind of man I'd choose for my best friend."

"He's a good guy. Loyal to a fault. Children and puppies love him." Miles put his hand in the middle of her back and guided her away. "He's just a numbnuts sometimes."

Maybe she could find Krista and Betty and ask them what they thought. But if she did that, there was no chance it wouldn't get back to Fawn, and she might resent their gossiping about her.

Realizing it wasn't the right time, Lucy continued walking with Miles toward the lodge, a throbbing pain growing between her eyebrows. "If I don't get my coffee I'm going to kill somebody."

The big man next to her grunted his agreement, and they set off side by side, two of her fast steps to one of his.

They arrived at the lodge just as Betty and Krista were coming out, each holding a bagel and a white ceramic coffee container, the kind that looked like paper but was non-disposable. Krista was in a form-fitting cotton beige track suit with Uggs, her hair tied up in a batik-patterned bandana. Betty, looking hungover and pissed, wore a huge gray Cal sweatshirt and baggy jeans.

When Betty saw Miles, she tilted her head back and whistled. "Looky there—it's Paul Bunyan."

Miles hesitated only a second before saying, "Damn. I didn't think anyone would recognize me without the ox."

Krista, who had been studying him, smiled suddenly and gave Lucy a questioning look.

"Betty and Krista, this is Miles, the best man. Miles, Betty and Krista," Lucy said.

"Paul Bunyan's got nothing on you," Krista said. "Though if anyone could pull off flannel…"

"Krista is straight, unlike me," Betty said, not even looking up from her coffee.

"My loss," Miles said politely.

Lucy sighed. "Behold the blushing bridesmaids."

Through a mouthful of bagel, Betty said, "I'll be blushing because of that damn dress. Can you believe she chose pink? Does she want to be a cliché? I suppose she's wearing *white*, too."

"At least you don't have red hair. Poor Lucy is going to look

—" Krista saw Lucy's raised eyebrow and bit her lip. "Not that it matters. Nobody's going to be looking at us."

Betty snorted into her coffee. "Somebody will be looking at Lucy. Somebody special. Somebody right back there." She rolled her eyes toward the lodge.

Lucy's stomach clenched. "He's in there?"

"Who?" Miles said.

The women froze and stared at each other in silence. Lucy wanted to slap them. The whole thing was embarrassing enough.

Krista cleared her throat. "Is that what you're wearing today?"

Lucy wasn't going to discuss her private life in front of Miles. "You know, I think I forgot something back in my cabin."

"Would you like me to help you look for it?" Krista, an aspiring fashion designer, had given Lucy a hard time about her "monochromatic palette" for years.

"Thanks, no. Finish your coffee and I'll try to see you at—what did Fawn say?—the Yoga Yurt at eleven-thirty."

Krista looked around. "Where is Fawn, anyway? Or is that a silly question?"

Should she tell them about what she'd seen and heard? Lucy could feel Miles's gaze on her. "She's in his cabin."

"Silly question," Betty said, pulling a pair of black Ray-Bans over her eyes. "Come on, Krista, let's eat. I'm freezing my ass off out here."

Lucy nodded toward her own cabin in the other direction. "I'll see you later, then."

"You know, I've changed my mind," Krista said. "I think I'll stay here, maybe meet some new people. Miles, are you going in?"

Holding Lucy's gaze, he put his hand on the door. "Yeah. If I don't get my coffee I'm going to kill somebody."

"Great! See you gals at yoga!" Krista said.

Lucy and Betty walked a few steps together before the path to their cabins split in opposite directions. "I wonder who Fawn picked out for *me*," Betty said. "Should be easy to pick out the lesbian in this crowd. I swear, I haven't been around so many aggressively straight people since high school."

"Fawn didn't pick out Miles for Krista. She doesn't even know the guy."

"But he's Huntley's best friend, and look at him—she could wear ten-inch heels and still look like a shrimp. She loves that," Betty said.

Lucy hesitated, not sure she wanted to leave Miles and Krista alone together, then reminded herself what she was doing. "So, the man I'm—"

Holding up her hands to her ears, Betty pivoted away. "Sorry! I swore I wasn't going to get involved."

"But he's there? In the lodge?"

"Not involved." She waved and walked away,

Lucy lingered, staring at the lodge. The two of them had looked good together. Just walking side by side, Miles and Lucy had to look ridiculous. A mismatched set.

With a shake of her head, she went back to her cabin to change.

Chapter 6

The woman—he didn't know which it was, Betty or Krista—walked ahead of him into the lodge. He recognized the warm interest in her eyes, but he wasn't in any mood to reciprocate, no matter how attractive she was. Tall, athletic, quick to smile.

"Have you known Huntley long?" she asked him.

"Since we were teenagers."

"Oh, you're from back East, too?"

"Just when I was a kid. I've been in the Bay Area for ages."

She glowed at him, leading him to a small circular table near a back window overlooking the shadowy forest. "Save this spot and I'll get you something. How do you like your coffee?"

He stayed on his feet. "No, please sit. I'll get my own. Yours is getting cold."

She started to protest but he insisted and strode off to the coffee service, gently touching the burn on his hand from earlier that morning. He realized he was starving. After he found a bagel and a glass bowl of cream cheese, balancing a hard boiled egg in the middle of the bagel, he rejoined the friendly bridesmaid.

"Forgive me, but I didn't catch your name," he said.

She grinned and held out a hand. "Krista Lang. I went to high school with the bride. And Lucy and Betty, of course."

"Miles Girard," he said. "High school is good at bringing people together."

"Like battle." She took a small bite of her bagel. "What doesn't kill you makes you stronger."

He looked around the lounge, wondering in spite of himself what man the other woman had been talking about, a man who would be looking at Lucy, but he only saw a few staffers walking around tidying up, carrying towels, refilling the coffee service. "I wonder how many of us are here this early in the week," he said. "I wasn't really given a choice."

Krista sipped her coffee. "I would love it if it weren't for—" Music suddenly blared from her midsection. She put down her cup and fumbled with a zipper on her sweatshirt, pulled out her phone, and the warmth drained out of her face. She twisted around and hunched over it, facing the window. "Yes? No, it's no problem…"

While she became engrossed in what was obviously a call from work, Miles wished he'd escaped to his cabin. He ate his bagel in three bites, gulped down his coffee, and wondered if the hiking trails were any good. The Pacific was fewer than three miles to the west, the rocky coast largely untouched up here, wild and gorgeous. He wished he had a group of his kids with him to show them the tide pools, make sandcastles, freeze their asses off.

Just as he was working through ideas for fundraising and chaperones to make a field trip possible, Krista put her phone away. "I am so sorry, that was totally rude. It's just—she's really difficult. My boss. Not that *she's* my boss. I report to somebody else, but I have to do whatever she says, no matter how irrational, you know?"

Miles gave her a sympathetic nod.

"I've got to find a way to use the lodge Internet without Fawn kicking my butt. Being totally out of the loop for a whole week isn't an option. I'm a designer for a new knitwear company. Very original, groundbreaking designs. Well, I'm an associate, which is why I can't really disappear for a week. The woman I work for is notorious." She reached forward and rested her slim fingers over his hand. "Anyway, I wanted to ask you about Alex."

"Alex? Oh, Alex Sargeant." One of the guys from their freshman dorm at Stanford, Huntley's other groomsman. He looked around the lodge again. "Has he arrived?"

"I met him right before I met you, inside the little shop back there. He was really nice, joked about Huntley having his own house in Atherton for whenever he got sick of living in the dorm. His own house, all to himself, when he was just eighteen."

"Not all to himself," Miles said, smiling into his coffee. "He had to share it with the servants." And then with Miles when he'd split from his father, dropped out of school, and didn't have anywhere else to go.

She laughed. "I can't imagine what it would be like to be rich like that."

"Nobody can unless they're born that way."

"That's exactly what Alex said." She dropped her gaze to the table. He could feel her hesitating over what she said next. "He mentioned he was the only groomsman to grow up without money."

He knew what she was asking but didn't bite. If she wanted to know if he was as rich as Huntley she'd have to ask outright, though she might leave him alone if she learned how modest his income really was. "Did you hear about the fourth 'groomsman'?" he asked.

She grinned. "That's so cute—to ask his sister! Isn't that great? She's threatening to wear a tuxedo, Alex said. Something about pissing off their mother." Wrapping her uneaten bagel in a napkin, Krista shifted in her seat and pushed out her chest a little bit, smiled more broadly. Flirting. "Alex made it sound like your parents were similar. Would they have a problem with a lesbian in a tuxedo at your wedding?"

Miles shook salt over his egg. "My mother died when I was three, I haven't spoken to my father in over fifteen years, and I think people should be able to wear whatever the hell they want to a wedding." He popped the egg in his mouth. "It's not Broadway."

"I'm so sorry. I didn't mean—I don't think Alex meant— oh, shit."

Seeing the stricken look on her face, he realized he was being a jerk. He swallowed the egg and wiped his mouth with a napkin. "No, I'm sorry. That was rude of me. I know what Alex meant."

"We were just talking about how nice it is here, that's all, and how nice it is for some people to be able to afford it and share it with people close to them."

"Of course. And he's right, I did grow up more like Huntley than like Alex." Alex had come to Stanford with a Goodwill wardrobe, a full need-based scholarship, and stories about living part of his teen years in a homeless shelter. "I had all the privileges in the world. I can't complain."

"He seemed really nice. I liked his eyes. Brown and warm, you know? I inherited my dad's gray eyes—he's white—but I really wish I had my mother's. Brown eyes are so warm and deep, you really feel like you can see into a person." She licked her lips. "His were like that, which is a good sign."

"A sign?"

"Oh, right." She clapped her hand over her mouth, peeked at him over her fingers. "Promise not to tell? I thought maybe you'd heard already, being friends with him."

"I haven't talked to Alex in years."

"Forget I said anything." She forced a smile and looked out the window. "I wonder if the sun will come out at all today?"

Sometimes people thought that because he was big and quiet he wasn't very smart. "I take it Alex and Lucy are being set up together?" he asked gently.

Krista's eyes went wide, nodding. "I'm not supposed to know who Fawn picked out, but I can totally tell."

"Picked?"

"Lucy has terrible taste in men, so she asked Fawn to choose."

The thought of earnest Alex and the intense redhead together made him frown. "I just don't see it."

"You're going by the Lucy you saw this morning, which I can understand. She doesn't realize what a turn-off it is to look like an angry teenager, especially when you want to be taken as wife material."

He choked on a mouthful of coffee. "Wife material?"

"See, that's what I mean. All that black denim and leather and boots—it's scary. Men like someone a little softer. At least, the kind of man she wants to settle down with does."

"Which would be"—he wiped his mouth with a napkin —"Alex?"

"If they hit it off. I only just met him, but he looked adorable for her. I hope she changed into something good back in her cabin."

Miles had a sudden image of Lucy shapeshifting like a mutant in the X-Men. "Change?"

"I took her shopping." Krista sat up tall, patted her fluffy curls, grinned. "I've been dying to do it for years. Get her out of that Elvira black into something fresh and appealing. We found the most gorgeous celadon wrap dress that really brings out her eyes. And it's cotton, so not too elegant to wear it here. The lodge, anyway, which is pretty nice in a rustic sort of way." She looked around.

"Your friend—Lucy—she's agreed to this? She doesn't seem the type to go along with that sort of thing." He wondered what celadon was. It sounded like a prehistoric mammal.

"I know, but it was all her idea. She really wants to get married. She was engaged for years and the guy bailed at the last minute." Her voice dropped. "Left her for somebody else. No warning. Lucy's really pissed."

"I bet." It didn't sound like the right frame of mind to get engaged to somebody else, though. Casual sex—sure. Definitely. His own experience was all for that. He followed that train of thought while Krista went on.

"She wasn't hurt, not like you'd think. Just furious he screwed up her *plan*. She wanted to be married at thirty and on her second child by now. So he wasted a lot of her time, and that bothers her more than anything, even cheating."

An unwelcome vision of Felicia obsessing over wedding websites flashed in his head. He knew what it felt like to be the token penis in a tuxedo. "I see," he said.

"She's totally type-A, dotting her T's, everything nice and tight, no surprises. When I took her shopping, she brought her laptop into the dressing room and recorded each thing on a spreadsheet. No shit." She laughed merrily.

He nodded, not too surprised this woman he'd just met would be sharing so much with him. Something about his face, his size, maybe his silence, made all kinds of random people, not just single women, open up to him. Like a bartender. Wherever he went, people latched on to him and told him things they really shouldn't have. Every once in a while he wondered if he should have become a spy. Or a priest.

Krista went on. "If she hadn't been so eager to make up for lost time, she never would have let me put her in turquoise, believe you me."

"She's lucky to have your help." Rising to his feet, Miles

held out his hand. "It was nice meeting you, Krista. Forgive me, but you've got me wanting to see if I can find my old friend, Alex. Catch up on lost time."

She sat up straight, eyes wide. "Oh, of course!" She bit her lip, looked like she was wondering if she'd said too much. "Look, you won't repeat anything I told you about Lucy, will you? I don't know why I blabbed all that. I get that way when I'm… Anyway, I don't think he even knows they're setting them up and I'd never forgive myself if I prejudiced him against her."

"No, no, don't worry about it. I won't say a word. It was nice talking to you." He escaped out of the lodge without asking at reception for Alex's cabin number. He and Alex had never gotten along. Overcoming so much adversity had made the man an insufferable bore in his opinion, and Alex thought Miles was a spoiled dumbshit who burned bridges he would've killed for.

He tried again to imagine Alex and Lucy together. His brain was quick to get Lucy naked, short and curvy, more red hair, climbing on top of him—

No, wrong *him*.

So, she thought she wanted a husband. He was surprised Alex wasn't married already; he was also the type to have a plan like that, down to the genders of his theoretical children. Always scheming, measuring, campaigning, working. Eyes on the future.

He got tired just thinking about it. Reflecting that ambition was for other people, Miles went to his cabin, determined to spend the rest of the day in the hot tub.

AROUND ONE O'CLOCK THAT AFTERNOON, Lucy noticed Krista

waving at her from a bench in a grove of redwoods behind the lodge.

"Where were you?" Krista asked. "Yoga was awesome!"

Patting down the filmy green dress flapping around her legs, feeling frozen and ridiculous, Lucy tip-toed through the ferns to meet up with her and Betty. The wet fronds soaked her silk ballet flats. Her idiotic, impractical, *beige* silk ballet flats. "Fawn isn't with you? I thought we might catch some lunch."

Krista shook her head, eyes shining. "Getting a jumpstart on the honeymoon, I bet."

"The yoga instructor is hot," Betty said. Her short, round body flushed and shiny, she splayed out on the bench wearing only a red sports bra, black boxer shorts, and purple flip-flops.

Lucy wrapped her arms over her chest. "I'm not. Aren't you cold? I feel stupid just sitting around the lodge, but then I go outside and it's freezing out. I never should have let you pick out my clothes, Krista. I'm uncomfortable and immobilized."

Krista got up and took her arm. "Meet anyone interesting?"

She thought of Miles, shoved that aside. "Nobody new. The resort is deserted."

Krista frowned. "I figured he'd be in the lodge. The yoga class was empty, too—just me, Betty, and Jaynette. She's the yogi."

"Three felt like a crowd to me," Betty said.

Lucy fumbled at the knot at her waist. "Once I figured out how to tie this thing I wasn't about to take it off. But I've changed my mind. I'm going to get back into my normal clothes so I can enjoy this place better. Go for a hike after lunch. There's supposed to be a river leading to the coast, just past the last cabins on the north side."

"No, you're not." Krista squeezed her arm to hold her back. "Any minute now you're going to meet this guy and you have to make a good impression."

"I agree. And I don't want that impression to be 'stupid girly-girl.'"

"You look gorgeous, doesn't she, Betty?"

"I'd hit it," Betty said, chewing on her thumbnail. "Actually, no, but I'm not your target demographic."

"My target demographic is a man who appreciates a woman with the sense to wear thick boots in the wilderness," Lucy said.

"At least wait until after lunch." Krista pointed at Betty. "And I am not going into the restaurant with you in your underwear."

"Fine." Betty stood up, pulled her bra over her head, and gave a vigorous, topless, nipple-shaking shimmy. "I was burning up anyway."

Krista swore, took Lucy's arm, and pulled her off into the trees.

Laughing, Lucy glanced back at Betty. "Should we save you a seat?"

"No, I'm going to check out Jaynette's hot yogi *asanas* again," Betty said, pulling her bra back on. "Meet me for a massage at three? At the Relaxation Yurt. It's on the map."

"Sounds great. See you then." When their friend was out of hearing range, Lucy turned to Krista. "That girl needs to get laid."

"So do you, which is why you're going to stay in that dress instead of donning the Ensemble of Doom again."

Maybe Krista was right about her preference for black clothes. Lucy had asked her friends to take over this, this—she would not call it husband-hunting, which implied conquest and destruction, and she didn't want anything that dramatic, God knew—this *introduction*. If Krista thought pastels and synthetic fabrics would accelerate the courtship process, she'd give it a shot.

They walked down a narrow walkway through a thick

grove of redwoods that cast the carpet of ferns below into deep shadow. In a sunny meadow ahead, Lucy caught a glimpse of a sign pointing to a large white building: *The Snowy Egret.* "Oh, thank God. Food."

Krista stopped and pointed to a fork in the path. "Hold on. I have to go back to my cabin first. I'm still in my workout clothes and I don't have my wallet."

"You don't need a wallet. It's all-expense-paid, remember?" Lucy pulled out her phone from between her breasts and studied the sweat-slick screen while Krista gaped at her. She stared back. "What? The dress didn't have pockets."

"Where's the matching clutch we bought?"

"That stupid thing didn't have a strap. I'd lose it in a second."

"That's why it's called a clutch."

Lucy reached over and used Krista's sweatshirt hoodie to wipe the sweat off the screen. "The Snowy Egret is open at eleven-thirty to three every day for lunch, then at five until ten for dinner," she said, reading the file she'd downloaded the week before. "They serve omnivorous, vegetarian, gluten-free, and vegan delights to the discerning palette—"

"I'll still have to change."

Lucy frowned at the designer track suit, brand new and embroidered with sequins. "You look great and nobody's around. Come on."

Krista made an unhappy noise, probably debating which was better: wearing the wrong thing herself or sitting with a friend who wasn't wearing anything at all. She followed Lucy to the white door.

A pale waitress with white hair, wearing a white apron over her white blouse, white slacks, and white Keds, led them over to a table draped with a white tablecloth and handed them each a white menu.

"I'm feeling very African American right now," Krista said

in a low voice, looking around without moving her head. The walls, curtains, and floor were also white.

Lucy studied the menu, stifled a snort. "Check out the food."

Krista scanned it and her jaw dropped. Then their eyes met across the tops of the menus. They burst out laughing.

"Mind if I join you?" a man said from behind Lucy, just as she was pointing at the special.

"Chicken with wine sauce, jicama salad, artichoke soup," Lucy said, still laughing. She twisted around to see a man with dark brown hair in a long-sleeved navy T-shirt. Early thirties, laugh lines around the eyes, nice lips. She took in the rest of him, the slim fit of the shirt over his toned biceps, his flat stomach. He wore fashionable dark jeans and thick-soled Keens.

"Alex!" Krista pulled over a chair from the next table. "Please! We were feeling lonely." It was a small table, barely room for two, but he nodded his thanks and sat down. His knees bumped Lucy's and she shifted away to give him more space.

So, she thought. *This is… Alex.*

The man she was going to marry.

Chapter 7

Lucy studied the guy and realized he was studying her right back. Suddenly uncomfortable, Lucy buried her face in the snowy-white menu.

Krista kicked her under the table. "We were just noticing the theme of the restaurant."

"Yeah?" He glanced around. "Ah, I see it now."

Smiling, Krista leaned over to show him the menu. "Halibut, endive, coconut broth, and skinned new potatoes. Get it?"

The waitress brought him his own menu and rearranged the table to make room for his place setting. He studied the first page, then said to Lucy, "Albino beets. I've never heard of that."

Lucy smirked. "Wouldn't that be a turnip?"

"No, I imagine it's a just a type we've never heard of," Alex said. "Perhaps an heirloom."

Lucy stared at him. "Perhaps."

"I'm having the chicken breast and jicama salad with vichyssoise," Krista said.

"Good, they've got a vegan entree," he said. "White cannellini and gnocchi with cabbage."

Which would have had Lucy reaching for the Beano, so she settled on the chicken. And, because Alex had shifted over to eliminate the space between them, she decided to ask for wine too, even though it was early and she was freezing and they only had chilled whites.

After they'd ordered, Lucy put on a warm smile and turned to Alex. "You're an old friend of Huntley's?"

"Not too old. Only since college."

"We're not *old*, Lucy," Krista said, and Lucy wished she'd let her go back to her cabin.

The waitress placed a goblet of coconut water in front of each of them.

"I meant I haven't known him as long as Miles has." Alex sipped the coconut water. "They went to prep school together, the whole bit—fathers belonged to the same country club, summer home in the Hamptons, spring break in Costa Rica, that sort of thing."

"Miles didn't mention that." Krista looked thoughtful.

"He's always been in denial," Alex said. "There was a lot of that at Stanford. Kids realizing how good they had it, not wanting to feel guilty about it."

The waitress placed a painted wicker basket of crustless baguette slices on the table. Lucy slathered a piece with butter and put it in her mouth, uneasy with Alex's tone. "Isn't he an old friend of yours?"

"Not really. We were roommates very briefly. Freshman year. Stanford makes a big deal about residental education. You're supposed to learn as much from each other as from your classes."

"It didn't work out?" Lucy said.

"He dropped out of school right after Christmas break. Moved into Huntley's mansion in Atherton, which is where Huntley spent most of his time too, since he hated his roommate. But then the spot opened up in my room, and he started sleeping with a girl on the third floor—" He closed his eyes for a second then laughed, looking embarrassed. "My God, listen to me. Not the sort of stuff I should bring up at the man's wedding. Point is, I got to be great friends with Huntley, but Miles left before I got to know him."

"Why'd he drop out?" Krista asked.

Alex sipped his drink. "You'd have to ask him."

Krista glanced at Lucy. "But you must know something."

"It's not my place to say," he said. "And really, I only heard about it secondhand."

"He never went back?" Krista asked.

"Krista," Lucy said, "It's really not any of our business."

"No, he never did, and it killed me. To have that opportunity—" Alex cut himself off again, ducked his head. "Sorry. I'm kind of irrational about education. And access to it."

Krista gave Lucy a meaningful eyebrow wiggle. "Alex is a lawyer for an educational non-profit in San Francisco."

"Great," Lucy said. Small talk was not her thing, especially when the other person was chatty. Easier just to nod and listen.

Breaking the awkward lull in the conversation, Krista said, "I had breakfast with Miles this morning. He seemed like a really nice guy."

"He is, he is," Alex said quickly.

"I kind of talked his ear off," Krista said.

"Easy to do," Alex said. "He's not much of a conversationalist."

Lucy was finding it harder to keep the smile on her face, so she looked down at the plate that had appeared in front of her and speared a potato. She really was going to have to think of something to say. Chewing, she caught Krista's eyes on her, the silent entreaty to speak. She swallowed and said, "Not that you knew him very well."

Krista closed her eyes.

"You're right." Smiling, Alex sipped broth from his spoon and nodded. "You know what my problem must be?"

"No," Lucy said, and Krista kicked her again. Lucy snapped her head around to glare at her. "What?"

Krista smiled tightly at Alex, who laughed.

"It's okay, I have it all figured out, and it's not flattering." He toasted them with his goblet of coconut water, then stared into it without drinking. "I'm jealous."

"Of all the privileges they had?" Krista reached out to touch his arm, grabbed her goblet instead. "We totally get that. Lucy and I grew up with the basics, but not much extra. People think academics make tons of money and it just isn't true."

"No, I'm jealous of something far more humiliating." Alex set down the glass, set his palms on the table to either side of his plate, and leaned back in his chair. "I, Alex Sargeant, am jealous that I am not the best man. There. I admitted it." He picked up his fork and scooped some gnocchi into his mouth, smiling at Lucy. His brown eyes were warm and amused.

Krista put her hand on her chest. "Oh! How sweet. Of course you would be." She gave Lucy a warning look. "It's funny, because I had the same problem."

Alex gave Krista a quick, polite smile. "Really?" The way he'd been staring at Lucy until then had made her wonder if she had white sauce on her nose.

Krista leaned forward. "Yes. We've all known each other since junior high, even earlier, and Fawn and I have always had a special friendship because of the fashion thing. She's a model, I'm a fashion designer—you know? I thought the wedding would be, uh, our place to really bond."

Lucy had to look at her plate to keep herself from laughing out loud. Fawn and Krista were friends, but not very close ones, and Krista's ambitions to be a fashion guru had put a strain on the relationship. Being her maid of honor would have led to homicide.

"So you know how ridiculous I feel," Alex said. "And I'm a guy, so it's even more embarrassing. We're not supposed to care about this sort of thing, which is of course a sexist delusion. Men are secretly, hopelessly sentimental."

"That is so true," Lucy said with conviction. "I've always known that."

He beamed at her. Really, he had very nice eyes. His hair was a nice, deep brown color too, and his skull looked nicely shaped if and when he lost his hair a couple of years down the line. He wasn't difficult to look at. No weird tics that might get distracting during a conversation. And he didn't have any obvious hygiene issues.

"Which is why it was so, so nice that Lucy offered to step aside so I could be the maid of honor," Krista said.

Burying her shocked cough in a napkin, Lucy averted her eyes back to her plate and couldn't see Alex's face when he touched her hand and said, "That was very generous of you."

Krista sighed. "Of course, I refused. But please don't say anything, okay? Especially not to Fawn."

His hand was warm over hers. She pulled hers free, patted his, and buried it in the napkin in her lap. Lucy didn't like lying. Lies unbalanced everything, fogged up the view. She was a scientist and believed in it. Lies were human; truth was divine.

"She's joking," Lucy said. "Fawn would never—Krista wouldn't—" Crap. What could she say now?

"I understand. We won't talk about it," Alex said, but Lucy could see he believed Krista. His knee was bumping her thigh again.

Nice skull, she thought. *And no obvious hygiene issues.*

They finished the meal—joking about the lack of a bill— and went out into the clearing in front of the restaurant. The fog had crept back in, blurring the tops of the trees, and white tendrils snaked through the trees looking like a side dish for The Snowy Egret.

"We have to go. We have a spa appointment at three." Lucy held out her hand. "It was nice meeting you, Alex."

His gaze darted down to her hand, lingering over the rest of her, and came back to her face. He held her fingers, then enveloped her hand between both of his and looked into her eyes. "Very nice."

She made herself smile back, but she didn't like two-handed shaking and was concentrating on holding her hand still inside his grip instead of jerking it free. "See you around," she said, nodding, smiling harder.

Looking amused, he let go of her hand and stepped back. "Yes, you will." Nodding to Krista, he pivoted on his comfy-looking leather shoes and strode away through the redwoods.

When she was sure he was out of sight, Lucy sighed loudly.

Krista whirled on her. "*See you around?*"

"I didn't like him."

Gaping, Krista pointed off into the woods. "He was totally hot."

"He didn't get my turnip joke."

Her big gray eyes got bigger. "Are you kidding?"

Lucy sighed again. "Do I seem too picky?"

"Oh, no. Totally reasonable. Turnips are really important."

"I'm not sure I could live with a guy who didn't laugh at my jokes."

"Even the bad ones?" Krista shook her head and started walking. "You're hopeless. Come on, I'm cold and these trees are dripping on me."

They found the path to their cabins and didn't speak for a few minutes. Lucy regretted having told Krista what she was thinking. Krista was so quick to overreact and jump to conclusions.

"I didn't say I wasn't going to try to like him," Lucy said finally. "Or that I couldn't learn to like him."

"You're impossible, you know that?"

"How am I impossible? I'm capable of changing my mind. You tell me I care too much about him laughing at my jokes. I'm willing to consider you're right. In the scheme of things, if his other qualities add up, it won't be a problem. But it would be dumb to go into a long-term relationship without knowing as many potential problems as possible."

Krista kicked a bark chip off the path. "Very romantic."

"Since when is having your friends pick out your spouse romantic?"

"Since you came to us for help, since we love you and want you to be happy, since we're in a totally gorgeous place to witness our best friend getting married to a billionaire out of a fairy tale."

"There weren't really billionaires in fairy—"

"Shut up!" Krista stopped and buried her face in her hands.

Lucy watched her for a minute. When her shoulders began to shake, Lucy put her arm around her waist. Like Fawn, Krista was almost six feet tall, and Lucy had to peer up at her. "This isn't about me, is it?"

Face still in her hands, Krista shook her head. "I'd be happy with any of them. Any one of them." She lowered her hands, exposing the tears streaming down her cheeks. "My neighbor. Huntley. Miles. Alex. Hell, even the guy driving that golf cart. Why don't any of them want me?"

This was a moment when Lucy wished she didn't hate lies so much. "I don't know," she said lamely.

"I'm thin and pretty and have nice clothes and a real job and I'm friendly to everybody—"

"Hold it right there," Lucy said. "For one thing, your list is screwed. Take it from me, I know lists."

"You don't think I'm—I'm—"

"I wouldn't want to be friends with the chick you just described."

A flash of anger displaced some of the despair in her eyes. "How would you describe me, then? Fat, ugly, and unemployed?"

"If you put on a hundred pounds, were disfigured in a fire, and went on disability, what would you have left?" Lucy held her arms and looked up into her face. "In addition to me and Fawn and Betty and your family?"

The tears began to flow again. She blinked, gazed into Lucy's eyes. "What?" she whispered.

Lucy smiled. "Figure that out first. Then worry about finding somebody to share it with."

Her voice wavered. "I'm so lonely."

Holding her tightly, Lucy nodded into her armpit. "I know." She patted her back. "Me too."

TUESDAY MORNING WAS as foggy as Monday had been but colder, with a wind that reminded Miles of riding his motorcycle over the Bay Bridge. Hiding out the day before had refreshed him enough to venture out of his cabin, get some air, interact with the rest of the wedding party. The hot tub had soothed his muscles, Fawn had soothed Huntley, and he was ready to admit that Huntley was right; it was past time to rebuild some bridges with his father.

Perhaps not a bridge. An infrequent ferry with one-way service. At least until he could get used to the idea.

Huntley had recovered from his paralysis and gone off hiking with Alex at dawn. Miles normally didn't get out of bed before nine unless he had to, certainly not during a vacation, and had no desire to be in Alex's company for a twenty-mile hike, so he'd begged off. Shivering in his thick sweatshirt from the short walk from his cabin to the lodge, he was glad he had.

He noticed her the moment he walked into the lodge.

Curled up in a slipcovered chair in the lodge, a laptop open in front of her, Lucy appeared deep in thought. Since she didn't see him, Miles paused near the door to take the opportunity to study her.

She was in black again, though today's sweater was a turtleneck that covered that pointy little chin of hers and set off her pale skin. And while she stared at her screen, nose wrinkled with concentration, she nibbled on the hem of her collar like a rabbit.

She was the cutest thing he'd seen in a long time.

He wondered why she was in here working instead of enjoying the free goodies at the spa. He wasn't into it, but most women were. Hell, he'd spent the entire afternoon the day before soaking in the hot tub, drinking his way through the mini-bar, having meals delivered to his cabin on a white tray.

Just as he was about to walk over and say hello, Alex Sargeant came out of the small store in the back of the building carrying a cloth grocery bag over one arm and two steaming coffee mugs. He didn't notice Miles, either because too many years had passed or because his eyes were fixed on Lucy. She hadn't noticed either of them yet.

Miles paused and turned aside to get himself a coffee, studying Alex from behind the branches of a large potted tree. He had to admit Alex looked pretty good—still had his hair, wore an expensive watch, looked like he worked out at the gym.

Miles found himself sucking in his gut and turned his attention back to stirring his coffee, laughing inwardly at himself. If that's what Lucy wanted, she could have him. He would be a perfect husband. He wouldn't tolerate anything less in himself. If he discovered any flaws he would have to kill himself, and then she could collect the hefty life insurance policy he'd be certain to buy.

Alex came up behind Lucy's chair. "Care for a peach?"

Lucy jerked upright, slamming down the screen of her laptop before twisting around in her seat. "Alex! Good morning."

"Mind if I… ?" Alex gestured to the seat next to her.

Taking his time, Miles got out a tub of cream cheese and picked through the bagels.

"Of course not. It's nice to see you again," she said.

Alex sat next to her, his back to Miles. "You brought your work with you?"

"No, just playing around. You know, killing time."

Alex handed her a mug. "I noticed your cup was empty. Yesterday you took cream but no sugar, so that's what I got you."

"Thanks, Alex," she said, sounding genuinely pleased. "I was too lazy to get up for another one."

Miles stabbed his knife into the cream cheese and smeared it over his bagel.

"If you're killing time, does that mean you might be glad to go for a walk?" Alex asked.

"A walk?" The way she hesitated and patted her laptop, Miles assumed she was about to turn him down, but then she said, "Yes. I'd like that. Right now?"

"We could have our coffee first if you'd like."

"Actually, I'm well caffeinated already, but if you—"

"No, the coffee was just a bribe to get you to talk to me." He reached into his bag. "I've got peaches if that didn't work."

Miles rolled his eyes. What a smoothie.

"I'll have to put my laptop in my cabin." She looked over at the door and suddenly noticed Miles behind the tree. Naturally, no man his size could hide for long behind an indoor plant. Her smile fell and her ears turned pink. "Oh, it's Miles."

Alex spun around in his seat. "Is it—Miles!" He jumped to his feet, strode over with his arms wide.

Was Alex really going to hug him? Miles was glad his hands were full. "Hi there, Alex, Lucy. Sorry to interrupt. I was just —" He took an enormous bite of his bagel and spoke with his mouth full. "Eating."

Alex slapped him on the arm. "Some things never change, big guy."

Now, Miles didn't mind when Huntley called him that, or even Ronnie or the kids, but when guys like Alex said it he had to make a conscious effort not to deck the little prick. "How was the hike?"

"Huntley bailed on me. Too cold, he said." Alex turned to Lucy, who had joined them with her laptop tucked under her arm. "I was disappointed at first, but not so much now, given the upgrade in my hiking partner."

"You guys can catch up while I put my laptop in my cabin," Lucy said.

Not sure how long he could keep the bland smile on his face, Miles stuck his hand out. "I'll drop it off for you. I'll be heading back there in a minute."

Alex slapped is shoulder again. "Thanks, big guy." He reached over to take the laptop from Lucy, as though to hurry or guarantee the transaction, but she clutched it to her chest like a freezing man with a heating pad.

"No, I'd rather do it myself. I didn't bother with the case."

"I'll be careful." Miles held out the right side of his unzipped sweatshirt. "I'll nestle it in here like a baby."

She glanced down at his chest, in the shadows of his body, and he felt his heart began to thud. He wasn't ashamed to admit he was sucking in his gut, or that he thought she was hot and adorable.

"Well, sure. Thanks." She handed it over.

He let his fingers brush against hers, enjoying the flash of sexual awareness in her green eyes. "You're welcome."

Alex practically carried her out of the building. "We'll catch up later, Miles," he said, hooking an arm around her back and pulling her away.

"Fawn should be in the cabin, so you can just knock and she'll get it," Lucy threw out over her shoulder.

"No problem," Miles said.

Alex looked back at him. A message passed between them, ancient and hostile and male, before Alex smiled and shut the door between them.

Ah, well. Better luck next time. Letting out the air he was holding, Miles lugged his inadequate breakfast and the laptop over to a couch in the corner and put his feet up on an ottoman. An older couple was just arriving, led by the golf cart guys in their white uniforms, but Miles didn't recognize them. More and more guests were trickling in today, though most weren't officially invited until later in the week. The spa had too many perks to waste, Huntley said—not that Lucy seemed to be taking advantage of them.

He lifted the screen to see what the serious redhead would be working on instead of having her soft, naked body rubbed with scented oils.

Or maybe he could play solitaire, distract him from the image of Lucy having her soft, naked body rubbed with scented oils. Or worse, the thought of Alex doing the rubbing.

The screen lit up in the middle of a spreadsheet of all things, and he remembered she said she was some kind of analyst for a drug company.

But this was no work spreadsheet.

He looked up at the door where she'd disappeared. If she suspected he'd open this up, she never would have left it with him. No wonder she'd hesitated.

He wiggled his butt deeper in the chair to savor the delightfully incriminating document in front of him. Quickly, so he didn't miss a thing if she came back early.

Her manhunt was documented.

The columns were color-coded, which was a nice touch. He especially appreciated how PHYSICAL APPEAL was a bright, garish red—though she'd numbered that as seventeen, putting it in a row at the bottom, far below such important characteristics as LIKES AQUARIUMS and REGULAR FLOSSER. Maybe the red stood for stop. Or danger.

He couldn't help but grin. The worst impulses in his nature were in motion like a wind-up toy. Lucy thought SALARIED JOB was more important than GOOD WITH KIDS? That was bad enough, but having RECYCLES rated six rows above TONGUE?

And did that mean what he thought it did?

Another quick glance at the door, then Miles had his fingers on the keys to make a few revisions. As a favor. It was obvious she was going about her husband selection the totally wrong way.

He hesitated, realizing how invasive and immoral it was to do this. He was a private person. He'd be furious if anyone ever did this to him.

Then again, he wasn't the one comparison-shopping men as though it was no different than buying a camera on Amazon.

Were all women like this? Or just women freaking out about passing thirty?

Like Felicia.

As a compromise to his conscience, he did a SAVE AS and began moving columns and adding fields that were both helpful, suggestive, and honest.

Really, it was the least he could do.

For her, Alex, and men everywhere.

Chapter 8

"Thanks for the walk," Lucy said as they approached her cabin.

Alex had his hands in his pockets, watching the pavement at his feet, and he glanced at her with a smile. "My pleasure."

She didn't say anything else, unable to hide her happiness that the hike was over. The wind was cutting through her clothes, even her usual jeans and sweater. The hot tub called to her.

"I suppose you've guessed by now," Alex said.

She paused with her foot on the bottom stair to her cabin. The wind battered the wood chimes hanging from the cabin's overhanging roof, and she had to shove aside her vision of steaming water for a moment to realize what he was talking about.

She had to appreciate his direct approach. Fawn had tried to complicate things, but it defeated the benefits of getting friends involved. She turned to him and smiled. "That we're interested in each other?"

He laughed softly. "Nicely put."

Shoving her numb fingers deeper into her jeans pockets,

Lucy tried to twinkle, but really, her ass was ice. "I enjoyed our hike."

"How about dinner?" He looked at his watch. "After the tree ceremony. Unless that's too early?"

Lucy only had a vague memory about a tree ceremony being on the schedule that afternoon. Something Fawn had set up. "No, that's fine."

"That gives us time to catch the movie afterward. It's an old film about modern life being out of balance. The score's by Philip Glass—"

"*Koyaanisqatsi*," she said. "Where? In the lodge?"

He looked pleased with her again. "No, they've got a separate building with a stage and seating for that sort of thing. Live music on Thursday night, I hear."

"Oh, you know, I'm much more into music than a movie. Let's plan on dinner tonight though, after the tree thing."

"Great. Now get inside—I can see you're freezing." He hesitated. Then, still smiling, leaned over and gave her a quick kiss on the cheek. His lips were cool and light, nothing sloppy.

She smiled and slipped through the door, grateful he was already turning to walk away.

Damn.

He was just fine.

She'd have to try harder.

"Hey, welcome back!" Fawn stood on the bed wearing a gray knit dress that skimmed her knees, staring at the open armoire. "The only mirror in the entire cabin is in there. Totally annoying. Too small and too high." She bounced down to the floor and pulled the dress over her head.

Lucy kicked off her boots, peeled off her jacket, and walked past her to the bathroom. "It's beautiful here, Fawn, but I admit I'm having longing thoughts for a tropical paradise." She slipped out of her jeans and folded them over a chair, noticing they were soaked up to the knees.

Fawn frowned. "What happened to you? You've got mud on your face, and not the expensive kind."

"I was a little too shrimpy to make it over that river without getting wet."

"What happened?"

"The stepping stones are for long-legged folk such as yourself. I fell in. Got wet, it was cold, we had to come back."

She put her hands on her naked hips, eyebrows wiggling. "We?"

"Me and Alex."

Fawn put her hand over her mouth as though trying to hide her tell-all grin of triumph. "How was it?"

"Fine, but freezing. I'm going to use that hot tub now." Peeking out the rear door window at the vinyl-covered spa on the private wood deck, she unhooked her bra and slipped off her underwear.

"Would you mind putting on a bathing suit? I've got Huntley coming over here in a few minutes to… talk."

Lucy slipped on a white terrycloth robe that fell to her ankles. "Can't you *talk* in his cabin?"

"No, no, we really are just going to talk. His father's watching some game because Huntley's the only one with a TV in his cabin and Huntley Junior—oh crap, I'm going to have to stop calling him that, but then what am I going to call him? Mr. Sterling is so formal. Huntley is my Huntley, you know?" Fawn grabbed fistfuls of her hair. "They just got here, his parents, a whole day earlier than we thought. So I'm kind of freaking out."

"That's why you're having a wardrobe crisis?"

"Exactly." Fawn reached into the armoire and pulled out a white blouse and black slacks. "What do you think? I want to look serious, you know, not like some bimbo."

"That kind of says 'catering.'"

"Even with a bright scarf? Yeah, you're right." She shoved

them back on the bar, pulled out a red pantsuit. "How about this?"

Lucy bit her lip and peeked outside at the spa. Getting her swimsuit out of a drawer, she said, "Look, Fawn, I'm not really the one to ask, you know? I'm sure Krista would love—"

"I should call her, but I don't have time." She pushed her blond hair out of her eyes. "Shit. I need to be put together for this."

"You always look beautiful, Fawn. And that's the truth."

"No, I mean to talk to Huntley. I'm a wreck and I need to be calm. I so wish the yoga vibe lasted longer."

Lucy put on her black one-piece Speedo, gearing up her courage to ask Fawn if she feared Huntley might get cold feet around his parents, when the door suddenly banged open and the handsome groom stepped inside.

"Honey, I'm home!" he cried, then saw Fawn wasn't alone. "Oh, hey there, Lucy. Miles was just asking about you. Did you get your laptop?"

She looked around the room, saw it on the little desk by her bed. "Yeah, it's right there."

"He wanted to make sure you got it. Guess you went for a little walk with somebody this morning?" Huntley strode over and punched her gently on the shoulder.

Lucy had to smile. "I did. Didn't you get the memo?"

He shifted his happy gaze to Fawn. "Not yet."

"I'll let you get to it, then." Tugging her swimsuit up, Lucy opened the door to her hot aquatic sanctuary and stepped outside. Surrounded with a tall wood fence and shielded by the cabin, the deck wasn't very cold at all. Actually, she thought, inhaling deeply, it was quite pleasant. Lavender, sage, something white and floppy that might be jasmine. Wonderful.

She flipped back the cover and sank into the bubbling water.

Just as she was about to close her eyes, Fawn appeared.

"Just so you know, we're going for a walk, so you can get naked if you want. We'll go straight from there to the tree ceremony."

Lucy noticed she'd settled on khakis and a sweater. With her hair back in a tight ponytail and the pinched look around her mouth, Fawn looked like the librarian in a porno who was about to take it in the ass. "Are you going to be all right? Is he giving you any reason to worry about… anything?"

"No, no—" Fawn glanced behind her. "A little. But we're talking about it."

"Okay. Good luck. If there's anything—"

"No, of course not. And wasn't he sweet to ask about your laptop? In the middle of all this garbage with his parents, he remembers stuff like that. Anyway, got to go. See you at the tree. Wear something comfy. It's on the map."

And she was gone.

Lucy sank back into the water, uneasy about her friend and her choice of husband but optimistic she could work it out. Fawn wasn't the type to give up.

Alex's comments about the Sterling family ran through her brain. All that money, all those connections—just like Miles. She thought about the big, quiet man in his sweatshirt and sneakers and just couldn't picture him in some New England prep school. In fact, she had trouble imagining how he became Huntley's friend, let alone his best man.

She sank deeper into the water and let the bubbles touch her nose. The jets pounded the tension out of her shoulder blades. Exhaling with delight, she reflected that the last time she'd been in a hot tub she'd asked her friends to find her a husband. Ergo the freezing hike with Alex.

What if they'd tried to set her up with Miles instead?

She realized she was still sitting in her bathing suit. After a moment, she peeled it off and slung it onto a chair next to the spa.

Much better. She flipped over onto her stomach and folded

her arms over the edge, rested her cheek on her hands. The jets kneaded water into her chest and down her stomach while her legs floated up behind her. She felt the cold air on her bare bottom and smiled, finally enjoying her day.

It was nice of Miles to bring the laptop back to her cabin. She'd been startled when Alex came up right behind her while she worked on her personal stuff. She hadn't even had the chance to quit the file.

She lifted her head and looked at the back door of her cabin, alert and wondering, then rested back down. No, he would never open somebody else's computer—

But what if he was desperate to get online for a few minutes? It might not seem like a big deal to pop up the lid and check the news, like turning on the TV.

She crawled out of the spa, cursing herself, but unable to rest until she closed out the file. It would be embarrassing if Fawn were to see it too—hell, anybody. She knew she was a little OCD sometimes but it was her own business and she wasn't hurting anybody.

Dripping wet, she slipped on the robe and jogged across the floor of the cabin to the desk. Just one little CTRL-Q and she could get back in the water.

She wiped her hand, lifted the lid, and felt the blood drain down to the damp jute rug at her feet.

She wore her heaviest black boots to kick his balls through his teeth.

BamBamBam. Hands on her hips, Lucy waited for him to answer his door, hot, mortified rage stiffening her spine.

The door opened a crack, and a gray-blue eye peered out. He didn't seem surprised to see her.

"Open up, you coward," Lucy said.

Laugh lines appeared. The door started to close.

She flung herself against it. "Don't you dare—"

The door swung open and she lurched inside. A strong hand found her elbow to steady her, then released her before she could shake it off.

"I suppose I should apologize right now and save us some time," Miles said.

Chest still heaving with her anger and the run over to his cabin, Lucy braced both her legs as though muscle tension could make her taller and glared up at him. "You were totally out of line."

He looked at her for a minute, not smiling anymore, and sat down on a white slipcovered sofa near the front windows. "You're right. Will you sit?"

Her anger banged around her chest like a bee trapped in a car. The way he was looking at her, passive and mildly apologetic—that wasn't enough, damn it. A few hours ago he'd invaded her privacy and—and—violated it. Her most vulnerable thoughts, unwillingly exposed, but then he had to take it a step further and—and—*mock* her. He must have spent an hour writing up that spreadsheet.

"You'll have to do better than that," she said through her teeth.

"You're right." He got up and went over to the cabinet above the mini-fridge. "Organic Oreos?" He saw the look on her face, shook his head, and squatted down to the fridge. "Something stronger."

"How dare you?" Her voice had lost too much of its anger. To her annoyance, she almost sounded hurt.

"It was a bad thing to do." He held out a bottle of Sam Adams. "There's no excuse. I tried to go back and undo it but Fawn was in your cabin and I didn't want to ask Huntley for help. I figured I would just make things worse if I confided in anybody what I'd done."

"Thank you so much."

"You're right to be angry. I was an asshole."

She glared at him, momentarily robbed of her righteousness. Finally she grabbed the beer and flung herself down on the sofa. The bottle was cold in her hand, and hard, and she had a vision of hitting him over the head with it. Instead she drank and let her pulse settle. She had to admit to herself she was grateful he hadn't shared his mockery with Huntley. She'd been imagining the two of them laughing at her. Then Alex might hear about it and that would ruin everything.

She finished the beer, aware that he was standing there, watching her, looking like he had all the time in the world. She wiped her lips with the back of her hand, noting her buzz, and he took the empty bottle from her.

"Who are you to give romantic advice, anyway?" She slumped back into the couch and put her feet, boots and all, on the coffee table.

"I wouldn't exactly call it 'romantic.'" The corner of his mouth twitched, but he suppressed it, got two more beers and handed her one.

"You're not allowed to call it anything at all." She took the second beer and nestled it on her stomach, giving him the evil eye as he sat down on the sofa next to her. It was only two cushions wide and he had to knock pillows onto the floor and scrunch himself over to the opposite arm to make room for his frame.

Sighing, he sipped his beer and regarded her muddy boots on the table. "How was your hike?"

"Lovely," she said. "Why did you do it?"

He flinched. "I'm not sure. Moment of weakness. Cynical about the wedding. Bitter about my ex. Forgot we weren't on those kind of terms."

"We barely know each other."

"My point."

She took a sip of her beer and moved her boots to the floor, regretting the clump of mud she'd left on *Cottage Living* and the footprints on the bamboo floor. She bent over to take off the boots, then settled back in the sofa with her beer. "I wasn't entirely serious, you know, about my numbering. But you had no right—"

"Yes, yes, we've established that. But answer me this, since when are aquariums more important than—" He looked down at his beer. "No, forget it, I shouldn't say anything. But for the record, I never would have done anything if it hadn't been for the aquarium thing."

"It was very lightly weighted in my calculations," she said.

Mid-sip, he choked on his beer, caught his breath, and shook his head. "Not as lightly as tongue."

Not a cheap drunk, Lucy chugged the rest of the beer and stood up, triumphantly steady on her feet. "I'm going to kick your ass now." She glanced at her black socks. "After I put my boots back on."

His gray eyes went wide. He had great cheekbones, a sensual mouth, and a hint of five-o-clock shadow, and she realized for the first time how good-looking he was. When he was standing up she'd been too far away to get a good look at him. But now, displayed before her in arm's reach, she got a very thorough look.

Neither of them spoke for a long moment, and she noticed absently that she could see the pulse in his throat, the way his chest rose and fell with his breathing.

Slowly, he leaned forward, set his bottle on the table, and held out his hand.

She stared at it. "You want to shake before I beat you up?"

A grin flashed across his face before he leaned forward and pulled her down into his lap.

Stunned, she sat frozen on the tops of his knees and gaped at him. She held herself as upright as possible, ignoring the heat pooling low in her belly, how her breath was coming tight and fast.

His gaze dropped to her mouth. She felt the skin of her palm tingle where it touched his, felt the warmth of his thighs through his jeans.

After a long moment, she let herself slide down his legs into the valley of his body. She could feel the fly of his jeans under her bottom. His chest was hard and broad against her arm, and her fingers twitched, wanting to stroke him.

"Lucy," he said, his rough, low voice sending electricity down her spine. "I'm going to kiss you, all right?"

She shook her head.

"Then you can kick my ass all you want."

"You bet I will," she said, slipping her hand behind his strong neck and pulling him down to her mouth.

Chapter 9

In the limited history of her life, Lucy had never kissed anyone the way she kissed him. She did it because she was angry and because she was hurt, because he had apologized and because he had warm, hard thighs.

But the second he cupped her jaw with his big hands and tilted her head to take the kiss deeper, she forgot everything except the soft pleasure of his mouth. She felt one hand slide behind her neck, fingers warm, then trail down over the bump of her bra strap into the small of her back and pull her closer.

She wriggled sideways until her chest was twisted against his and she was lifting her leg over his lap to straddle him. God, he was big. She knelt on either side of him, pressed her pelvis into his stomach, kissed him some more. She wanted him to lift the back of her shirt and touch her. She wanted to feel skin on skin. Her own hands left his face and explored down over his broad chest, amazed at the sheer scale of him.

He kept kissing her, nibbling, licking, slowly and gently. It had been months since she'd been with a man. The smell, the stubble-roughness, the hardness. He wore a thick sweatshirt that bunched up around his waist between them, preventing her from finding out if his chest was hairy or smooth. She hungered for the feel of his warmth under her fingers, and all the while she kissed him, she shoved everything else out of her mind.

He trailed his mouth across her cheek to her ear. "Beats… aquariums," he rasped.

Her hands, which had been making their way under the bottom ribbing of his sweatshirt, froze on his stomach. The haze in her mind cleared and she opened her eyes. He was nibbling lightly on her ear, which was almost enough to send her back into mindlessness, but then she realized consciously how relatively motionless he was under her onslaught. His hands hadn't moved from their firm grip on her hips, and his posture—leaned backward against the sofa with his legs kicking forward—was that of a man under attack.

She jerked her hands out from under his sweatshirt and tried to stand up, but she was trapped between his legs and his chest and he wasn't letting go.

"I'm an idiot," he said, bending forward to nuzzle her collarbone. "Forget I said that."

She broke his hold on her and flung herself onto the floor, her breath coming fast. Desperate to get away, she stumbled once before she got to her feet and hopped to the other side of the small table. "We shouldn't have done that."

He gave her a sad smile. "Why not?"

"All right. I shouldn't have done that."

"Because it wasn't what you planned?"

All the anger flowed back into her like water into a glass. "Exactly. You are not in my plans."

"Maybe your plans suck."

"Maybe it's none of your damn business."

His gaze dropped down and perused her body. "You seemed interested in making it my business."

That was too much. Dan's words popped into her head.

Shoving her feet into her boots, she gave him a cold look. "I was drunk and pissed off and trying to teach you a lesson."

"You're a very good teacher," he said. "Can I have another class?"

She clomped over to the door without lacing her boots and yanked it open. He was just playing around. Like he'd said, he was cynical and bitter.

She turned to him, calming herself enough to study him with her brain and not her hormones. He was a good-looking guy and she was lonely. It would be a fun week and then it would be over and she'd regret it. "No," she said. "No, you can't."

"Too bad." He sighed and got to his feet with a loud exhale. "I would have liked to work through the rest of your list."

She leaned a hip on the doorframe and crossed her arms over her chest, unpleasantly aware her pulse hadn't yet settled at a normal pace. "Really? You want to buy a house and save up for retirement with me? Be the father of my children?"

"Admit it, Lucy. Your list is bullshit. You're freaked out about getting older and want to bag a husband before you think it's too late."

She couldn't speak for a moment. "Did you have problems with your last girlfriend? Is that it? Because I think you're flinging a lot of snap judgments at somebody you just met."

"Maybe. Or maybe I heard about your setup with Alex. Maybe I read over your little spreadsheet and know more than I want to about what makes you tick." In two steps he was right next to her. "Maybe I noticed you're more interested in me than him."

She lifted her chin. "Not in any way that matters," she said, and stormed out.

Miles was late.

He still had no idea what a tree ceremony was, but he'd never intended to blow it off. Since Lucy had left his cabin, however, his mind had been elsewhere. When he finally took a break from his brooding over what had and hadn't happened, he looked up at the clock and scrambled to find the map and the steep path through the forest before he lost his nerve to see her. Now he was hiking up a trail through clusters of towering trees and inhaling the damp silence. He wished he could absorb the quiet into his body.

He never, ever should have poked around her computer. He'd done worse things, like pulling her into his lap and kissing her, but none of that would have happened if he hadn't started the flirting in the first place.

He wasn't going to lie to himself; that's what he'd been doing. Breaking into her computer and teasing her was flirting. He thought she was cute, he thought Alex was a tool, and he thought her blender-shopping approach to finding a spouse was shallow and annoying and, yes, reminded him of his ex-girlfriend. Maybe he'd wanted to take her down a peg because his pride still stung from Felicia dumping him.

Or maybe he'd taken one look at her flushed pink cheeks and her compact, fierce little body, and he'd wanted a taste.

He picked up a curved stick and swiped at a fern blocking his path. He had to cool it. The last thing he needed was another woman who wanted a husband more than she wanted a man.

The path looked simple and natural, just a smooth ribbon of earth switchbacking up through the trees, but he could see it was carefully maintained by human hands to be free of mud or rocks, fallen trees, poison oak. Every couple of minutes he passed a wooden marker with a hand-carved image of a tree. Just as he was breaking a sweat, he reached the top of a ridge. In the center of a clearing was a massive coastal redwood at least ten feet in diameter. Built right next to it was a timber platform, about twenty feet high, with a zip line extending off into the forest.

A zip line? And the Sterlings? His mood lifting, he approached the tree.

A dozen or so people stood around it in small groups, looking up at the platform where a man and a woman were preparing harnesses. Two snub-nosed electric cars were parked off to the side. The climb was probably too much for the golf carts, and not everyone could hike up mountains.

Or ride on zip lines.

He hoped the ceremony involved Huntley's parents flying through the air at fifty miles an hour. And that the wedding videographer was around to capture it.

Lucy was there with her friends and a handful of people he didn't recognize. He told his body to calm down and went over to Huntley. "I can't believe they haven't made a run for it."

Wedged between his parents, Huntley smiled at him, but his eyes looked anxious. "They know I can't make them," he whispered. "They didn't even want to get in the car to ride up here."

Fawn stood awkwardly off to the side, clearly excluded, while Huntley's parents gave Miles the once-over of people who'd known him when he was very young and still couldn't believe how much he'd grown. It always made him feel like a Saint Bernard.

The elder Huntley strode over and held out his hand. "Still slumming it at that nonprofit, Miles?" He squeezed hard and gave him a serious look. "What kind of security do you have in a place like that? Oakland, isn't it?"

"Nice to see you again, Huntley the Second," Miles said with a half smile. "And the clubhouse is in Berkeley." The "Second" nickname had started when Miles was eleven and he hadn't been allowed to call him anything else since. The younger Huntley said it probably made him feel like a regular dad—the kind who coached soccer teams, not the kind who owned one.

Miles nodded at Huntley's mother. She had never wanted to be regular. "Mrs. Sterling."

"I think you're old enough to call me Rosalind, Miles." She took his hand and leaned in for an air kiss. Softly, audible only to him, she said, "Save him, will you?"

Miles smiled noncommittally and broke away to stand with Fawn. She was clearly eager to win over Huntley's parents, with clothes off the set of a L.L. Bean catalog shoot and a big smile in spite of the obvious hostility aimed her way.

"So, who gets to go first?" he asked her. "Strapping people to wires and pushing them off a cliff had to be Huntley's idea."

"Actually, it was mine," Fawn said. "The wedding coordinator here at the spa made it sound unforgettable."

"I imagine it will be," Rosalind said.

Miles glanced at Huntley to see if he would jump in to stand up for Fawn, but he had a hand on the platform for the zip line, tapping it as though checking its stability.

The dork. Miles was tempted to grab his ankles and shake him upside down again. Even if the best man wasn't thrilled about the bride, the groom had to be.

Miles gave Fawn a smile. "It looks really fun," he said. "What do we have to do before we ride? The note said 'ceremony.'"

Huntley's father snorted. "Whatever it is, I hope they get on with it. They should have warned us about the athletic features of the event." He scowled at the guides and their harnesses. "Not to mention the cold."

He and Rosalind were wearing summer-weight shirts and slacks, no jackets, leather shoes. The fog had never burned off and a wind was picking up.

"We were waiting for Miles," Fawn said. "I'm sure they'll start in a second."

The elder Huntley squeezed his shoulder. "So we can blame you, Miles. I hope you don't teach those children of yours it's all right to be late. Hardly the message they need to make a place for themselves in the world."

"They're better than I am with the clock, I admit," Miles said.

The elder Huntley patted him on the back. "All that basketball, eh? But you didn't answer my question about security. What kind of staff do you have?"

"The clubhouse isn't in a dangerous neighborhood, just industrial. Lots of biotech companies, factories, warehouses, that sort of thing."

"The kind of kids you're trying to help bring problems with them, don't tell me they don't. What's your age limit? Thirteen? Twelve?"

Miles gave him a steady look. "They're welcome to come as long as they want. I pay the older ones to run the summer camps. I've got a girl right now who comes in every Thursday afternoon to help with grant proposals. She's going to Cal in the fall."

"A girl, one with that kind of ambition, sure. But aren't you dealing mostly with delinquent males?"

Miles saw Huntley close his eyes and could almost hear him praying. But Miles was used to the insults and the snap dismissals. "No," he said calmly. "They're just kids who need a place to go after school. All walks of life."

"You telling me the professors and doctors pay to send their children to your inner-city gym?"

Miles managed a smile. "Some of them."

Rosalind made an impatient noise and took her husband's arm. "It really is freezing up here. Fawn, could you please go and see what's holding them up? Any longer and I'll have to request a ride back to the lodge."

Fawn hesitated, but when Huntley said nothing, she blasted them all with her stunning smile and strode away toward a group of people on the other side of the clearing.

"Pretty girl, Huntley, but not very bright, is she?" Rosalind said, watching her walk away. "When the looks go—and they will, even with all the help your money can buy—what will be left to hold you to her?"

Huntley laughed nervously and put an arm around her. "My mother the romantic."

"I'm serious. Even with a prenup, marriage is nothing to joke about."

"Even with a prenup." Huntley winked at Miles, pretending his mother was just being her usual comic self. "I better go see what's holding us up." He scurried away.

"That boy needs to grow some balls," the elder Huntley said.

"I'll go see if I can help him with that." Miles strode after his friend and caught his arm just as he was about to climb up the ladder to the platform. As though he could just fly away, leaving Fawn behind to talk to the staffer with the walkie-talkie. "Don't you dare."

"The sooner we get this moving, the better," Huntley said.

"The sooner you stand up to them, the better."

Huntley choked out a laugh and ran his hand through his pale hair. "Really? And then spend the rest of the week trapped at the resort with them? No, thank you."

"You owe it to Fawn."

"I owe it to her not to cause a scene with my parents over her in public," Huntley said. "My parents have been brilliant about maintaining the family's privacy. Even when my sister started her gay rights campaign, she always kept it classy, never let on Mom and Dad were privately giving her shit. I'm not going to be the first Sterling to screw that up."

"You want to keep it *classy*?" Miles gripped his shoulders and swiveled away from the platform. "Go stand next to the girl you're going to marry. Show everyone whose side you're on. Which, in case you've forgotten, is hers."

"What's your problem? I thought you didn't even believe in marriage anymore."

"Not bad ones." Miles gave him a shove and turned his attention to the one person standing near the tree he couldn't ignore any longer.

LUCY WATCHED Miles talk to the Sterlings on the other side of the platform. They looked happier to see him than they had anyone else.

"Kind of standoffish, aren't they?" Geri, Fawn's mother, asked her.

After a brief introduction, the Sterlings had moved away to the other side of the tree. No friendly chitchat between the parents of the bride and groom. Not even a smile.

Geri lowered her voice and gestured down at the waterproof jacket and hiking boots she wore. "Were we supposed to dress up? I thought this was just some fun nature thing."

Lucy gave her a squeeze. She'd spent a lot of afternoons in Geri's kitchen, eating normal foods her eccentric, academic father never learned how to cook—things like chicken with bones, fresh vegetables, anything more complicated than toast. "You look fine. They're just from the East Coast. Probably thought all of California was hot. And I think the zip line was a surprise to everybody but Fawn and Huntley."

Fawn's father, Larry, was remarried, and stood with his wife Val a few feet away talking to Betty and Krista. They were all dressed in warm clothes—fleece, jeans, hiking sneakers. Lucy waved but stayed with Geri.

"You'd think all that money could pay for better manners," Geri said, still watching the Sterlings.

"Their way of showing they're not thrilled about the marriage, I suppose."

"I meant Richie Rich," Geri said through her teeth.

"Don't you like Huntley?"

"Look at him over there. He's not even looking at her. Like he's ashamed of her."

Lucy had been too distracted by the large man in the navy sweatshirt next to Huntley. Miles seemed to be arguing with him about something.

Geri sighed. "Ignore me. It all just happened so fast. I'm just surprised they didn't elope. Sudden weddings between strangers should happen on the cheap in Reno. You know how much this week must be costing them? I had breakfast in that restaurant—did you know every stupid thing in there is white? And afterward I'm sitting there waiting for the check and then finally learn, oh no, it's all paid for!"

Lucy nodded. Forced herself to turn so Miles was out of her line of vision. "Ate there last night."

"I wish they'd told me. I felt like an idiot. Tried to pay for my free oatmeal with a debit card." She squeezed Lucy's arm and whispered in her ear, "I should have gotten the crab omelet with champagne!"

"Tomorrow. I'll eat it with you."

They laughed together. "How are you, Lucy? Fawn told me you broke up with Dan. It was so many years. Is it bad to say I'm relieved?"

"I don't know. Is it bad for me to *be* relieved?"

"Thatagirl." Geri squeezed her again. "I always thought you were settling. I know how badly you want a family, but take it from me, some men just aren't worth it." She glanced at her ex.

"But without him," Lucy said softly, "you wouldn't have Fawn."

Geri sighed. "True enough. And look at her, so lovely. Never ceases to amaze me that gorgeous creature came out of my body."

Lucy smiled at the old joke but then noticed the hostility in Huntley's mother's face. "Don't worry. If Huntley doesn't stick up for her I'll key his private jet."

Geri's face twisted with worry. "She even signed the prenup. I told her, whatever you do, just make sure he loves you. And don't sign anything!"

Suddenly Miles was there at her side. "They're going to start in a minute. A staffer stopped me to apologize for the delay."

Pretending her heart wasn't pounding, Lucy stepped away from Miles and introduced him to Geri. Geri admired him with her sharp brown eyes and gave Lucy a raised eyebrow before drifting away with her ex-husband and his wife. They got along pretty well as long as nobody was drinking.

Miles and Lucy stood there awkwardly, saying nothing, watching Huntley and Fawn doing the same thing a dozen yards away. Lucy knew her cheeks were hot and was grateful for the chill in the wind.

She felt his gaze on her but pretended she didn't notice. "I should have warned Fawn. About Huntley's parents."

"She knew."

Lucy sighed. "Yeah, I guess she did."

Another silence. "It's not going to be a very fun week if you won't even look at me." He lowered his voice. "And you know you want to."

Chapter 10

She turned her body toward him and glanced up at his face, noticing with alarm how the overcast sky matched the gray of his eyes. She dropped her attention to the zipper pull on his sweatshirt halfway down his chest.

"Chicken," he said softly.

"I am not going to talk to you anymore." She took a step back.

He put a hand on her arm and her body responded with a rush of blood to the spot where he touched her, an acceleration of her breathing, a tingly feeling down her spine. "Party's starting," he said, gesturing past her.

Grateful for the distraction, she turned to watch a woman in white, arms upraised, jog to the base of the platform. "Greetings, fellow human beings of Earth. I am Celeste. Before we climb up the platform, we're going to link hands in a Welcoming Circle around Bahbbe—the tree—and let the life force that is so powerful here rise up through the roots, down from the canopy, sharing with us a Life Blessing for the future."

Lucy's snort came out before she could stop herself. She covered her mouth and coughed.

"And then we're going to go for the ride of our lives!" Celeste whooped and pounded her fist in the air.

"It's almost worth being here just to watch Rosalind Sterling's face," Miles said in her ear while they watched Celeste greet them. "She looks like she's chewing something nasty."

Fighting the impulse to cover her neck where he'd breathed on it, Lucy stepped away. "I'll link hands, but no way am I getting up there."

"It is pretty high." Miles looked up. "Are you afraid of heights?"

Her stomach lurched. "That would be silly."

"Not it's not. It's pretty common—"

"I'm not afraid. I just… don't like to be strapped in like that." Hurling through the air. A hundred feet above the ground.

He leaned down, touched her shoulder, dropped his voice. "No harnesses on your list? How about *straps*?"

"There's still time to beat you up."

He grinned.

Celeste herded everyone toward the tree, smiling and addressing each one of them by their first name: Fawn and Huntley, their parents, Lucy and Miles, Krista and Betty, then stopping and gasping in alarm. "Where is Alex?"

Lucy frowned and looked around.

Miles grinned. "You didn't notice he wasn't here, did you?"

She ignored him. But she hadn't. "I don't see Huntley's sister either."

"Is she your backup if this arranged marriage with Alex doesn't work out?"

"Will you please shut up?"

At that moment Alex's head appeared, climbing up from below on the trail. He was short of breath and had a bloody streak across one cheek. "I hope I'm not late. I took a detour and had a little tumble. It was steeper than it looked!"

"You dumbass," Huntley said, walking over and slapping him on the shoulder. "Trying to ruin my wedding by getting yourself killed?"

Alex put a hand on his cheek. "It was nothing. Just afraid of missing the ceremony." He scanned the group and beamed when he noticed Lucy. He strode right to her. "Have I missed anything?"

"My sister won't be here, so let's get it going," Huntley said.

Celeste faltered at that news. "It won't be the same without her—"

"She's in London until tomorrow. Please continue."

Celeste looked around and seemed to finally absorb the lack of enthusiasm. "Well, she'll be here in spirit! Everyone link hands."

It took a few minutes, but eventually everyone was circling the tree. Miles had Lucy's right, and Alex had her left. Fawn's family was next to Miles, and Krista and Betty closed the circle with Fawn and the Sterlings on the other side.

"New Age bullshit," said Larry, Fawn's father, just as Celeste began to sing.

Alex shushed him and tried to share a disapproving look with Lucy. Lucy was too busy trying to ignore how warm and strong Miles's big hand felt around hers.

"My God, I can't wait to ride that line," Alex whispered in her ear. "Ten minutes soaring over the redwood canopy. Awesome."

Her throat went dry. "Ten minutes?"

"Maybe more. They've got gondolas and platforms strung all over the forest."

"It wasn't on the website," she said.

"Huntley made them keep it a secret for the wedding. It's brand new."

So new it probably hadn't been tested properly. "Wonderful," she muttered. She craned her neck back, estimating the top of the platform was twenty feet up from where they stood. That was bad enough.

The path the line took through the trees and over the creek below, however, was an impossible journey into groundless green and blue space.

Celeste began to sing in a language she didn't recognize. Somebody was playing drums.

There was no way the Sterlings would climb up there. Geri had a bad hip, so she wouldn't even try. Fawn's dad, Larry, weighed over three hundred pounds; they probably wouldn't let him ride even if he wanted to. And his wife, Val, never left his side. Krista and Betty would be good sports, and the groomsmen. And Huntley, of course, though he sure was shaping up to be a disappointment in the stand-by-me department.

Fawn needed visible support. And Lucy was the maid of honor.

Celeste stopped singing and clapped. The group dropped their hands, most backing away from the tree, and some lined up below the platform. Betty was first. She climbed up right before Krista, who asked if they could go more than once. Huntley assured her they could as long as nobody died.

While the first volunteers climbed up, Fawn went to talk to her family.

Alex put his palm on Lucy's back. "You can go in front of me." He had a camera around his neck. "This is going to be incredible."

"No, please," she said. "I'd rather you went first."

"I don't mind, really," Alex said.

"No, I'd like to wait for Fawn."

"If you're sure…"

Lucy assured him she was and he left her to climb up the ladder after Huntley.

After a couple of minutes, Fawn waved at her mother, father, and stepmother as they got into one of the electric cars.

The Sterlings just stood there, watching. Their flat and unreadable eyes followed Fawn wherever she went.

Lucy *had* to participate in the activities and look like she enjoyed them.

Miles touched her arm. "Are you sure you want to do this?"

Just the thought of climbing the ladder made her knees buckle. But she had to, especially now that Miles thought she couldn't. "Of course." She walked over to the base of the platform. It cast a dark shadow. The wooden rungs were damp, a little slippery.

Her body released a panicked dose of adrenaline into her bloodstream. Focusing on the rungs one by one, only the ones she could see, she made her way up slowly.

Very slowly. Her nerves vibrated.

Eventually, with her heart hammering against her ribs, she saw flat planks. A railing around the top. Other people.

She wouldn't look at the harnesses. How Huntley was getting strapped into one, Alex right behind him.

Sucking in shallow breaths, she stepped forward. Just another person waiting to go on the fun little ride, no big deal.

Sweat dripped down her forehead. She tried to focus on the horizon and not the ground below, not the delicate cable stretching out over nothingness. All that open air. Birds gliding beneath them.

She put her hands on her knees.

"Lucy?"

She heard Miles's voice through a fog, felt the ground tilt.

"I've got her," Miles said. "Stand back."

She realized somebody was lifting her. Her head bumped against a big, steady chest—a wall of fleece.

Miles.

She blinked away the stars. "Put me down. I'm fine."

"Of course you are. You just need a minute." He took his time setting her down on the platform.

She was relieved to sit. More points of contact between her body and solidity. If she closed her eyes she could pretend she was on a deck only a few inches above ground. "Thanks."

His hand settled on the back of her head and guided it down between her knees. "Breathe deeply. Slowly."

"I'll be fine. I'm fine."

He didn't say anything, just waited. She drew in more air and waited for the black edges of her vision to recede. When her head felt like it had reattached itself to her neck, she lifted it up slowly and gently pushed his hand away. "Really, I'm fine now."

This time he did move back. Just a little. She met his gaze and they stared at each other for a moment, not smiling, not speaking.

She could look at him forever.

"Lucy!" Fawn's head appeared as she climbed up onto the platform. "What is it?"

"I'm fine. Fine. Just needed to sit down for a minute."

Alex strode over wearing a half-attached harness. "I didn't realize what was happening."

Miles held up his hands, palms out. "She needs a minute and some space. So she can climb back down."

"But—what's the matter? Are you hurt?" Alex asked.

"Lucy, I'm sorry, I didn't think," Fawn said.

Alex squatted down next to Lucy and pointed at the zip line. "You really should just try it once. He's pretty far now, but can you see Huntley just—there!—can you see him? Look at him soar! He's got to be two hundred feet in the air. Higher than the *redwoods*! Just *flying*—"

Lucy's vision went sparkly at the edges.

"Down you go," Miles said, gently pushing her head back down.

"Alex, Miles is right," Fawn said. "She's got a… thing. I'll explain later. You go. They're ready for you."

"Well, okay," Alex said. "I'll see you at the bottom."

When she was pretty sure he was gone, Lucy asked Miles, "How did you know?"

"I've seen that look before," he said. "Been that way your whole life?"

She grunted. "Little bit. Got worse when I was a teenager."

"I had this one kid, real tough. Dodging drug dealers in West Oakland didn't faze him, but he wouldn't go near a Ferris wheel."

She nodded. "They make me tingle in all the wrong places."

"I'd like to hear more about that later."

"I bet," she said weakly.

He patted her on the back. "Sorry. Keep taking deep breaths."

She obliged, glad she hadn't eaten much. No way was she going to watch her best friend dangle around on some dental floss in the sky. "I'd like to get out of here," she whispered.

"All right. Can you walk?"

"I'm looking forward to it."

"I'll go first and clear the way."

She toddled after him, gripping the railing and staring at her hands. Giving up on the zip line did wonders for her composure. She was able to turn around and find the rungs with her feet without another wave of dizziness or nausea. The descent was slow, full of pauses, but she made it.

She let him help her to the ground at the bottom but was grateful when he released her without comment. He had every right to make fun of her.

The Sterlings were gone, as were Fawn's father and stepmother. Geri was looking up with her hands over her eyes, peeking through her fingers. "I can't watch," she said.

"Me neither," Lucy muttered on her way to the path.

An unexpected wave of dizziness hit her when she eyed the trail down the hill. Climbing up, the ridge hadn't seemed so high and steep, but now—

"This is so annoying," she said, putting her hands on her knees.

Miles put an arm around her. "We'll take the last car."

He waved down the staffer with the mustache.

In a few minutes they were side by side in the little electric car and heading down a paved, narrow path, not nearly as steep as the foot trail. She didn't risk a look up at the platform, not even when she heard Fawn scream.

It was a long, dwindling scream. The kind a person might make while they hurtled to certain death.

"She's fine. She's just having fun," Miles said.

Lucy always felt ridiculous when she had an episode like this. Her father said her mother had been the same way, and sometimes she let that thought comfort her, that she had this connection to her. A genetic phobia.

A slow, winding drive later, the car reached the lodge. Groucho—no, Miles called him Shawn—parked in front. "There's a free wine tasting until six. Would you like to get off here?"

"No, thanks," Lucy said. "I just want to go to my cabin." She was recovered enough to be distracted by the long, muscular thigh pressed against hers. Miles wasn't intentionally touching her; he was just too big not to. He looked uncomfortable, all hunched over.

"Ceanothus coming up," Shawn said, and the cart puttered back onto the path.

When they reached her cabin, Lucy stepped out onto the ground. Nice ground.

Miles joined her and sent Shawn on his way. "You should eat," he said. To her relief, he didn't try to help her inside, though she was still feeling a little lightheaded as she climbed the stairs and unlocked the door.

"I just need to lie down."

"Want me to get you something from the restaurant? It's dinnertime."

"No, thanks." She bent over to unlace her boots but Miles got there first, surprisingly quick for such a big man.

"You don't want to be leaning over like that just yet." He slipped off each boot and set them neatly by the door. Her socks were thick but she felt naked having him touch her feet. She took off her jacket and padded over to the bed while he hung it up.

She sat on the edge. "You don't have to do that. I usually just throw it over a chair."

He lingered by the door. "You really should let me get you something to eat."

"The thought of all that white food just makes me feel worse."

"Fun gimmick they've got going on. Makes me want to order ketchup."

"Man, I'd kill for a burger, and not a turkey one." She lifted her feet up onto the bed and pretended to yawn. Having him around was uncomfortable. What they'd done that afternoon was still too fresh in both their minds.

"Mendocino is only a few miles but the bike wouldn't be safe for you just yet."

"No, really. I'm fine. You can go."

He watched her from the door for a moment, then turned to leave. "All right."

"Miles."

"Lucy?"

She stared, not sure what she could say. "About this afternoon…"

"Sorry about that."

"We just want different things. It wouldn't work," she said.

"All right."

She couldn't read his expression. He didn't look angry, but she felt like she'd hurt him somehow. "Thanks for helping me get back to my cabin."

"You're welcome. Now get some rest. You have an iPod or something you want me to bring to you? No TV here in paradise."

"I'm fine."

He opened the door and nodded. "Right. Sorry. I'll get out of your way."

When he was gone, Lucy let out a long breath and sank back on the pillows.

Her mind swam with images and impressions of him. The feel of his lips, the smell of his skin, the gentle patience of his tree top rescue mission.

Did he have to be so nice on top of all that sexual charisma?

Damn it, it wasn't enough. She needed the boring stuff that would last. Long-term compatibility. Mutual goals.

She couldn't give up on having a family. All her life she'd wanted that simple thing: two people living together in legally binding, semi-permanent domestic harmony.

So she wasn't so special. So she was a walking cliché, maybe like his last girlfriend, wanting to catch any guy before her body gave out.

But growing up in the upstairs corner of a Berkeley four-plex with her father, without regular meals or a garden or siblings—hell, or even a goldfish—had left a hole inside her. Life was lonely and unreliable when your only family was an antisocial widower with borderline Asperger's. Dad hid out in his office and left her to deal with everything else, uninterested in most of the real world. No grandparents, no cousins, no mother.

It was just common sense to seek out another person looking for the same things she was.

If only Miles…

She dozed off. When she woke to a knock on the door, the windows were dark. Disoriented, struggling to shake off a deliciously hot dream about Miles kissing her, she put her feet on the floor.

Another knock. Heart beating a little too fast, she went over to the mirror and patted down her hair before opening the door.

Alex stood there holding a tray draped with white linen. "I took the liberty of bringing the restaurant to you."

She let him in and tried to hide her disappointment. Of course it wasn't Miles; she'd sent him away. "I forgot. We had a date, didn't we?"

"Don't worry, I'm not offended." He set the tray on the small circular table near the mini-fridge and pulled off the white cloth and white ceramic cover with a flourish. "Tilapia Alfredo. With fresh sourdough and artichoke soup."

The smell of the fish made her stomach turn over, but the bread and soup looked all right. "There's only one plate. Where's yours?"

"I hope you don't mind, but I ate with the Sterlings. After that little ceremony in the woods they looked like they'd enjoy some civilized conversation."

"I thought you liked the zip line."

"It was incredible. Just inappropriate to the occasion. Anyone would know Rosalind and Huntley Sterling wouldn't appreciate it."

"You know Huntley's parents?"

"I made a point of it when I met him in college. His father is quite the altruist, especially as he enters his golden years, and I've been very lucky to know him." Alex pulled out a chair in front of the meal and Lucy felt obligated to sit in it. "I wasn't likely to meet many billionaires where I grew up."

She picked up her fork. "So few of us are."

"Indeed."

"Please sit. You're making me nervous."

Alex laughed and sat on the edge of the bed near her. "I thought the soup was a little too salty, but it's all they had. Cute idea, though, all the white."

She dipped a corner of bread in the soup and took a bite. "Cute."

"I've actually developed quite a relationship with Huntley the Second over the years." He leaned over and plucked a slice of sourdough off her plate. "That's a nickname a few of us have the pleasure of using. Truth is, I think of him as the father I never had. Even though he's on the other side of the country, that isn't a problem when you've got unlimited funds and technology at your fingertips." He chewed off a corner of the bread.

Lucy nodded and tried to eat while he talked. It was probably good to get something inside her stomach, though she had to shove the tilapia to one side and focus on not breathing in the fishy steam smell. Alex went on about the nonprofit work he'd done over the years and she pushed the food around, trying to look like she was listening. After a few minutes, though, her mind drifted to the scene near the tree and she wondered how Fawn was doing. She hadn't come back to the cabin.

I wonder if she survived. He'd tell me if she fell to her death, right?

"You don't eat much, do you?"

She realized she'd been sitting there staring off into space. The plate was still buried under the mounds of white, lumpy rubble that had been her meal. "I'm sorry, I'm just not hungry."

"Oh, I don't mind. Totally makes sense that a petite woman like yourself wouldn't need to eat very much."

"Don't get the wrong idea. Usually I chow down like a horse. Just not right now." She stood up, looked at the phone to see if the message light was blinking. It wasn't. "I wonder if Fawn's okay. I expected to see her by now."

Alex picked up another slice of bread. "She was at the restaurant. I told her I was coming over." He met her eyes and held them. "She's probably happy to be with Huntley, anyway."

Lucy sat back down at the table. *She better be happy, or some pretty blond head is gonna roll.* "Good. I didn't want her to worry about me."

"I'm sure she's not. She told me you'd always had a fear of heights. In fact, I'm surprised you even climbed up to make the attempt, knowing you might, you know——"

"Puke or faint?"

He smiled. "Sorry. I didn't mean to be insensitive. Peer pressure can be tough to resist."

"You know, Alex," she said, getting up, "I think I'll need to take a raincheck on our date. I'd like to crash for the night so I can"—she paused—"do the sunrise yoga class in the morning."

"Fantastic, I was hoping to see you there. Tell me about your practice."

"My what?"

"Yoga. Have you been practicing long?"

"Now and then I drop into a class at the Y. Nothing fancy."

"Oh, you really should give yourself more time to benefit from it. I've found yoga to be a great gift," he said. "Six times a week is ideal, but I tell myself if five is what the universe can give me, five is what I'll take and be grateful for it."

She smiled politely and wished he'd get off her bed. If she changed into her pajamas would he get the hint and leave?

There was a knock on the door. She went over and jerked it open, reflecting that staying home was a lot more relaxing than this rejuvenating, renewing resort.

"Hi," Miles said.

____

Chapter 11

____

*S*he stared at the broad figure filling the doorway. His hair stuck up on one side of his head and his cheeks were pink. Under one arm was a motorcycle helmet, and the other—

He held out a paper bag. "I got you a hamburger. Sorry it's a little squished, I had to put it in my tank case."

After a split second, she took the McDonald's bag from him and felt a wave of confusion so acute it made her feel like keeling over again. The paper was slightly warm and sagged at the bottom.

"I couldn't get you a soda on the bike," he continued, "which left milk and orange juice, which, given the color thing, was a no-brainer." He searched through the pockets of his leather jacket until he found the little bottle of juice and held it out to her.

Their eyes met. She felt a funny pressure in the middle of her chest. "Thanks." She took the juice, her mind going blank, not knowing if she should invite him in or—

"What are you doing here, Miles?" Alex was right behind her in the doorway.

The faint smile on Miles's face disappeared. He stood up a little taller. "Alex."

"He brought me dinner too," she said, still surprised.

Alex leaned closer, then laughed. "McDonald's? Going all out, eh, buddy? Well, sorry you wasted a trip, but Lucy's already eaten. Fresh local fish and vegetables can't compete with"—he took the bag out of Lucy's hands, looked inside—"a Big Mac, but she didn't have much appetite anyway." He thrust the bag at Miles.

"I kind of asked for it." Lucy gently retrieved the bag and touched Miles's arm for a second. "Thanks."

He stepped backward, tripping down the top step and grabbing the railing for support. "No problem. I went out for a ride and happened to pass it. It's probably cold by now."

"It was nice of you. Really." Why did she feel like he'd caught her in a criminal act? She had no reason to feel guilty. She hadn't asked him to get her a hamburger, hadn't asked him to do anything.

He was already turning away, arm raised in a wave. "Hope you feel better. See you around."

She felt silly standing there watching his back, so she closed the door and turned back to Alex, the bag still in her hand.

She was ready for Alex to go. Her head ached again and she didn't think it was because she'd fainted earlier. "Alex, would you take that tray back to the restaurant for me? It was nice of you to bring it here. Very nice."

The annoyance on Alex's face flickered only for an instant before he went and got the tray. "You want me to take that for you, too? It'll stink up the cabin."

Her fingers tightened on the wrinkled paper. "No," she said, walking back to the door and pulling it open, "I don't mind. He was sweet to get it for me."

"Worried about his feelings? Tough guy like that?" Alex walked past her onto the landing, pausing when he was closest to her. "Well, I'm glad you were able to be honest with *me*." He leaned over the tray between them and kissed her lightly on the cheek.

It was fine. Just fine. "I was. You're right," she said. "I'll see you tomorrow?"

"First thing."

He walked off with another wave and she bolted the door after him.

The Big Mac was delicious.

———

THE SOUL OF MUIR RESORT had designed many of their public buildings to resemble those of traditional Native Americans yurts. The small brown buildings huddled under the redwoods were shaped like gumdrops and had rough, unpretentious exteriors, but inside each was decked out with all the modern amenities of health-seeking rich people everywhere.

Miles wasn't seeking health so much as release. After he'd left Lucy, he'd stripped down to a T-shirt and shorts and found the Cardio Yurt—a miniature 24-Hour Fitness in the forest.

He'd pushed himself like a bat out of hell on the treadmill, way past his usual pace, trying to obliterate the image of Alex and Lucy together in her cabin, trying to forget the feel of her warm little body in his lap.

It wasn't working. When Alex strode in after an hour of endurance training, Miles was dripping wet and half-crazed with a runner's high that wasn't nearly high enough.

Alex walked over, placing himself next to the treadmill. "I've been looking all over for you."

He thought about slowing his pace and discarded the idea. Maybe Alex would get the hint he wasn't in the mood to chat. "Here I am," he said between breaths.

"So, you'd rather run in here on a machine than hike outside through one of the most beautiful places on earth?"

Miles glanced at him, then back at the status screen.

"Listen, I wanted to talk to you."

"Not a good time." Anger gave him another wind, and his feet pummeled the belt, every ounce of his two-forty pounding into the machine like a techno dance hit.

Annoyance flashed over Alex's face. "Could you slow that down for a minute? It'll only take a minute."

It was already taking too long. Miles stabbed the green downward-facing arrow button and waited for the belt to slow to a walking pace. The plantar fasciitis in his left heel was flaring up and he'd probably be limping tomorrow. Wouldn't be able to carry any more swooning maidens. From the looks of him, Alex spent a lot of time in the gym; no doubt he'd love the opportunity to show Lucy that Miles wasn't the only manly man around. Even if he was a shrimp.

"Thank you," Alex said.

Miles grabbed his towel and wiped it across his face while he walked and tried not to stumble off the machine due to exhaustion. "Well?"

"I think you must have some idea what I want to talk to you about."

"If Huntley's asking for a stripper again, tell him he shouldn't have trapped us in rural Mendocino for his bachelor party."

"No, Miles, I didn't want to talk to you about strippers. Quite the opposite."

"He wants a nun?"

"Very funny. I know this is awkward, but I felt it was my obligation to warn you about something. So you don't make a fool of yourself."

Pressing his molars together, Miles looked down and jabbed the speed up again. "That does sound awkward."

"It's about Lucy."

"She's cute, isn't she?"

"More than that, I think. Huntley tells me she used to be in a doctoral program in biostatistics."

"Sounds hard."

Alex gave him a pitying look. "I'm sure it was. She's quite brilliant, he said."

"Guess she wasn't brilliant enough."

"Miles, not everyone drops out of school because of a lack of intellectual power."

"Like me?"

Alex looked at his hands, shifting his weight between his feet. "Sorry, I didn't mean that."

"Oh, that's good. I thought maybe that was a dig about me bailing after one quarter at Stanford."

"No, of course not. I meant that Lucy had realized a master's was ideal for her corporate career, and she'd be better served devoting her energies to working her way up in the private sector since she never wanted to be an academic like her father." Alex ran his hand down the front of his button-down yellow shirt. "You did know about her father?"

He knew very little about Lucy, but Alex didn't need to know that. He picked up his water bottle and took a big gulp. "You've lost me, dude. Why tell me all this?"

"Unlike her father, Lucy has goals. Her father never had the ambition to get tenure, find a management job, make a salary anywhere near his talents." Alex sighed, his eyes bright. "She's the type to appreciate hard work and long hours, because she's done the same and she knows what it'll get you."

Miles toasted him with the water bottle. "She has a nice ass, too."

"This is what I'm talking about. You don't—you don't understand."

"Don't you think she has a nice ass?"

Alex closed his eyes for a second. "I saw the look on your face tonight. You were hoping your little fast food offering would get you somewhere. Before you get hurt, I wanted to warn you that it's hopeless. She and I have already agreed to start seeing one another."

"Exclusively? Seems kind of fast. Didn't you just meet yesterday?"

"In person, yes, but our connections are more complex and go back for years."

"Meaning your friends set you up."

"Some of us value our friendships very highly."

Miles stared at him, looking for malice but only seeing a cloud of smug. Did Alex really think he was too stupid to be insulted? "I value my friendships."

"Of course. Though you gave Huntley a hard time about being his best man, I hear."

"Just looking out for him."

"Of course, of course."

Wrapping the towel around his neck, Miles hit the stop button on the treadmill and let it come to a slow creep before stepping off. His legs were wobbly, but he held himself up to his full height and looked down his sweaty nose at Alex. Getting Lucy the burger had been his version of an apology, not a come-on. He wondered what Alex would have called the way he'd pulled her into his lap. A marriage proposal?

He shook his head and sent sweat flying onto Alex's cheek. "She mentioned she wanted a burger, I was glad to get out for some air, end of story."

"Right. Good. So we understand each other?"

"I'm trying to understand you, Alex, but you're not making it easy."

"I'm not trying to be a dick here, man. I just didn't want you to get the wrong idea. She might have seemed grateful when you helped her down from the zip line, but that doesn't mean what you might have thought it meant, you know?"

"She doesn't want to fuck me, you mean."

The smarmy concern drained out of Alex's face. "Exactly," he said tightly.

Miles almost said, *Then why did she stick her tongue in my mouth?* But unlike Alex, he wasn't an asshole. He wouldn't kiss and tell. "Too bad," he said instead. "She's hot."

The condescension came back into Alex's features. "More than that, my friend." He forced a smile and slapped Miles on the arm, then drew back and walked to the door, surreptitiously wiping the sweat on his hand onto his khakis. "Thanks for taking that so well. I wasn't sure how you'd handle it."

"I'm pretty bummed, actually."

"There are other single women here. I'm sure one of them is looking for the same sort of thing you are."

"Pussy?"

Alex blinked, his face turning red, but he managed to force another smile. "You never grow up, do you, Miles? Must be fun." He opened the door and stepped out with a wave. "Maybe tomorrow we can talk to Huntley about stripper alternatives."

Miles watched the door for a few minutes after he'd left, more confused than ever. The urge to seduce Lucy was, as Yoda would say, strong in him. If anyone deserved to be taken down a notch it was Alex. And he liked Lucy, really liked her. It would be no sacrifice.

He rubbed the towel roughly over his face and cursed into the thick organic bamboo fibers. Alex couldn't have any influence over him. If he went back on his previous decision to stay away from her just because Alex had insulted him, he'd be a loser. He had more spine than that. If the smug little lawyer wanted to think he was a shallow, womanizing dimwit, let him.

Lucy knew better.

Didn't she?

THE YOGA CLASS was at six-thirty the next morning. Wednesday was looking identical to Monday and Tuesday: white sky and damp, cold air, an unlikely August anywhere else in the country but typical for the northern Pacific coast. Lucy wore black yoga pants, black tank, black sweatshirt, and black flip-flops with a large silver rosette over her big toe, wishing she'd packed her black puffy vest and maybe a black cap to keep out the chill.

If Krista didn't like her *palette* she could bite it.

She hadn't slept well. The nap after the tree ceremony had messed up her biorhythms, and she'd stared at the dark room for hours, burping up McOnions and hoping Fawn and Huntley were having cathartic make-up sex in his cabin because she'd never come back after dinner.

She viewed her indigestion as a reminder of another kind of incompatibility. Something could taste good going down but would kill you in the long run.

Not that she was thinking about going down.

"Lucy! You made it!"

Krista jogged over from the path ahead, looking bright and perky. The Yoga Yurt was in the cluster of spa buildings to their left, the morning so early and dark the solar-powered lanterns still glowed from each rounded doorway, casting off a faint blurry light through the fog.

Lucy waved half-heartedly. "Where's Betty?"

Smile turning sour, Krista glanced at the treetops overhead. "Naked, hungover, and snoring like a lawnmower."

"At least somebody had a good night."

"Why, what happened to you?" Krista looked her up and

down, then grabbed her wrist. "Oh, that's right, you totally fainted yesterday. Are you better now?"

"Fine. Just didn't sleep very well. And Fawn didn't come back to the cabin."

"Well, duh. I wouldn't expect her to."

"She'd intended for them to spend the nights apart this week."

They walked up the stairs into the yurt. "Knew that wasn't going to happen," Krista said. "The night before, sure, but all week? He'd never make it."

Lucy paused at the door. "Did you notice how standoffish he was yesterday?"

"Just because his parents are a little conservative. I'm sure it'll be fine." Krista pulled the door open and warm light poured out over them, illuminating Lucy's inky ensemble. "Didn't we buy you a pink tracksuit?"

"Did we?" Lucy avoided her gaze and walked past her into the small studio, relieved to see Alex there, sitting cross-legged on a mat near the front mirrors. His presence would stop Krista from giving her a hard time.

Sure enough, as soon as Krista saw him, she squeezed her lips together and gave Lucy an eager, bright-eyed stare. "You know, I just remembered I promised to have breakfast with Betty. I'll have to catch you later."

She really didn't want to be alone with Alex just then. Wasn't anyone else in the wedding party awake yet? "Krista—"

"Sorry!" Krista shoved the door and hurried back outside, leaving Lucy alone inside the quiet, bamboo-floored studio with Alex. Krista may have been desperate for a man of her own, but she was a generous person willing to live vicariously through her friends.

Alex rose from sitting to standing without moving his feet, a smooth maneuver that had Lucy momentarily staring. "Feeling better this morning?" he asked.

She glanced around, confirmed there was nobody else there, and got a mat off a rack near the door. She unrolled it several feet away, parallel to his, hoping her eyes didn't give away what she thought of his outfit. His white T-shirt and navy bike shorts reminded her of the time a Shakespeare company had performed at her high school and caused a giggle riot. There was just something about men's fabric-molded genitals that bugged-out her modern American eyes.

"Much better, thanks." She sat down in the middle of her mat and smiled at him in the mirror, grateful when he sank back down to the floor, and his reproductive organs disappeared behind his folded legs.

Don't be ridiculous. It wasn't anything personal, she just didn't like seeing penises mushed up with testicles under tight, shiny Spandex. Even if Miles came in wearing a Speedo that was three sizes too small…

She twisted around to look at the door.

No, of course he wouldn't come to yoga at six-thirty in the morning. Or any time of day. He probably couldn't even reach the floor from way up there.

Big Mac.

Just then a forty-something woman came into the yurt wearing Uggs and a big smile, her brown hair tied up in short pigtails and her long, lean body draped with an off-white tunic and matching harem pants. "Morning, yogis, I'm Mary. Sorry I'm late." She strode over to a rolling stereo cabinet. In a moment the sound of rushing water filled the air. "Middle of your sticky mats, please, and I'll come over and you can tell me about your practice."

"Don't worry," Alex said to Lucy. "Just tell her you're a beginner."

"You don't have to tell me what to do," Lucy said.

Mary walked over to him and squatted down; they began talking so quietly, their voices were drowned under the sounds of synthesized rushing waves. He held himself bolt upright, hands on his knees with the palms up, and never opened his eyes.

Lucy felt a huge yawn rise up inside her, swamping her like the waves in the music, and she had to fight the urge to lie down and go back to sleep. She heard a squirting sound and smelled lavender; Mary was spritzing the air with a small bottle as she walked over to her.

Mary kneeled down and looked into Lucy's face with small, amber-colored eyes that didn't blink. "Tell me about your practice."

Alex turned his head without moving his shoulders, like a doll that could swivel a three-sixty. "She's a beginner."

"I've gone to a class at the Y a few dozen times," Lucy said, hearing the defensiveness in her voice.

Mary patted her on the shoulder. "If it hurts, don't go there."

"I won't."

They began with a long period of closed-eye meditation that had Lucy yawning uncontrollably. The only reason she'd said she was coming to the class was to get rid of Alex the night before, and now there they were.

She opened her eyes a crack and studied him. He had a nice profile, a strong chin, a healthy body. He had a nice sprinkling of brown hair on his arms and legs, and strong-looking hands and feet.

He was well-educated, ambitious, had a good job, wanted kids. If he'd had drug or gambling or mental problems, Fawn wouldn't have set them up.

Perfect in so many ways.

The door opened, bringing in a gust of cold, damp air and a large, damp man. Wearing a fleece sweatshirt and jeans, Miles met her gaze from the doorway for a moment before he bent over to unlace his boots.

Lucy's heart began to pound. She turned back to the front of the room and squeezed her eyes shut, but she could still see him in her imagination—the combed-back hair just out of the shower, the calm intelligence in his eyes, the hint of a smile on the lips she'd tasted just the day before.

She had to admit it. Her hormones were jonesing for the wrong guy. It was like her web browser kept sending her to the wrong link. No matter how many times she clicked "Alex," her body redirected her to "Miles."

She had to look at him again.

"Nice jeans," Alex muttered, turning back to the front of the room.

"Should I change?" Miles asked Mary. "I've never done this before."

"Well… why don't you stay and we'll see. Once you go, you might be reluctant to come back. Getting here is so often the biggest challenge."

"Great." Miles grabbed a mat and strode over to Lucy's other side, ignoring Alex. "Morning."

She felt her face flood with heat. Closing her eyes, she ducked her head and told her respiratory system to calm the hell down. "Morning."

He unrolled the mat and fell down on top of it with a grunt. After manually arranging his legs into a cross-legged position, forcing his knees down with his big hands, he swore under his breath. "Sorry. Sore from a run. Don't mind me."

"Maybe you need a recovery day," Alex said.

"I thought yoga might be the perfect thing to loosen me up." Miles looked up at the teacher, excessive innocence in his gray eyes. "Is yoga good for flexibility?"

"Absolutely. Just give it time." Mary beamed at him with evangelical good cheer. "Take it slow and you'll find yoga is a path away from injury."

"Sounds good to me," Miles said. "Batter up."

Lucy folded her lips between her teeth to hide another smile.

Alex exhaled loudly through his mouth, sucked in more air, let out another one.

"You can get started now," Miles said. "I'm ready."

"We already started," Alex said tightly.

"Really? Awesome. I can do *this*."

He sounded so sincere and looked so proud to sit cross-legged on the floor; Lucy caught his gaze in the mirror and smiled at him. He had such a friendly face, broad and open, nothing pinched or held back. When he smiled back at her, a dimple flashed in his left cheek and she gazed at it for a long moment.

Smiling, Mary settled herself in front of them. "Wonderful. Now, reach your hands forward and stretch to the top of your mat, keeping your sitz bones grounded—"

"Sit bone?" Miles bent forward, but just barely. His arms pointed rigidly ahead like a kid learning how to dive.

Alex stopped pretending to be self-contained. "Miles, if you think this is so funny, maybe you should leave."

A quick frown passed over Mary's face. "We've got a place for everyone here. Nobody should be worried about what his or her neighbor is doing." She got up and went over to Miles, touched his shoulder. "That's it. You just need a little support." She padded off to the racks behind them and returned with two large cork blocks. She set them under Miles's hands.

Alex snorted.

Mary shot him another displeased look.

Miles appeared to be making a genuine effort to fold himself forward, then from side to side as Mary instructed, and didn't say another word. Nevertheless, Lucy could feel the tension building in the room like a kettle over the stove.

The next postures had them on their hands and knees, and that was no problem. They all arched their backs and hunched themselves over and breathed as Mary told them, Alex with obvious enthusiasm, exhaling his air out with a *hunh* that was so loud Lucy glanced at Miles to see what he would do. He caught her eye and winked.

Hunh! Alex went again, and Lucy had to bite her lip and stare at her hands pressing into the mat to stop herself from laughing out loud.

Hunh!

The laugh burst out of her. Alex swung his head sideways to look at her in dismay.

"Sorry," she said, swallowing air and staring at the floor again.

She kept it together for another few minutes, even during the Modified Plank, and then Child's Pose—for which Miles required the addition of another pair of blocks under his forehead.

But then came Downward Facing Dog.

Miles watched Alex, Lucy, and Mary position themselves, then tried to lift his own butt in the air. He didn't come close to looking like an upside-down V; his knees were bent, his head was lifted, and his chest was parallel to the floor.

"Woof," he said. "Does this work for you?"

Mary stood up from her own pose, went over to him, tried stack the blocks higher so he could straighten his legs. "It's not what works for me, it's what works for you."

He grunted, dropping his knees to the floor. "Maybe I'm more of a caterpillar. Is there a caterpillar pose?"

She touched his broad back and smiled. "We'll do Cobra in a minute."

Should the instructor be touching one of her students so much? It's not like she could imbue his body with flexibility through the power of her skinny little fingers. And why did she keep smiling at him?

Lucy's thoughts continued along these lines throughout

Triangle Pose and all the Warriors. It was like Mary chose poses she knew Miles wouldn't be able to do so she'd have to stroke his big, strong, inflexible muscles. And then get him hot and sweaty so he had to take off the bulky sweatshirt, exposing the thin, skimpy T-shirt he wore underneath.

His jeans strained against his thighs, his back stretched the jersey of the T-shirt, his strong arms lifted over his head. He looked like Atlas himself.

Lucy lost her balance and fell to her hands and knees.

"Listen to your body," Mary said.

The instructor might have been surprised to know what Lucy's body was saying; it had nothing to do with yoga. Lucy got back to her feet and tried to balance with her legs three feet apart. *Just don't look at him.*

They folded over and got down into Plank Pose, which was a little more than Lucy's arms were up to. She slumped down to her knees and then flopped onto her belly.

In spite of Miles's jokes about being a caterpillar, he wasn't having any trouble with holding himself off the ground in the Plank's pushup position. His broad shoulders flexed with muscle and his legs stretched out behind him, firm and immobile.

From her bellyflop position on the floor, Lucy watched Mary with narrowed eyes to see if she would find an excuse to go touch him again. "Readjust" him.

Hunh!

Lucy looked over at Alex, caught him looking at her, and smiled politely.

"Try Child's Pose if you need a rest," he said.

"I'm fine right here." She closed her eyes and put her cheek on the mat, forced to listen to Mary's footsteps pass by her and hover next to Miles again. Hussy Pose.

Okay, you've officially lost it, Lucy.

She joined in with the rest of the positions as well as she

could, grateful when they moved onto their backs for leg stretches and twists, and she could stare at the ceiling instead of at Miles's body. And later, when they went limp, closed their eyes, drifted off into a state of total relaxation.

Yeah, right.

As soon as Mary told them to wiggle their fingers, Lucy got to her feet and rolled up her mat. Miles was still sprawled out on his back next to her, a peaceful calm on his face, and she felt a powerful urge to adjust him.

He opened his eyes, those smiling gray eyes, and made a face. "I think I'm stuck."

Before Mary could rush over to help, Lucy bent over and held out her hand. "Here."

He raised an eyebrow. "You got superpowers I don't know about?"

"Try me."

He grinned and her stomach did a *chaturanga*. "I will." He lifted one hand, put it in hers, and pulled. She tumbled forward and landed on top of him, her face in the crook of his shoulder and her butt in the air. "Whoops," he said.

"Déjà vu," she muttered. She could feel his heart pounding under her cheek, smell him.

"Ah, French. The language of love," he said softly in her ear.

Her free hand in the middle of his huge chest, she pushed herself up to kneel next to him, unable to look away from his face. His sensuous mouth was curved up in a smile, but his eyes were serious and dark.

Alex appeared on his other side. "How the mighty have fallen." He grabbed Miles's opposite shoulder and rolled him over onto his side, facing away from Lucy. "Yoga's not for everyone."

The hem of Miles's sweatshirt had risen up, exposing the

base of his spine and the hint of two dimples above the waistband of his jeans.

The blood rushed out of Lucy's head. She stumbled onto her feet and carried the mat over to the rack, her mouth dry.

Holy Moses.

"Are you all right?" Mary asked her.

Nope. "A little lightheaded."

"That's normal. Go slow. Drink lots of water. Remember your breath."

"Right." Lucy inhaled deeply. "Thank you."

She couldn't look at him or it would be obvious. Exaggerating her weariness, Lucy put her hand to her head and caught Alex's eye. "I'm going back to my cabin to, uh, hold on to this feeling for a while. See you later." With a vague wave, she fled out of the building into the chilly morning and began to run.

$\mathcal{M}$iles left the yoga studio before Alex could say anything that would lead to violence.

One thing: he was glad he'd worn jeans instead of the shrink-wrapped number Alex had on because he'd been fighting a hard-on for twenty minutes.

Damn, the feel of her when she landed on top of him...

Where did she go? He stepped out onto the path and looked around, but she was gone. Not eager to continue what they'd started. Afraid.

At least she was beginning to realize how wrong Alex would be for her. The more time she spent with him, the better.

No, the more time she spent with *Miles*, the better.

He pulled his sweatshirt over his head and set off into the woods before Alex would catch up with him for another little chat.

Where would she have run off to? She probably sensed he was going to hunt her down, which would eliminate her cabin as a hiding spot. The lodge was getting crowded; every day, more and more guests arrived, lingering there, especially in the morning for a quick cup of coffee.

He yawned, feeling a tightness behind his eyeballs. He could use a shot of caffeine himself. Maybe she'd be desperate for java, too.

As soon as he stepped inside the lodge he knew he'd guessed correctly. Her black hood was pulled up over her distinctive hair, but he recognized her dark, pear-shaped silhouette entering the gift shop past the sitting area.

His body responded optimistically. He tried to relax, but he'd spent the last hour stealing glimpses of her round ass and perky breasts bouncing around right next to him on the floor and it was impossible to pretend he wasn't halfway to heaven.

He caught up to her by the refrigerated case across from the cash register. The store was only about ten square feet, with the usual sweatshirts and hats and postcards displayed on the walls and a few shelves of toiletries and snacks in the middle. The staffer at the cash register was ringing up all the purchases but explaining to Fawn's mother that no payments were necessary.

"For God's sake, I wish they'd put up a sign or something," Geri said to Lucy, putting her wallet back into her purse. She had a bottle of water and a small box of condoms, which she quickly shoved into her purse after the wallet. "I could've stashed them away without making such a scene."

Lucy laughed. "I think it's cute you met somebody."

Miles wondered what kind of guy would send his woman out to buy condoms at eight in the morning.

"Cute? Have I gotten so old that it's *cute* I have sex?" Shaking her head, Geri went over to the shelves, helped herself to a box of crackers and a bottle of wine, and went back to the register. "Wait until you meet him. 'Cute' isn't the word."

Lucy still hadn't noticed Miles standing in the doorway behind her. "When does he get here?" She sounded amused.

"Not sure. He has to get time off work."

"One box enough?" Lucy asked.

Geri swung around, looking like she had a retort on her lips, but froze when she noticed Miles. Lucy hesitated, then turned slowly and saw him.

"Morning, yogi," he said, then nodded his head to Geri. "Mother of the bride."

"Aren't you a vision," Geri said. "I was just telling Lucy here how cute it is to have sex."

Lucy gasped.

"Now we're even." Geri thanked the cashier for the items she'd bagged up and smiled at Miles on her way out.

Lucy turned her back to him and thunked her bottle of water and apple on the counter.

He grabbed the closest thing to him—a crystal window decoration—and joined her at the register. "Nice lady."

"Very."

"Fawn's parents been divorced a long time?"

"Since fifth grade. Right before we met."

"I didn't realize you'd known each other so long. That explains a lot."

She frowned at him, clutching her purchase to her chest. "What does it explain?"

"How a supermodel and an analyzing processor would be best friends."

"Process analyst."

He grinned. "Right." He handed his crystal thingie to the cashier and hoped she didn't take too long wrapping it up.

But Lucy was already out the door. "Sorry, never mind," he told the cashier, abandoning it there to run after Lucy.

"Sorry to rush off, Miles, but I've got an appointment in a few minutes."

He strode after her through the lodge and out the door. "What kind of appointment?"

"Massage. Then a facial. I'll probably just sleep the rest of the day."

"Aren't the massages in the buildings back there? Near yoga?"

She stopped and looked through the trees behind him, shook her head. "Yes, of course. Silly of me." Without meeting his eyes, she scurried past him in the opposite direction.

"You know, I've never had a facial," he said. "Does it hurt?"

She dug her hands into her pockets. "Only when you pay for it."

"Do you do it to yourself, or is there help?"

She ducked her head under the hood and kept walking, but he thought she might be laughing a little.

"Can I come?" he asked.

After a pause, she stopped and glanced up at him. Her cheeks were pink, her green eyes bright but wary. "Why?"

"I have a face, don't I?"

She bit her lip, studying him. "You do."

He took a step closer. Not for the first time in his life, he wished he weren't so damn tall. Trying not to look obvious, he bent his knees a little. "Think they'll know what to do with it?"

"Y—" She cleared her throat. "Yes, I imagine they will."

One of her coppery curls had escaped her hood and was poking her in the eye. Slowly, not breathing, he lifted his hand and brushed it aside with the tip of his index finger. Her skin was buttery soft. Warm.

"I don't want to be late," she said, but didn't move.

He kept his hand near her cheek, feeling huge and clumsy, and looked for something in her expression that would give him permission to touch her some more.

But she stepped back and turned away, and Miles felt the opportunity evaporate like the haze overhead. Nevertheless he said, "Would you like to have lunch with me?" and waited a long moment before she slowed her steps and glanced back.

"I can't."

"Dinner?"

She smiled but shook her head. "I should probably eat with Alex. To make up for last night."

"A hike this afternoon, then."

"Miles—"

"You've got to do something. Might as well be with me. I'm sure you like Alex a lot, really I'm sure you do, but you probably don't want to spend the entire day with him." Her mouth dropped open to protest, so he hurried on. "Until after you're married. Then you won't be able to spend a minute apart, of course. You wouldn't want to."

"Just because—" She crossed her arms over her chest, lips in a flat line. "That's not the kind of relationship I was looking for anyway."

Maybe it should be. "How about three this afternoon?"

They stared at each other a couple of seconds too long. He felt his body respond with excessive hope, especially when she said, "Have to do something, I guess. All right."

He smiled. "I'll come by your cabin."

"I can meet you at the West Side trailhead. It's on the map."

"I'll come by your cabin at three."

"It's out of your way. We can just meet there," she said.

"I'll be at your cabin."

She rolled her eyes but was fighting a smile. "Yes, Camp Leader."

"Bears," he said. "There might be bears."

She snorted, looked him up and down, and turned away. "Something like that."

Man, how he wanted to pick her up and do wet, happy things to her body.

He shoved his hands in his pockets and watched her walk away. It was almost worth having her leave to be able to study that ass move like that. He wondered if she had a tattoo. Bet she did under there somewhere. Somewhere good.

Readjusting his jeans, he headed back to his cabin where he found Huntley sitting on the steps with his chin propped in his hands.

"Need your help," Huntley said.

Miles went past him into the cabin and kicked off his shoes. "It's too early. Come back after noon. I'm going back to bed."

"You need to talk to my parents."

"Close the door. I'm taking off my pants." Miles sat on the bed and shoved his jeans down to his ankles. The bed was still unmade from the night before, but it was soft and cool and didn't demand any unusual flexibility on his part. He slid under the covers and let out a deep sigh.

"Please, Miles. They'll listen to you."

He closed his eyes. "No. Your job. Past time. Good-bye."

"What's the matter with you? Not like you were out drinking last night." Huntley hesitated. "Right?"

"Jealous?"

"All you have to say to them is that you've changed your mind about Fawn. You realize she loves me. That she's brilliant and hard-working and wonderful and everything."

Miles pulled a pillow over his head. It was only Wednesday, and early morning at that. That left at least twelve hours today, and all of Thursday and Friday. "What time is the wedding on Saturday? Morning or night?"

"Morning," Huntley said.

"Thank God." He might even make it home in time for the game. And all of Sunday would be his, quiet at home in blissful solitude.

Miles thought of Lucy and sighed into the down pillow.

What would she think of his apartment in the city? Would she call it a dump in the ghetto like Felicia had?

He was sick of defending himself and the choices he had made. Lucy wouldn't ever see his apartment because Lucy wanted a husband. Whatever fun they might have over the next few days, it wouldn't follow them into their real lives. They'd spend the afternoon together, then he'd try to extend it through dinner and many hours past that—but next week? Her spreadsheet didn't have room for him next week.

How ironic. He'd like to pursue his attraction to her, hers to him, see where it led—but she'd fight him at every step of the way because she was the one who wanted a commitment.

"Women are irrational creatures," Miles said, his voice muffled by the pillow.

"Fawn's got a point, though," Huntley said. "I've been paranoid about any public displays of affection because I don't want to push my parents over the edge."

Flinging the pillow aside, Miles looked at him. "There's a lot of wiggle room between treating her like a leper and going down on her while they watch. Maybe hold her hand. I know that's a big step for you, but I think your parents can handle it." He pulled the covers up to his chin. "She deserves at least that much."

"You're right, you're right." Huntley sat on the bed, crushing Miles's toes. "Think how much more effective it would be if you warmed them up a little bit beforehand."

"You want effective? Man up." Miles pulled his feet out from under Huntley's bony ass and kicked him off the bed. "You're too old for this. Handle it yourself."

"Some best man you are."

"We've established that."

Huntley ran his hand through his pale hair and walked to the door. "I know you're right. I just wanted a little backup."

"This is your backup."

"Just one little conversation—"

"The only conversation I'll be having is right here with Mr. Pillow."

Huntley snorted and slammed the door on his way out.

Miles rolled over to dream about an irrational, round-bottomed redhead.

HE WAS at her door at two fifty-nine, smiling at the blue sky with a bounce in his step. He'd put on new hiking boots, a fresh sweatshirt, and shaved a second time—he wasn't James Bond or anything, but at least he smelled okay.

She came out before he knocked, her cheeks flushed, and didn't hold his gaze for more than a split second. But he saw the spark there and smiled again.

"How's the face?" he asked.

She glanced up at him, a smile twitching in the corner of her mouth. "Fine."

"I agree."

"Miles—"

"Sorry. I'll tone it down. I thought we could stop by the lodge for water and trail mix. I brought my pack."

"Is that really necessary? My plan is to be back by five-thirty."

"What's at five-thirty?"

"It's only three. Do you think we'll be gone that long?"

"Easy. I was just curious." If she had a firm date with Alex, she'd say so, wouldn't she? "You want to be back at five-thirty, we'll be back by then. I'm very punctual." He held out his wristwatch. "See? Got here right at three. Reliable guy, Miles Girard."

She snorted and walked ahead. "I suppose it would be a good idea to have some water."

"And an energy bar or something. Bears like me have to eat frequently. Storing fat for the winter." He patted his stomach, watching her carefully to see if she look disgusted, but she was fighting down another smile.

The sun slipped through in a white diagonal stripe through the trees, illuminating a vast spiderweb that stretched between the redwoods across their path. Lucy paused, glanced back at him to see if he noticed it, and they both set to discover the orb weaver at its center. When they found her, a surprisingly small creature for such an enormous web, they silently admired her and her miraculous accomplishment for a long moment. However hopeless the gesture, they both ducked below the web to continue walking down the path.

With a deep, contented sigh, he followed her the rest of the way to the lodge, reflecting that Huntley had picked a nice spot to get hitched. Miles had backpacked through the north coast before, but he had to admit it was nice to enjoy the beauties of nature after sleeping in a heated cabin with all the perks of a luxury hotel.

He watched Lucy's bouncy step, the way her bottom swayed, the hint of skin at the nape of her neck under the copper-bright hair.

She was one perk he hadn't anticipated. They had rare chemistry—mutual, sudden, instinctive attraction—and they were in an oasis away from their normal lives where they could actually enjoy it.

It would be stupid to waste it.

He jogged ahead of her to open the door to the lodge, holding her gaze with his as she came up the steps, sliding his hand down her back to usher her inside. Pretty sure he saw her shiver, he grinned.

But as soon as he stepped inside after her, he felt a sixth sense prickling the back of his neck. Smile falling, he looked over to the right.

A woman stood with her back to him. Tall and fashionable, she had honey-blond hair, tight jeans, and a lean figure that would be the envy of a woman half her age. She was only— Miles clenched his jaw, remembering—in her mid-forties now.

Of course she still looked good. Heather had always looked good. That's why his father had married her.

Then he saw him.

Alan Girard, looking shockingly older than the last time they'd seen each other. His hair was white, not a hint of dark brown remaining. The pale skin of his scalp was visible through the fine strands. Miles had always thought of him as a giant, bigger than he would ever be, but today, with fresh eyes, he saw the slight sag to his father's shoulders, a thinness in his cheeks, the whiff of weakness. He'd been a middle-aged man when Miles was born. No longer.

Miles had to wait until his breathing steadied and he was in complete control of himself before acknowledging him. The last time they'd seen each other, neither had spoken—in rare accord that his half-brother Chas's wedding was no place to end a cold war and start an open one.

But Huntley wasn't family, years had gone by, and all bets were off.

Miles shoved his hands in his pockets and gave him a cool stare. He hoped the emotion flooding his body wasn't obvious. "Father," he said carefully.

Neither took a step toward the other.

His father stared, frozen in place, unblinking.

Just as he looked as if he might say something, Heather swung around and flung up her hands. "Miles!" she cried. "We hoped to see you here!" She walked over.

Warily, Miles watched Heather approach, distastefully aware of how she checked him out. He wondered what she saw when she looked at him. The one that got away? Her lucky escape?

Jailbait no more?

"Heather," he said roughly. His face felt hot. Childish shame washed over him.

At least his father wasn't going to pretend this was some lighthearted reunion. He stayed on the other side of the room and stared into a coffee cup.

Heather's pale blue eyes flicked over to Lucy. "Who's this?"

Without thinking, Miles put a protective arm around Lucy. "We're late for our hike. See you later."

But Lucy held firm and stuck out her hand. "Lucy Hathcoat. Maid of honor."

"Heather Girard." She gave Lucy a slow once-over, her gaze lingering on her heavy black boots. She turned her attention slowly back to Miles, making a show of tilting her head back as though the journey from Lucy's face to his had taken her a while. "Old friends, you two?"

"Very. Have to go." He squeezed Lucy's shoulder.

This time, she got the hint.

"Sorry, Miles knows I'm pressed for time. The bride needs me in a few hours but I'm dying to see the ocean while the sun's out."

"The beach is close by?" Heather turned back to his father, still standing there like a secret service agent, cold and important and silent.

"Close enough," Alan said.

They stood awkwardly for another moment.

"We'll see you around." Miles took Lucy's hand in his and pulled her back outside. When the sun hit him in the face, he realized he'd fled without buying anything at the store. "I forgot to get water and snacks."

Lucy didn't pull her hand free. "We'll be fine."

He forced a deep breath and turned his attention to the soft, warm palm pressed against his.

"Yeah," he said.

Chapter 13

He didn't say much. Lucy didn't mind. The afternoon was bright and clear, and feeling the sun on her face for the first time in three days made her realize how much she'd missed it. Everything seemed lighter, warmer, easier.

For her, anyway. Miles was obviously shaken by his family reunion back at the lodge. She pulled a field guide to birds out of her pack pocket and flipped through aimlessly, not really caring about the difference between Great or Snowy egrets but not wanting to force unwanted small talk.

The physical resemblance between Miles and his father had been striking. Both were linebacker-sized men with gray eyes and broad faces, each visibly tense and unhappy to see the other.

"Sorry I didn't introduce you," Miles said suddenly. They were walking along a narrow path next to the creek, sheltered from the wind by the hills to the northwest. Soon they'd be passing out into the open, grassy wetlands that led to the coast. "He and I aren't very close."

"I heard."

"What did you hear?"

"No details. Just that you had some falling out years ago."

"Alex tell you that?"

"He might have mentioned it. And Fawn, too." She picked up a long stick and snapped off the thin side branches one by one. "We love to sit around gossiping about you, of course. Exchange notes. Secret pictures."

He snorted, but some of the gloom faded from his eyes. "I'd like to see your secret pictures."

"It's amazing how small they can make cameras these days. I've got a great one of you doing Downward Facing Caterpillar."

"Now I'm really interested. Was this a hidden camera? Any self-portraits?"

"Afraid not. All of you."

He grinned. "None of Alex?"

She'd walked right into that one. Throwing the stick into the bushes, she smiled brightly at him. "Loads. I don't have to hide, so I just click away."

"Hmph. I bet he'd love to pose." He shoved his hands in his pockets and strode over a jagged crack in the path. "A born poser, Alex."

"That your snobby upbringing shining through, Miles?"

"Me?" Miles turned to her. "You have been listening to Alex."

"You call him a poser because he's ambitious. Determined to make something of himself."

"I call him a poser because he's a poser."

"Snob."

"That too."

"I mean you."

"I'm not a snob, but you'd know that if you were processing your analysis with a little more objectivity."

She laughed. "I'm processing just fine."

"No, you're indulging in heavy bias. You want to like him, ergo, you'll ignore the evidence before your eyes. You don't want to like me, ergo"—he raised his eyebrow and held out his arms—"you ignore the evidence before your eyes."

She brushed past him. He thought he was so damn cute. "'Poser' implies somebody pretending to be something he's not, as though he's not entitled to be educated and respected—"

"He's a phony, Lucy, always has been. He cares more about how he looks than who he is. He's been putting on the show so long I bet he's even fooled himself."

"What about him is a lie? You met him at Stanford yourself. He must have gone to law school—or do you think he made that up?"

"Forget it. The more I say about him, the more you'll convince yourself he's Mr. Right."

"I'm not like that."

He looked at her. "Maybe not. Never mind. I shouldn't say any more. He's the last person I want to be thinking about. Well, maybe not the last. Second to last." He kicked a rock. "Third to last."

She studied the tension in his broad shoulders as he walked ahead of her, debating how much she could pry. The sun was still high but tilting west, shining in their eyes—at least until the blanket of fog crept back in.

"Is your father in first place?" She remembered the scary blond woman with the mean eyes. "Or would that be your stepmother?"

He swung his head around to look at her. "How do you figure that?"

She stared back, lifted an eyebrow. "Just processing the analysis."

"Hmmph." He gestured for her to walk ahead of him. A fork in the path was marked with a tidy wooden sign; a couple of miles ahead was the ocean, to the left a single loop trail through the wetlands and back to the lodge. He looked at his watch then up at the sky. "Fog's coming in again. If you want to get back by five-thirty, maybe we should just head back now."

"Nice try. Ask one little question, and you're already trying to get rid of me." She began striding down the path to the ocean. "It's an easy trail. Two miles won't take very long."

"It's a lot colder than I expected."

"Look, it's all right if you want to take a rain check, but I'm going to keep going. I can handle a little walk by myself. I'm a big girl." Looking back, she saw the look on his face and stuck out her tongue. "In all the important ways." That made his look get even more suggestive so she went back to him and poked him in the chest.

Capturing her wrist, he held her hand against his heart and looked down at her, a small smile on his lips. "Wherever you go, I go, big girl."

She froze. He felt warm and vital under her palm, a living mountain of a man. Something old inside her soul rose up in recognition. *I know this one.*

His grip softened. His thumb stroked the back of her hand, sending tendrils of sensation up her arms, to the back of her neck, down her spine.

Then he released her hand and lightly touched her shoulder. "Let's go see this ocean. Find out what all the fuss is about."

She let her breath out slowly and swallowed. He waited for her to resume walking, and in a moment they were on their way single file down the path, through the golden, matted grasses. The creek met up with a widening river, and Highway 1 came into sight on an elevated bridge. They walked under the road, into the wall of wind.

Lucy used the time to reboot her brain. Reattach the

cranium to her nerve endings, apply overrides to the hormonal malfunctions going rampant in her body.

Yes, he was adorable. He was big and sweet and charming, had dimples she wanted to touch, a trustworthy demeanor, sensuous hands, gentle eyes.

All wonderful qualities, qualities that would be great in a pal or a boyfriend, but she was looking for a different kind of man. She'd wasted eight years waiting for Dan to be "ready" for marriage. There wasn't time to waste eight more. Men had it easy; they could dawdle. Women might have more years at the end of their lives, but her ovaries didn't know that. They hadn't even realized the Ice Age was over. They wanted her to have babies before her stone tool wound got infected or she got eaten by a giant prehistoric bird with obsidian-sharp claws.

Lucy glanced back at Miles, reflecting that he would be a good candidate for continuing the species. She could easily imagine him whacking a flying predator with a club, a heavy fur pelt on his broad, powerful shoulders—

He grinned at her, his dimple flashing. "What?"

This was why she had to use her brain, not biochemistry, for decision-making. Flying predators were not on any of her lists.

She swung her head around and focused on the path ahead. "Nothing."

He tromped up next to her. "What?"

"You and your dad look alike," she said, if just to make that dimple go away and stop tempting her.

Sure enough, his smile fell. "There's an evolutionary advantage to looking like your father. Helps pressure the man to stick around. Not that it always works."

"Just thinking about evolution myself."

"Yeah?" A twinkle came back into his eyes. "Was that when you were admiring my body?" He patted his chest, wiggled an eyebrow. "Millions of years of natural selection went into this physique, baby."

She bit back a grin. "It's very nice."

His gaze raked down over her body, came back to her face. "You think so?"

"Of course," she said, now smiling, amused he looked a little insecure. "I'd kill for a little of your... stature."

The wind blew the hair across her face. He reached out and tucked it behind her ear, staring down at her. Then he lowered his hand and cupped her face. Her heart thudded, expecting a kiss, and she told herself to reach up and pull his hand away and keep walking. But when he dropped his arm and strode past her, she was tempted to complain.

"What kind of birds are those?" he asked her briskly, pointing at the beach.

"Seagulls."

"Ah. Right."

She snorted, passing him, in control of her biology again. She jogged ahead to look for tide pools.

***

"Thanks for not prying," Miles said.

Barefoot in the surf, Lucy turned and caught his gaze, her green eyes matching the ocean behind her. Her cheeks were flushed pink from the wind. He noticed freckles along the bridge of her nose and he lost his train of thought, absorbed in the details of her face.

"I'm a little curious, I admit," she said.

He dropped to his knees in the sand and dug a hole until he hit water. He mounded up hills of wet sand, imagining it was her body, wondering if that made him a creep. "My father and I haven't spoken to each other for a long time."

Lucy sank down to the sand next to him and began digging

her own hole about two feet away. They worked in parallel, each making a tower just out of reach of the waves. Finally she asked, "What happened?"

Should he tell her? He glanced up and saw she wasn't watching him but staring at her hands, submerged in a sandy puddle. The wind whipped her coppery hair around her cheeks. He saw she had a triple piercing in her left ear, and was surprised he hadn't noticed earlier. Three little pearls, not much larger than the freckles on her nose, outlined the curve of her ear like stars.

"I wouldn't think you'd like pearls," he said. "Kind of old-fashioned for you, aren't they?"

Now she looked up. "They were my mother's. She died when I was nine."

He saw the calm challenge in her eyes. *If I can talk about it, you can*, she seemed to say.

He bent down for another handful of sand. "I was three. Barely. I don't remember her very well." His memories of a little apartment with a huge, smelly dog were more vivid than his memory of his own mother's face, which had always both-ered him. "That's when I went to live with my father, but it was my stepmother—not Heather, but a couple of marriages earlier—who really took me in. I still think of Pat as my mom. She lives in Arizona now, a great human being, generous to a fault. I spend the holidays with her."

"How old were you when—" she stopped herself. "Sorry. Prying again."

"It's all right. I was in sixth grade. He dumped her for an 'on-air personality.' A TV reporter. That one only lasted a year. Then, when I was in high school, he married Heather."

"Ladies' man, your dad?"

"To hear him tell it, he's just very honest. Not one to sneak around. When he wanted to be with a different woman, he said so." Miles pounded the tower of sand he was building. "I've never bought that, but maybe that's because he seemed to have different standards about different kinds of women. As if the women who worked for him didn't count."

"Your mother…"

"One of the secretaries at the firm. In case you're keeping track, that would have been after wife number one and during wife number two," he said. "More proof Pat—my ex-step-mother—is a wonderful human being. She never ever let on that I was anything but one of the family." He cleared his throat, fighting down unwanted emotion. "Even though I was a reminder of my father's disloyalty. If my mother hadn't died, Pat might never have found out I existed."

Lucy traced a circle in the sand with a stick. "What happened?"

"Car accident. Yours?"

"Cancer." She shrugged. "For a long time I was terrified of being an orphan. My mom had died and I knew my father was much older than any of the other kids' dads. He'll be seventy-five this year."

Miles realized with some discomfort that he didn't know precisely how old his own father was anymore. His half-brother had mentioned a big seventieth birthday party a few years back, maybe hoping he'd come. "I suppose I felt a little vulner-able too. My father's about that age. Heather… Well, she's obviously much younger. Your dad remarried?"

"Just recently, thank God. Trudy is a little younger and is the type to alphabetize her spice jars. Managing my father's life is a snap." She smiled weakly. "Before she came along, I had a lot less free time. My dad is a stereotypical absent-minded professor—he'd lose his own butt if it wasn't attached. My stepmother is a gift from heaven."

"They can be. Especially if you have a large pool of step-mothers to draw from."

"So, what's the story with Blondie?"

"Heather?" He jabbed his finger into the sand to make a doorway to his castle. "I don't like her."

Lucy choked out a laugh. "I gathered that."

He hesitated. Was he really going to tell her? He watched her work on her own castle. Very carefully, she dripped wet sand from her pinched fingers, making an impossibly delicate column reach up to the sky like a tower in a fairy tale.

He scooped up a handful of wet sand and tried to imitate her technique. "The problem," he said slowly, "was that she liked *me*."

Lucy moved her hand away from her fragile creation and stared at him. "How old were you?"

He shrugged. "That wasn't the problem."

Her eyes bored into him, deadly serious. "How old?"

"Old enough. I was a big boy. Just had an issue with her being my father's *wife*."

Lucy crossed her arms over her chest, ignoring how her hands left clumps of wet sand on her clothes. Her eyes narrowed. "You were in high school when they got married. Then dropped out of college your freshman year. So you couldn't have been much over eighteen."

"Alex loves to gossip, doesn't he?" He dug his knuckles into the sand to make ramparts. "I would've felt exactly the same way if I'd been twenty-five. It was the disloyalty that offended me."

"You were just a kid," she said fiercely.

He laughed, amused by her protectiveness. "You're cute when you're angry."

"What did your father do when he found out?" she asked.

Time to change the subject. He swiped his sand castle into the hole and climbed over it on hands and knees. She leaned back, arms still folded over her chest, but the fierce gleam in her eyes turned into something else. When his face was only a few inches from hers, she licked her lips.

His hands were too cold, wet, and sandy to touch her, but his mouth wasn't. He moved closer, smiling as a tendril of her hair tickled his cheek, and kissed her gently on the lips. She was so sweet. Her mouth was soft under his, yielding, and he tilted his head to deepen the kiss.

Two cold, sandy hands clamped onto his face and pushed him away. "Nice try, but I'm not so easily distracted." Her voice was low, shaky.

"My father blamed me, we fought, I moved on. End of story." He broke free of her grip and kissed the side of her neck right under the constellation of pearl earrings. He could feel her pulse racing under his tongue. "This was my plan all along, you know."

Very slowly, she tilted her head to the side. "Telling me your life story?"

He nibbled her earlobe, letting his tongue trace each individual pearl, feeling her tremble as he blew air across her damp skin. "You smell so good," he whispered.

She moaned and leaned into him. "You're evil."

Chuckling, he kissed his way across her wind-blown cheeks to her lips, his hands still braced in the sand. Hers were gripping his shoulders—whether to hold him back or keep him close, he wasn't sure.

She let him kiss her. Unlike the time in the cabin, however, she didn't jump on top of him. He wanted to tap into that passion again, feel her come alive, not hold herself still and rigid and careful.

At least she wasn't fighting it anymore, this chemistry between them. While his mouth explored hers, he tried to figure out how to get her back to his cabin.

Stupid of him to start anything on the cold beach. It was like making out on a sandy glacier. His hands were going numb in the wet sand. He could hardly push her onto her back next to the piles of decomposing kelp and rip her clothes off in twenty-mile-an-hour gusts with the tide coming in.

"Shall we continue this at my place?" he asked in her ear.

"I have a date with Alex."

He pulled back, his mind dulled from the blood pooling elsewhere. He must have misunderstood. "He'll understand if you cancel. After you explain."

She sighed and rolled away from him. Her cheeks were even more flushed now, and her lips looked damp and swollen. Kissed. Scooping up another handful of sand, she went back to making her castle without meeting his eyes. "There's nothing to explain."

Still on his hands and knees, he ducked his head to make her look at him. "Lucy…"

"We'll just stop doing this. You promise to stop initiating, and I'll promise to stop responding." She patted the base of her tower, still not looking at him. "'Kay?"

He gaped at her. "And why would I agree to this?"

"You know there's no future between us. Unless you're looking to settle down." She gave him a bright, fake smile. "Want to get married?"

"You don't mean that. With me or with Alex." He got to his feet and slapped the sand off his knees. "You don't even *like* Alex."

"I don't know him well enough, which is why I'm not going to give up on the idea just because"—she waved her hand between them as if she were dispersing a bad odor—"part of me isn't governed by reason."

"Yeah," he said, "I like those parts."

"Sure you do." She stood up, walked away from him into the surf. She bent at the waist to rinse the sand off her hands.

Miles was struck by the perfection of the view. He strode over, grabbed her from behind, pulled her against him.

"I'd give you time to chuck Alex on your own, but there is

none," he said, bending over to brush his lips against the earrings again. "Take advantage of what we've got here. We should enjoy each other. You can bag a husband any time."

She wriggled away and swatted his arm. "Any time? Please. Clock's ticking here, buddy. You don't want to deal with a woman in a hurry? Bark up a younger tree." She gave him a big, toothy smile that didn't reach her eyes. "I'm sure there are lots of twenty-two year-old women who would love to have you."

If they'd been in a cozy, dry, comforter-filled spa cabin when he'd made his move, they'd be naked by now. He slapped the sand off his feet, watching her do the same, and they put on their shoes.

Getting to his feet, he gestured to the path up the beach. "Let's head back."

She fell into step beside him. "Look, I know I'm sending mixed signals. I'm sorry."

"No problem, I understand." *So long as your signals to Alex are mixed in the opposite direction.* "You've been very up-front with me."

She sighed, apparently relieved, and he let her walk ahead of him up the path. "Thank you. It would be selfish to have any drama between us stress out the lovebirds this week. They're having enough trouble with his parents."

Watching her bottom sway as she hiked, Miles realized he'd almost forgotten about his own parent trouble. That was the great thing about lust. The ultimate amnesia. He was dreading the next few days, how he'd feel like a dumb, angry kid every time he saw the coldness in his father's eyes, the measuring hunger in his stepmother's. Getting Lucy naked just might make it bearable.

They hiked back to the spa, only breaking the silence to comment on the birds or terrain. When they reached the fork in the path leading to her cabin, he took a deep breath and asked casually, "Want to have some tea at my place? Just to warm up?"

But she wasn't fooled. She glanced at him and shook her head before striding away.

He stared after her. *Has she ever given in to that passion before? Just let loose?*

She thought she wanted a husband, but her body knew better.

It would thank him for showing her the truth.

***

WHEN LUCY THOUGHT she was finally out of Miles's sight, she glanced back over her shoulder.

Just the trees.

She sighed, both relieved and disappointed. It was like being fourteen again to have a craving for someone so inappropriate. Back then she would've called it love if she thought about a guy fifty-nine seconds out of every sixty; if the hair on the back of her neck stuck up just because he touched her; if she couldn't control herself around him.

I'm too old for this. As long as she reminded him of her goals, she'd be able to keep him away. Mentioning marriage was like flinging a crucifix at Dracula. Begone, servant of Satan! Tongue to yourself, hands at your sides, spawn of the devil!

Time to get serious. She hurried the rest of her way to her cabin, deciding to call Alex and push their date to seven. That would give her time to wash the sand out of her hair.

She rested her head against the door, overwhelmed with the memory of Miles kissing her over the sand castles. She'd almost jumped him again, right there in front of the gulls and the kelp. If he'd touched her, if he'd pushed it, Lucy would have done anything.

She heard a gasp and spun around. Fawn was running

down the path to the cabin, barefoot, tears streaming down her face. The pretty silver heels that matched her floral chiffon blouse and designer slacks dangled from one hand.

Lucy flung open the door and helped her inside. "What happened?"

Fawn threw herself face-down on the bed and began to cry.

Gritting her teeth, Lucy kicked off her muddy boots as fast as she could and fell to her knees beside Fawn on the bed. "What did he do?"

"It's what he didn't do," Fawn choked out.

"Because his parents were there?"

She pounded the duvet. "I *hate* them."

Lucy rubbed her back, cursing the Sterlings under her breath. "Oh, Fawn. You deserve so much better."

"Dinner last night was bad, but lunch today was worse. They just won't give it up! They're horrible!"

"Is it the modeling? They'd rather you were an investment banker or lawyer or something?"

Fawn flipped over and sat up, wiping her eyes. "I was all prepared for that, even had a little suck-up speech about my degree from Cal being so important to me, how I could casually mention my SATs and my net worth just to show them I'm not just some stupid bimbo."

"Don't even say 'just.'"

"Yeah, well, it doesn't matter. They don't even look at me, not once, let alone insult me. It's like I'm not even there. I couldn't tell you the eye color of either one of them." She leaned forward. "Any of them. Huntley was the worst of all."

Lucy grabbed her hands and squeezed. "I'll kill him."

"He was ashamed of me." She glared at Lucy through her tears. "How can I marry a man who's ashamed of me?"

Lucy swallowed. *Oh, shit.* "You can't."

Chapter 14

Lucy banged on Betty and Krista's cabin door. It was past six. Hopefully they hadn't already gone over to the Snowy Egret for dinner; she'd rather not track them down in front of a crowd.

Betty opened the door wearing only a towel and a smile. Her black and green hair was wet and combed back away from her forehead, emphasizing her bright eyes. Then she saw Lucy, and her smile fell. "Oh, it's you." She glanced over Lucy's shoulder.

"Waiting for somebody?"

"I thought Jaynette might come back." Sighing, Betty opened the door wider and stepped aside to let Lucy in. "Probably for the best. Easy to overdo it, you know? I wouldn't want her to get the wrong idea. I like yoga, but I'm not about to shack up in a spa for the rest of the year to find out how much."

Lucy didn't have time to get into Betty's love life. "I need your car," she said. "Fawn needs to get away for a while."

"Away from here?"

"Huntley's being a dick."

"Shitty timing."

"Yeah."

Chewing her lip, Betty strode over to the bedside table, shoved aside a purple vibrator, a bottle of lube, and a bag of Cool Ranch Doritos to unearth her cell phone. "Krista's got it. She was going through retail withdrawal. Went to Mendocino with Fawn's mother to shop, have dinner." She dialed, glanced up. "They wanted to ask you to come but couldn't find you."

"I was hiking." Lucy rubbed her lips, remembering what else she'd been doing. "Maybe we can catch up with them. Fawn would love to be with her mom, get away from this place for a while."

Or longer. They could brainstorm together on how to get Fawn through this. Worst-case scenario, they could reschedule the wedding—not like money was an issue. Hell of a lot easier to cancel a wedding than a marriage.

Betty shook her head and dropped the phone back on the bedside table. "No coverage. Want me to try at the lodge?"

"I'll call her myself if I can get out of here. Who else has a car?"

Smirking, Betty tucked the towel more tightly around her breasts and stuck her hand in the bag of Doritos. "We could ask Jaynette. She wanted to take me for a ride down the coast tonight and I turned her down."

"That would be great. If she could drop us off in Mendocino, we could get a ride back with Krista and Geri."

"If Fawn wants to come back," Betty said, mouth full of chips. "She should pack her bags just in case. Shows him she's serious and gives her an escape hatch." She picked up the spa phone and dialed.

Sighing, Lucy glanced at the clock. What a mess. They never should have taken Huntley's limo up here. She hated being dependent upon other people.

"Hey, babe, it's the Green Hornet," Betty said into the

phone in a throaty growl. "I've got a favor to ask. Groom's an asshole and the bride needs a ride. One-way to Mendo. Your offer still good?"

Lucy turned away and walked to the door to tune out the low-voiced sex talk that followed. After a minute, Betty dropped the towel and the phone and jogged around the bed to a pile of clothes on the floor. "Your cabin, ten minutes," Betty said, bending over.

"Nice love bites," Lucy said, staring at the red marks on Betty's bare thighs.

"No shit," Betty said, pulling a T-shirt over her head. "You'd think I'd been snakebit and she was sucking out the venom."

"Glad somebody's having a nice time," Lucy muttered, adding her thanks, then ran back to her cabin to tell Fawn about their plans.

A mountain of suitcases at her feet, Fawn sat on the edge of the bed with an open bottle of champagne braced between her thighs and a fierce scowl on her face.

"I'm not coming back," she declared, lifting the bottle to her lips.

"One step at a time," Lucy said. "Let's get out of here, talk, clear our heads." She plucked the bottle out of Fawn's two-handed grip. Surprised it was half empty, Lucy took a closer look at her friend's face. "I was gone five minutes."

"I'm in mourning." She reached out for the bottle.

Lucy marched into the bathroom and poured it down the sink. "You need to stay clear-headed. Figure this out rationally."

Fawn burst in behind her and grabbed her arm. "That was two hundred dollars' worth!"

"Just saving it the trip through your kidneys," Lucy said. "Come on, Betty's new girlfriend is giving us a ride to the coast. Mendocino's not far."

"I want to go home."

"We'll talk about it."

They dragged Fawn's luggage outside just as Betty and the yoga instructor were driving up in a golf cart.

Jaynette was much younger than Lucy expected, a pretty, wide-eyed blonde with a delicate steel nose ring. For all her cynical remarks, Betty looked dopey and pleased to be back with her new squeeze. She jumped out to help load up Fawn's luggage.

There was too much. "We're going to need a bigger boat," Betty said, eyeing the pile of suitcases.

Jaynette pulled out a walkie-talkie. "I'll call Shawn. He owes me a favor."

Sure enough, in two minutes the staffer purred up in another cart. When he saw who needed the ride, and all the suitcases at her feet, he hesitated.

"Not for us to meddle, Shawn," Jaynette said. "The Lord works in mysterious ways."

With a nod, he jumped out and loaded up the rest of Fawn's luggage. The women got into the cart with Jaynette, and they puttered off to the Greeting Lot in silence.

Except for Fawn. She was coping with her grief by indulging in drunken revelry. "It's just like Thelma and Louise," she yelled, grinning.

"Good thing she's not driving," Jaynette said to Betty.

Jaynette's car was an early '90's Subaru wagon, mostly red except for a silver hood. The rear bumper was missing. She scurried over and ran around the car to unlock the doors and open the trunk.

"Nice key action," Betty said to Jaynette. "Very retro."

"It gets me where I want to go," Jaynette replied, wiggling the keys at her, giving her a suggestive look.

Betty grinned. "Smart woman. Excellent priorities."

While Shawn loaded up the bags, Lucy noticed Fawn was

frozen in place, biting her lip, staring behind them into the darkness.

"We're just going to Mendocino," Lucy said. "You can come back tonight if you want to. Or tomorrow morning."

"I won't be able to come back. Not after this." She wiped away a tear. "I am such an idiot."

"Don't talk that way." Lucy got her into the old car. Put her seatbelt on for her, pulled her head down to her shoulder. "Though if you throw up on me I'll never forgive you."

Fawn sighed, sagging against Lucy, and they drove off through the trees. Hopefully half of Jaynette's attention would be enough to master the sharp curves of the road, because Betty couldn't keep her hands off of her. While Fawn cried silently at her shoulder, Betty and Jaynette giggled and stroked one another, obliviously happy with their own moment.

Maybe marriage does ruin everything, Lucy thought. She and Dan had been happy together for years. Unexciting, maybe, but peaceful. It wasn't until Lucy pressured him to make it official that they began working more, going to bed at different times, eating meals alone.

The car swerved and barely regained the road before an oncoming pickup sped past them. Jaynette squealed, slapping Betty's hand away, and they continued on their way.

"I'm going to puke now," Fawn said quietly.

Lucy clutched Jaynette's shoulder. "Pull over."

With a squeal of tires in the gravel, the car slid off the road. Lucy fumbled with the door and pulled Fawn out with her, grabbing her before she tried to spill her guts into the oncoming traffic instead of the bushes.

Three miserable minutes later, Fawn crawled back into the car.

"Any water?" Lucy asked the others.

"Cold coffee from this morning?" Jaynette held up her travel mug, but Fawn shook her head.

"We'll get something in town. But thanks."

A half hour later, they drove into the picturesque coastal village of Mendocino, a wealthy enclave of B&Bs, jewelry stores, art galleries, restaurants, and boutiques. The sun was sinking down to the Pacific horizon, hazy behind the bank of fog.

Lucy had been texting Krista, and finally a reply came through. "Not good. They've gone back to the resort already." She squeezed Fawn's knee. "I'm sorry. Her phone was off. Did you want her to get your mom on the line?"

Fawn moaned and put her face in her hands. "I can't talk to her right now. I'm not sure what I'm doing."

Lucy addressed the cheerful women in the front seat. "Can we just keep driving for a while?"

"I was headed up to Fort Bragg," Jaynette said, "but with all the twists and turns on Highway 1, I don't think your friend is up to it."

"I'm fine," Fawn said. "I need a minute to figure out a plan. Please."

In ten minutes Lucy and Fawn were sliding back and forth along the back seat with each bend in the road. The Pacific, cold and vast and wild, crashed into the rough coast to their left.

"I take it back. I need to get out," Fawn said.

"There's a B and B in Pajaro. Nice bar. Popular with the locals," Jaynette said. "Right up ahead."

"There's a vacancy sign," Betty said as they drove into the lot, fondling Jaynette's thigh.

"This will do," Lucy said. "Thanks for the ride."

The lovebirds didn't hesitate to dump them at the front door. Within two minutes Fawn and Lucy stood alone with the bags at their feet, eyeing the old Victorian on the cliff, while Jaynette's Subaru zoomed away. Loud music from a bar on the ocean side drifted across the broken asphalt of the parking lot.

Luckily, Fawn threw up before they got inside.

***

MILES SIPPED his potato soup in the Snowy Egret and thought about white bras and cotton panties, bracing himself to see Alex come in with Lucy on his arm for dinner. On their "date." Pretending to "like" each other.

Shit.

He'd been waiting for two hours, chewing slowly, eating a series of pale appetizers, plotting his moves. How he would seduce her with his bedroom eyes from afar while Alex bored her to death. He wore the shirt his ex had said made him look handsome, and he kept looking down to make sure he hadn't spilled anything on it.

I'm pathetic.

Just as he was signaling the waitress for a coconut water refill, Huntley burst into the restaurant, his eyes wild. He saw Miles and rushed over. "Have you seen her?"

Miles almost said, *I can't get her out of my mind,* then realized he must mean Fawn. "Nope."

Huntley grabbed a chair and sank into it. "She's hiding. Can you believe that? *Three* days before the wedding and she's hiding."

"Can't blame her. She met your parents."

"Shit." Huntley buried his face in his hands. "I'm so screwed."

"Mm-hmmm," Miles said, mouth full.

"She was kind of upset with me after lunch. We were with my parents at the restaurant, and it wasn't great but nothing bad really happened, I thought. It was quiet. You know how my mother gets when she's trying to punish me, kind of cold—"

"Calling your mother 'kind of cold' is like calling Fawn 'kind of pretty.' She makes a living at it."

"Yeah, well, so she was kind of extra chilly. But I thought I cheered Fawn up afterward. You know, the hot tub and the wet bar, girl stuff—"

Miles nodded grimly, remembering Lucy's girl stuff.

"But then she starts crying, right after the good parts, and I'm like, 'What the hell?' I figure it's just stress and… you know, it was a long day and I'd just gotten off. I must have dozed a little."

"So, she was upset and crying, naked in bed with you, and you fell asleep."

"It wasn't like that!" Huntley cried. "Okay, but I didn't mean to. And she took it personally, like I meant to hurt her intentionally, because when she woke me up later she was totally pissed. I was in the middle of this nice dream—about her!—and I realize she's talking to me about leaving or something, and before I'm totally awake, she's gone."

"You couldn't find her at her cabin?"

"I wasn't going to just run after her. I was practically asleep! And kind of pissed, too, that she would just start a fight while I was sleeping. It wasn't really fair."

Miles pinched the bridge of his nose, headache at war with laughter. "Dude, you're fucked. When did you go and look for her?"

"It doesn't matter. She's gone now."

"Gone?"

"Gone. Cabin's empty."

"I thought you said she was hiding, like in the sauna or something."

"You think I'd be this freaked out if she was still here at the resort?" Huntley helped himself to Miles's glass, took a mouthful. "She packed up. Clothes, bags, everything—cabin's empty."

"Empty?" Miles felt his stomach drop. "How about Lucy?"

"Oh, her clothes are still there." Huntley rolled his baby blue eyes. "But she's not. I assume she's with Fawn. Probably was jealous of her all along, getting married and being the pretty one and everything."

"Excuse me?"

Huntley drew back, apparently surprised by his tone. A sheepish look came over his face. "Fawn told me she got dumped by her own fiancé. Maybe she's bitter." He caught Miles's eye. "You know all about that."

"Lucy's been a hell of a lot more loyal than you have." Miles shoved a crusty piece of sourdough baguette in his mouth. "And she's prettier, too."

Huntley stared. "Interesting."

"You want to blame somebody, blame yourself. Even your parents are just trying to look out for you." Miles looked at his watch. Lucy didn't have a car and it was too late to rent one, even in Fort Bragg. And since it was unlikely anyone would drive her all the way back to the Bay Area, she couldn't have gotten far unless— "Are her other friends still here? Krista and the one with green hair?"

"Krista took Fawn's mother to Mendocino for shopping and chow hours ago."

"So Fawn might have tried to meet up with them?"

Face lighting up, Huntley popped back up to his feet. "Of course!" He pulled out his cell. "I have to give some story to my parents before they suspect anything. I'll meet you—"

"Find her yourself. Show her you're serious." Frowning at the glass Huntley had stolen, Miles dumped his napkin on the table.

"Serious? Would I be going through all of this with my parents if I weren't? I'm going to marry her!"

"If she'll have you. Your parents showed her how they felt about her, which wasn't good. You didn't say anything."

"They just don't know her yet. And this isn't going to help." Huntley shook his head. "I'll book them for a mud treatment in the morning, just in case. That'll buy me a few more hours."

Miles got up from the table and nodded his thanks to the waiter. Grateful for the two hours of service and the free food, he left a twenty for a tip before following his pathetic friend out of the restaurant. "You worry too much about what they think and not enough about what Fawn thinks," Miles said. "And she noticed."

But Huntley, already sucking up to his parents on the other line, wasn't listening.

Miles walked back to his cabin with the annoying realization that he was going to help him out because he didn't want to risk letting Lucy get away just yet.

IN THE END, they decided to search for them separately—Miles on his bike and Huntley in a car, splitting up at the coast to search a wider area. B&Bs and restaurants littered the rocky coastline along Highway 1, and Miles was pessimistic that they would be able to find them without more information.

Miles went to Fort Bragg, a real city with more services, not just a gourmet ghetto for tourists, but he didn't have a clue what he was supposed to be looking for. Krista drove an old Subaru, they'd learned. That would stick out about as well as a Ford pickup. Or a blue Prius.

Miles wondered what Lucy drove. Something black, he bet. Small and black—a VW or a Japanese hatchback, nothing expensive, something practical. Something he wouldn't fit in.

He wanted her. He wanted to find her, wanted to hold her.

Damn it.

Why didn't Huntley ask Alex to go look for them? They could have turned it into a nice little four-way.

Alex. Miles didn't blame her for holding out for her dream guy, the one sticking out his ankle for the ball and chain with a smile, but Alex was not the one. She knew that. She had to know that.

Huntley reached him on his cell when he was getting gas. "Score!" Huntley cried into his ear. "Pajaro!"

"You found them?"

"I found their ride. A yoga instructor at the spa called in with the manager. With Fawn's friend with the green hair," Miles said. "They're in Pajaro!"

"Where the fuck is that?"

As it happened, it was just a few miles south from where Miles was getting gas, a tiny town with a B&B and a view and not much else. Miles followed Huntley's directions and parked in front of the run-down Victorian hugging the cliff, wondering if he should wait for Huntley.

Nah.

Chapter 15

He wouldn't touch her again. She'd have to come to him this time. If he backed off, she'd face the reality of Alex's utter unattractiveness just in time to find Miles there ready to console her.

He heard a happy crowd—big for a Wednesday—coming from the large bar on the ocean side of the building and wondered what game was on. He'd been in other bars like it up here, local hot spots, usually filled with fishermen and service workers on their nights off, and it did sound busy. Shouting and laughter, loud music, women squealing. Not the kind of place he'd expect to appeal to two unlucky-in-love city girls on their own.

There was a game on the big screen over the bar but nobody was watching it. Instead, two dozen burly men and a matching set of burly women stared at a short, bright-eyed, very loud redhead perched on top of the bar belting out a song and slapping something metal against her knee. Spoons, Miles realized. Sitting next to her on the bar, a very tall, lanky blonde was refilling a pint glass from the tap herself while the bartender grinned and clapped his hands to the beat. The beat of the spoons, which Lucy slapped like a horse's gallop along her thigh.

Nobody spared Miles a glance. He froze, too surprised to move, and tried to absorb what he was seeing. And hearing.

"Come on, Lucy," a woman's voice yelled out. "Sing that Irish one again. The one that made Jake cry!"

Lucy shook her head, making her bright curls bounce, and sang something folksy about "ain't a gonna be feelin' that way no more." Fawn held out the refilled pint glass to her, and Lucy bent over to give the spoons one last, frenzied flourish before tossing them aside and grabbing the beer. The crowd broke out into applause. Lucy laughed, stood up on the bar, and bowed, beer foam on her upper lip.

A brown-haired guy in an orange Giants sweatshirt tugged on her leg, no doubt annoyed to have her feet near his plate of fries, but when she climbed down, he hooked an arm around her waist and hauled her into his lap.

Whoa there, buddy. Lucy was obviously too drunk to fight him off. Maybe she didn't even realize why her bar stool had gotten so well-padded.

The thought that the stool might not be so soft made Miles push away from the doorway and stride over through the crowd to the bar. "Lucy," he said loudly. "I've been looking for you."

The guy frowned at him and looked down at Lucy. "You know this dude?"

Lucy gave Miles a slow, sultry once-over. "Coulda shoulda didn't," she said, then threw her head back and laughed.

Miles put a hand on the chair-guy's shoulder and nodded darkly at Lucy. "She's drunk."

He gave Miles a look that said *no shit* and put a second arm around her, grinning. Then he dipped his nose into the mop of curls on top of her head and visibly inhaled, an intimate act that made Miles want to reach over and stab one spoon up each hairy, trespassing nostril.

"Hi, Miles!" Fawn waved and jumped down from the bar onto the floor, her eyes darting over his shoulder to the door.

He should have waited for Huntley, let him make the big heroic gesture, but he wasn't thinking about other people's happy endings right then. He leaned closer to the Giants guy, tightened his grip on his shoulder. "Get your hands off of her."

"Who the hell are you?"

Lucy unwrapped the guy's arms but stayed in his lap, although with better posture. "Yeah, who the hell are you?"

He took the beer out of her hand and put it on the bar. "A friend," he said.

"Pffft!" She slid her arm around the Giant's sweatshirt. "What I need is a man."

"Oh, yeah," the guy said.

Miles turned to Fawn, who looked like she didn't like the Giants guy much more than he did. "Huntley wants to talk to you," he told her. "Let's get out of here."

"He's here?" Fawn squinted over his shoulder, smiling, gripping the bar for balance.

He really should have waited for Huntley. "No, he's on his way."

"Pffft." With a contemptuous hand gesture, Fawn went back to her beer. Miles felt a powerful temptation to join her. After he beat the crap out of the orange octopus who kept sniffing Lucy's hair.

"Lucy," he said. "This loser is not in your plans."

"Oh, now you care about my plans."

"You want a lap to sit in, fine." Miles took the stool next to them and held out his arms. He'd never started a bar fight, but wasn't that just the sort of thing he needed to spice up his life? Beating the crap out of the guy would be like therapy. He'd spent years talking to teenagers about self-control and nonviolence, but the sight of hairy Giants arms wrapped around Lucy would have made Ghandi bust out the baseball bat.

Cricket bat.

Lucy pushed the guy's hand away from her rib cage but stayed where she was. "You're no different than this loser, just wanting sex, sex, sex."

"Hey, don't call me a loser," the guy said.

"You know I'm different," Miles told her. He let his gaze sharpen, put some of his soul in his eyes. He waited, sitting on the stool next to them, not blinking, feeling on the edge of something.

The bar roared at something on the TV and Lucy's chair wobbled to the side to watch. She unwrapped the orange arms around her again and slid down to the floor, never taking her eyes off Miles, and he heard his heart pound louder than roar of the crowded bar.

She turned away from him. At least she wasn't rubbing her ass into that creep's lap anymore. The nice, round ass in a pair of jeans he hadn't seen before, still black but with something shiny on the pockets. Like bait.

Then she stepped back until her bottom brushed against Miles's knees.

His mouth went dry. His sober reflexes were fast and sure, and he hauled Lucy's curvy deliciousness up into his lap before she could reconsider the impulse.

She was stiff at first, back arched as though she'd just climbed up into the top row of bleachers and was trying to see over somebody else's head.

Miles was feeling pretty stiff himself. He hadn't stopped thinking about the way her body had felt under his mouth, how right she felt in his arms.

Now she didn't seem like a woman who had her eyes on the prize of a 30-year fixed mortgage and a dependable, pompous bore.

Because now she was shit-faced.

He palmed her thighs and slid his hands up to either side of her waist, pulled her closer to his chest, and rotated her away from the crowd facing the TV. If she felt his hard-on through his jeans, she didn't seem to mind. With each moment he held her, she relaxed a little more until her back melted against his chest and his mouth settled against her ear. "I shouldn't be doing this. You're drunk. It's not good." He inhaled her scent for himself and fresh possessiveness exploded in him.

"You feel good."

He groaned inwardly. If they weren't in public he'd be getting her naked by now, drunk or no. "I'm not good," he said.

"Promise?"

Sharp desire stabbed through him. His thumb found the curve of her breast and he caressed her, hearing her gasp, savoring the way her nipple hardened. His lips found one of the pearls in her earlobe and he rolled it between his teeth.

Whack. Miles drew back, stars exploding in his head. "Hey!"

Fawn stood in front of them wielding a studded purse. "What are you doing to her? Lucy? Are you all right?"

"I'm letting him be bad," Lucy said. "Give him a minute."

Readjusting his grip on the hot, soft body in his lap, Miles glared at Fawn through Lucy's curls. "You have a license for that thing?"

"What are you doing here?" Fawn's eyes glistened with tears.

Miles heard her real question. "Huntley sent me. He's on his way."

"Why didn't he get here first?"

With the pain in his skull and a different kind of pain in his lap, Miles struggled to speak over the noisy bar. "He thought you'd be in Mendocino with your mother. I took the northern route."

Lucy leaned back and he slipped his hand under her shirt. When he felt bare silky flesh, all words left him. He buried his nose in her neck and licked the pulse thrumming there.

"Oh," Fawn said, sinking against the bar. She watched them for a long moment, then said, "Should you really be doing that here?"

Miles's hand moved down her body, seeking the heat between her thighs wrapped in tight denim. *Oh, definitely.*

"Lucy, I want to go back," Fawn said.

Lucy's hips were making little circles in his lap, driving him on, but then she sighed and stopped. "Hold on. Need to think."

He cupped her.

Some other metallic object connected with his skull, not quite as hard as the purse, and Lucy broke free of him. She tapped him with the spoons one more time and dropped them on the bar. "Fresh air. Need some." She took Fawn's arm and stumbled away through the crowd while Miles waited for some blood to return to his brain.

No time. That blood had other plans. High hopes. Hot, hard hopes.

Miles took after them, holding his jacket over his crotch. He found them in the parking lot. Icy wind blew off the shore, blasting away some of the lusty confusion of the bar. The two women had found their coats somewhere and looked a little more sober, standing tall in the cold night, waiting for him.

Lucy's pale face and bright hair stood out sharply against the black jacket, jeans, and boots she wore. He knew her tall friend next to her was stunning, famously beautiful, but he only wanted to look at Lucy.

Pulse still racing, Miles tried to catch Lucy's eye, but she stared at the ground.

He had to get her alone.

Now.

He dug his cell out of his pocket, dialing quickly. "I'll get Huntley on the phone for you, Fawn. You can talk while he drives here." Not the best idea on the hairpin curves over the coast, but he had to cull Lucy from the protection of her herd.

Huntley's voice burst into his ear. "You got her?"

"She wants to talk to you." Miles strode over and shoved the phone at Fawn. Lucy looked up at him then, eyes dark and wide, lips parted, so damn hot. He slipped his hand down her arm to entwine her fingers with his and pulled her away, across the lot to a dark corner under an arbor near the building's entrance.

He tucked a curl behind her ear, though the wind blew it right back into her face, and hunched down to kiss her.

She pushed him away, leaning back on a fence post, breathing deeply. "Look, I'm sorry to lead you on back there, but you didn't follow the plan. Remember the plan? You don't touch me, I don't... you know..."

Bending his knees to reach her, he brushed his lips along the soft curve of her cheekbone. His body responded to her scent, sparking to life, remembering. "I'm pretty sure I didn't agree to any plan."

"Exactly! My point. You don't like the plan. My plan." She put a hand over her heart. "It's a really good plan."

The outdoor lights lit up her face, and she looked beautiful, otherworldly, and very not sober. He brushed another curl off her forehead. "Did you check into a room?"

"Yes, but we left the bags at the desk." Then she scowled. "No. No room." She shoved him in the shoulder.

He grabbed her fist, held it softly against his chest. "Huntley should be here soon, and looks like Fawn's going back with him."

Frowning at her captured hand, Lucy made a feeble effort

to pull free. "He'd better suck up. I want to see major sucking up."

"You like sucking up?"

She met his gaze. "If Fawn goes back, I go back with her." She forced a laugh. "Obviously. I mean, I'm her best woman. I mean man of honor. Maid of woman. Shit."

He tugged her close. "You are definitely made of woman," he growled.

Sinking against him, she sighed, wriggled closer.

Desire sliced through him. "Let them have their reunion in private," he said in her ear. "We'll go back in the morning."

Her free hand slid around his waist and cupped his ass. "God, I'd like that."

He pulled her hips against his and bent down to taste her hot, sweet mouth again. Her tongue met his, slick and eager, soft, open. He tilted her face to deepen the kiss, shocked by the way his legs buckled, how his body cried out for hers.

But she broke away and stepped back.

"See, this is why you need to follow the plan," she said, gasping. "It's very simple. You don't initiate, I don't respond. See? Simple. Excellent plan."

He blinked, breathing heavily, his vision clouded with desire. "One night, Lucy. When's the last time you just had a really, really good time, just for the hell of it?"

She arched away from him, her hand still on his chest, small but firm. "Oh, sure. Funny you mention hell. The devil is from hell. You're the devil. You can make hell sound good, pull me down with you, but then what? Then I'll get all burned up, smell like brimstone, suffer forever and all that." She spun around. "Forget it, Lucifer. I'm going with the other shoulder." Then she walked away.

She was killing him. He strode after her. She'd run in the wrong direction, noticed her mistake, and weaved back to get back to Fawn.

"Shoulder?" he asked, falling into step beside her. He rubbed his lips, desperate to taste her again.

"You know, the devil on one, the angel on the other." She shot him a dark look. "I know which one you are."

He managed to grin. "I like the sound of that." He put an arm around her, encouraged when she slowed down. "I'll tell you what your devil is. And it isn't me."

She lifted her chin, tried to stare at him down her nose even though he towered over her. "Here we go again, the I-hate-Alex song."

He shook his head slowly, cupping her cheek in his palm, savoring the contact again. He wondered if she could feel his hand shaking. "Your devil is fear. Not me. Fear."

She rolled her eyes, laughing nervously. "Oh, right."

His thumb traced her lower lip. He savored the softness, the hint of moisture, and bent closer. "Fight for what you want. Don't let fear beat you."

"So if I don't screw you right here in the parking lot it's because I'm afraid?" She grabbed his wrist. "Nice try, buster, but I'm not that drunk. You're just one big hormonal organism looking to score. Your pop psych arguments have no effect on my superior intellect."

He pulled her hand up to his mouth and rubbed his lips across each soft, delicate knuckle. "How about my physical arguments?"

Watching him through half-closed eyes, arm extended, her lips parted, she managed a frown. "Unfortunately, those are more effective."

Her skin was so soft. He caressed her fingers in his, stroking, kissing, smelling her. "I think you need to modify your plan." He separated her index finger from the rest and sucked it into his mouth like a lollipop.

Her eyelids fluttered. She moaned.

He licked the pad of her finger, sucked it in deeper. "One

night," he whispered around the prize in his mouth. *And then I'll talk you into another.* "What are you afraid of?"

She pulled her finger free. "Are you kidding me?" She twisted away, staggering in Fawn's direction. "Afraid. Of course I'm afraid. I'm not an idiot."

Miles watched her, fighting for control before he joined them.

So close.

Fawn was smiling when she handed him the phone.

He knew he wasn't. Clenching his teeth, he went over to his bike, zipped himself back into his jacket.

Maybe he was crazy. She said no. She really didn't want to give in. Whatever reasons she had for avoiding a little fun—fuck that, a lot of fun—were probably good ones. No question she'd been clear about what she wanted.

He took out his helmet and looked at her, standing as tall as her short height made possible, chin defiantly up, hands on her round, sexy hips.

No, her plan sucked. That was a fact.

"Is that jacket leather?" he asked her. His gaze slid down her body and admired her thick boots. Sensible woman.

"Yeah, why?"

"Good for the bike."

She shook her head. "Nice try." She turned to look up the highway. "I'm going with them."

"I don't think they'll want your company."

She snorted. "Too bad."

"I've got an extra helmet."

"Your skull is so thick I'm surprised you'd need one at all," she said.

Fawn's dopey smile fell, and for the first time since getting off the phone, she turned her full attention to Lucy, then to Miles. "What's going on between you two?"

"Not enough," Miles said roughly.

"He wants to have sex with me. As if that's going to work." Lucy waved her hand up and down in his direction. "Look at him. It'd be like a poodle with King Kong."

While Fawn laughed into her hand, Miles smiled and pretended that shot hadn't hit home. "More like a Great Dane, baby," he said through gritted teeth, grabbing the handlebars of his bike.

"There he is!" Fawn cried, just as Huntley's Porsche pulled into the tiny pot-holed parking lot.

"Tone it down," Lucy said, putting a hand on Fawn's arm. "Give him a chance to grovel. You want to see some major sucking up."

Still annoyed, Miles watched Huntley pop out of the slate blue sports car and run over to his fiancée. While Lucy held on to her arm, Fawn stayed where she was, silent, not rushing to meet him though her face was bright with love and relief.

To his credit, Huntley fell to his knees in the broken asphalt and clutched her hand. "Forgive me," he said, pressing his lips to her knuckles.

Lucy glanced over at Miles who, having just done the same to her, was also watching the gesture with more lust than the scene justified. She looked at him and their eyes met and held. Her tongue darted out, moistened her lips.

She *so* wanted him.

Instead of throwing his leg over the seat and taking off as he'd planned, he gave the bike a pat and waited, watching her.

"Lucy!"

She looked away from Miles to the other man's voice.

No fucking way.

Jogging out from the other side of the Porsche was Mr. Marriage Material. Looking slick and dependable in a white button-down shirt, khakis, and loafers, Alex gave everyone a little wave before coming up to Lucy's side.

No. Fucking. Way.

Throwing a scrawny little arm over Lucy's shoulders, Alex regarded Huntley with an incredulous smile. "You're ruining your trousers."

Trousers? He sounded like a grandmother.

"What are you doing here?" Lucy asked.

"Huntley can't let his bride escape, can he? Come on, man. She gets the point," Alex said, using his free hand to pull Huntley up from the ground.

Huntley didn't take his eyes off Fawn, and though he got off the ground, he didn't stand up all the way. Head low, he nuzzled Fawn's neck, hooked an arm around her waist, and pulled her away from the others to the shelter of the arbor where Miles had had such great luck.

What the hell was Huntley doing, bringing Alex after making such a big deal about having Miles on the road searching, even though he seemed to have realized Miles had a thing for Lucy—

Miles shifted his gaze from Alex's scrawny arm to the Porsche. The 911. Not the limo.

He sought out Huntley in the shadows of the B&B, not surprised to see Fawn's legs wrapped around his waist and her tongue down his throat.

Suddenly feeling magnanimous, Miles smiled and walked over to join Alex and Lucy. Sure, Huntley should have groveled more, but the guy had charm. Forethought.

And a very, very small car.

"Guess you'll have to come with me, Lucy," Miles said, watching the way Alex pulled her more tightly up against his side.

She made a rude noise. "You wish." Without seeming to care how it unhinged Alex's arm from her shoulder, she spun sideways and pointed at the Porsche. "I'm going in that."

Miles shook his head. "Don't think that's going to be possible. Didn't Fawn bring all of her bags with her? Her suitcases?"

Her eyes widened, darted back to the car, then to Alex.

"There's room for two in the back." Alex lifted his hand as though he was going to put it back on her shoulder, but Lucy was already marching across the lot to peer into the back seat.

He bit back a grin. Alex was catching on. He frowned into the darkness, where Huntley and Fawn were still going at it.

"I'll get Fawn's bags," Miles said cheerfully. "She said they're at the front desk. Lots of them."

Alex wasn't stupid. He snapped his jaw shut and eyed Miles. "She'd need a helmet."

"I always carry a spare." Miles strode around him, past the necking lovebirds and into the front office of the B&B. He smiled down at the huge pile of suitcases.

Fawn came up behind him, her hair in a tangle around her face. She talked to the lady at the front desk for a minute while Huntley joined them.

His face was smeared with lipstick. With a grin to Miles, Huntley said, "Alex insisted on coming, so I had to improvise."

"I appreciate that," Miles said quietly.

"Quid pro quo, my friend."

Fawn came over from the front desk and hooked a hand around Huntley's waist. They all stared at the pile of bags at their feet.

"I kind of brought a lot," Fawn said.

Miles bent over and lifted the two largest bags. "No problem. Really. Very understandable, given your profession."

"Absolutely," Huntley added. "We wouldn't think of leaving a single thing behind. Not even for the night."

Fawn ran her hand through her hair, looking amused at their enthusiasm to haul all of her suitcases out to the Porsche. She slung a garment bag over her shoulder and let them carry the rest, a lopsided smile on her face.

Halfway out to the car, his arms laden with the suitcases, Miles asked Huntley, "What did you say to make it up to her?"

Huntley glanced back at Fawn. "That I loved her. That I'd stand up to my parents. How sorry I was."

"That's it?"

"What else was I supposed to say?"

Miles dropped the suitcases near the trunk and went back for more just as Fawn caught up to Huntley and pressed him against the car for another kiss.

There were at least six suitcases, each with wheels and handles that took up extra room. Miles lugged them out to the car, wondering if Lucy would be sober enough to get on the bike or if he should make his move here.

"I'll go on the bike with you," Alex said, putting a firm hand his shoulder. "Lucy can go in the car."

Miles nudged Huntley and Fawn, still in each other's arms, away from the car bumper. "Pop the trunk, Huntley the Third?"

Without taking his mouth off of Fawn's, Huntley reached into his pocket. The trunk popped open and Miles got to work filling it up.

"Nope, definitely not enough room for all the bags. Some will just have to go in the back seat." Miles went around and shoved the biggest suitcase behind the driver's seat so Alex would have to sit behind leggy Fawn—who would obviously need to have her seat pushed all the way back, being so tall and everything.

"Come on over, Lucy," Alex called out, waving wildly. "I'll go on the motorcycle."

Miles couldn't see Lucy clearly enough in the darkness to read her face but she wasn't rushing over.

If she wanted Alex, she wouldn't stay as far away from him as possible, right? She wouldn't be fighting the urge to grab Miles's butt?

Which he'd enjoyed quite a bit.

"What's her problem?" Alex muttered, frowning across the

car at her.

"You'll have to go in the car," Miles said. "I don't take anyone on the bike without proper gear."

"Lucy doesn't have—"

"She has the boots and the jacket. No armored pants, but it beats an oxford shirt and penny loafers."

Alex looked down at his feet then up at Miles, his jaw set. "I'll take full responsibility."

"My bike, my rules."

"I know what you're trying to do. Give it up."

Miles glanced over at Lucy, who was finally walking slowly toward them, carefully avoiding the potholes underfoot, her arms stretched out to either side for balance.

She was a cute drunk, but he'd have to sober her up a little before he got her on the bike.

His body tightened. There were empty rooms inside. A bed now, breakfast in the morning, and all the hours in between.

"Break it up, you two," Lucy said to Fawn and Huntley, who were still making out on the other side of the car. "Huntley has to get back to the spa and tell his parents to fuck off." She poked Huntley in the ribs.

Huntley squealed and jerked away from Fawn. "Hey!" He seemed to be only vaguely aware of the rest of them standing there.

"Right?" Lucy demanded.

Huntley sighed, gazed into Fawn's eyes. "I'll talk to them."

"Let's get going," Alex said. "Lucy, we've pushed the suitcases to one side so you'll be pretty comfortable. It's only a few miles, really."

Eyes on Lucy, Miles stepped forward and rested an elbow on the car, completely blocking the entrance with his generous figure. She met his gaze and held it a long moment.

He thought about mentioning the safety issue again, how Alex was wearing flimsy clothes and shoes, definitely putting all that marriage material in jeopardy—but he wanted her to choose. Right now, in front of both of them.

She turned to Alex. "You'll freeze to death. Go on, I'll go on the bike. It's not far."

Miles silently let out the breath he was holding and found it was difficult to suck in another one.

"It's hardly safe for you to get on a motorcycle when you've been drinking," Alex said.

She raised an eyebrow. "I'll be the judge of that." She walked away from the car, arms extended to either side again, weaving through the potholes toward the bike.

Flinching, Alex watched her go. He turned on Miles, eyes narrowed, his lips pressed in a flat line. "At least get her a cup of coffee first." He climbed into the back seat.

Smiling, Fawn got in the front.

Huntley gave him a cheerful thumbs-up over the top of the car. "Have fun, Jolly."

LUCY'S HEAD WAS SPINNING. The hard, cold wind off the shore wasn't enough to clear her mind. She leaned back against the railing that divided the parking lot from the gentle slope down to the beach and stared at the way Miles's jeans hugged his thighs. Her whole body was hot, tense, ready for more of what they'd started.

She couldn't sleep with him, but she could look.

The Porsche roared out of the lot, spitting gravel. She sighed. That wasn't cool how she'd sent Alex away—not because she'd stayed, but because she hadn't been candid with him. He was just so irritating. Aggressive, anal-retentive, goal-oriented.

She was aware of her hypocrisy.

"I'm too much like him," she told Miles. He was only three

feet away, eyes dark, moving closer. She ignored the sexual tension crackling between them. "Maybe it could work if I were different."

"Of course it could work if you were different." He stepped close to her, almost touching, leaned next to her against the railing. "A different woman."

"I could change," she said softly.

"For what? For him?"

"For me."

He bent closer. His lips were so close she could feel his breath. "I'm going to kiss you now."

"I want a husband."

His hand slid around the small of her back, pulling her hips up against his. "I don't," he said, and his mouth came down hard on hers.

Chapter 16

*L*ucy froze, stunned by the fierceness of his kiss. Unlike before, he wasn't teasing, sweet, passive, cute. His tongue swept into her mouth, tangled with hers, demanded she respond. His large hands, so gentle before, grabbed her ass and lifted her up to grind against him, hard and hungry.

She was too shocked to kiss him back or worry about pushing herself on him or think about the future. Her heart pounded in her chest, her nipples hardened, her legs went weak. While her mind froze, at war with itself, her body sparked to life.

His hand slipped down between the cheeks of her ass and lifted her higher. She realized he was stroking her between her legs from behind, urging her thighs apart.

Right there in the parking lot, the noisy bar only twenty feet away, Lucy gave up the fight. She hugged his neck and let him lift her higher. Straddling his hips, she wriggled close and hooked her ankles behind his back.

He groaned into her mouth. His hands were too busy holding her up to explore her face, so she took over the kiss, tunneling her fingers through his hair and controlling the angle of their mouths.

It was hard and fast and crazed. She could feel him thrusting the erection under his jeans into her crotch. Two layers of denim between them, a maddening obstruction.

She slipped one hand down his hard chest, down his stomach between their bodies. His jacket was in the way, the thick leather bunched under her breasts. She shoved it aside to reach his belt.

Miles leaned back on the railing and she slid down his body to stand tiptoe on the ground, her attention now on the damn buckle. She had to break the kiss, her breathing fast and uneven, to see what she was doing.

The bulge below was too much to resist. Hard, warm, big under her palm, she stroked him—

"Wait," he gasped. "Oh, God." He put his hand over hers and pressed down. She felt him jump under her fingers as they explored the shape and length of him.

"There's a path right over there," Lucy said, caressing him. "Down to the beach."

He leaned back and looked into her face, doubt battling lust. She could see the moment he caught up to her and his expression hardened with determination.

He grabbed her hand and pulled her toward the path. They tripped over the curb, too eager to watch their step.

If they didn't slow down they were going to get hurt.

It wasn't a swimming beach. Even surfers stayed away from this rocky spot. But people couldn't resist beauty, and many feet had worked their way down the rocks to the nooks that formed at low tide. Though it was cold and the air was misty from the crashing waves, they hurried to get even closer to the frigid shore that was dark and secluded and invisible from above.

The moment their feet hit level sand they were back in each other's arms. Miles leaned back against a rock that was taller than him and pulled her up against his body. He slipped his hand between her legs and kissed his way down her neck to the hollow of her throat, licking and nipping and taking.

"Do you really want to do this?" he asked. She could feel his breath against her skin. "I mean, here? We could go to the room—"

She stroked him again. "Do you have a condom?"

He leaned his head back. Sucked in a breath. "Wallet."

Taking her time, she searched his front pockets, slowly and carefully, then slid her hands to the back and pulled it out.

He shuddered. Through his teeth he said, "You're killing me."

The wallet was thick leather, like his coat, soft and warm. He snatched it out of her hands and had the condom removed and out of the foil before she took another breath. Not wanting to be outdone, slightly annoyed he'd grabbed it so roughly, she unzipped his fly and wriggled her fingers inside.

He froze. Let her unbutton his jeans and free him.

"I want you," she told him.

"Glad to hear it." He grabbed her wrist. "A second. Need one."

Grinning, she rubbed up against him and reached her hand behind his neck to pull his mouth to hers. He got the condom on and surprised her by tugging her down sideways onto his lap where he sat in the sand, the rock at his back. He unbuttoned her jeans.

"You've got the best ass in world, you know that?" His hands were under the denim, under her panties, pulling the fabric down her thighs. She knelt in the sand next to him. Felt icy wind on her exposed bottom. Then warm, strong hands.

With him sitting on the ground, it was easier to kiss him, to reach all of him. While she licked his jaw, savoring the roughness under her tongue, kissing his racing pulse, he was struggling to get her out of her pants.

He held her face in both hands and pulled her away from him. "Take off your boots," he said roughly.

It was the most erotic thing she'd ever heard.

She managed to stand up on her shaking legs, her jeans and underwear sinking below her hips, and turn to face the ocean. She bent over and pulled the lace on the first boot.

A large hand clamped down on her calf, but she swiveled to the other boot and took her time.

His hands moved up her calves, the backs of her knees, hooked into the fabric to expose the rest of her. Before she could shake off the first boot, one palm circled her ass and his fingers were—

"Oh, *God*," she said. He was between her legs. Delicate, tickling, eager.

"Could you please hurry the fuck up with the footwear?" he asked softly, adding a finger.

Three seconds later and she was barefoot in the gritty sand. Then naked from the waist down, facing the ocean and suddenly shy about turning around.

Powerful hands grabbed her hips and pulled her down into his lap. Strong arms turned her around, hooked one leg over his other side, clamped on either side of her and positioned her on top of him.

His mouth was on hers again, demanding and hot, and she wanted him. She needed him to touch her again. The wind was cold at her back, there on the public beach with the noisy crowd inside just above their heads. She'd never done anything like this before in her life. Never thought she would.

"*Miles*," she groaned. He was rubbing his cock between their bodies, not inside yet but slowly separating her while he lifted her hips up and down, up and down, working them both wild.

She shifted, trying to get the angle right, clutching his shoulders.

And then he thrust inside. Filled her. Huge, hard, sudden.

Throwing her head back, she let him drive deeper, lift her up, impale her again. His fingers clamped onto her hips, unwavering, pushing her up and down in a building rhythm, impossibly strong and relentless.

She'd never known pleasure like it in her life.

No longer trying to anticipate his speed or do anything in return, she let go. She flipped the switch and went blank. If she hadn't been so tense, spiraling down into a whirlpool of the best orgasm of her life, she would have laughed.

Miles thrust into her, tireless, watching her with black, black eyes. When his arms buckled and his rhythm faltered because he'd hit the wall, was jerking with his climax, she threw her head back and let her thoughts go white with blinding, shuddering joy.

A SHARP STICK was poking Lucy in her left knee. He was still inside her, his arms holding her tightly against his chest.

They were both fully clothed from the waist up. Miles wore his boots, and even his thighs were mostly covered by his jeans. The madness was fading, but they didn't move or say anything. Was he waiting for her to speak first?

I'm drunk, Lucy thought. Her bare ass stuck out under her jacket, probably visible for miles around. A white moon on the beach. Miles's hands had released her hips, and one gently stroked her hair.

Not drunk enough.

Tension was building again, and not the sexual kind.

Reluctantly, she pushed herself off his chest and lifted herself free of him. While she got to her feet and scrabbled around in the sand for her clothes, he cleaned up, giving the beach and the used condom a pained look before stuffing it in his jeans pocket.

Afterglow was a bitch.

Silently, he watched her pull on her underwear, jeans, and boots, and she felt increasingly uncomfortable. "Miles…"

"You don't have to say it. I know." He shrugged, stepped closer, out of the shadows. He had a little smile on his face.

"How could you know? I don't even know."

He took her hand and squeezed gently. "Sorry. Go ahead."

"I want to return to the resort tonight. I know we just did this and the room is right up there, but I want to go back to the resort."

He nodded, squeezed her hand again. "Of course. Should we grab a drink before we head back?" He zipped her jacket up to her throat, smoothed the leather over her shoulders. "Coffee, something else warm?"

"You think you knew that's what I was going to say?"

"It's okay, Lucy. I just fucked your alcohol-soaked brains out on a public beach. You're entitled to whatever you want." He pushed a strand of hair out of her eyes, then dropped his hands to his sides. "Let's get out of here before the tide comes in."

She exhaled loudly, annoyed that he seemed to think she was some kind of victim. "I don't regret what we did."

"Not yet."

"I'm not going to."

He put a hand in the small of her back and nudged her toward the path up to the parking lot. She waited for him to say *me neither*, but he didn't.

He didn't touch her during the walk up the bluff, not even when they got to the railing and climbed over into the lot. His motorcycle huddled there, away from the cars, the silhouette of its handlebars sticking up like antlers, and she had the funniest feeling that she was jealous of it, this vehicle of his that he rode every day—

She dropped her face into her hands and sucked in a deep breath. Too much beer, too much everything.

Miles was already striding over to the bike. He unlocked the rounded case on the back and took out a helmet, then another one, acting like nothing at all had just happened.

"I have to use the bathroom," she told him, turning on her heel and striding away.

He jogged to catch up to her, the helmet under his arm. "You sound angry."

"I just have to use the bathroom."

"Sure," he said, still following her.

She stopped under the arbor, not sure what she was feeling. "I'm fine."

The light from the front door slanted across his left eye. He looked tense. "I didn't plan for it to be that way."

"I told you, I don't regret it. You didn't push me into anything."

"I just—I got a little carried away," he said.

"Will you listen to me? I was right there with you. It was something that happened." She dropped her gaze to a sliver of bare skin visible low on his throat under the layers of T-shirt and leather. Gently, she touched him there with an index finger, felt warmth, soft hair, his pulse. "It was pretty great."

He put a hand over hers and held it to his chest. "Let's get a drink before we go back. Water, coffee, whiskey, whatever."

"I don't want to go back in that bar," she said.

"We'll stop somewhere else on the way."

She shook her head, freed her hand, and went inside. Just a quick bathroom break and she'd be fine. Splash some water on her face, wash the sand out from under her fingernails, shake the sand out of her shoes. Tomorrow she would figure this out.

"There you are," the lady at the desk said, slapping a key

on the desk. She was blond with gray roots, and wore red cat-eye glasses and a tight plaid flannel shirt. "I was about to close up. Breakfast is from eight to ten-thirty, but the chocolate waffles go fast, so I'd get here before nine if I were you." She saluted her with a steaming coffee mug.

Lucy paused. She thought Fawn had settled everything. "I'm sorry, but I'm not staying. I just need to use the bathroom."

The woman froze with the mug halfway to her lips. "But it's our best room. I told your friend we didn't do refunds. She said you wouldn't want one anyway." Her glance slid past Lucy to Miles, who had come in behind her.

Lucy didn't move. The key was the long, old-fashioned metal kind, attached to a narrow wooden tag labeled "9." It sat there, splayed out on the scarred wooden counter in a V shape. Like two legs spread apart.

Lucy ran her hands over her eyes. "I just want to use the bathroom. We don't know if we're staying."

She could feel Miles approach her from behind. *We don't know…*

"Up to you, of course," the woman said. Her study of Miles seemed to explain something to her, because her slightly offended look had warmed into bland amusement. With a faint smile, she tapped the key with one nail-bitten finger before turning off the desk lamp. "Like I said, the chocolate waffles are real popular." She winked at Miles. "Worth sticking around for."

Lucy grabbed the key. "Where is it? The bathroom is en suite?"

"Yup. Right up those stairs, far left corner, ocean side," the woman said.

"Thanks." Lucy jogged up the stairs without looking back, not sure if Miles would follow her or not but certain she didn't want to put on a show in front of the proprietor.

The Victorian building had a long, narrow upstairs hallway with a worn runner down the middle and a handful of rooms on either side. Framed images of dogs of all kinds lined the walls—some photos, some illustrations. The floorboards creaked.

She found the west-facing corner and let herself in just as Miles appeared at the end of the hallway behind her.

"I'm just going to use the bathroom," she called out.

He nodded, striding closer, glancing around. "I'll go after you," he said. "If you don't mind."

She pushed the door open to let him inside. "Understandable."

He was big. He had to duck, brushing against her in the doorway on his way in. "Given what we were up to," he said in a low voice.

She swallowed. "Yeah. Anyway. I'll go first. Thanks." Barely noticing the shabby-chic decor, (except for the enormous four-poster bed in the middle of the room), Lucy scurried over to the bathroom and locked the door behind her.

While she cleaned up, she had to face facts.

That was the best sex she'd ever had in her life.

She was a little sore, but in a good way. Letting herself smile, she shook the sand out of her underwear, jeans, and boots into the lined wicker wastebasket. Got dressed again.

Feeling less gritty, she went to the pedestal sink to wash. She froze when she saw her face in the mirror.

No wonder the front desk lady was amused. Wild hair, unfocused eyes, razor-burned cheeks, puffy lips—she was quite a sight. Soap and water just wasn't enough to wipe away the evidence of what she'd obviously been up to.

Miles knocked on the door. "Are you all right?"

She ran a hand through her electric-socket curls. *Never better.* She dried off with a fluffy towel and pulled open the door. "Let's stay."

He didn't react. Face impassive, he asked, "Here?"

"Of course, 'here.' What else would I mean?"

"Sorry, it's just you were quite insistent a few minutes ago about going back."

Lucy put her hands on her hips. A tiny voice inside her suggested he'd already gotten what he wanted. "Don't you want to stay?"

"Sure." He ran a hand through his hair, then wrinkled his nose and looked at his fingers. "I've got sand in my hair."

"It's just—" She stopped herself, not liking the way his face had closed up. His eyes were watching her, but not like before when he seemed to want to consume her.

Of course he wasn't falling over himself with lust now that they were in full lighting. Hadn't she just looked in the mirror? She looked like a slutty mermaid the ocean vomited onto the beach.

There was a pitcher of water with glasses on a small round table by the window. She walked over to it and poured. "The room's already paid for. It seemed like a waste. But it's nothing special, and of course the resort costs a million times more."

She was babbling. She needed a shower and a long night's sleep and tomorrow she wouldn't feel so insecure and vulnerable.

"I don't mind staying," he said.

Mind?

"No, forget it," she said. "Wash up, and I'll meet you downstairs."

He stared at her from across the room, one hand on the bathroom door. "Do me a favor and stay here. I'll just be a minute."

"I mean it, Miles. Forget what I said. I'm a mess, obviously. I just want to get back to the resort so I can figure this all out tomorrow."

He smiled a little. "I know what you mean," he said.

"Please stay in the room? Some of those guys down there were a little rough."

She waved him off and poured herself a second glass of water. "Fine. Go on."

He disappeared behind the door and she let out a long breath. What was her problem? It wasn't like they hadn't already had sex. Hot, hard, crazy, pounding sex. *Just down there,* she thought, looking out the window.

She thought he'd go wild again at the suggestion they stay. Not shrug like he was doing her a favor.

He's not Dan.

And he wasn't Alex, either. Alex, who wouldn't ever speak to her again, at least not with baby strollers in his eyes. Alex, who'd followed her out here, who she'd shoved into the backseat of a Porsche so she could be with another guy.

Hoping Fawn left her credit card on file for incidentals, Lucy popped open the mini-bar cabinet and found a bag of M&M's. With peanuts. Which made them nutritious, she decided, tearing the wrapper apart.

She washed those down with a Diet Coke, keeping her back to the door. It was late, but the bar was still noisy. People's voices and music vibrated through the building. This B&B hardly compared to the Soul of Muir Resort. Even the water glasses were mismatched, one of them chipped. If she hadn't been blinded by alcohol and lust, she would have noticed right away the room was hardly the quaint haven the proprietor had assured Fawn hours ago.

Miles came out, only glanced at her as he zipped up his jacket.

It was that aloof gesture that made Lucy set down her drink and stride over to the door. "I've been on a motorcycle a few times before," she said, pulling it open, "but not recently."

He cleared his throat and followed her into the hallway.

The door slammed behind them. "It's a good bike for a second rider. You'll be fine."

They walked down the hall, past the puppies and dogs smiling at them from their framed posts on the walls. Just as they slowed at the top of the dim, narrow staircase, Miles touched her arm. "Careful, there's a loose floorboard. Three steps down."

She hesitated. He hadn't removed his hand. "Thanks."

"I'm surprised Fawn settled for this place," he said softly.

"We liked the bar and the view."

His fingers softened on her arm. His hand moved to cup her shoulder. "Lucy…"

Her heart began to pound. "It's okay," she said, imagining the heat of his palm through her thick jacket.

"It's not how I imagined—"

She turned. "Look, if you want to regret it, fine, but I'm not going to."

He moved ahead of her down the stairs and faced her. Soft gray eyes fixed on hers, he captured both her shoulders in his hands. Slowly, he grinned. "I don't regret it. Are you kidding?"

"Then stop moping around. Just because I want to go back to the resort doesn't mean—"

"Yes?"

She poked him in the chest. "Doesn't mean anything about you. I rushed out with Fawn so fast I didn't even bring a toothbrush."

He nodded and turned, gesturing down the stairs. "I apologize. I will stop moping around and commence playful post-sex banter."

"Thank you." The wood creaked under her feet as she made her way back down to the main floor. Luckily, the front desk was empty, and the two of them slipped out into the night without another word.

Miles got a helmet out of the rear case of his motorcycle and sized her up. "You sober enough to hold on?"

"I held on to you, didn't I?"

He didn't smile. "Yeah."

"Hey, playful post-sex banter, remember?"

He took a deep breath. "Yeah, I remember." He looked down at her, patted her wild hair. "Let's see if this helmet will fit you."

The foam interior of the helmet slipped over her skull. "It's tight," she said, trying to poke her hair into it, out of her face.

He nodded. Tapped his own.

She swung a leg over the bike and climbed aboard, wiggling her bottom to get comfortable. "You should know I can't hear anything, okay?" Just because they were there and he was staring at her, she grabbed the handlebars and bounced up and down, pretending to rev the engine.

He didn't move to get on in front of her. Finally, he said something she couldn't hear.

"What?" she yelled.

Closing his eyes for a moment, he stepped up to her, unbuckled the strap under her chin, and took off her helmet. "I almost made it. Later, I hope you give me credit for that at least."

"Made what?"

He cupped her face, his gaze dropping to her mouth. "You didn't really think I'd drive you back tonight, did you?" He traced her bottom lip with his finger and his voice fell. "When I've finally got you all to myself?"

Chapter 17

When he first met her, Miles thought Lucy was cute. Down on the beach, he thought she was smoking hot. But now, watching the moonlight reflect in her wide, soulful eyes, the only word for her was… beautiful.

Beautiful.

His heart was beating too fast again. He wanted her, was afraid he wouldn't get her. Not for another quickie, but a slow, comfortable night together, far from rich, needy friends.

Luckily, she didn't have a car.

"You didn't seem so eager a few minutes ago," she said, her bottom lip plumping out a little bit.

He rubbed it with his thumb, bent down closer. "I was trying to be a gentleman."

"A gentleman doesn't make a woman feel like she's asking for it."

He put an arm around her waist and lifted her off the bike. "You can ask for anything you want, sweetheart."

She wriggled down to the ground but didn't push him away. Taking that as a sign, he caressed the small of her back, slid around her hip, squeezed the swell of her ass.

Earlier he'd worried about being able to perform again so soon. Now he hoped he'd be able to go slow enough to make a better impression this time. He kissed her quickly on the cheek and took her hand. "Back to the room."

"You should have made up your mind earlier. I turned in the—" But she hadn't. Slowly, she reached into her pocket for the large room key and stared at it. "I forgot to turn it in."

"I noticed." He grinned at her and tugged her across the parking lot. "That's what sealed your fate."

"I can't believe I forgot. I never forget things like that."

Her hand was small compared to his but not the least bit frail. He didn't have to worry about hurting her. As they passed the front desk, his mind was thinking ahead to what he would do first to her body, what parts he'd kiss, taste, take. When she went ahead of him up the stairs, his conscious thoughts fled, replaced by the vision that was Lucy's ass swaying closely at eye level.

He grabbed her hips to feel her as she climbed. A forty-something woman in a hooded sweatshirt appeared at the top of the stairs, coming down with a telescope over one shoulder. Miles quickly dropped his hands.

"Partial lunar eclipse tonight," she said, nodding as she passed. "Hope the fog doesn't come in."

"Yes," Lucy said vaguely.

"Good luck," Miles said, grabbing Lucy's bottom again.

They stumbled onto the landing and made their way down the hallway to their room, weaving from side to side as they progressed from light groping to heavy petting with each step. By the time the key was in the lock, Miles had unbuttoned Lucy's jeans and slipped his hand underneath her underwear.

"The—key—doesn't work," she said, leaning her back against his chest to let him touch her.

Warm, soft curls under his hand, then wet, slick heat. His breathing was fast and shallow. "Maybe you're distracted."

"Huh," she said. "I'm usually very focused."

Reluctantly, he removed his hand and unlocked the door. "Maybe you're focused on something else right now." Gently, he pushed her ahead of him into the room and shut them inside.

Alone, quiet, together. The metal bed looked big enough, but old. He hoped there wasn't anyone directly below them because it looked like a squeaker.

He turned Lucy around in his arms and captured her face in his hands and nuzzled. "Are you a squeaker?" he whispered.

"I can squeak." Her hands were at his throat, tugging down the zipper to his jacket, and then she was on tiptoe trying to push the armored leather from his shoulders.

He bent down and let her tear it off of him. "I like the way you do that."

Next she went after his shirt. And his jeans. His knees began to shake. "Easy," he said, holding her hands just as she reached for his underwear. "We've got all night."

She jerked her hands free and ran them up his chest under his T-shirt. A jolt of exquisite pain shot through him as she found a nipple and pinched. He yelped, and she pushed the fabric up and kissed him softly. "Sorry."

He ran his hands through her hair and held her against his heart. "No problem."

"Boots?"

"Yes, please."

She bent down and unlaced them, then her own, and in ten seconds he was in his boxer briefs, barefoot and erect, watching her peel off her own shirt while he felt his heart stop.

"On the bed," she said, pointing. She wore a black, silky-looking bra that shoved her breasts up and out, and black bikini panties with a yellow smiley face right over the jackpot. Her hair was wild and bright around her flushed cheeks and pointy chin. She looked like an aroused, sexually dominant fairy.

He was all hers. Tearing off his underwear, he hopped over to the bed and flung himself down on his back.

Doubt flickered across her face as she stared at his cock. "You're kind of huge all over, aren't you?"

He reached down and stroked himself, firm but slow. "We already had a trial run," he said through his teeth. "Remember? No need to worry."

Licking her lips, she raked her gaze over him from head to toe, one hand lightly circling her left nipple through the fabric. "I remember." She dipped a finger in her red, swollen mouth, sucked it, then rubbed the saliva over the fabric until her nipple was hard and visible.

She repeated this on the other side while Miles watched and clutched fistfuls of fabric. "You are so hot."

That seemed to please her. She smiled and looked down at herself, then up at him. "What do you want to see first?"

"Whatever you got, baby."

She turned around, tilted a hip, looked at him over her shoulder. "You like?"

"Very much." Jaw clenched, he gathered more fabric in his fists.

With a teasing smile that made his heart lurch, she pushed down the elastic over her ass, exposing a round expanse of perfect, womanly flesh. Then she caressed herself, pulling the rest of the fabric down her hips. "Still happy?"

"Come over here and I'll show you how much."

She bent over and slipped the panties off.

He lunged, grabbed her around the waist, and threw her down on the bed next to him. Smiling, her green eyes hot with desire, she wrapped a hand behind his neck and tugged him down for a kiss.

The playfulness faded and serious lust took over. While his

tongue swept into her mouth, he unhooked her bra and reached under the cups to free her breasts. He broke away from her mouth to kiss his way down her neck, nipping and breathing hot against her skin to her breasts. Stroking his hand between her thighs, he sucked one nipple into his mouth, hard then soft, and licked his way to the other.

"Lift your knees," he said, his mouth only an inch from her skin. He pushed her thighs apart and settled himself between them. "Put your feet on my shoulders."

Soft toes curled around his neck and settled on his collarbone. "You don't have to—"

"Do too," he said, going down.

She was as responsive and passionate as any woman he'd ever been with, generous and lusty, open and free. He'd begun with a goal of getting her off so he could move on to his own release without feeling guilty, but soon he lost track of any plan and became obsessed with teasing her. He brought her close to the edge and pulled back, stroking, penetrating her with his tongue, his fingers, until he finally gave her what she wanted. She screamed out and he crawled back up her body, triumphant but close to the edge himself.

Hands shaking, he got a condom on and settled himself on top of her. Sweaty and dazed, she looked up at him with raw tenderness in her eyes. Then her fingers wrapped around his cock and guided him down He thrust into her, unable to wait any longer, and she felt so good and so right. He shouted out her name.

Though it wasn't an easy fit, she tilted her hips to take him deeper. They fell into a rhythm together, pulsing back and forth. He couldn't stop looking into her eyes. His body began to shudder, his arms flexed on either side of her beautiful face. Surprisingly uninhibited, she cried out and dug her nails into his skin.

He came, shaking, not a thought in his head. A moment

later, muscles buckling, he sank down to rest on his forearms, buried his face in the crook of her neck, and breathed in her sweet skin.

Long minutes stretched by. His heart finally came to a manageable speed. His vision cleared. He savored how right it felt, resting there between her legs, her pulse blending with his own. So right it couldn't last.

"I suppose you want to go back to the resort again," he muttered into her shoulder. "Any minute now you'll be telling me you were drunk and I'm an asshole… and you'd be right."

She captured his face between her hands and pushed his head up to look into her eyes. "You're not getting out of here until morning, big guy," she said huskily.

Before he knew it, she'd flipped him onto his back and was attempting to tie his wrist to the bed with his T-shirt.

"Would it ruin the moment," he began, feeling his blood start to simmer again, "if I said you make one hell of a cute dominatrix?"

"Easy, tiger." She trailed a finger down his sternum. "I'm just making sure you don't escape while I use the bathroom."

Grinning, he closed his eyes and sank back into the mattress.

As if he'd try.

***

HE WATCHED HER SLEEP. Her short, wild curls framed her face on the pillow. Carefully, he moved the hair off the left side of her face and studied the light shadow of freckles across her skin, the way her reddish eyelashes rested against her cheeks.

They'd used four condoms, the latest in the shower a few hours ago. He hadn't thought he was capable of that last one, but sure enough, feeling her wet body rub up and down his was enough to get him going again.

And now it was morning, and he couldn't stop looking at her.

In his career working with children he'd known plenty of families that began unexpectedly. If Lucy was so eager to get married and have kids, would she be on the pill? Or was a thin layer of latex the only thing between them and parenthood?

He couldn't help but wonder what a kid of theirs might look like. A redheaded giant? A shrimpy brunette with a tragically hopeless dream of playing pro basketball?

You're losing it, dude. In the air above her body, so as not to wake her, he traced her shape with his hand. She had generous hips compared to the rest of her, but any baby of his would be so huge he didn't want to think about what it would do to her body. Split her in half. Not to mention how it would make her hate him forever—if she didn't kill him out of revenge first.

He couldn't give her what she wanted. In this alone, it seemed, she was willing—no, eager—to be reckless.

He would never be reckless about marriage. Let alone children.

He sighed and sank onto his back next to her, staring at the ceiling. A water spot stained the corner near the window.

Relax. You weren't the one she wanted to marry, anyway.

The truth of that brought little comfort.

———

THE SOUND of the shower turning off woke her up. After a drowsy delay, she bolted upright, clutching the sheet over her chest, and struggled to get her bearings.

Shabby bedroom, sound of the ocean, splitting headache.

The bathroom door opened and Miles stepped out with only a towel slung around his hips. His broad, muscled shoulders and upper arms were damp from the shower. Dark hair trailed down over his stomach, pointing south under the folds of the towel.

"Morning," he said, drawing her attention up to his face.

Such nice eyes. Great laugh lines. And now that she knew what that mouth could do to her, she couldn't stop staring. Sensual lips, but not serious. The type to smile between kisses. Hot, wet, tireless kisses.

She sank back and flung her arm over her eyes, groaning.

"Coffee?" he asked.

Not moving her arm, she nodded.

"The breakfast room should still be open."

The thought of food made her stomach growl. She peeked out and looked for a clock. "What time is it?"

Still hovering near the bathroom door, Miles shrugged one massive shoulder. "Not quite ten."

"Oh, shit." She started to jump out of bed but stopped when she remembered she was completely naked. "I promised Fawn I'd do a spiritual retreat thing with her this morning."

"Call and explain."

Giving up on modesty, Lucy slid down the tall, creaky bed to the floor and scrambled around on the floor, picking up pieces of her discarded clothes from the night before. "Explain what? That I spent all night having sex with somebody other than the guy she set me up with?"

"Like she doesn't know." He bent over and found her panties under the bed, handed them to her. "You want me to go get you something to eat while you get dressed?"

"What do you mean, 'like she doesn't know?'"

"She was here last night. She knows."

"But she left." Rubbing her eyes, Lucy remembered the look on Alex's face when she stayed behind with Miles. "With Alex."

"Yup." He came over and kissed her quickly on the cheek.

"Take your time. Fawn will understand. I'll get you some coffee and chocolate pancakes."

"Waffles."

He kissed her again, this time on the lips, and tried to linger but she pushed him away. "My teeth are furry."

He stroked her cheek with his thumb. "I don't mind," he said, but smiled and released her. "Back as soon as I can."

In five minutes she was dressed in yesterday's clothes and brushing her tongue with a washcloth. Her cheeks were chafed from the night before, her eyes bloodshot—making them even greener than usual—and it stung to wipe.

She didn't regret a moment. She'd been drunk, impulsive, shortsighted, and illogical, but for the rest of her life she'd have this night to remember. Dan's bitchy comment about her being too sexually needy for him couldn't hurt her anymore. A handsome, virile guy with more testosterone in one eyelash than Dan had in his entire body had found her irresistible not just once, but—she turned off the water and stared at her face in the mirror—four times.

She blinked back at herself wonderingly. Was that biologically possible for a man more than a decade past adolescence? Maybe that last time nothing really came out.

The door slammed. "Honey, I'm home!"

Her body reacted instantly. In the mirror, she could see her eyes widen, the way she blushed and licked her lips.

She squeezed the washcloth into a ball and threw it down onto the sink. Sex was great fun but she couldn't get carried away. "Out in a minute!" She paused with her hand on the door. It wouldn't look good to rush out as though she'd been dying without him.

"Success," he said. "There's even enough for me, and that's saying something."

She peeked out. He was trying to fit a few overflowing

plates onto the small table by the window. The last one kept toppling sideways. Giving up, he put it on a chair before stepping back and brushing his hands together with pride.

He was so damn cute. And he'd made the room smell like hot sugared starch and caffeine. Heaven. She walked over, suddenly shy, and took the empty chair. "Where's yours?"

He came close and tilted her chin up to look at him. Little jolts of electricity went through her as he stroked the tender skin of her throat. Then he bent over and brushed his lips against hers. "Right here."

She froze. "Miles—we need to talk. I'm not sure—"

He smiled faintly, nodding at the steaming feast. "After breakfast." He lifted the plate off the chair to sit down.

The waffles were smothered with butter, chocolate chips, whipped cream, cinnamon, and fresh raspberries. She picked at it, hyperaware of him, a mountain of man sitting across from her. He had delicate table manners. He cut his food into small bites and used a cloth napkin to dab at a dollop of whipped cream that graced the corner of his sensuous mouth—

"I don't think I can do this," she blurted out.

His eyes smiled at her over his coffee cup. "You're doing fine."

"No, I'm not. I'm *nervous*. It's ridiculous. After everything we did to each other all night, why would I be nervous?"

His smile grew, stretching from ear to ear and taking over his entire face. "Because you know we're about to do it again?"

She tried to muster up something coolly dismissive, or even lighthearted and flirtatious, anything to show she wasn't feeling raw and exposed and totally, completely terrified.

Instead, all she could say was, "We are?" and stare at him blankly.

"Yup." His smile was gone now. He glanced down at her plate. "Done?"

Numbly, she nodded. He took her plate and dumped it on top of the others.

"We'll have to talk later, then," Lucy managed to say. Right before he lifted her up in his arms and threw her on the bed.

Chapter 18

*L*ucy climbed up on the bike behind Miles. She couldn't stop smiling.

"We're never going to talk about this, are we?" She gingerly adjusted her weight on the seat. Sore, but the good kind of sore. Happy to have her arms around him again, she squeezed his waist, savoring the delicious realness of him.

The engine sputtered to life under them. He turned his head, but in the helmet she couldn't see any hint of his face. "Did you say something?"

Shaking her head slightly, she reached down between his legs and stroked him.

"Hate to say this, but you can't do that now," he said. He was half-shouting through the helmet visor.

With one last little pat, she took her hand away, grinning. She'd never felt like this before. Like nothing mattered. She could float away with the fog, she was so light.

"Hold on!" he shouted, and they were off.

And damned if the ride didn't get her all turned on again. Was good sex like eating potato chips? She'd devoured his whole bag and now was trying to get the last crumbs out of the bottom corners with a wet finger.

A sharp curve in the road, with a sharp drop-off to the rocky shore below, made Lucy grab onto Miles like a baby koala.

Yet more proof she wasn't herself; the height only gave her a few butterflies. And she was already lightheaded.

There was another curve, and another. They passed an RV, then a trio of cyclists, and she lost herself in the rhythm of the journey and the beauty of the ragged, wild coast.

Later. She'd think later.

"I THOUGHT we were going to do a spiritual retreat," Lucy told Fawn that afternoon, stifling a yawn as she stepped into the large public hot tub next to the lap pool. The pool complex was covered with a protective tent about fifteen feet high at the center and looked like a giant, hollow marshmallow. The warm, quiet humidity inside was a nice change after the relentless wind outside.

Fawn glanced at the pool tent entrance, then settled down under the water. Tendrils of steam rose up around the hair she wore on either side of her head in two round, braided pigtails —Princess Leia the supermodel. "I wanted to talk to you privately first."

Uneasy with the serious tone, Lucy slipped down into the water to hide her face. She'd called from the B&B to admit her descent into sin, but Fawn hadn't said anything other than "Okay," and "Can you be back by four?"

"Are you angry with me?" Lucy asked her finally.

She looked at the door again. "Oh, no, of course not."

Lucy wasn't convinced. "I'm sorry about Alex."

Fawn's eyes were suddenly on her. "Are you?"

"I know how awkward it might be…"

"For him? Or for you?"

"For you," Lucy said. "I asked you to set me up, and then I blew him off in front of everybody. Well, not that I blew him at all. Ha, ha."

"You had a lot to drink. Was that it? You weren't quite yourself?"

A vision of riding Miles on the beach flashed through her mind. She felt her already rosy body get rosier. "You could say that."

"Because I don't think it's too late to explain that to Alex—"

"I'm spending tonight with Miles. In his cabin."

Fawn stared at her, face blank. Her beautiful android-of-the-runway look.

"You're angry," Lucy said.

"If it's not meant to be…" She bit her lip.

The high-pitched whir of the pool bubble's zipper opening caught their attention. Krista stepped in wearing a white bikini, Betty right behind her in a black wetsuit that went down to her knees.

Fawn swore. Her eyes darted between them and Lucy.

"What?" Lucy whispered at her.

But their friends were already at the edge of the hot tub, stepping down to join them.

"Damn, it's hot in here," Betty said, reaching for the zipper at her neck.

Krista held up her hands. "Please don't get naked again. I can't take it anymore."

"I'll melt!"

"Why didn't you just wear a bathing suit?" Krista jumped down to the bottom of the pool and strode through the water to Lucy's side. "I have seen that girl's boobs enough for a life-time, God help me. I deserve a medal."

Betty stuck out her tongue and peeled the suit off. After a shimmy for Krista, she stepped down into the bubbling water, completely naked, while the rest of them openly stared.

"Is that a tornado under your belly button? I've never seen that one before," Lucy said, studying her tattoos before they disappeared under the surface.

Betty wiggled her eyebrows. "The vortex of love," she said. As they laughed, she went on, "Speaking of which, where were you last night? Not to mention—ouch!"

Fawn bobbed over and put an arm around Betty's bare shoulders. "Sorry. Guess I slipped."

"You stuck your foot in my vagina!"

Biting her lip while the others laughed, Fawn said, "Sorry," and bent down to say something in Betty's ear.

"Fawn, what's going on?" Lucy asked. "You've been acting funny all afternoon. If it's about me, forget it. They obviously know already."

"Know what?" Krista asked, looking alarmed.

Fawn ducked her head.

Did she really think, after last night, there could ever be anything between her and Alex? Lucy hadn't made her decision with the clearest of heads, but it was done now.

"I slept with Miles last night," Lucy declared, understating the events for the sake of simplicity and what shred of privacy she had left.

Krista gaped at her. "What?"

"Miles," Lucy said. "We spent the night together. Just wanted to get it out there."

Krista continued to stare. After a long moment, she asked in a little voice, "Alex was there?"

With an awkward laugh, Lucy said, "Only at the beginning."

Krista closed her eyes. "I see." She sank down into the water and disappeared. Only her curly, dark hair was visible, floating on the surface.

"Your hearing aid!" Betty cried, splashing over. She jerked Krista to the surface. "Your hearing aid!"

Eyes downcast, Krista shook her head. Water trickled down her face. And a few tears.

Betty hopped out of the pool, displaying a labia piercing that made Lucy flinch. Then she grabbed a pile of white spa towels from a nearby basket. Squatting down, ignoring Krista's tears, she popped a hearing aid out of one ear, then the other, and wrapped each carefully in a towel. "You dork," she said affectionately. "Not that you can hear me."

Wishing she knew what the hell was going on, Lucy tried to read the glistening faces of her friends. "Did she… like Miles?"

Ignoring her, Betty jumped back in the water, her naked breasts bouncing, and took Krista's face in her hands. Face to face, so she would read her lips, Betty said, "He wanted you. You. Are. Hot."

Krista shook her head. "He was drunk!"

"It gave him the excuse he needed," Betty said.

"I was just a rebound girl!"

"You're the one he really wanted."

Lucy met Fawn's eyes across the pool, finally understanding. "Alex and Krista?" she asked, and Fawn nodded.

That was fast. Lucy sank deeper into the water and pondered the steam rising up between them. She felt a funny surge of relief. If Alex had slept with Krista, she was off the hook. They were even. Neither of them wanted the other.

"He was after Lucy, not me." Krista looked at Betty and wiped her eyes.

"He wised up," Betty said.

Lucy frowned. That didn't sound very nice.

"And I was going to have Miles!" Krista continued.

Uh-oh, Lucy thought.

Betty started to put a hearing aid back in her ear before Krista took over and put them in herself.

"I had it all figured out," Krista said. "Now it's a mess."

"Was it that bad?" Betty asked. "Last night? Because sometimes those preppy ones are rockin' in bed. All that pent-up energy. Give them a chance and they explode. Oh, was that it? I'm not an expert on penises but I can imagine the letdown if he starts squirting too soon all over the place and you haven't even—"

"It was fine!" Krista said, while Lucy and Fawn tried not to laugh. "Really good, actually."

Betty threw up her hands. "So what's the problem? Did he text you pictures of himself naked? Put a secret video online? What?"

"I had it all figured out but at the first opportunity I jumped in bed with another guy just because he showed a little interest in me." Krista dropped her face in her hands. "What's my problem? What if I can't be faithful because—"

"It's kind of early to worry about faithful," Betty interjected, then added under her breath, "Of course, in my opinion it's always too early."

"—because I'm so friggin' pathetic I need to please every man who might want me?"

Betty put an arm around her. "Of course you're pathetic. Everyone's pathetic about love."

"But I don't love him," Krista said. "Maybe I could, but—"

"Not that kind of love. The need to be loved. You've always been a little extra deprived in that department. Your parents are okay, but they're kind of cold. Measuring everything out like you owe them something."

"They're a million times better than your parents and you don't have a problem," Krista told Betty.

Betty removed her arm. Sank back into the water. "I've slept with two different women since Monday."

Lucy exchanged glances with Fawn. The chance to slip away had long passed.

"Two? How? You were with Jaynette both nights," Krista said.

"Jaynette's a teacher. She's used to working in a group."

That broke through Krista's funk. She put her hand over her mouth to smother a laugh.

"Krista…" Lucy didn't know what to say. "I'm really sorry, I had no idea."

"No, it's fine," Krista said, not sounding like it was. "I just don't get it, though. He's so big. Wouldn't you be more comfortable with somebody your own size? It's kind of a waste."

Krista had always had body image problems. Lucy didn't believe a woman should have to choose her partners based on height. "I didn't waste an inch of him."

Krista closed her eyes. "Thank you so much for sharing."

"You hooked up with Alex! Besides, I had no idea you were interested in Miles," Lucy said. "And neither did he, I'm sure."

Krista pulled her hair back and squeezed out the water. "I gave him a pretty good idea." She climbed out of the hot tub. "Forget it. What's done is done. I think I'll go get a salt scrub. No, Betty, stay where you are. Please." She smiled crookedly. "You'll never get back in that wetsuit."

The three of them watched Krista stride away and climb through the pool bubble.

"Damn," Lucy said. "I should have seen that coming."

"I tried to tell you," Fawn said.

"You should have talked faster."

Betty floated over to Lucy. "Didn't waste an inch, huh?" She grinned. "About time you found someone who could satisfy you. Guess you just needed to think big."

Miles slept through the afternoon to recover from the night before. When he woke to a banging on his door it was almost six in the evening.

Assuming it was Huntley, he shouted, "Go away!" and pulled a pillow over his head. The only person he wanted to see was Lucy and she wouldn't knock that hard. Smiling, he tried to reclaim the erotic dream about her he'd been enjoying before the interruption. Whatever Huntley wanted, it couldn't be remotely as important as Lucy licking maple syrup off his testicles.

The banging continued. Then, "Miles! I know you're in there!"

His father. Miles cursed as Lucy slipped away and he was stuck with reality. The sheets were tangled around his legs, half off the bed, and he had a raging hard-on.

"Not a good time!" he shouted. He untangled his legs and sat up.

"I know she's in there!"

That woke him fully. Why would his father care who he was sleeping with—

Oh, lord. Did the man never learn? Miles pulled his jeans on and trod to the door. He took a deep breath before he opened it to his father's red face.

"Where is she?"

Miles sighed. "I should pretend I don't know who you're talking about, but you're too predicable."

Alan pushed him aside and stormed past the mess of the bed to the bathroom. He even looked in the closet before striding out to the rear patio.

Miles grabbed a bottle of water and sat on the edge of the mattress. When his father came back, Miles just stared at him.

Still red in the face, Alan paced in front of him. "She probably jumped over that fence. God knows she's capable of it. Working out all day." Jaw tight, he glanced at Miles. "You think I'm stupid enough to think that body is for my benefit?"

Miles saw the pain in his father's eyes. He didn't want to feel sorry for him but he wasn't used to seeing the charming, mighty Alan Girard look like a wounded old man.

"She wasn't here. Never was."

His father slumped down on the bed next to him. "Right."

"Never. And I mean never."

"You don't look like a man who spent the night alone."

"I didn't."

He glanced sideways at him. "Who, then?"

Miles hesitated, then shrugged. "Lucy. The maid of honor."

His father mulled that over. His face was reverting to its normal color. "You were together earlier. When we met."

"Yes."

"I thought you were using her as an excuse to get away from me."

"No, I used *you* as excuse to get away *with her*." Miles gulped down a mouthful of water. "And Lucy or no Lucy, I wouldn't touch Heather with a ten-foot pole." *Unless it was electrified.*

Alan massaged his face and sighed. "All right." He got to his feet. "I'll go."

He made it to the door before Miles said, "Wait."

Alan turned. Once again, Miles was struck by the difference in the man he'd feared and revered all his adolescence. "I've been stupid," he said finally.

Mouth flattening, his father closed his eyes. "So she was here. I knew it."

"Oh, for God's sake. Give it a rest." Miles was going to tell him he regretted running away. That he should have made him believe the truth, that life was too short. But his father, even now, was too blinded by jealousy. "Check the staff housing. She always did like them young."

His father slammed the door on his way out.

Chapter 19

This wasn't where Miles wanted to be.

The sun had disappeared behind the redwoods, casting the path to the lodge into premature night at just past seven o'clock.

He was going to find Heather and deal with this once and for all. Then he'd be able to spend another night with Lucy. Right now he was too angry to be fit company for anyone.

The lodge was very warm. Though high summer, a fire burned in a cast iron woodstove near the seating area. A handful of people sat there, most with a glass of wine in their hand. He didn't recognize any of them. They looked rich. Part of his father's generation.

One of the staff, a fifty-something woman in a baggy beige dress and chunky jewelry, hailed him with an outstretched glass. "Good evening. I've got a wonderful Shiraz here tonight."

He scanned the rest of the room. No sign of his lovely step-mother. "No, thank you." He strode past the group to check in the little store before he tried the pool.

Bingo.

Heather stood in the aisle talking to Fawn's mother, Geri. He resented how the sight of her always made his palms sweat.

"Heather," he said. His determination to get this off his chest made his voice harsher than he'd intended.

She jumped and spun around. "Miles, you scared me." Smiling, she looked at Geri. "Have you two met?"

That's when he noticed Heather was holding a box of condoms and a small black bottle of lube.

A surprisingly forceful wave of pity for his father washed over him. "I want to talk to you," he said.

Geri raised her eyebrows. Heather put the contraceptives back on the shelf. "Of course, Miles. I was just telling Geri how we've got a lot of catching up to do."

Geri looked at her watch. "Lord, look at the time. I've got to be going. Nice meeting you, Heather." She gave Miles a funny look on her way out.

Great. The condoms, the flirtatious greeting… now Fawn's family thought he was having sex with his stepmother.

"Fantastic to see you, Miles. You look gorgeous. I didn't get a chance to tell you the other day." She walked up to him and patted his chest.

He grabbed her wrist and squeezed. "We're going to go for a little walk."

Her eyes narrowed. "You're hurting me."

"The path to the parking lot is lighted. We'll walk there," he said, releasing her.

"How romantic." She strode ahead of him.

They both waved the wine lady away and stepped out into the night. The temperature had already dropped in the few minutes he'd been inside. Wind blew Heather's hair into her face.

"Lovely night for a stroll. How nice of you to think of me," she said.

"My father was looking for you."

"If you're so eager for me to see him, perhaps I should leave you and go to him right now."

"He thought you were with me."

"And so I am," she said.

"He nearly knocked my door down."

"He does like to throw his weight around."

"Damn it, Heather—" He gritted his teeth, waited until he was in control of himself. In a calmer tone, he continued, "I know he must have made you sign some killer prenup, but maybe you could do the right thing… just because it's the right thing to do."

They'd been walking side-by-side down the narrow path, but now she stopped and turned to face him. "You're lecturing me? You haven't spoken to your own father in sixteen years."

"And you haven't been loyal to him for one day."

All hint of warmth drained out of her face. Her eyes narrowed. "You don't know shit."

"I know plenty."

"You know shit." She continued walking.

"What happened then is hardly something I'd forget. Or are you going to tell me I misunderstood why you stuck your hand down my pants?"

That shut her up. They walked past the last cabin. A beam of sunlight sliced through a gap in the fog and the trees and lit up a small meadow to their left. His heart pounded. He felt on fire. He should have confronted her years ago.

"I don't remember doing what you say I did—"

"Liar."

She snorted. "But if I did, I apologize."

"You *apologize*?"

"Yes, I apologize. Though honestly, you've certainly milked it over the years, walking around with that big chip on your shoulder when really you should be thanking me."

"Listen to me. I don't give a damn about what you did to me."

"Now who's a liar?"

"It's my father you're hurting. And God knows who else."

"Please. Don't pretend you suddenly care about dear old Dad." She turned and started walking back the way they'd come. "This conversation is over."

He strode after her. "I'm not through with you."

"Give it up. If you want a real conversation, talk to him. It's been almost two decades. I think you're due."

"I already talked to him. He's upset his wife sleeps around." Disgusted, he stopped where he was, letting her walk away, talking to her back. "I don't get it. Why would you stay married when you're so miserable?"

She stopped and gave him a small smile over her shoulder. "Who said I was miserable?"

FIGHTING a yawn and feeling dead on her feet, Lucy knocked on Krista and Betty's cabin door. She'd intended on taking a nap instead of having dinner to rest up for another night with Miles, but she felt too guilty to sleep. She kept seeing Krista's stricken face.

Krista had always been an odd combination of needy and invincible. Much more popular in high school than Lucy, she'd always known what to wear, what to say. She'd been in the student government clique, starred in several plays, dated the best-looking guys.

But it was never enough. She never seemed satisfied. Something about Krista—no matter how many people liked her, it was never enough.

Over the years those popular friends hadn't stuck around but the motley crew she'd known since elementary school—

Betty, Fawn, and Lucy—had. To her credit, Krista never turned her back on them when it might have made her more popular with her exclusive crowd. In high school, she ate lunch with Betty—whose hair had alternated between pink and platinum blond—and always chose Lucy for her team in P.E., no matter how much grief her cooler friends gave her.

Krista got on Lucy's nerves, but she was a good person. She was a good friend. It bothered Lucy that she'd hurt her, however unintentionally.

Lucy knocked harder. "Krista? It's Lucy. I know you're in there. I saw you go inside!"

And she'd been alone. If Krista had been with Alex, God knows she never would have interrupted.

The door opened a crack. Krista's tear-streaked face appeared. "Lucy?"

"Hey. Can we talk?"

"We don't have to talk. It's my issue, I'll deal with it."

Lucy hesitated. If she tried to force a conversation it would seem like she was only there for her own sake, not Krista's. "Are you sure? You seemed awfully upset."

"I probably just need to be alone." But she opened the door wider and moved a little to the side.

Lucy got the hint. She stepped into the cabin. "I just wanted to tell you how sorry I am I didn't understand what you were going through earlier."

"But I did tell you. Right after I talked to Miles that first time. And you told me I had to figure out what might be worth loving about me before I expected a man to want me."

Oh-oh. "That's not what I meant." Lucy rubbed her temple and gestured near the rear of the cabin. "Do you have a private patio back there like mine?"

Krista nodded.

Lucy got first aid out of the mini-bar. She hadn't planning on drinking any alcohol tonight but that was apparently unrealistic. "Let's have a glass of wine and talk about how awesome you are."

"No, I'm not, obviously I'm not—"

Lucy nudged Krista with her knee and herded her onto the back patio. She set the bottle and glasses on a small table near the hot tub and smiled at her old friend. "You want to know a secret? I'm not kidding about it being a secret, either. You'll have to promise not to tell anybody. Really. Anybody."

Krista sat on the edge of a teak bench across from her and crossed her arms over her chest. "Even Fawn?"

"Especially Fawn," Lucy said, dead serious.

Interest sparked in her eyes. "All right. What?"

Lucy took a deep breath. "Promise?"

Krista sighed and drew an X over her heart. "I promise."

The wine wasn't chilled, but Lucy poured a glass and handed it over. She hoped her confession didn't come back to bite her. "I've always thought you were the one who should have been a model."

Krista froze with the glass at her lips, eyes wide. She took a sip. "Really?"

"Really."

"Why wouldn't you want Fawn to know that?"

The wine was excellent. It was worth drinking at any temperature. "You're right. I left off the juicy part."

Now Krista was smiling a little. "Yeah?"

"I still don't understand why Fawn is an internationally known supermodel and you aren't. I think you're the most beautiful person I've ever known. In person, I mean."

Krista looked around as though they might be overheard. "But Fawn is gorgeous. She's six feet tall, thin, blond, those eyes, that skin, she's so graceful—"

"All true. Which just goes to show what I think of your total hotness," Lucy said, swallowing another mouthful. "Not to get all Betty on you. This isn't, like, me trying to be the most promiscuous bisexual slut in the wedding party or something. Collecting as many of you as I can."

Krista stared at her. Finally a corner of her mouth twitched. "Saving Betty for last?"

"No. She was for tomorrow night at the rehearsal dinner. I was saving Huntley's lesbian sister for the wedding itself. If I'm going to gay, I might as well go for an heiress."

"She's cute. I've seen pictures."

Lucy saluted her with the wine glass. "Good. I'm very picky."

Krista laughed out loud and shook her head. "I'm not sure I believe you."

"All right, I wasn't really going bi on you. I've got enough trouble with men to start multitasking."

Still smiling, Krista drained her glass and put it down. Then she lay down on the bench and stared up at the darkening sky, her hands folded over her stomach. "Thanks. I guess."

"You've already started to dismiss what I said. I never said anything before because I didn't think it should matter what people look like, especially between friends, and I didn't want you to think I was judging you that way," Lucy said. "But you're so damn insecure and it makes no sense. Of course guys want you. Of course Alex wanted to sleep with you. The question I wish you'd ask yourself is, 'Is he worth it? Is he worth *me*?'"

Krista tilted her head and looked at her. "Is that what you do?"

Lucy thought about how she'd measured and weighed every man she'd ever known, estimating their sum total of qualities against her requirements. "Yes. Too much."

"I agree."

Lucy snorted into her glass. "You're supposed to reassure me I'm doing what's right for me."

Krista pushed herself back up to sitting. "But you're not." She leaned forward and put her hands on her knees. "You wanted Alex because he was good enough for marriage. Then you wanted Miles because he was good enough for sex."

The wine dripped onto her lap as Lucy lost her grip on the glass. "That's not fair. That's not—"

"Not once did you ask yourself if you were good enough to use other people for what you wanted, no matter how they might get hurt when your experiment was over." Krista pushed up to her feet. "I'm flattered you think I'm pretty. I know I'm pretty. But what I want goes deeper than that, and I think it's really sad you can't even see that. For me or for yourself."

Stunned, Lucy put the glass down and stood up. "Of course it goes deeper than that. And why shouldn't I think about what I'm worth and what I need? That's what everyone else is doing."

"But it's always an experiment with you. You're so heartless. Calculating. Dan left you for another woman and right away you started looking for a new victim."

Lucy sucked in a breath. "You don't mean that. You're just upset."

To make things worse, Krista began to cry. "Oh, God forbid somebody gets *upset*. Of course I am. Every guy I like would rather be with women like you. Women who treat them like *shit*."

This was not what she'd come over for. "Your theory is flawed," she said, reaching out to the cabin's back door. She'd have to walk through the bedroom to get out. "As you yourself pointed out, Dan left me."

"He would have come back in a flash if you'd shown the slightest feeling about him leaving you. He was *testing* you, Lucy. Making sure you loved him before you got married. And you failed the test."

"He started living with somebody else. That was quite a test."

"Extreme measures, maybe, but you yourself said they weren't even sleeping together."

"You don't know what you're talking about. You've got this idea about me because you're unhappy, and now everything has to fit into your hypothesis. It has no bearing on reality." Lucy strode into the cabin and tripped over one of Betty's bras. She had to put a hand on the unmade bed to regain her balance. Great, now *she* was upset. Couldn't even walk.

Krista was right behind her. "You're the one who's twisting reality. One of these days you're going to get hurt and realize I'm right!"

Where was this coming from? Lucy frowned at her, not believing so much crazy resentment had been simmering under the surface. "You'd *like* me to get hurt?"

"Maybe. Yes. It would be good for you to know what it's like."

She knew well enough what hurt felt like. Lucy shot her a cold look before striding out of the cabin and hurrying down the stairs. She marched off into the forest.

How long had Krista been bottling up that little rant? Maybe they'd never been the closest friends in their group, but Lucy never suspected she'd been harboring such... venom. And because of men, no less. This gorgeous, popular woman was bitterly jealous of Lucy's relationships with men—Lucy, who had slept with three of them in her entire life.

It was too ridiculous.

Irrational. Krista was unhinged.

What had happened between Lucy and Miles had been extremely consensual. Four—five if you count the beach, which she certainly did—times. Five very consensual times. The idea that she was using him was absurd.

And Alex? They'd met a few days ago and had barely

spoken. Not like she and Miles had, not with the immediate click of understanding and friendship. Who was the user? He slept with Krista without even knowing what Lucy had done with Miles. He could guess, but he didn't know. Hardly a trustworthy type. Probably jealous, too, the kind of guy who'd want to know where you were every minute, like you were his property. She would *hate* that.

What she and Miles had was fun and healthy and wasn't hurting anybody. He didn't make demands on her. He didn't need her.

In fact, she was going to find him right away and remind herself of that.

***

ALAN GIRARD LAY on his stomach on a massage table, fully dressed and immobile. If Shawn hadn't tipped him off, Miles never would have looked for his father in one of the massage yurts; he didn't think of him as the type. Then again, he was still wearing his wool trousers and Italian loafers, and no spa staff was in sight. So he was was just… waiting? Resting? Drunk?

"Dad?"

"Go away." He didn't move, just spoke through the hole in the padded table.

Miles stepped deeper inside the round building and closed the door behind him. Only tiny bluish lights along the floor lit the room. "I don't want to talk to you any more than you want to talk to me, but I guess we'd better."

"I'm busy."

In spite of himself, Miles laughed softly. "I can see that." When his father didn't say anything else, he added, "I tracked Heather down."

Silence.

"Look, I don't know what's going on between you and your current spouse—"

Alan snorted. "'Current spouse.' Nice." He didn't lift his head.

"Could you please sit up and talk to me?"

"We're talking."

"You're face down and I'm staring at your back. Hard to have a conversation."

"Now you know how I feel."

Miles closed his eyes for a moment before walking across the room and sitting down on the floor under his father's head. For a moment their eyes met through the hole in the table. "See? With a little effort the conversation becomes possible."

Alan sighed. He lifted his head and rubbed his eyes. "What the hell do you want?"

"Reconciliation."

"Hell of a time."

"Why? What's going on?"

"None of your business."

Miles stretched out his legs. "I'm not going anywhere."

"Great. Sixteen years you won't have anything to do with me. Now you won't leave me the hell alone."

"You told me when I was eighteen you never wanted to see me again."

His father pushed himself upright. His face was flushed. "That is such bullshit. You know I didn't mean that."

"Oh, you meant it."

His hand came down on the table with a loud slap. "Grow up! Two years of chasing after you was enough to prove my point. Phone calls, letters. No, three years. As far as I'm concerned, the day you turned twenty-one my debt to you was paid."

"Not once did you say you were sorry, Dad. That's all I wanted to hear."

"I'm not going to apologize for one stupid remark I made at a moment of great distress."

"You can't apologize because you can't admit you were wrong," Miles said.

"You know what your problem is? An inability to forgive. You get that from your mother."

"You can't forgive somebody who doesn't ask for it."

His father made a rude noise. "Your mother loved her high horse too."

Miles shifted his weight to get up. "I was stupid to think we could ever talk to each other."

"She laid all the blame at *my* feet, just like you're doing," his father continued. "Well, it takes two to tango, my friend. Not one person on God's green earth is perfect, not even you."

Miles pointed at the door. "I'll just go back to my little love nest now. Heather and I wanted to get in another quickie before you tracked us down."

"She'd like that," his father said roughly.

Miles stood directly in front of him and met his eyes. "I never touched her. Not then, not now. Not ever."

"This isn't about you, son."

Miles jabbed a finger toward the door. "You just barged into my cabin looking for her. You assumed she'd be with me because you never believed what I told you—"

"I assumed Heather was with you because she's pissed at me, you idiot!"

After a pause, Miles asked softly, "And you thought I was with her for the same reason?" All these years, his father still didn't know him. "I would never do that. Even if I liked her. Even if I hated you. Which I don't."

His father stared at him before dropping his gaze to his hands. He twisted the thick gold wedding band between his fingers, his face as intense as if he were defusing a bomb. "She caught me," he said finally.

"With another woman?"

"You'd think so, from the way she reacted. But I haven't cheated since, well, your mother. No, she caught me on the computer." When Miles continued to look blank, Alan grimaced. "Porn. Don't tell me you don't like to look at naked girls. You can't be that perfect."

Miles bit his lip. "No. Not that perfect."

"Hmph. Funny thing is, I was just curious. Only peeked around a bit. Got too much time on my hands since I retired. I'm not a young man anymore, with my... you know." He slapped his thighs. "Certainly not young enough to know how to cover my tracks. I'm an intelligent man, but technology, well, it's beyond me. Unfortunately, Heather's a different generation. A whiz on the computer. Somehow she saw that I'd been to a few websites, and ever since then I've been tied up in the doghouse while she keeps taking young pups for walks right in front of me. I'm chained up well enough. Don't even have much of a bark anymore. Just have to wait until she gets it out of her system."

"Let her get it out of her *what*?"

"She caught me. I was looking at other women. What else can I do?"

Miles shook his head, amazed. "What do you mean? You know how to get divorced. You do it all the time."

His father's sad, tired eyes met his. "She'll get tired of torturing me eventually."

Miles ran his hand through the hair. He never thought he'd see his father so... *defeated.* "You've really met your match with this one, Dad." He thought of Patty, his favorite stepmother. His mother. The other wives. None of them could have looked at another man without finding themselves in divorce court. "You finally married a woman who was more ruthless than you are."

"Oh, she's much worse."

"You're really going to just wait for her to get tired of sleeping around?"

"She's already getting bored with it. I'm starting to think it's all for show. Like hinting she would be with you," his father said. "She wouldn't really do it."

His confidence worried Miles more than his dejection. "She would, Dad. You need to know that she would."

"You haven't seen her since you were a kid. You really don't know her at all."

Miles sighed heavily. What else was he refusing to see about his wife? What other men, what other lies had there been? "I need to tell you exactly what happened. What she did back then. I tried to tell you but you wouldn't listen."

"Whatever she did is between the two of you."

"She claims she doesn't even remember what happened."

His father nodded as if he believed it, which infuriated him. "She doesn't *remember* sticking her hand down my pants," Miles said. "At my high school graduation. Then at my freshman dorm. I don't care if she doesn't remember it, I sure the fuck do. It ruined my—"

Miles stopped himself and looked away, realizing what he'd been about to say. And it wasn't true. His life was good. He'd been free to pursue what made him happy.

But it had cost him all the years away from his father. Which, he had to admit, had been his choice.

Now, though…

His father watched him intently. "She wasn't in AA then. Now she is."

He wasn't denying what she did. Just making excuses for it. "So she's an alcoholic? That makes it all right?"

"She's been sober for twelve years. Before that she had a few missteps, but she kept trying. She's had to make amends to quite a few people." Alan slid off the table and grabbed Miles's shoulders. "If she said she doesn't remember it you have to believe her. I hope you can talk to her about it again. Both of you need to give it a rest."

"You make it sound..." Miles trailed off. Like it had nothing to do with him.

"I didn't believe you at first. Yeah, I admit it. She was so beautiful, why wouldn't you want her? I was too jealous to see you were my spitting image. I should've been flattered." He sighed. "And I figured you were angry about your mother. Patricia, I mean, like your brother. Chas hated Heather too, though time healed that one. A little, anyway."

Miles pulled away from him. "I need to think."

"To hell with thinking," his father said, slapping his back. "Let's get a drink and you can tell me all about this youth foundation I keep hearing about. I'm buying."

"The Sterlings are buying."

Alan gave him a wicked smile that took thirty years off his face. "Even better."

"Miles?" Lucy rapped on the door again. It was almost ten. Where was he?

She pinched the elastic of her underwear to pull it back over her butt cheeks. The one time she wore the uncomfortable kind, the kind that looked good but felt like a sequined hair scrunchie, and she ended up wearing it for hours.

Where was he? She pressed her ear to the door. Nothing.

Fighting her growing embarrassment, she turned and went back down the steps.

Something with Huntley must have come up. The wedding rehearsal was tomorrow, and the wedding first thing Saturday morning. Maybe the guys jumped the gun on a bachelor party.

But wouldn't Miles have called her? Sent a message?

They'd parted with kisses and giddy groping. They hadn't set an exact time, but it was understood they both wanted more.

Dread pooled in her stomach. Was this just her overactive libido talking? Maybe five times was enough to tide him over until—

Until next week. When they both went home.

No, no. That wasn't it. There hadn't been any hint of goodbye when he kissed her over his motorcycle. And they'd specifically discussed how nice it was that he had private cabin.

She marched up the path. She couldn't go sit around in her own cabin waiting for him. She could go get a drink, maybe. And something to eat.

She pivoted and headed for the Snowy Egret. A half-dozen people were mulling about the resort, most in pairs. Still older people. More of Huntley's socialite pals had arrived, flooding the Soul of Muir with the Soul of Moolah. Maybe Miles had been roped into meeting them.

Roped. That was a fun image. Like Gulliver. He was such a sport, she knew he'd be up for anything…

Except right now, apparently.

Damn it.

She paused at the door of the Snowy Egret, looking in, and let out a long sigh of relief to see him sitting at the bar with his father.

The two large men mirrored each other. Both had their elbows on the bar and faced each other, foreheads nearly touching, and after a moment Miles reached out and patted his father on the cheek.

Lucy let go of the door handle.

That was great for Miles. She was glad. Hungry and lonely, but glad.

She went back to her cabin, telling herself how happy she was for him. Hadn't she liked him precisely because he didn't put any demands on her? Well, it cut both ways. She didn't own him either.

The calculator in her brain reminded her how few hours she had left with him before they went home. How she'd just lost a third of that time because he'd chosen to reconcile with his father instead of getting naked with her.

She told the calculator to shut up.

Chapter 20

Friday morning Lucy had breakfast early. Still no sign of Miles. Fawn had dropped the pretense of spending her nights away from Huntley, so Lucy had the cabin to herself now.

What a waste.

After Krista's tirade, and the fruitlessness of donning a sequined hair scrunchie on her private parts, she'd felt a little unpopular and had slept badly. Every bump in the night sounded like Miles at the door. None was.

Eating her white breakfast alone didn't help, and as soon as she'd taken the last bite of her egg white omelet, she marched to Miles's cabin.

They only had today and tomorrow. Sunday morning at ten, a Sterling limo would take her home. Nothing in her plans allowed for continuing strings-free sex after that. As soon as she walked into her apartment and did her laundry and cooking for the work week ahead, reality would come crashing back. She was alone and single and getting older than she'd ever thought she'd be without a mate, kids, the whole bit. She could ignore that hard truth while surrounded by cedar and egrets, but not forever.

She had to enjoy her time with him here and now.

Miles's scruffy broad face appeared in the crack in the cabin door. "Lucy. Oh, shit."

Hardly the welcome she'd been looking for. "I'm sorry to wake you. Thing is, we don't have much time left."

He squinted at her. "Time? What time is it?" He rubbed his face with both hands.

"It's only nine. But it's Friday." She heard the whiff of desperation in her voice. "Never mind. Maybe I'll see you later."

He leaned forward and grabbed her arm as she took a step down. "Hold on! Just give me a minute."

"It's okay. I'm going for a walk. Find me when you're up." She glanced down at his boxers. "Awake."

"Oh, God. Last night. I fucked up. My dad and I—"

"It's okay. I saw you at the bar."

"But I should have told you. I never meant for it to go on as long as it did. Then when we finally got out of there, I was in no condition to—"

"No problem. Really."

"But you must have come here looking for me. How long did you wait? I hate to think of you knocking on the door and me not answering—"

"Actually, I didn't even make it this far. I saw you at the restaurant and figured we'd have to reschedule." She felt her face get warm. She couldn't stand the idea of him feeling sorry for her because she'd wanted to have sex with him and he hadn't bothered to show up. "Did you have a good talk with your father?"

"Light on substance, but it was good. Lots of scotch and sports talk."

"Male bonding."

"Exactly." He rubbed his eyes again. "Where are you headed? I'll catch up."

"Thought I'd hike out to the ocean."

"I'll catch up." Then he flinched. "Oh, damn. No, I can't. I promised my father I'd have breakfast with Heather."

It was already nine. Breakfast would probably tie up the rest of his morning. Why did that fill her with panic?

She didn't cope well without structure. She knew this about herself. They just needed plans, however short-term. "Lunch?"

His face fell again. "Can't. Promised to eat with Huntley's parents." His lip quirked. "Unless you'd like to join us…"

"Do I get to tell them off?"

"Fine with me."

She swallowed tightly, feeling rejected, which was silly. "Tempting, but no. Maybe this afternoon."

"Definitely. Except—I might have to spend some time planning Huntley's bachelor party. I can't put it off any longer." He scrubbed his face with his hands. "Shit, the wedding's tomorrow."

"If you're having a bachelor party tonight, you won't be able to commit to anything later, either. I wouldn't want—" She cut herself off. *Wouldn't want to wait up all night for you again.* "Well, I imagine we'll both be at the rehearsal tonight."

He reached out and touched her cheek with the backs of his fingers. "Not quite what I had in mind."

After a pat, she moved his hand away. "Can't be helped. Good luck with that breakfast. It's great you're working through these family issues."

"Thank you. But maybe—"

"Sure. See you around." Forcing a smile, she gestured up the path. "You know where I live."

But only for the next forty-nine hours.

As she walked past her cabin on the way to the West Trail, Lucy ran into Alex.

Eyes lighting up, he stood directly in front of her. "There you are. I've been looking for you. Have you had breakfast?"

Lucy glanced past him through the trees. Mist sank through the branches, coating the air with dew. The sun hid behind a thick layer of morning fog.

She looked back at Alex. He had an uncertainness about him that hadn't been there before. Dark circles under his eyes. Unshaven jaw. Wrinkled button-down shirt, half undone, with a faded T-shirt hanging out underneath.

"I'm sorry, but I have."

He glanced behind her, his gaze drawing a line between her and Miles's cabin. "Right."

"But I was just about to go for a walk out to the beach. Would you like to join me?"

"A walk?"

"We won't get a chance tomorrow. The wedding's early."

He nodded. "I'd like that." He stood up taller, gestured down the path. "Shall we?"

They hiked in silence for ten minutes until the buildings of the resort were out of sight behind them. The fog grew heavier with each step. Lucy walked ahead, wishing she'd chosen a shorter hike. She'd imagined Miles at her side. All night she'd wanted him, and now she ached to reach out and take his hand, feel his big palm in hers.

When they got to the stream that had soaked her before, she stopped abruptly, and Alex bumped into her. Poor man, she'd almost forgotten he was there.

"I'm sorry about how things turned out," she said.

"Sorry, as in you regret it?"

"If I hurt you, yes."

He studied her. "That's nice of you. I'm sorry if I hurt you, too."

How would he have…

His laugh sounded forced. "Can I help you get over to the other side?"

Disconcerted, she turned her attention back to the shallow, ten-foot wide ribbon of water at their feet. Flat stones formed a bridge that a toddler could cross.

"I'll be fine." She stepped across easily. "I think I was just nervous before."

"Funny, I wasn't nervous until right now." Alex came across behind her and jumped onto the bank. "I need to tell you something."

Oh, lord. He's going to tell me about Krista. "Please don't. You really don't have to."

But he was reaching into his pocket. "I didn't realize how little time we'd have to get to know each other, or I would've told you sooner." He pulled out his wallet. "I thought it might make you uncomfortable, so I didn't. Now I wonder if it might've helped me… stand out, so to speak. Though it's foolish to speculate."

Lucy frowned at the square of paper in his hands. Slowly and carefully, he unfolded it to reveal a page from a glossy magazine. He handed it to her.

A photograph. Fawn getting into her Volvo in Berkeley, paparazzi swarming around her—and Lucy at her side. She wore her usual black and was jabbing one of the photographers with an umbrella.

"I thought you were beautiful," Alex said.

Oh. "You noticed *me?*" She looked back at the photo, wondering how that could be possible. The red hair did stand out, of course, and she was looking straight at the camera. She looked pissed off. Fawn was a blazing beauty who lit up the picture like an angel in a Renaissance painting.

"Huntley gave me that to show me how beautiful his new girlfriend was, but all I could see was you."

"Alex." Lucy put a hand on her chest. Her mind went blank. "I'm—"

"Sorry. Yeah, I got that." He took the paper back from her and folded it just as carefully as before. "You don't owe me anything, Lucy. I just wanted you to know."

"I'm still not sure what happened, but it wasn't something I planned."

He nodded, not meeting her eyes. "Being away from home can make us forget who we are. Especially in a place so"—he waved his hand at the lichen-draped trees—"primordial."

"Thank you for understanding."

"You probably heard I spent the other night with your friend Krista."

Damn, he sounded so casual about it. Like they'd shared a pizza. "Yes. She's…" She tried to think of something flattering to say but was still too annoyed with her. "An old friend," she finished lamely.

"And you spent the night with Miles."

She nodded. She wasn't going to talk about that.

He held out another piece of paper. She looked at it. His business card. "This whole week is already starting to feel like a dream," he said, pressing it into her hand and putting his other hand over it. "I'd still like to be friends. We'll be seeing each other occasionally, I'm sure, given our close friendships with the bride and groom."

She looked up into his face. A nice face, with kind, patient eyes. Even now, even though he possessed emotions she hadn't expected, he was determined to approach the situation calmly.

He really was the type of man she'd been looking for.

So why didn't she want him?

"Lucy!"

She swung away from Alex. Miles stood on the other side of the creek.

After what Alex had just said, Lucy felt like an impulsive

child. Although her body twitched to jump across the creek and climb up into Miles's arms, her mind, for the first time that week, had a grip on the situation.

She reclaimed her hand and the business card from Alex's grip but didn't move away from him. "Thank you," she told him softly.

Alex nodded.

"Lucy!" Miles yelled again.

"What?" Lucy asked him.

"What do you mean, 'what'? You just came by and asked me to go for a walk!"

"What about your breakfast with your stepmother?"

But Miles wasn't looking at her. Face flushed with color, he glared at Alex as he strode over the stream to join them, completely ignoring the rocks or the water, the way he got soaked up to the shins. "What the hell are you doing here?"

"*We* were walking," Lucy said. "What's your problem?"

"You weren't walking just now."

"For God's sake!" Lucy looked Miles over, disgusted to see his chest puffed up and his hands balled into fists. As if preparing to beat Alex into the muddy bank. Poor Alex—his body mass was probably fifty percent smaller.

Maybe she didn't want the guy who'd just told her she was beautiful to be pounded into the ground.

"I came as fast as I could," Miles continued. "Guess I should have run faster." He loomed over Alex with a snarl on his face.

"What is the matter with you?" Lucy poked him in the ribs. Hard.

But Alex looked eager to take him on. Shoulders back, hands fisting, he mirrored Miles's aggressive posture. Lucy could smell the testosterone flying through the air like aerosol sunscreen at a swimming pool in July.

"If you think this is attractive, acting like violent, macho idiots, you're wrong," she said.

They ignored her.

"I think it's time you gave up," Miles growled at Alex, no hint of his usual gentleness in his eyes. "She doesn't want you. Stay the fuck away from her."

"She *invited* me, big guy. Wrap your little brain around that."

"She felt sorry for you," Miles said.

Alex paused, then shoved him in the chest with both hands.

Miles, unmoved, lifted one of his fists and pulled his elbow back to swing.

Chapter 21

"No! For God's sake, no!" Lucy flung herself on Miles. "Hit him and I'll never touch you again!"

Frozen, not looking at her, Miles said to Alex, "Hear that? All I have to do is not beat the shit out of you and she's mine. *Mine*."

Lucy shoved Miles as hard as she could. "You arrogant *bastard*!"

He didn't budge, but her choice of insult made an impact. He looked down at her, pain at the edges of his eyes.

"You heard me." To hell with his sore spots. "Get out of here. Alex and I are going to finish our walk." She took Alex's arm. It was rigid with tension but she forced him to hook it through hers. "Without you," she told Miles.

"One night was enough, is that it? Think you had your fun and now you're ready to settle for this pompous little shit?" Miles flung up his hands. "Am I the last person in the world who believes in monogamy?" He spun on his heel and splashed through the creek to the other side.

Lucy watched him storm away. What was she supposed to do, just let him beat Alex up?

Macho idiot. He stood her up, didn't make time for her, and now he wanted to control her? To hell with him.

She wished she hadn't called him a bastard, but she didn't mean it in the offensive, archaic way. She had to find better insults that weren't politically loaded. If only she'd brought her smartphone so she could look up good words on her thesaurus app.

"You care about him," Alex said. He made no effort to walk alongside her, so she had to stop and stare at him.

"I'm *pissed*, that's what I am. Can you believe the way he *freaked* about us taking a walk?"

He untangled his arm from hers and held onto her hand for a moment.

Lucy's mind still raced through her mental thesaurus. *Oaf. Bully. Dorkbutt.* That's it. She'd make a spreadsheet with her ideas and title it "Miles Dorkbutt."

Alex squeezed her hand before releasing it. "You're not quite what I expected."

Reluctantly she set aside her mental spreadsheet to give Alex her attention. "How so?"

"I mean no criticism. More of an apology." He stepped back. "I've never been attracted to dramatics. It's completely my fault for assuming that a woman in your profession would be of a particular personality type."

"What the hell kind of *type* were you expecting?"

He sighed, smiling. "See? There you go again. You've got a temper. I hate to say it, because it implies such a stereotype and I certainly don't mean it that way, but you're kind of... hotblooded, aren't you?"

"Like a typical *redhead*, you mean?"

"Please don't be offended. I'm just sharing an observation. And it's totally my fault for being so eager to settle down that I ignored the obvious." He stuck his hands in his pockets. "You're not ready to settle down."

"Just because I didn't jump at the chance of being with *you*—"

"It has nothing to do with me." He pointed down the path to the resort. "You picked the most immature, commitment-phobic male you could find and went to bed with him."

"You are way out of line."

"Fine. Maybe so. But if I'm wrong, you're about to get hurt. And that would be a shame." He held out his hand. "I only wish you the best."

He was just trying to soothe his ego, imagining how badly she was going to get hurt by liking a guy he didn't approve of. Accusing *her* of being a hothead. Lucy Hathcoat, the number-crunching databot. If only her friends had heard him.

She didn't really want to touch him again, but he was right about having to see each other again over the years. Reluctantly, she squeezed his hand quickly then folded her arms over her chest.

"See you around." He turned to go back over the stream.

How could a man so perfect in so many ways be so completely annoying?

"Hey, Alex!" she called, just as he stepped onto the first rock.

He glanced back.

"Don't hurt Krista," she said. When he frowned, she added, "After all, you don't like it when I lose my temper."

"THIS IS POINTLESS," Heather said, getting up from the table. She wore a white sleeveless blouse, skin-tight white jeans, white sandals with white bows around her ankles. She should have blended into the pale decor of the Snowy Egret, but somehow, with her toned and tanned skin, her blond hair, all the gold jewelry, she made heads turn. "I told him you wouldn't be capable of this."

Miles let her walk away, past the newly arrived wedding guests having breakfast. Every table was filled with the young and the old, the bright and the beautiful. A few looked familiar, perhaps from movies or TV. Perhaps from a random game of basketball with Huntley. Perhaps both.

He didn't get up to follow her until she'd reached the door. Then, deciding he *had* been rude, arriving late and then barely speaking two words during the meal, he got up and strode after her.

"Sorry. I've got something on my mind." He flinched at the bright sky as he stepped outside. "And I'm a little hung over."

And depressed. He wasn't quite sure, but he thought he'd screwed up out there at the stream.

But she'd been standing there holding hands with him. Looking deeply into his eyes.

You screwed up.

He knew she didn't want Alex, would never want Alex. He knew, just like he'd said, that Lucy just felt sorry for the striving twit. She was trying to let him down easy.

"Lady trouble?" Heather asked.

They stood outside the restaurant facing the trail west. Alex and Lucy would come back that way if they hadn't already.

His head ached. "I don't want to talk about it."

"How's that working out for you so far?"

He gave her a warning look.

"Because from where I'm sitting, not talking about what's bothering you has caused a lot of problems. For everybody."

"You're the last person who should be giving relationship advice."

"Is that what you've got with her? A relationship?" Heather patted him on the chest. "Because from where I'm sitting, it looks a little early to be calling it anything at all."

Heather didn't know anything; she was just fishing. Looking for weak spots. He made a show of looking at his watch. "Actually, Lucy is expecting me now. Sorry to eat and run."

"Your father told me how you stood her up last night." She patted his chest again, this time leaving the fingers splayed across his heart. "Is she the forgiving type?"

Why had he told his father about Lucy? And why had he shared that with this vindictive woman? "She is, actually. I already explained."

"That you preferred drinking an elderly man under the table?"

Miles stilled. "He's not that old."

"He's seventy-three, Miles. Way past middle age. In fact, who could say how many years he has left?"

He wasn't going to admit how concerned he'd been the night before about his father's age. After their fourth drink, his dad tripped over the bar stool and would've fallen if Miles hadn't caught him. Not many people could stop a Girard man from hitting the floor—they were big suckers.

He captured her wrist and squeezed. "We had a really nice time. You got a problem with that?"

"Why should I? Now I'll get to see you more often."

Miles pushed her hand away from his chest. "Why can't you stop being such a bitch?"

Heather's eyes lit up as if given a precious gift. "Now who's giving advice?" She smiled at the sky, inhaling deeply and arching her back. "Such a lovely day. The cold takes a little getting used to, but I'm starting to like it. Maybe I can talk your father into moving out here."

"You'd hate it."

She laughed. "It is so nice seeing you again." Before he could step back, she went up on tiptoes and kissed him on the cheek. "Son," she whispered in his ear.

He recoiled instinctively. "Stay away from me."

She was still laughing as she strode away.

MILES WENT IMMEDIATELY to Lucy's cabin and banged on the door. His conversation with Heather had shaken him more than he'd like to admit. That woman was poison. His father needed to see her for what she was.

He corrected himself. His father's choice was none of his business. Certainly nothing he could do anything about. If he was going to have a relationship with his dad, he couldn't dive in being critical of Heather. His dad had already shown whose side he would choose.

He knocked on the Ceanothus cabin door again. No question he owed Lucy an apology.

But it was Fawn, not Lucy, who answered the door. "Hey, Miles! Just the man I wanted to see."

"Not Huntley?"

She pulled him inside. "Not at the moment." She shut the door and pinned him with a serious look. "What did you do?"

Every transgression Miles had ever committed flashed before his eyes. "Do?"

"To Lucy."

He lowered his voice. "I thought you knew about what we did."

She rolled her eyes. "Not *that*. Give me a break. This morning."

"We had a fight."

"Like I said, what did you do?"

Miles sighed and sat on the edge of the bed. "I screwed up."

"That's what I thought." Fawn went over to the mini-bar and pulled out a diet energy drink. "How are we going to fix it?"

"We?"

"Tell me what happened."

"She was getting all lovey-dovey with Alex, and I flipped."

"She was *what*?"

"They were holding hands."

"Brother. You think that was her idea?"

"I admit I overreacted."

Fawn sighed. "Here's the deal. I don't know you well, Miles, but I knew from the way Huntley talks about you that you'd be perfect for Lucy. Sure enough, right away she's all hot and bothered. A great sign."

"Hold on. I thought you were setting her up with Alex."

She smiled over the rim of her Monster Lo-Carb. "You've got to be a little sneaky with Lucy."

He stared. His mind flew back over the last few days. "Not very nice to Alex."

"He jumped to his own conclusions. I didn't do a thing."

Miles stood up. "I have to talk to her."

She got between him and the door. "Listen to me first. I have some advice."

"Fawn—"

"I'm her best friend. I understand her like nobody else."

"I don't need your help."

"You do."

"I just need to explain how crazy I am about her."

"That's the last thing you should say."

"She's all I can think about. Even though it's only been a few days."

Fawn sucked in a breath. "No. *That* is the last thing you should say."

She was so certain, so genuinely horrified, Miles sat down again. "It is?"

"She can't stand it when guys are all gushy. That's how she

ended up engaged to somebody who didn't like having sex with her."

Some loser shared a bed with Lucy and didn't even like it? "Was he gay or something?"

"We've been wondering. Point is, Lucy seemed to prefer that kind of relationship. And I knew she'd look for the exact same thing again if we didn't interfere."

"Wasn't it risky to set her up with Alex?"

"I didn't! She just assumed he was the one." She took a sip of her drink. "But it was you. Not that I could say that, because then she'd get skittish and weird and you'd never, ever have made it this far."

"But Alex seemed to know she was looking for a man."

"Maybe Huntley said something to him. Or maybe he just picked up on her signals." She shrugged. "Anyway, it's over now, thank God. Maybe Krista can sort him out."

"Krista."

She threw the empty can in the recycling basket near the door. "They slept together. The other night. After we left you at the B and B."

He looked at his hands. Hot damn. "And Lucy knows?"

"Oh, yeah."

Grinning, he looked up at her. "Then I'm set."

She sighed in exasperation. "Alex was never your problem. *Lucy* is your problem. She hates big displays of emotion. Lots going on under the hood, as I'm sure you know, but she likes everything on the surface to be calm and controlled."

He thought of the way she screamed his name and squeezed his hips with her thighs. "Not as much as you might think."

Face breaking into a stunning smile, Fawn sat down next to him on the bed. "I know you're what she needs, Miles. A man who can give her real passion."

"You just told me I was too *gushy*."

"In bed you can be as wild as you want. But the rest of the time you have to play it cool. No angry outbursts about her being your woman. If she thinks you want a long-term, exclusive thing without a baby at the end of it, she'll run. As long as you're fun and casual and great in bed—and not too easy—she'll keep you around."

Easy. She made him sound like a slut. "Maybe I do want a long-term, exclusive thing without a baby at the end of it."

"Maybe. Who knows? You just met. One thing I do know? Lucy needs at least one hot, passionate fling in her life. Something to dream about after she's married to some boring guy who can't light her fire."

The thought of her married to a cold, boring guy made him clench his teeth. "How am I supposed to 'light her fire' and be a jerk at the same time?"

She patted his knee. "You just have to do what I say."

To Lucy's surprise, the rehearsal dinner late Friday afternoon was neither a rehearsal nor a dinner. Like the tree ceremony, the spa had a tradition of gathering the bride and groom with the important people in their life and having some kind of New Age ritual that made everyone uncomfortable. This time it would be in a spa building called the Peace Yurt. Lucy went over with Fawn a few minutes early to make sure everything was ready.

Vibrating with nerves, Fawn kept tripping over the dirt path. Lucy didn't want to add to her stress, but she was worried about being forced to hold hands with both Alex and Miles and sing love songs or something.

Other women might've liked having a man fight for her, but Lucy hated it. She wasn't anyone's *thing*. Not her father's, not some guy she just met. Why did men think a little affection meant they owned you? Was it because they were so incapable of taking care of themselves?

Neither of them was what he seemed. Alex, ambitious and anal-retentive, should have been too self-absorbed to get attached to a stranger in a photograph.

And Miles! Preening around like the alpha gorilla. They hadn't made each other any promises. Now he seemed to think he owned her.

Nobody owned her. For the first time in her life, she was free. Her dad was safely hitched to an excessively capable woman who seemed to enjoy the exhausting job of taking care of him.

No adult should need that much from another. Children— sure. But a grown man? Or a woman? What kind of life was that, to live at the mercy, skills, whims, emotions, or fortunes of another?

Fawn stopped suddenly and put her hands on her stomach. "I feel sick. I'm so nervous I'm going to barf."

"Don't worry. It'll be fine. Who's going to be there?"

"Bride, groom, maid of honor, best man, parents," she said in a monotone. "Am I wearing too much concealer? Of course I had to break out this morning. All the sugar and stress. Look at my chin. It's like a 'You Are Here' dot right on my face."

"I can't see anything."

"Don't lie to me!" she snapped, then bit her lip. "Sorry."

Lucy put an arm around her. "Go ahead. Say anything that makes you feel better. I can take it."

"You are so great," Fawn said slowly, looking up at the sky and blinking fast. "I hope you find as much happiness as I have."

I was kind of hoping for more. "How are Huntley's parents behaving?"

"Same. It's okay. They're probably too old to change."

"And Huntley?"

Fawn didn't look at her. "He's willing to live on the west coast so it doesn't come up very often."

"But Fawn—" Lucy stopped herself. Should she tell her that wasn't going to work? She was marrying into a family that didn't like her. That was going to be awful no matter where they lived.

After checking her makeup in her compact and putting on more lipstick, Fawn plastered a smile on her face, pushing her shoulders back. "My mom went to meet her new boyfriend at the Greeting Lot. She might not make it here in time, which I told her was totally fine." She lowered her voice. "It's hard enough for *me* to suck up to the Sterlings. She doesn't have it in her."

"We just want you to be happy."

"I am happy." She put her hands over her chest and sucked in a deep breath. "I can do this."

Lucy hugged her. "Of course you can. Huntley will be here. And I'm here."

Fawn took her hand and squeezed. "I can't expect Huntley to turn against his own parents, but if you're here, at least I feel like there's somebody prejudiced to take my side."

"That should be him, Fawn."

"He's not a fighter, but he is loyal underneath. I love that about him. I do. I just have to keep reminding myself that it's going to be enough. His parents obviously hate my guts and always will."

Fawn opened the door to the Peace Yurt and gave Lucy a funny look. "Wow, I guess they weren't kidding."

Lucy peeked inside and groaned. "We're going to be naked?"

"Not the whole time, I don't think."

"I'm not getting naked, Fawn. I love you, but—"

Fawn pushed her inside. "I don't see why you're getting

prudish now. You seemed pretty eager to get naked the other night."

"Er—"

Another push. "If I can do it, you can."

So says the supermodel.

A naked female staffer greeted them with a white candle in each hand and a big toothy smile. She was in her fifties, had breasts more perky than Lucy's had been in high school, and sported gray pubic hair that was trimmed short. Like hedged lavender.

Lucy imagined her serving mashed potatoes and bean sprouts at the Snowy Egret and started to giggle. "I'm sorry, but I can't do this." She turned to flee and ran into a big, familiar chest.

Miles wore a fitted black sweater that emphasized his strong build. She inhaled the scent of him and hung on for a second before stepping back.

He kept his hands on her. "Where's the fire?" he asked. Then he saw the nude staffer. "Oh. There it is, right behind you."

"She wants us to get naked," Lucy said.

Miles frowned. "I don't do naked in groups. It's bad for fundraising." With an arm tight over her shoulders, he guided her back inside. "Maybe it's the wedding *night* rehearsal dinner. In which case, I think they could skip it since they've been practicing a bit already."

Then he dropped his hands and walked to the other side of the yurt.

"Hello, friends," the naked woman said. "I'm Denise, and yes, I'm nude. I'm going to invite all of you to join me. It's a simple but profound step to illustrate your unlayering. To bare yourself to me, to your committed partner, to each other, to yourself. I've got towels—"

"Thank God!" Fawn said, holding out her hand.

"—for you to lie down on. I'll come by with scented oils for your feet and hands. I do ask that you not touch one another, as that may increase the discomfort of everyone else."

Fawn held the towel to her chest for a moment, then shrugged and started unbuttoning her dress.

"I really can't do this," Lucy said.

"Oh, boy," Miles said, looking at the door.

Lucy turned around to see Huntley and his parents walk in.

Behind Huntley, Rosalind Sterling had on a cream pantsuit and a gold necklace as thick as a Twizzler. The elder Huntley wore a navy blue pinstripe, but had left off the tie—which, next to his wife, made him look as naked as Denise.

"Why is that woman in the nude, son?" Rosalind asked.

Wild-eyed and grinning, Huntley got a good look at Denise and Fawn. Then saw his father's face and his smile fell. "I'm not sure, Mom."

"And your friend. She's also taking off her clothes," Rosalind said. "Perhaps you have some insight in that area?"

Fawn was frozen in the middle of taking off her underwear. She'd already pulled off the dress and bra, which pushed her blond ponytail off to the side. Bent over with one knee in the air, she looked like she was posing for a photo shoot. Like Lucy, she watched her fiancé. Waiting.

"Must be part of the ceremony," young Huntley said, and went over to Denise to grab a towel. Then he stood there and didn't take off a stitch.

"Welcome!" Denise said. She handed towels to Huntley's parents and peeked outside the door. "Any more coming?"

Now naked and glorious, Fawn stood up with her back straight and said, "My mother can't be here until a little later. She's with her new boyfriend. I wanted him here at the wedding because she really likes him and I love her and that's how people act when they care about each other." She met the Sterlings' cold stares with a steely gaze of her own.

You go, girl, Lucy thought. Standing buck naked in front of your fiancé's parents would take guts even if they'd picked you out at the bride store and arranged the marriage themselves— let alone when they hated you. Even if you were six feet tall and gorgeous and posed in front of strangers for a living.

My best friend, the warrior princess.

"So, it's just us for now." Denise closed the door with a bang and turned back to the room with her hands together. "As I was saying, obviously, I'm nude. I invite you to join me. We get so many letters about this ceremony I can't even tell you. I know it seems strange. We are conditioned to be ashamed of our bodies. I admit, even I used to feel uncomfortable when we started this. But each and every day I get a letter from a former guest of our spa telling me how meaningful it was, how helpful, and I'm motivated to share this joy with you."

"Like hell you will," the elder Huntley said.

"This was obviously her idea," Rosalind said, fingering the necklace at her throat. "Perhaps Huntley could explain to her that marriage is a serious business, especially for a man like him, and then we can all forget this ever happened."

The room fell silent, most of them staring at Huntley. He studied the floor. Fawn's proud bearing was beginning to waver; Lucy could see tears shining in her eyes. But her jaw was hard and she didn't make any move to cover herself up.

Lucy didn't know what to do. If she took off her own clothes she might make the situation more ridiculous—she was one of Fawn's friends, and they'd write her off as another California nutjob. But if she ran over and covered Fawn with a towel, it would undermine the bravery of her stance, imply she had something to be ashamed of.

Suddenly, Miles said, "What the hell," and dropped his pants. He was wearing tight black boxer briefs; she admired them and the ass underneath, got lost in the memories of the feel of it under her hands. "Because marriage is a serious business." Then he kicked off his shoes, his jeans, pulled the shirt and sweater over his head. He didn't smirk or laugh with his eyes, just stripped down as though he were doing something important.

I love you, Lucy thought, watching him. And then, *No, I can't.*

"You're right, Miles," the younger Huntley said, breaking out of his trance. He went over to Fawn, stood a few inches away from her, not touching, and looked into her eyes. "Forgive me?"

Fawn let him squirm for a long moment before reaching out to unbutton his shirt. Slowly her fingers made their way down his chest, loosening each button to his waist. "Tell them," she said.

He nodded but didn't look away from her face. While he wriggled out of his shirt, he said, "Mom, Dad, this was all my idea. All of it. This place, this ceremony, this wedding, this woman." He kicked aside his shoes, pulled off his pants, then his underwear. He was naked, his bare white bottom aimed at his stunned parents. "I don't regret any of it."

"Jesus H," his father said. "About time."

"Give your trainer a bonus, dear," Rosalind said, smirking at his naked backside.

And then the two of them smiled at each other and went out the door.

Leaving Lucy the only one in the Peace Yurt with any clothes on.

Chapter 22

"Isn't that it?" Lucy asked wildly. "You got the groom and his parents to face up to the love between him and Fawn, so now we can all just go and maybe have something to eat—"

"Lucy." The warrior princess was staring at her now with the Gaze of Command.

Her face burning, Lucy turned to the side and took off her sweater. Then kicked off her shoes, her jeans, and eventually, when nobody told her she didn't have to, the rest of her clothes. After all, the only ones who hadn't already seen her naked were Huntley and Denise, and they couldn't care less.

Miles grabbed a towel and sat cross-legged on the ground on the opposite side of the yurt. Never looking at her, he put the towel over his lap and reached for one of Denise's bottles of oil.

Huntley and Fawn followed suit, forming a loose circle, and Lucy had to do the same or she'd be the only one standing up. Like she was It during a game of Strip Duck-Duck Goose.

Denise began chanting something but Lucy was lost in a daze.

First, there was the love thing. That was a problem. But she would just have to admit she was human and thus capable of infatuation and give herself time to get over it. Or see it as the natural progression of a quick, valuable friendship. He was a hot, sexy guy, but he was a human being first. She didn't have any trouble loving human beings. For instance: Fawn. She was a human being. No problem there.

The second issue, however, was how her new valuable friend (who was a human being) was totally ignoring her. This same person who was eager to fight over her like a rutting ape was now rubbing oils over his well-muscled calves, and thighs, and now upper inner thighs, without even glancing her way.

Instead he smiled at Denise, who was droning on about some flaky spiritual garbage.

Those breasts couldn't be real. And who trimmed their pubic hair like that? Sure, young girls posting videos on the Internet. Not post-menopausal therapists trying to get commitment-minded adults to discuss their deepest fears.

And my God, did she have to sit cross-legged? It was like Georgia O'Keefe down there.

Lucy flopped down on her stomach and buried her face in her arms. They could bring her to water but they couldn't make her look.

At Denise's nagging, Huntley began speaking about his fear of being worthless. "I've never had to prove myself," he said softly. "I can't imagine what Fawn sees in me. Not the money or, you know, my looks. The real me. What if there isn't anything there?"

"You dork," Miles said. "How many pretty billionaires do you see me hanging around with?"

"Maybe I'm the only one you could find."

Miles snorted. "I wish."

"If we could keep the tone more peaceful," Denise said.

Fawn scooted closer to Huntley and put a hand on his bare

knee. "I'm exactly the same way. That's what I feel when I'm with you—that sameness. Nobody's ever seemed to understand that."

Lucy lifted her head. "Hey."

"You're different. You knew me before. Plus, you're like a sister. Of course you love me. But would we be friends if we met today? Would you like just the grown-up me, if that's all you had to go by? I don't know."

"All right. I would, but I understand what you're saying." As long as she wasn't telling her she was too poor and ugly to understand the real Fawn.

Huntley moved closer to Fawn. "I love you."

"I love you," Fawn said, starting to cry.

Did they really have to do this in a group? Naked?

Lucy looked up at Miles. He stared back expressionlessly. She was suddenly aware of her bare ass jutting up while she splayed face down on the floor. Yet his gaze kept slipping away to Denise.

This was the guy who'd just lectured her about monogamy?

She decided to sit up. He'd been eager enough to get her naked before; he'd kissed and fondled her breasts with hungry enthusiasm. She'd give him a little reminder.

Arching a little as though her back had been cramped on the floor, Lucy stretched out, nipples aiming at Miles's eyes, and wiggled her legs. That would have ripple effects for sure.

Miles did glance at her, but instead of smiling, or staring, or fainting dead away from lust, he frowned and turned back to Denise.

Well, hell.

Huntley leaned in to kiss Fawn, but Denise stopped him with a warning *eh-eh-eh* sound.

"Sometimes touch is the avoidance of true intimacy," she said.

Huntley withdrew slightly, smiling. "You're so incredible," he told Fawn. "I can't wait to be married to you."

"I can't wait to be married to *you*," she replied, gazing into his eyes.

Lucy crossed her arms over her breasts. Sat cross-legged. Arched her back again.

He never even peeked.

"Can't we give them some privacy?" Lucy asked finally.

Miles glanced at her, but only for a second. "You want us to leave, guys?"

"My mom should be here soon," Fawn said. "It might be awkward if it's only us."

"Yeah, we wouldn't want it to be *awkward*," Lucy said.

Denise frowned at her. "Sarcasm is another layer that distorts and disguises. Try to set it aside as you would your garments."

Just as Lucy opened her mouth to tell her she was a phony busybody, she noticed the smile on Miles's face. While he stared at Denise's breasts.

That's it. Fawn was obviously doing fine with her new soulmate and didn't need a cynical maid of honor ruining the love-in. "Sorry, guys, but I'm not feeling well."

She grabbed her clothes and put them on as fast as she could without looking back. In thirty seconds she was outside.

She lingered on the threshold of the Peace Yurt for a few seconds. Okay, minutes.

When it was clear Miles wasn't going to follow her, she marched back to her cabin.

MILES WAITED TEN MINUTES, each one tougher than the last.

"This is ridiculous," he said. "She'll just think I'm an asshole."

Fawn and Huntley gazed into each other's eyes, obeying the rule not to touch each other only in the most literal sense. There couldn't have been a millimeter of air between their bodies.

"Fawn knows best," Huntley said, sparing him a glance. "If she said you should cool it, you should cool it."

"All right, so I won't try to beat anyone else up. But I'm not going to sit back while she goes after other guys."

Denise, who had been frowning and smiling simultaneously during this conversation, finally broke in. "Perhaps we should return to the relationships between those present in the circle. Discussing souls that are not present is not usually productive."

Now Miles knew how his older kids must feel, being forced to talk about their feelings with somebody who was being paid to care. Or pretend to.

Keeping the towel around his waist, he lumbered to his feet. "Fuck it. I'm going after her."

"Perhaps that's for the best," Denise said.

"No!" Fawn cried. "Just give her another few minutes. Enough to realize you're not chasing her."

"I am chasing her."

"But she can't know that or she'll freak out," Fawn said. "You need to play hard to get."

"Like Alex?" He got his clothes on, glaring right back at Denise. "He practically proposed after their first conversation. I wouldn't even call it a date, though I'm sure he does. Probably already planning their first anniversary."

Denise dropped the fake smile. "*Please.* This is not about you."

"Then why the hell was I invited?" He stalked over to the door, pausing to turn back and give Huntley an apologetic shrug before he went outside.

Fawn might know a lot about Lucy's family history, but she couldn't know how terrified she was of being alone in the world. Only a fellow near-orphan could relate to that. Miles could see it in her eyes. Mom dies, and the other isn't quite enough. No other blood relations to depend on, only the mercies of the few big-hearted people in your social circle.

Then you get older and you're not supposed to care anymore. You're supposed to be tough and independent, immune, invincible. If you want a family, just make one.

But families you *make* are the most fragile of all. Just pieces of paper. She needed to see how it was the emotional connection that mattered, not their legal status. The relationship itself.

I can't play games. He could barely stop his feet from running the rest of the way to her cabin. *I need to be honest with her.*

So he jogged through the woods to her cabin, knocked on the door with the most polite level of force he could manage.

Lucy appeared in the cabin doorway. Her hair was pulled back by a black headband, exaggerating her wide forehead and pointy chin, the green of her eyes, the pearls in her earlobes. Her lips were slightly parted, pink and shiny. Her T-shirt was low-cut and hugged her curves. She was barefoot.

Miles was taken aback for a moment by the sight of her. Just looking at her reduced his IQ by fifty points.

Easy, buddy. No more games. Be a man.

"It was all Fawn's fault," he said.

HER COPPER EYEBROWS FLEW UP. "FAWN?"

Rubbing his temple, he hung his head. "Sorry. No. My fault. Can I come in?"

Lucy had just poured herself a glass of wine and was looking forward to drinking it—and a few more—but she couldn't deny the thrill that went through her at the sight of him. Even as angry as she was.

What did he mean about it being Fawn's fault? "This isn't

the best time," she said. "The bachelorette party is tonight. I need to rest up."

"Sure, of course. Me too. I mean, for the bachelor version. But"—he rubbed his mouth, looking distressed—"back there. I've got to explain. The way I was acting… ignoring you…"

She could hardly admit she was jealous about him looking at another woman. That was just the sort of possessive stupidity she'd called him out on earlier. She looked down into her wine. "It's fine. You don't have to dote on me every second."

"But I was trying to… look, can I come in? Or could we go for a walk or something?"

"I think I've had enough walks."

He sighed. "And I'm sorry about that, too. Fighting with Alex. I overreacted."

"You think?"

"Lucy. You need to know I'm not usually like this."

"I'd like to believe that, but—"

"I know. Fawn explained. She told me lots of things. That's what I want to talk to you about."

Lucy groaned inwardly. "Just what did she explain?"

"She gave me some advice. About not coming on too strong."

Fawn? Coaching Miles?

"How long?" she asked, stepping away from the door and moving inside.

"How long what?"

"How long has Fawn been giving you advice?" She was going to kill that girl.

He flinched but said, "Just today. We'd never spoken before then." He started to come inside after her but she held up her hand.

"You can walk with me to the lodge store." She could survive a short stroll without losing her head, but not if he was inside her cabin. He couldn't think she would jump into bed with him whenever he felt like being friendly.

She pulled on her socks, found her boots. "I need to see if they have some industrial-strength hair gel. I can't have millions of pictures taken tomorrow with it frizzy like this."

"It looks great."

"It's the bane of my existence."

"It's beautiful."

She gave him a look. "Try surviving junior high with hair like this. See if you like it then."

"Kids can be cruel."

"It was the adults who laughed the loudest." Especially Mrs. Bergman, a sadist disguised as a science teacher. She stepped outside next to him and closed the door. "But I'm glad you like it."

He reached up and stroked the soft curls at the back of her head. Suddenly he pulled her close. "I love it," he said, brushing her cheek with his lips.

Boy, did she miss him. She froze, letting herself enjoy his touch just for a moment. "Is this part of Fawn's plan, too?"

"No. She told me not to come. She wants me to play hard to get. She really drilled it into me. How I needed to back off."

"Maybe she's still hoping I'll hook up with Alex."

"I doubt that."

Lucy moved away from him. "I wonder."

While they walked in silence, Lucy tried to set aside her emotions and study the facts.

Back on Monday, Fawn had laughed at the idea of Lucy being attracted to Miles. Tuesday, she'd seemed happy about her spending time with Alex, though Alex wasn't the type of guy Fawn usually liked. Wednesday, she'd intentionally left them at the B&B with a paid room. Now she was giving Miles confidential information and advice.

"That sneaky bitch," Lucy said suddenly, coming to a full stop in the path. "She's been manipulating me."

Miles nodded. "Looks like it."

"What exactly did she tell you?"

He glanced around. The lodge was still out of sight through the trees. Other cabins flanked either side of the path, but though there were distant figures walking around, nobody was close enough to hear. "She told me about your father."

Sighing, Lucy looked at the gray sky. "Let me guess, he's the reason for everything that ails me."

"Something like that."

"Fawn took too many psych classes in college. Totally unscientific garbage."

"Hmm," he said.

"You don't believe me."

"She's known you a long time."

"What did she say?"

He ran his hand over his eyes. "Look, I don't want to come between the two of you."

"What did she say, Miles?"

He peeked out at her. "Promise not to storm off and yell at her. She's getting married tomorrow."

"I don't yell."

His eyebrow went up.

"You think I'm a hothead?"

Smiling, he put an arm around her waist and hugged her closer. "Yes."

"I can't believe this."

"You're passionate." He bent down buried his face in her neck. "Full of life."

"And you're full of something else." But she tilted her head to let him trail kisses up her neck. "You're just trying to distract me."

"Funny, I was thinking the same thing about you."

She put a hand on his shoulder and held him back. "What else did Fawn tell you?"

He tried to kiss her again, but she put another few inches between them.

Sighing, he lifted his head. "She told me I should back off a little. So you don't think I'm obsessed with you and scare you away."

That was Fawn's doing? Brides weren't supposed to be thinking about anyone but themselves. "I got the impression you were obsessed with Denise. Maybe you should worry about scaring *her*."

He pinched the bridge of his nose. "That was embarrassing. I never should've listened to a woman who thinks Huntley is a catch."

He sounded so mournful, so sincere. She moved a little closer to him, relieved to have an explanation. And to feel his big, strong body under her hands again. "What else did she say? I might as well know it all."

His hand slipped down her shoulders, down the curve of her spine, over the swell of her backside. "She thinks you avoid real relationships with men because you don't like them to lose control of their emotions."

"And how do we define 'real?'"

His mouth searched the tender skin under her ear, kissing and licking. "For starters, a healthy sexual interest."

She stiffened. Fawn had told him about Dan. "I see."

"And it also includes"—he wrapped his arms around her and squeezed—"a little natural possessiveness."

"Is that what you call trying beat up some guy who talks to me?"

"I lost my temper because I care about you." He inhaled the smell of her hair, brushed her forehead with his lips. "A lot."

Alarms went off inside her head. It felt much too good to hear him say so. "We just met a few days ago."

"Exactly. Too soon to say goodbye." His fingers lifted her chin, stroked her neck, held her for a tender kiss on her mouth.

Breathless, she managed to say, "It's only Friday. We don't leave until Sunday."

"Lucy," he said, lifting his head to look into her eyes. "Be serious."

"That's exactly what I am. Serious. Ask anyone. I'm very, very serious."

He shook his head, his smile warming his eyes. "I want you to see my apartment, even though I'm afraid you'll think it's a dump. I want to meet your dad and see if he's as eccentric as Fawn says he is. I want to take you to my favorite taqueria in the Mission and I want to see how you decorate your place."

"You want a wife and kids, big guy? A mortgage, life insurance—"

His smile broadened. "I'm onto you, Lucy. You can't scare me away with that stuff anymore."

"It's not a game!" She pulled away from him. "I'm not fooling around. I've let myself enjoy a little fun with you this week but it's nothing that can last."

"It's been more than fun and you know it. And whatever *this* is, you need it as much as I do."

She began walking. "No. What I need is somebody who wants the same things I do. From the start. So there's no confusion." Or worse. She was already infatuated with him after four days; what would four weeks do?

"What do you think you need? Let's hear it."

"Don't patronize me. I'll tell you exactly." She held up her hand and pointed at her fingers as she counted. "One, marriage. Two, children. Three, a home. This is it for me, Miles. I mean it."

"I'm not buying it."

She threw up her hands. "It's impossible for you to believe I might want something you don't?"

"It's impossible for me to believe you don't want to see me again after we go home."

Her chest ached. This had gone much too far. She walked faster.

"Look at me, Lucy. Stop running away."

She spun around and faced him. "I'm telling you what I want and you don't believe me. It's infuriating."

"You don't want a man like your father, Lucy."

She gritted her teeth. *I'm going to kill that supermodel.* "One psych class and she hangs up her shingle," she muttered.

"What's the big deal about planning on seeing each other next week? Why is that so hard for you?"

"Don't pretend this is all about me. You're so freaked out about following in your own father's footsteps the thought of marriage gives you hives."

"I'm talking about going on a date next week and you need me to propose first!"

She shook her head. "I know what would happen if we dated. It would be great for a few months, maybe even a couple of years. We like each other, we're great in bed, et cetera. But then I'd start talking about the future and you'd start pointing out all the problems we had together. About why we're not ready to put down money on a house. Why you're not ready to become a dad." She took a deep breath. "I'd be a sucker for all these arguments because I'm very practical. I'd agree with many of them. And next thing you know I'll be forty and you'll be just about ready to maybe have a kid, except now I'm kind of old and I'm having trouble conceiving, so another year goes by. Next thing you know, some young thing is pregnant with your child and I'm looking for a studio apartment that allows cats. Since you've run off to Reno to marry the mother of your child. The end."

He blinked. After a long moment, he laughed. "You almost had me."

"I'm not kidding. I have never, ever been afraid to see the hard realities. Especially when they're six foot five and staring me in the face." She gave up the pretense of walking to the lodge and turned back to her cabin. "Alex warned me, you know. He said I'd jumped into bed with the most commitment-phobic male I could find."

Mentioning Alex wiped the smile off his face. He caught up to her easily, his long stride dwarfing hers. "All right. So I'll propose first."

"Very funny."

"I'll ask you to marry me, you say yes, then we date. How about that? Or do I need to cough up a ring first?"

"Don't be a jerk."

"Nice. I propose and you call me a jerk."

"You're mocking me." She walked faster. "Go away, Miles. The wedding's tomorrow. Don't you have a bachelor party to deal with?"

"Why should I mock you when you're refusing to go out on a date before I promise to be the father of your children? You're right. You are totally reasonable."

"If you're trying to change my mind you're failing miserably," she said.

He got ahead of her and grabbed her by the shoulders. "I know you care about me. Me, not the idea of me as your husband. The real guy who wants you. The real you, for yourself, not what role you might play in my life. How can you throw that away?" His voice softened. "How can you throw me away?"

Her throat tight, she lifted her chin and met his gaze. "I want a family. A real one. That's what I've wanted since I was a kid. That's what I've wanted as an adult, and that's what I want to have when I die." She put her hands over his where they held her shoulders. "That's what I don't want to throw away."

"But you've got no problem chucking me?"

Her breath caught. She had a huge problem with it. So big it was going to swallow her alive. "If you had any interest in… settling down some day… even theoretically…" She looked deep into his eyes, tilting on the edge.

"You want a guarantee, Lucy. I can't give one. I won't."

"Not a guarantee, just a possibility. Can you imagine…" She trailed off, finally realizing how angry he was. His jawline was rigid, clenched.

He can't imagine. He can't because it's not what he wants. From me or any woman.

Ever.

"I'll see you tomorrow, then," she said dully, stepping away from him. "Before we go home."

Chapter 23

There was no bachelorette party. Fawn decreed the evening free of any obligations and insisted her friends go and enjoy themselves—after the four of them shared a last meal in the Snowy Egret.

"But it's bad luck not to have a party the night before!" Krista said. "We've been planning it for months."

"The whole week was all about me," Fawn said, toasting each of them with her chardonnay. "I want all of you fresh and happy in the morning. Not sick of me. Or hung over. We'll be posing for lots of pictures."

Lucy, who'd been struggling to put Miles out of her mind, looked up at her. "Don't you get enough of that at work?"

Somebody kicked her under the table. Probably Krista, given the constipated look on her face.

"We'll keep it simple, don't worry," Krista said, putting her hand on Fawn's arm. "Just a *little* drinking and a *few* games and I promise we'll get to bed early."

"I'm so sorry, but no," Fawn said. "I love you guys but I'm spending tonight all by myself. I arranged it with the staff an hour ago. I'll have my own cabin and nobody will know where

I am. I've got a hot tub, my music, a nice book, lavender oils, and the stars. The real ones, not the famous kind." She smiled at each of them. "I'll see you first thing tomorrow at seven. No makeup—I'll take care of that. Hair, too, and dresses. And I want to give each of you a little something."

"Tux. You promised a tux," Betty said.

"Of course. You and Huntley's sister both." Fawn grinned. "I can't wait to see how Dear Old Mom reacts when the two of you walk down the aisle arm in arm."

"So long as we don't have to get ceremonially hitched at the altar in some kind of straight liberal guilt fest, I'm cool with it," Betty said. "Is she as hot as her brother?"

"Touch her during the service and you die," Fawn said.

Betty laughed.

Pushing the gratin around on her plate, Lucy tried not to think about having to endure the ceremony at Miles's side. All day, having to smile and act happy for Fawn and Huntley when all she wanted was to get the hell out of there and forget the disgusted look on Miles's face when she suggested a future together.

"Come on, girls," Krista said, looking around the table. "We had a plan!"

"Now you sound like Lucy," Fawn said.

"We've wrapped the party favors and everything!"

Lucy lifted her drink. "It's just chocolate. In obscene shapes."

Another kick. This time it was obviously Krista, because she followed it up by taking away Lucy's gin and tonic. "Stop drinking. Save your meager tolerance for the party."

"There isn't going to be a party." Lucy snatched it back so roughly it spilled over her knuckles. "Because that's what *Fawn* wants and we *love* her."

"Fawn's just saying that because *some* of us have made such a *mess* of our lives we can't handle being with other people."

"I'll be fine," Betty said. "Jaynette will be psyched I'm free tonight."

"I meant Lucy!" Krista cried.

"Oh. Well, she's earned a little sexcapade, don't you think? Being engaged to that gay guy all those years." Betty ran her hand through the green side of her hairdo. "If she wants to spend another night with a straight man, I say we let her. Hell, I'll set up the mood lighting."

"Dan was not gay," Lucy said, wondering if that was true. "And I'm not sleeping with anyone tonight."

Fawn gave her a sharp look.

"His eyebrows were skinnier than mine are," Betty said.

"He was fastidious, that's all," Lucy said.

"Wouldn't go down on you, would he?" Betty asked.

"Betty!" Krista gasped, looking around them at the restaurant. Betty's voice tended to carry. Especially when she was talking about female reproductive organs in public. "Just because you have a unibrow doesn't—"

"I do not. Look. Asian girl here." Betty gave Lucy a knowing nod. "He was gay. Have fun tonight."

Lucy focused on her halibut alfredo, not wanting to talk about how little fun she was going to have.

"Before I go, I need to tell you all something," Fawn said suddenly.

Lucy stopped chewing. Fawn looked nervous.

"Back when Huntley and I planned this wedding," she began, "we were afraid his parents would never really accept me. So we figured we'd move into my place in Berkeley for a while, take a break from our jobs, plan our life together." Fawn dropped her gaze to her wine. "And then, when his parents came around, we'd move to New York."

Lucy forced herself to swallow the lump of potato in her mouth. "You're moving to New York?"

Full of concern, Fawn's eyes met hers. She nodded.

"Cool," Betty said. "Can we visit?"

"Definitely. I insist," Fawn said.

Lucy smiled, but she felt hot tears threatening. "Right after the honeymoon?"

"I wanted to break it to you more gently, but all of a sudden Rosalind and Huntley are really nice and talking about buying us a place—in Manhattan!—as a wedding gift, and there was no time."

Krista had the nerve to nudge Lucy under the table again before reaching across the table to Fawn. "We're happy for you."

After returning Krista's kick in the shin, Lucy lifted a glass to the bride. Fawn travelled a lot, but her home base had always been in California. Now, with both her career and her new family on the East Coast, they'd grow apart. They'd learn about their lives from Christmas cards and emails, birth announcements. *People* magazine.

She would *not* cry. "To Fawn," Lucy said. "The most beautiful person I know, inside and out."

They all clinked glasses and drank, even Krista. Everyone was sniffling.

Fawn jumped up and went around the table to kiss each one of them. "I'd better go before I change my mind. On everything. I love you guys so much." She got to Lucy and whispered, "We'll talk later."

"I'm fine. Enjoy yourself," Lucy said, squeezing her arm.

When she was gone, Krista told Lucy, "This is all your fault." Then she scowled at Betty. "And yours."

"Make up your mind." Betty pulled out her cell, studied the screen, looked back at Krista. "Uh, any chance I can have the cabin tonight? Jaynette's roommate is back."

Krista rolled her eyes. "I swear, you are such a frat boy. What next, hanging your underwear on the doorknob to warn me you're busy?"

Lucy gulped down the rest of her drink and felt the fire course down to her belly. Clearing the air with Krista wasn't something she wanted to do, but it was on her to-do list. And it might help her feel better. "You can sleep in my cabin, Krista," Lucy said. "Obviously Fawn won't be there."

"What about the big guy?" Betty said.

Lucy shrugged, trying to look casual. She'd tell them all about it later when her feelings weren't so raw. "Not tonight."

"Actually, I don't need either cabin," Krista said softly. She glanced at Lucy before taking a big gulp of her wine. "I'll be with Alex."

It shouldn't have bothered Lucy, but it did. Everyone pairing up, moving on.

"What about the bachelor party?" Betty asked.

"After that. They're making it an early night, too."

"Sure they are," Betty said. "Watch him show up drunk and missing a front tooth."

"No, Huntley insisted he wants to keep it mellow."

"And you're not sleeping with Miles? Not even for one last fling?" Betty asked Lucy.

Both of them looked at her. They wouldn't be alone tonight, wondering if they'd done the right thing, if they were brave or a coward. She forced a smile and shook her head.

"Ah, well," Betty said. "There's always tomorrow night."

Chapter 24

Miles stood under the rose arbor in a flood of sunshine. The ceremony was only moments away, not on the beach but in a courtyard of an old Mediterranean-style villa that predated the spa by a hundred years. Only a half mile east of the Greeting Lot, through the forest and over a ridge, the villa and original vineyard was the spa's acknowledgement that wealthy guests would want convenience and glamor, not just rustic eccentricity, for their biggest events.

Golden stone walls surrounded them, semi-ruined but picturesque, overrun with vining jasmine and wild roses. Artful ruin was good ambiance, Miles supposed, though in his opinion the faux-distressed bricks were overdone. They could have used the cheap new kind and just bombed the place.

Shielded from wind and bathed in warm sun, he had to admit the courtyard was an idyllic spot for a famously photogenic pair's wedding. The guests sat in curved rows of white lattice-back chairs hung with floral garlands, their eyes fixed on the groom and his best man, waiting for the fun to begin.

The elder Sterlings sat in the front row, looking as pleased as Miles had ever seen them. No doubt relieved by the classy setting. Or maybe they were actually happy for their son.

In a row behind them, Miles's father sat next to Heather, who wore an enormous yellow hat. His dad looked tired and old in a gray suit, his body leaning away from his brightly colored wife. But for a moment, he glanced up and met Miles's gaze, and something vivid and affectionate passed between them. Remembering their night at the bar, maybe, or acknowledging the irony of celebrating another marriage when his fourth was in trouble.

And then he pointedly glanced at Heather and rolled his eyes. Miles swallowed a smile.

The groom, however, wasn't enjoying himself. Rigid and silent, Huntley stared down the aisle with his hands clutched in a vice grip in front of him.

Thinking of Lucy, Miles sank back into his own misery.

"She's not coming," Huntley said.

"Of course she is." Miles felt around in his pocket for Fawn's ring to confirm for the tenth time it was still there. Their little ring bearer, one of Huntley's cousins, had panicked and thrown up over the elder Huntley's shoes. He'd been mercifully relieved of his duties.

Though Miles would have appreciated a wild night of bar hopping, strip clubs, gambling, and other celebratory vice, Huntley insisted on dinner (one beer), a movie (French), and an early return to the spa. Alex enjoyed it (he chose the restaurant and the movie), but Miles would much have rather sat it out, alone, in his cabin.

To scheme.

He still couldn't understand where he'd gone wrong with Lucy. And how to make it right.

Sitting near a fountain near the back, the string quartet switched from Bach to Handel. Heads turned, bodies shifted, gazes moved up the aisle to capture the first glimpse of the bride.

"I'm going to be sick," Huntley said, smiling through a clenched jaw.

His skin did look a little green next to his slicked-back pale hair. Keeping the groom from upchucking at the altar was probably top of the best man's List of Duties.

Betty and Courtney, Huntley's sister, began walking down the aisle, arm-in-arm in their tuxedos. A mumbled reaction rippled through the crowd but the women were up for it. They approached with their chins high, dead serious.

"Not going to make it," Huntley muttered.

"Knock knock," Miles said quickly.

Next, Krista and Alex appeared. The two looked good together. Quite comfortable with each other, actually. Their hips brushed against each other's while they walked, and both looked happier than they had all week.

Guess Alex made a late night of it after all.

"Who's there," Huntley replied.

"Orange," Miles said.

"Orange who?"

"Orange I cute in a tuxedo?"

Huntley let out a little breathy laugh, but his heart wasn't in it. "Is it too late to move this to the beach?"

"I'm game," Miles said.

Then Lucy appeared and he forgot about Huntley. Just the other day he'd had her. The perfect woman. He'd always thought she was beautiful, but now—now she was breathtaking. Red hair, green eyes, pale skin, a knockout dress that plunged and curved in all the right places.

It hurt to look at her.

Give it up. She wants an aquarium-loving sperm donor, not you, he told himself.

"Knock knock," Huntley said.

Lucy's dress was pale pink, almost white. Like a bride. "Who's there?" Miles barely managed to say.

His bride.

He told his heart to calm down. It wasn't his wedding. Lucy was wearing *pink. Everything'sfinedeepbreath.*

Lucy looked nervous. She didn't have the carefree good humor of a bridesmaid. With her eyes fixed on the ground, she walked unnaturally slowly after Alex and Krista, a fixed smile on her face.

Everyone else faded away. His chest felt tight. Her cheeks were flushed with color.

His little redhead.

No, not his. Not anymore.

"Banana," Huntley said.

Her hair gleamed like fire.

Huntley nudged him in the ribs. "Banana."

Miles glanced at him. Sighed. "Banana who?"

"Banana I cute in my tuxedo?"

He turned his gaze back on Lucy. She was only a few feet away from them now, and apparently wasn't going to lift her eyes from the ground. "Very banana," he said vaguely.

"You're worse off than I am," Huntley said, just as the flower girl burst into the aisle holding her white basket.

Got that right.

They didn't go home until tomorrow. He still had a chance.

***

THE WEDDING ATTENDANTS flanked the bride and groom, three on each side, facing the important couple and the middle-aged woman who was officiating the vows.

Don't cry, Lucy told herself.

She was a capable, sensible person. It didn't make any sense to cry just because her friend and her friend's chosen mate were saying a few words to each other in front of hundreds of people.

"You complete me," Fawn said.

Oh, God, even worse. She was going to lose it with a *cliché*.

"You had me at hello," Huntley said right before he kissed her.

I give up, Lucy thought as the tears broke over her eyelashes, artfully lacquered with waterproof mascara, and trailed down her cheeks. At least she'd had the brains to smuggle a few tissues inside her bouquet. She pulled one out during Fawn's reciting of an e.e.cummings poem and dabbed at her eyes.

She risked a peek at Miles. Unfortunately, he wasn't absorbed with the ceremony and crying into a tissue.

He was staring right at her. Electric shocks tingled down her spine.

She'd always liked how he looked. Ridiculously out of proportion to her, his action-figure girth, the height that shrunk doorways—he was attractive. A fun adventure.

Not anymore. Now he was *scary*.

First of all, he was wearing a black tuxedo. Not the kind she was used to, the ill-fitting Hefty bags rented at the mall, but a gorgeous ensemble of perfectly tailored inky sleekness that turned him into a broad-shouldered, sophisticated *god*.

She'd always been a sucker for black. And now, with her heart all stirred up and her body remembering every inch of his? A body she'd never touch again?

It hurt to look at him.

Focus on Krista. Put him out of your mind.

But when she looked at her beautiful friend she saw the over-caffeinated brightness of a woman who'd had a hot and sweaty night. Good for her. No, really. They looked great together.

I wonder if Alex still has that picture of me in his wallet.

Alex's gaze slid away from the bride and groom and settled

on Krista. Teeth that Lucy had never seen before flashed in his face as he smiled at her. Bright, lusty happiness shone in his face.

That picture was in a garbage can somewhere by now. No—a recycling bin.

She shoved the tissue back between the Peruvian lilies and godetias in her bouquet. Good riddance. She was happy for Krista, or would be if it was what she wanted. If he *completed* her.

Pfft. Nobody was going to complete anybody, that was bullshit. Everyone was alone and needed to accept that. As soon as you started thinking you needed somebody else in order to be a whole person, you put an impossible burden on the relationship. Anchoring it to the ground, preventing either of you from moving forward, growing, living.

Like Fawn. Her best friend. Lucy would miss her, but she had a new life to begin. New York was far, but Fawn had spent many months of each year there since she was seventeen. With the Sterlings and her career, of course she should settle there. Lucy would just have to fly more often. Maybe get a frequent flyer credit card, work the system to accrue lots of points.

Her mind was already making the spreadsheet, tallying the dollars and points and months.

"You are my sunshine," Huntley said with a straight face. In fact, his voice cracked.

Lucy pulled out her tissue again just before they kissed. Unable to help herself, she glanced at Miles.

He was gazing at her, his own eyes shining.

Chapter 25

The reception was in the same courtyard as the wedding, though the white chairs were cleared away and replaced with the spa staffers in white uniforms carrying trays of food and drinks. Shawn had spiced up his outfit with a polka-dot bow tie and a big grin.

Lucy wasn't going to drink, not even a single glass of champagne. She had enough unruly feelings to deal with. Jealousy, loneliness, doubt, sexual frustration—a big, simmering stew of emotions she hadn't felt since seventh grade. Liquor would only weaken her grip on herself.

Because she refused to sink further into a pit of despair. Her best friend was so happy she glowed. Wherever the bride and groom walked, hand in hand, guests stopped talking and gazed at them with dopey smiles on their faces.

The romance in the air was infectious. Fawn's father, Larry, was beaming, stealing kisses from his wife at every opportunity. Geri was there with her new boyfriend, a handsome guy in his forties who looked like George Clooney and danced like Pacino in *Scent of a Woman*. No wonder she was hoarding condoms.

With all that joy around her, Lucy would be happy too. Even if it killed her.

Krista and Alex didn't need any help being cheerful, either. Even during the photographs, they'd stuck together. Both had been eager to have one taken of just the two of them, holding hands under a rose arbor.

The photographer was gone, but they still sat there, talking and smiling into each other's eyes.

Plucking a bottle of Calistoga off the bar, Lucy strode over to clear the air. They were probably going to see a lot of each other over the next... few weeks... forever?... so Lucy had better make it clear there were no hard feelings.

"It sure is beautiful here, isn't it?" she said as she walked up to them.

They both looked up at the same time. Alex frowned only for a split second before smiling back at her. "It certainly is."

"I meant to tell you how lovely you are in pink," Krista said. "I knew you would be."

"I admit I was skeptical," Lucy said, touching her hair. "But I look fine."

Alex stood up. "Better than fine. Lovely, as Krista said." He leaned forward and kissed her cheek quickly. "If you'll excuse me, I need to use the little boy's room. Can I get either of you anything from the bar on my way back?"

They assured him they were fine and he left them there alone.

"Isn't he sensitive? Almost psychic," Krista said, standing up. "I didn't even have to tell him I wanted to talk to you in private."

"I'm glad you're happy."

"You are, aren't you? Which is why I need to apologize. I was such a bitch."

"Oh, you were just—"

"No, I was a bitch. I thought you were starting something

special with Miles and all I could think of was my own emptiness." She folded her lips into her mouth. "I was jealous, Lucy. Green with envy. I am so, so sorry."

"Oh, God, don't cry. Krista, please."

But the tears already trickled down her cheeks. Lucy bent down and put her water bottle on the flagstones before putting her arms around her friend's waist. "You goose. Nothing to cry about."

"And now you're alone and I'm not and I feel so bad," Krista said.

Lucy released her and retrieved her water bottle. "Don't worry about me."

"Miles stared at you through the whole ceremony."

"I know."

"I don't know what happened, but I hope it wasn't my fault. Anything I said."

Lucy sipped her water. "No, just reality crashing in."

"Alex—sorry, I hope you don't mind that we talked about it —he says Miles has *always* run away from his problems."

However shit-canned her life plans were at the moment, at least she hadn't hooked up with that guy. "Alex has *always* been annoying. Hope you don't mind if I talk about it."

Instead of angry, Krista looked stricken. "He didn't mean anything—"

"Sorry. The thing is, Alex doesn't know the whole story. Why Miles cut himself off from his family, why he dropped out of school. He could've put money first and sucked it up with his father, letting him pay for everything, getting a free ride through life—but he chose to be true to himself and make his own way. Helping other kids like himself in the process. He's quite… amazing, actually."

Krista stared at her. "If you feel that way, why aren't you together?"

"He's not the marrying type."

"So you *do* agree with Alex."

Lucy paused. Did she? "About this, maybe. But not in general. I can't risk... What if we... I've done this before, you know? Years of waiting, being put off. Life's too short."

"Lucy, life's too short not to go for it."

"I've got to be practical."

"Fuck practical! Practical got you Dan! This is something different and you know it. You have real feelings for Miles. When's that ever happened to you?"

Unable to resist, Lucy looked over at the handsome giant in his tux. The one who saved her from zip lines and brought her Big Macs. The one who did yoga in jeans and couldn't even bend his knees. The one who kissed her like he'd never get enough.

To her horror, she felt tears pool in her eyes.

Krista squeezed her wrist, stopping Lucy from hiding her face in her water bottle. "You never cried over Dan and you were with him eight years."

"Of course I did. I cried like crazy."

"Really? But you were so casual about it. I never would have thought—so, you were really torn up?"

Uneasy with the sudden, eager look that flashed over Krista's face, Lucy said quickly, "I wasn't crying over Dan exactly. Just..." She trailed off, not wanting to spell out her humiliation. *What if the next guy who wants to marry me is even worse? How badly will I lower my standards just to have a family?*

"The idea of him. I get that. I totally get that." Krista laughed and tipped back a glass of champagne. "As I'm sure you've noticed."

She did. How far would Krista go with Alex just because he was there, convenient, willing?

Suddenly, not having a real drink wasn't going to work. When she spotted Alex returning, Lucy hugged Krista one more time and fled to the bar.

GULPING DOWN HIS THIRD—FOURTH?—GLASS of champagne, Miles sagged against a classical statue of a woman twice his size, trying to catch glimpses of Lucy's feet. The string quartet was gone, replaced by an apparently famous New York DJ and dance area in a tiled corner of the courtyard.

She'd taken off her shoes and was bouncing around with dozens of other guests who apparently didn't mind the bride and groom's taste in Top 40. Her toenails were the same color as her hair.

Her hair was the same color as heaven.

Huntley came over to him. Smiling, anxieties forgotten, the newly married man nodded at the statue. "Good thing that Amazon is there. She's the only thing big enough to hold you up." He held out a plate mounded over with something white on toothpicks.

"They've got it all wrong. Heaven gets the fire. The color. All that"—Miles waved his free hand, bumping the plate Huntley was extending—"passion."

Huntley glanced back and saw the object of Miles's gaze. "Easy, buddy. This is not the time to get stupid."

"Too late." Miles tilted the glass back to his lips before holding it up to his face to confirm its emptiness. "You'd think a billionaire could afford bigger glasses. Nothing but Dixie cups in this joint." He leaned down and propped it between the toes of the statue. Boring gray stone toes.

Huntley leaned over to rescue the glass. "These 'Dixie cups' are crystal imported from Ireland as a wedding gift from my mother's last client. She got six mil in the settlement."

"Figures." Miles moved to kick the glass but was too late. He hit the statue platform instead and had to grab the stone lady's massive knee for balance. "Getting married costs a fortune, but getting divorced gets you one."

"No, that costs even more." Huntley gripped his arm and spoke in his ear. "Careful, Miles. Eye on the prize. As long as you keep playing it cool, you've got nothing to worry about with Little Orphan Ann—shit, what was that for?"

"Don't call her that."

Rubbing his shoulder where Miles had hit him, Huntley stepped back. "No more drinking until Fawn and I are out of here." He looked over his shoulder. "I should leave Eric here to watch out for you, but I need him to get us to the airport."

"You will address Lucy with *respect*."

"Then again, I don't know anybody else here who can take down an elephant with his bare hands." Huntley sipped his own drink and looked him up and down. "Should it come to that. Just what are you so upset about again?"

"I told her how crazy I am about her and she told me bye-bye. Unless I pop the question."

"Christ. Fawn warned you."

Miles pushed away from the statue, straightening himself up to his full height. He swayed a little, but he just needed to take a deep breath, regain his balance, and he'd be able to walk across the short distance between him and Lucy just fine. "She doesn't need marriage. She needs *love*."

"Pound your chest again when you tell her that. Modern chicks dig that."

"No limits. No plans. Just two consenting adults with the guts to take it where it leads."

Huntley's mocking smile fell. He looked over the crowd. "Maybe Fawn can help me rein you in. She's worked too hard on this."

"Don't worry. I'll drag her somewhere private." He grinned. "I've learned my lesson. Get naked right away. Saves time and trouble. No time to waffle. Just eat waffles."

"My God, how much did you drink?"

On the dance floor, Krista and Alex began to kiss like both were headed off to war.

The pain on Lucy's face as she watched them made Miles's heart skip a beat. "I need to tell her again how I feel. This time so she believes me."

"Not the time," Huntley insisted.

"It's the perfect time. Look at her! She's so sad!"

"Look at you! You're so wasted!"

Miles smoothed his hair. "She won't mind. She needs me. I know she does."

"Damn. Fawn!" Huntley looked around wildly. "She's schemed for weeks to pull this off. Don't screw it up on her big day."

"She did pull it off. She's Mrs. Huntley the Third now."

"Not us, *you*. Promise me you'll stay here for five minutes while I go look for her. Just five. Okay? Wedding present to me?"

"This was all her doing. Me. Lucy. You knew that?"

"Where do you think she got the idea?"

"You have uncharted depths." Miles leaned down and wrapped his arms around his old friend. Then, overcome with the moment, he lifted him from the ground and squeezed. "Congratulations on the ball and chain, buddy."

Gasping, Huntley tried to wriggle free. "Fawn!" he cried. "Anybody!"

Unfortunately it was Alex who heard the call for help. Breaking his lip-lock with Krista, he came over with her in tow. He pried Miles's fingers loose. "You're ruining his suit."

Miles put Huntley down and gave him a final whack on the shoulder for good measure. He deserved to be happy, the little rich dude.

"He's about to ruin his life," Huntley said to Alex. "We need to keep him away from Lucy until he sobers up."

Alex and Krista looked at each other for a long moment. "I don't think we can interfere," Alex said finally.

"Hah! See there?" Miles patted Alex on the shoulder. "Finally came around, huh? Good man. First time you've minded your own business since I've met you."

Huntley put a hand on his other arm. "Please. Start an argument with him. Distract him. Just a few minutes until I can find Fawn so she can take over."

Alex stepped back and put an arm around Krista. "I don't feel like arguing with anybody."

"You owe me this, Alex," Huntley said. "The last night of my life as a single man, I wanted a burger and you made me eat seaweed. This is my price."

"I heard the sushi was fantastic," Krista said.

"He can eat there on your wedding night. Right now I need you to stop Miles from scaring the shit out of Lucy," Huntley said.

Miles grinned and patted his chest. "Too late." He turned his attention to Alex and Krista. Handsome couple. Easy to be happy for them, too. He could forgive them for publicly displaying their affection. Though it might make Lucy a little depressed to face the obvious collapse of her theoretical engagement, he'd be right there comforting her. Like, soon. With his body.

That was his mistake yesterday; he should've seduced her first. Wore out her defenses. She was a passionate creature, a woman with needs. He'd exploit every weakness to get through to her.

"I'm sorry, Huntley," Alex said as Miles strode past him. Lucy's bright head had disappeared in the crowd. "I can go look for Fawn if you like."

Miles didn't hear whatever was said after that.

She was only ten feet away. Her back was to him, but there was no mistaking the red curls. Her hourglass shape. The fantastic ass. He recognized a mole on her left shoulder, delightfully exposed by the open neckline of her bridesmaid dress. She'd giggled when he kissed her there that night in the B&B.

The cravings in his heart, inflamed by other more earthy feelings, became a physical ache. He needed to get her alone.

She was dancing with a touchy-feely jerk with big teeth. Miles fisted his hands. You weren't supposed to grope your dance partner during Top 40. Lady Gaga wasn't a fucking waltz.

He put a hand on the other man's shoulder.

"Hey!" The guy flinched under the contact, as if Miles had broken his collarbone.

What a wimp. Miles bit back a smile. "May I cut in?"

The guy frowned. "What?"

"It's not that kind of dance," Lucy said.

He hooked an arm around her waist and swept her up against him. "It is now." Ah, that was better. He ducked his head to smell her hair. So right, so nice. He didn't move his feet. Not everyone was a dancer.

"You're drunk."

"You're beautiful." He ran his hand down her back, savoring her curves. "Lucy."

"That's me," she muttered into his chest.

He nibbled her ear. Licked the pearls along the lobe.

She jerked free, glancing around at the crowd. "How much did you have to drink?"

"Why is everyone so interested in my fluid intake?"

"Gee, I wonder." She gave an apologetic smile to the guy with big teeth before walking away from both of them. With a single glance over her shoulder at Miles that he couldn't read, but set his heart pounding.

She's afraid to admit how much she wants you.

"You look like you need company," a silky voice said in his

ear as a hand slipped under his jacket. "What's the matter, Miles, didn't she want to keep you either?"

Distracted by Lucy, Miles hadn't seen her coming. Her heat-seeking, pointy fingers twisted under his cummerbund like an invasive plant. Even with him swatting at her skinny arms, she just wiggled closer.

"Not now, Heather."

She went up on her toes. "Good point. Too many witnesses. Tonight then?"

She had to be kidding. Or deranged. They were surrounded by all kinds of people she probably knew through her marriage or her shallow, plastic, manipulative life. Holding himself as still as a rock—or as close to it as he could get, given how buzzed he was—Miles let her paw and squeeze him while he did nothing at all.

She just wants the attention. Being with children all day had taught him a lot. Some people just wanted to get a rise out of you. What they hated most was to be ignored.

So he stared off into space and mustered up a yawn while Heather felt him up. Even when her bony pelvis began rubbing up against his hip.

Unfortunately, it didn't work. She kept at it, even moving her hand down to squeeze his ass. "I'm so glad you've stopped fighting it, sweetie," she purred.

She was a bully. A tease. *Somebody should call her bluff.*

He grabbed the hand on his butt and pressed it down on his cock. When she tried to pull away, he mashed his mouth against hers.

She went rigid underneath him, not enjoying his play at all. He released her with a sense of triumph.

But then he saw his father's face across the dance floor. Lips in a flat line, his eyes wide, Alan Girard stared at his wife and son groping each other and didn't move. As still as the archway over his head.

And then turned and walked away.

Lucy saw Miles's father walk past the DJ onto the gravel path that led to the garden. The anguish on his face was clear from the other side of the dance floor.

She went after him. What had Miles been thinking? Pushed too far, apparently. Lucy saw the way Heather had attacked him. Obvious to everyone around that her come-on was unwanted. More a parody than anything.

And yet… Lucy had felt jealous. Even knowing how Miles felt about his stepmother, knowing he would've rather punched the lady than kissed her, she felt jealous.

How can you throw me away?

She ran after Alan Girard, telling herself she had an idea of how he was hurting. If Miles had been off his rocker enough to kiss Heather, God knew what he might say to his father. And at this moment, it would ruin everything between them.

"Mr. Girard!" she called.

He was stepping onto a brick-in-sand path toward a formal herb garden. Rosemary and lavender were clipped into short, overlapping rectangles, punctuated with globes of boxwood every few feet.

He turned around, frowning. Then he seemed to recognize her, because he sighed and ducked his head. "Excuse me. I'm not feeling well. I just need a moment alone."

"Forgive me, but—it wasn't what you think. It was all… for show. Not what it seemed."

He smiled tightly. "Lucy, right?"

She nodded.

"It was exactly what I think," he said.

"No, please. Listen. It means so much to him that you… believe him. He wants you in his life."

He just stared down at her.

It may have been wrong for her to intrude, but she couldn't stand by and do nothing. If anything she said could help Miles reconnect with his dad, she had to try. "Please give him a chance to explain. Don't let—" She stopped herself, not wanting to attack a person's spouse, no matter how loathsome. "Don't let another decade go by without talking to one another."

His eyebrows went up. "You think—ah, of course." He managed a weak smile and put a heavy hand on her shoulder. "I hope Miles appreciates you. Tell him I said that." He started to leave.

"Wait. Please. I think—"

He turned around. Whatever else Lucy was going to say died on her lips as she looked into gray eyes so much like his son's. But these eyes were watery, broken, sad. She was struck by a vision of Miles sinking this low years from now, with an estranged son, a failed marriage.

Never. He should never look like this.

"It would be wrong to give up again," she said finally, softly.

His thick, silvery brows came down over his eyes. "No," he said, rising up to his full height and looking past her, the grief in his eyes morphing into fury. "It would be just right."

Poor Miles. She twirled around, prepared to separate the two men by any means necessary until they'd cooled down. *Pigheaded, stupid men!* Both had shown how long they could carry a grudge.

But it wasn't Miles behind her.

"Would you leave us, Lucy?" Alan said.

"Is she trying to give her boyfriend an alibi?" Heather said, tiptoeing her heels over the brick path. "How cute. Or is she trading up? Think there's a job opening coming up, honey?"

Lucy glanced at Alan. He watched Heather approach, his jaw clenched. Twitching.

He's through with her, Lucy realized. *Not Miles.*

"I need to get back to the reception," Lucy said quietly.

Neither of them watched her go, weaving around the tufts of thyme growing through the cracks underfoot on her way to find Miles.

Chapter 26

$\mathcal{H}$e had to reach his father before Heather did.

Where had he gone? Trying to get through the crowd on the dance floor without hurting anyone took time and grace Miles didn't have at the moment.

Ducking through an archway, he strode down the tiled great room of the half-restored villa. A handful of women lined up near a doorway suggested a bathroom. Other people lounged in a sitting area, laughing and drinking, while the music from outside blared through the open windows.

Not inside. Maybe the garden.

He strode out another door that led to a covered patio, where the cake was set up on an enormous table against the wall. Stone steps led down to the garden out the back.

Just as he passed the cake, Lucy popped into view. She was coming from the garden, jogging as if in a track suit and not a pink silk dress that reached her ankles. She still had flowers in her hair, though they bounced wildly with each step, sliding down over her vivid green eyes.

Damn, she's beautiful, he thought, stopping to stare.

As much as he wanted to talk—touch—be with her, he had to get to his father first. Who knew what Heather was saying?

He ducked his head, prepared to plow past her.

"Miles, stop!" She put both hands on his chest, short of breath, upset. "Don't."

She'd probably seen him with Heather, just as his father had.

Good.

He froze, stunned by the thought. *You idiot. Were you hoping she'd be jealous? Because you kissed your stepmother?*

"I know, I know," he told her, disgusted with himself but pulling away from her. "I'm so sorry. I suck, I really do and all that, but right now I've got to stop Heather from talking to my dad before I can explain."

"No!" She grabbed his arms. As if she had the strength to overpower a man his size. "You have to wait. He understands."

"He thinks he does—"

"I was just there. With him. And Heather." She sucked in a breath. "I think this is it. He's through with her."

Her confidence brought him no comfort. "She won't let him."

"He's really angry this time, Miles. I saw it in his eyes."

"Since when are you an expert on my father?"

Lips flattening, she moved back an inch but kept her grip on his arms. "Give him a chance." She squeezed. "Just a few minutes. They need to hash this out in private."

"He saw what I did—"

"And so did I. You lost your temper. That's all."

He gaped at her. "You freaked out when I wanted to punch Alex, but it's okay if I sexually assault my stepmother?" He pulled free. Of all the times to get drunk and stupid. Major donors to youth charities would be at weddings like this. He could lose everything, pulling stunts like that, no matter the context. Grabbing a woman and forcing himself on her. "If I hadn't looked up and seen my father, who knows how far I would have taken it?"

She snorted. "Obviously, since you were raging with lust, you were just about to pull out your penis and make love to her." She whacked him on the chest. "Give me a break. You kissed her. You pushed her away. Next thing you'd do, my dear, would involve high-tailing it for higher ground."

He studied her. She was laughing. At him. "You're not angry?"

"Of course not."

A weak part of himself suggested it was impossible to make her jealous because she just didn't care that much. "Why not?"

"It was like watching little kids fighting. Some name-calling, a push here, a push there. I was waiting for the hair-pulling to start." She reached up and straightened his tie, a small smile on her face. "Nobody—I mean nobody—could've thought that was a moment between lovers."

"I saw my dad. He was furious."

"With her, Miles. With her."

He wanted to believe her. Slowly, some of the tension drained out of him. He became aware of her closeness. The sweet smell of the flowers in her hair.

What difference could a few minutes make, anyway?

"I was chasing after you when Heather jumped me." He stepped close, sliding his hand behind her neck. "So actually, this is all your fault."

"Nice try." Her mouth was a flat line, but her eyes danced. And she didn't pull away.

<hr>

THIS COULD GET RISKY, *living in the moment*, she thought.

He leaned down and lightly brushed his lips across her

temple. "Did you have any champagne? I'll get you a glass. Two. They're small."

She shook her head. "Maybe later," she said softly. Her body came to life under his touch. Her mind… well, it couldn't remember anything bad about him either.

He lifted her arm, kissing his way down to her wrist. When he got to her watch, a sporty rubberized black thing that clashed with the pastels of her wedding uniform, he looked up at her with a smile. "I'm surprised Fawn let you wear this."

"I shoved it down my bra. Just put it back on. I like to know what time it is."

His smile broadened. "So organized, my Lucy."

He bent his head again. His lips brushed along the pale skin of her inner wrist, arousing a shiver.

"Remember," she began, her heart pounding, "how I said we had until Sunday to be together?"

Without moving his lips away from her skin, he looked up at her. Voice dropping, he responded, "Yes?"

"It's only Saturday," she whispered.

He closed his eyes for a moment as if in prayer. Then stood up and hauled her up into his arms. "I love a girl who knows her days of the week."

She laughed, gasping, wriggling in his arms, all the while hearing the word *love* reverberate in her skull.

Lifted up against his chest, she was able to see over his shoulder. Where the other large Girard man was standing.

"Excuse me," Alan said, turning to go. "I—I'll talk to you later, Miles."

Still holding her in his arms, Miles swung around. His gaze dropped to Lucy's, the conflict ravaging his face.

"Of course you can talk now," she said, shimmying her way down his body to the ground. "I'll just take a little walk."

"Are you kidding?" Miles clasped her hand and wove her fingers through his. "You're not going anywhere."

Alan managed a sad smile. "Good thinking, son." He ran a hand through his gray hair. "This will just take a moment."

"First let me explain—" Miles began.

"No. Enough of that. We both know what she was doing, and I've told her that. I'm sorry."

"No, Dad, don't say that. I never should've—"

Alan stepped forward and gripped his shoulder, anger resurfacing in his eyes. "Enough. There's more to say, but not that, and not now." His gaze moved to Lucy. "Maybe you can cheer him up. I've got a flight to catch."

No, not now. They were so close. "Are you sure you have to leave so soon? I'm sure Miles would love to spend some more time with you," she said. "It's only Saturday."

Miles squeezed her hand.

"Can't," his father said. "But I'll be back." He put both hands on Miles's shoulders, smiling tightly, and then, as if shoved by an invisible hand from behind, he lunged forward and embraced him.

Lucy slipped her hand free and watched the two large men in their tuxedos hug each other quickly but forcefully. Wiping her eyes, she struggled to think of another day she'd cried as much.

Blinking and scowling through tears of his own, Alan stepped back and tugged down his jacket. "Top of the Mark, next Saturday, seven." His eyes darted to Lucy. "Beautiful redheads encouraged to attend."

"You're coming back to San Francisco?" Miles asked hoarsely.

"That's where my son is, isn't it?" Alan said. "Well? Will I see you there?"

"Yes. Sure. Of course."

Then he turned his questioning gray eyebrows on Lucy.

That's the billion-dollar question, isn't it? she thought.

Before she could construct an answer, Alan bent down and

kissed her cheek. "I look forward to it," he said before he strode away.

"Well," Miles said. He reclaimed Lucy's hand in case she had some crazy idea about running away.

She looked up into his face. "That was beautiful."

He touched her cheek. "Were you crying?"

"Anybody would."

No, not anybody, he thought. "Old age has definitely mellowed him out. That right there was more emotion, except for anger, than I've ever seen him show in my entire life." Lifting her hand, wanting the softness of her skin under his fingers, he traced the band of her ugly black watch. "Then again, maybe it was just the champagne."

"I'm sure that was it."

He kissed his way up her inner arm until he got to the tiny silk sleeve of her dress. With one finger, he pulled it down to completely expose her round, lightly freckled shoulder. "Nice try getting rid of me, by the way. As if I'd rather hang out with my old man than you."

A flush rose up her neck, stained her cheeks. She glanced past him. "Everyone will be coming in here any minute to watch them cut the cake." Her voice wobbled.

He cupped her face in his hands and kissed her gently. "I like cake."

"Oh," she sighed.

He felt her shaking. Big green eyes stared into his. He caressed her hot cheeks with his thumbs, savoring their softness. He kissed her again, slipping his tongue into her mouth while his fingers dove into the short, silky waves of her hair.

She pulled back. "Any minute. People. Here. Lots of them."

The cake was about the size of Huntley's Porsche and sat on a rectangular table big enough for a shipload of Vikings. With the tip of his shoe, he lifted up the edge of the tablecloth and felt for empty space underneath. Plenty of room.

He grinned at her.

"No way."

He stroked her cheek, cupped the back of her head, brushed her earlobe with his lips. "Admit it. You want a little fun. Just this once."

"I am not getting under—"

His lips found the sensitive spot under her ear while his right hand slipped under the gaping pink silk of her dress and stroked her nipple until it puckered. "No one will know. Just us."

"You've had an emotional upheaval."

Squatting down, he lifted the tablecloth. "All the more reason to lighten up a little." He slipped a hand under her skirt and caressed her calf. "Or a lot."

He kept his expression playful, but he was shaking. This was the moment, this was the time. Raw, emotional, connected —she might never let him get this close to her again after they went home.

"I can't believe I'm going to do this." She shook her head and dropped to the ground. Her cheeks were pink, her eyes bright and alive. She reached up and caressed his thigh before she disappeared.

With renewed urgency, he crawled in after her and tugged the tablecloth down. Hunched over, his head bent at an angle under the table and his inflexible leg muscles complaining, he had a brief, sobering moment of doubt.

No bed. *Maybe a little planning is a good thing.*

But then Lucy pushed him down until he was flat on his back under her hands, and his doubt vanished. The table was long enough for him to stretch out his legs and gaze adoringly at her.

He ran a hand along her waist, up to the delicious mouthful of her breast. The neckline of the bridesmaid dress was low, and her breasts pushed up high. His fingers slid under the silk and lace and found a taut, tender nipple.

She groaned and pressed her lips against his.

He sucked her tongue into his mouth, continuing his caress. "Admit it. You don't always have to plan everything."

She found his own nipple and pinched it. "How do you know I didn't plan this?"

Choking back pain and laughter, he moved his hands down to lift her skirt. He heard the approving moan in the back of her throat.

Suddenly she pulled away, her body going rigid. "Uh-oh," she said softly.

Then he heard them. Voices nearby, getting louder. The dance music had stopped. And a voice over the speakers was saying something about…

Cake.

"Too late now," she sighed into his ear, then stuck her tongue in.

He shivered. Turned his mouth to capture hers, loving the feel of her on top of him. Solid, womanly, hot, real. The kiss went deeper, less playful.

More and more voices around them.

It was so hot, knowing they were surrounded by people who didn't know they were there. He hadn't thought she'd really get under the table with him. Just teasing. But now that he felt her warm skin under his palms… smelled her scent… heard the little gasps of her breath…

WELL, this wasn't on my list, Lucy thought.

She wriggled against his chest. The tile under her knees was hard, but his body took most of her weight, and being in his arms again was a powerful anesthetic. The flowers in her hair fell around Miles's head, tugged out by his roving hands.

The crowd got louder. Larger. The tablecloth was too thick to let in much light—or air—but at least it promised a certain amount of privacy.

Yeah, right. If anyone heard them and happened to look under the table… what a view. She'd never live it down. Everyone had a camera. Some of these people even owned newspapers. Cable channels.

She smiled. Never in her life did she think she was capable of having this much fun. Miles did this to her. Turned her on. Lit her up. Unlocked her. She might never have the chance to feel like this again.

She wouldn't think about that. And since they were stuck under the table until the last piece of fondant-encrusted dessert was served, they might as well enjoy it.

"What are you wearing?" he whispered, struggling with the control-top chemise under her dress.

She reached down and rolled the tight elastic fabric up over her hips to her waist. "Shhh." Thighs finally free, she spread her legs wider and wiggled against him, her skirts falling back down over them. A little privacy, anyway.

His hands journeyed up her calves, over her knees, up her thighs. He slipped a finger under the waistband of her panties. The way he touched her—confident, familiar—made all the blood pool in her belly. Lower. His fingers were surprisingly agile and quick, gliding under the satin, sliding down between her legs.

There wasn't enough air. The way he was looking at her, hot but tender—

She leaned down, kissed him. His whiskers were rough against her chin. He tasted like fine champagne.

And he was stroking her. "Relax," he whispered against her lips.

Sucking in a breath, she rested her cheek against his chest, all her attention drawn to the hot demands between her legs. Something about how wrong it was, what they were doing, how he was in a tuxedo flat on his back and she was sprawled on top of him with his hand up her dress…

Right under the cake…

With two hundred well-heeled people surrounding them, not knowing they were there…

He rolled her sideways so some of her weight was in the crook of his arm. Kissing her open-mouthed, he pushed her legs wider apart. Gently, quickly, his finger moved in and out, circled her, stroked.

She was going to come faster than she thought physically possible.

Vaguely, she heard people talking, clapping, laughing. Glasses clinking. Plates rattling.

Miles slipped his tongue between her lips. His fingers, down lower, moved faster.

The tension built, spiraling higher. She clung to him. Pressed against his hand. It was too much, too fast. He was pushing her too high.

"Let go, Lucy," he whispered.

She broke. He swallowed her cry with his mouth, eased her back to earth, caressed her gently.

On the other side of the tablecloth, the crowd cheered and clapped.

"To Huntley and Fawn!" a cry went up.

Miles patted her. Wrapped his arms around her and pulled her back on top of him, kissing her.

"To us," he said.

Chapter 27

After several minutes, still dazed, Lucy rubbed her cheek along Miles's jaw. "You can't be very comfortable," she whispered.

"I'm fine." He slipped his hands down her sides, caressed her hip. Shifted his pelvis. "Mostly."

Now that she was coming back to earth, she realized how crazy they were. "They're still out there," she whispered.

"Just the staff. The rest sound like they've moved back to the tables. Chowing down."

She rested her head on his chest and listened. He was right. The hum of the crowd was farther away. "How are we going to get out of here?"

He tangled his fingers in her hair. "What's the hurry?"

She hesitated, not wanting the moment to end. But it had to. "Doesn't the best man give a toast?"

Miles jerked up, dislodging her. "Damn!"

She got her feet underneath her and struggled to get into a squat beside him. Balancing on top of his broad hugeness may have saved her dress from the worst damage, but there was quite a bit of dust and grass on the silk. She brushed it roughly. "Hold on, you can't just crawl out of here."

He gave her a quick kiss. "Got to give that toast. I spent all night writing it. When I wasn't thinking about you."

She kissed him back. He tasted so good.

But he broke away with smile, reaching for the tablecloth.

"Wait! I can't go out there like this," she said, looking down at her dress.

"Stay. I'll be right back."

"I can't stay here. For one, I want some cake."

A hand appeared, lifting the tablecloth higher. "Hello?"

Lucy scrambled back and ducked her head under her hand.

"Shawn! My man!" Miles flashed Lucy a grin. "Don't worry. Shawn's cool."

The tablecloth went higher, and the staffer's furry face appeared. A fresh breeze blew under the table. "Mr. Girard. The groom was wondering if you were ready to speak, or if you need Mr. Sargeant to step in."

"I'll be right there. Tell Alex to chill."

"Yes, sir," he said, nodding as he disappeared. His gaze had never moved from Miles, as though not noticing the tousled woman squatting right next to him with her dress bunched over her knees.

Grinning, Miles goosed her thigh as he reached for the tablecloth.

Then he paused. Slowly looked back at her.

He held her gaze for a few deep breaths. Something in his eyes made her heart, already racing, trip over itself.

The playfulness faded away. No hint of a smile remained. She swallowed over the dryness in her throat as he reached up and cupped her jaw in his palm.

"I love you, Lucy."

She stopped breathing. "Christ," she whispered.

"I want you in my life."

She was shaking. "It's too soon."

At that, he smiled. "I thought you were in a hurry."

Not for that. "But we——"

"Tonight," he said, and left.

FEET SORE, dress rumpled, heart fragile, Lucy waved at Shawn as she opened the door to her cabin.

The golf cart guy raised a hand and drove off, the thick black mustache failing to hide the grin on his face.

Maybe I'm not the first slutty bridesmaid you've found under the cake table, she thought.

She shut the door behind her, leaned against it, closed her eyes.

Miles had given his toast to the bride and groom, hamming up his role as drunk, irresponsible best man. The crowd laughed and cried. Lucy managed to slip into a seat next to Betty at the head table without drawing too much attention.

Though Betty found some grass in her hair. "Nice bling. Have fun?"

Face burning, Lucy forked a huge bite of wedding cake into her mouth. "Is it that obvious?"

"I saw you come out. So to speak."

Oh, God. "Anyone else?"

"Who cares?"

Betty was right. It didn't matter what other people thought.

What Miles thought, however… saying he loved her…

He'd been drinking, turned on, caught up in high emotions of the day.

Well, the day was nearly over now. Fawn and Huntley were off on their honeymoon, happy and hitched and starting their ever after. Krista, a softball star in junior high, caught the bouquet before disappearing with Alex. And Betty took off with Jaynette in her old car to explore the Lost Coast up north for a few days.

Leaving Lucy alone in her cabin. Waiting.

She hung up the dress, a fruitless effort since it was badly wrinkled, frayed on one side, and streaked with dirt. Not that she had a place for such a dress in her normal life anyway.

Running her finger along the scooped neckline, she remembered Miles's touch and shivered.

Too much, too fast.

She peeled off the chemise and everything else and got into the shower. The hot water felt good, washing away makeup and dust, the soreness in her shoulders. But it couldn't touch the fear.

What if he regretted what he'd said?

If only they could go back in time. Meet years ago, when she was still in her twenties, uneasy with the cold bed she shared with Dan. They could have taken their time—

No. Stupid to speculate. She turned off the shower and stepped onto the soft mat. Pausing at the door to confirm the cabin was quiet, she jogged naked out the back door and flipped back the hot tub cover.

Steam billowed up. It was only mid-afternoon, and the sun was still uncovered by fog, but the coastal air was typically chilly.

She sank under the water and sighed.

Why am I smiling?

It was wrong, it was foolish, it was dangerous.

Eyes closed, she let her legs float while the jets pounded her back and she thought about Miles—and smiled.

She loved him too, and not just as a human being.

It should've been impossible.

And it could never last. Right?

The sound of a door slamming made her open her eyes.

"I didn't want to scare you." Miles stood next to the spa. He'd changed out of his tux into jeans and a snug black T-shirt. His brown hair was tousled, his jaw shadowed with the hint of an afternoon beard. Hands in his pockets, he watched her with a sober, slightly anxious expression on his face.

"Too late," she said softly.

The corner of his mouth curled up. "Is it?"

She stretched her arms out beside her along the edge of the spa, nodding. Her breasts bobbed at the surface.

His gaze dropped, along with his smile. "I thought we should talk."

Her stomach clenched. She didn't want to talk. He looked so serious, so worried. "Join me first."

"We should—we really should talk."

The sun sparked amber highlights in his hair, making him seem warm, young, vulnerable.

She floated over onto her stomach and held her hand out over the edge to him. "After."

"Lucy—"

"Whatever happens, I want one more time with you."

His brow wrinkled. "Whatever happens, I want more than one time."

She shrugged. Got her feet under her on the seat and slowly stood up.

His eyes drifted down to her wet, naked body. She ran her hands over her stomach to her breasts and stroked, squeezed, pinched her erect nipples.

His jaw clenched. "You don't play fair."

"Neither do you."

"I swore to myself we'd talk."

She grabbed a handful of T-shirt fabric and pulled him closer. Her other hand worked the lower hem free, slipped around his waist, found warm skin. Making a low growl in his throat, he stepped into her embrace. Emboldened, she lifted up his shirt and stroked the hard, broad muscles of his back, his shoulders. As the shirt went over his head, she rubbed her breasts against his bare chest. "We can talk, too."

"I give up. Come here." He reached down, moving his hands over her ass, and lifted her up to his mouth.

His hard, open kiss ended the conversation.

Chapter 28

---

er hair had dried in a funny tangle over her left cheek. Lightly, careful not to wake her, Miles brushed it aside and studied the little pearls dotting the curve of her earlobe. Her breathing was deep and slow, her mouth slightly parted against his chest. She was smiling.

Would now be a good time?

Sure, now would be great. Since she's asleep, *you dumb-ass.*

"Lucy?"

"Mmmm." The arm over his chest stretched. Pulled him closer.

"It's getting late. You want to go find some dinner?"

She cracked open an eye. "Storing up for winter again?"

"Something like that." He slipped his hand down her naked back, found the comforter, pulled it up over her shoulders. "And I did want to talk. We… what I said…"

His mouth went dry. He swallowed over the lump, licked his lips. *Wrong time. What if she says no? They're in bed together. Naked. Totally awkward.*

Both her eyes were open now. She lifted her head and

smiled. "You already went out on a limb. Let me go first this time."

He exhaled in relief. *You coward.* "Okay."

She ducked her head for a moment. Curls tumbled over her forehead. Then she looked up, her smile gone. "I'd like to see your apartment."

"Oh."

"Isn't that what you want?"

"Well, it wasn't my ultimate goal, no."

"But it means—we could, you know, keep seeing each other."

"Obviously we're going to keep seeing each other."

She pulled up into a sitting position, taking the comforter with her. "Obviously?"

"You think I was going to let you hide in Berkeley and never see me again?"

"So you were committed to stalking me?"

"If necessary."

"Even if I said I didn't want to see you anymore?"

"I'd be like that guy on the news. Hiding in the bushes outside your apartment. Calling you day and night. Visiting you at work."

She turned away, grabbed a water bottle on the bedside table, and drank. "Maybe we should get dressed before we have this conversation."

Suddenly that seemed like a very bad idea. "No, let's talk now."

"I don't like hearing about your detailed plans to stalk me when I'm in bed naked with you."

"It wouldn't have been against your will."

She rolled out of bed and went over to the armoire. "You're probably kidding, but I just can't joke about stuff like that."

The way she pulled on a T-shirt and underwear at light

speed reminded him of the other night at the Peace Yurt. He put his feet on the floor and looked around for his own jeans. Remembering they were outside near the spa, probably wet, he sank back onto the bed. "Come back here. I was just kidding."

She stared at him. "It was all the detail that got me. Like you'd really thought it out."

"Sorry. Believe me, I'm not thinking about anything except how to get you naked again." He stretched out on his side, patted the mattress.

"Sorry to overreact. I just, well, felt like you took the wind out of my sails. After our fight yesterday, I thought you'd be happy I wasn't… you know……"

"Will you sit down?"

She did. And took off her T-shirt too. "Happy?"

He grinned, so happy he almost forgot there was something big he wanted to say. "Actually, maybe you should put that back on," he said, staring at her chest. "Damn, you're pretty."

After a quick kiss on his lips, she flipped onto her side, nestling her bottom into his lap. "There. Now you can't see." She wiggled. "And we're both comfortable."

He held her, desperately trying to stay focused, painfully distracted by the delicious handful in his arms. "When I said stalk—"

"Bad word choice."

"Yes. Agreed. When I said it though, what I meant was *pursue*."

"Much better."

"But even that doesn't quite capture my intent, which—"

"Because 'stalk' is just creepy. Even when I'm totally in love with the guy saying it."

His breath hitched. He stretched up on one elbow and brushed the hair off her face to see her expression better. "Is that what you are?"

"Yes. Go on."

He sank back down, his heart thudding against his ribs. *She said it.* "You've derailed me. Again. Please don't interrupt. What I—"

"Sorry. I won't—"

He put a hand over her mouth.

"Great, first you stalk me, then you get rough," she said through his fingers, her voice muffled.

"What I mean to say was that I'd chase after you until you gave in and married me, though now that you're convinced I'm a pathologically violent, deranged maniac—"

She rolled out of his arms and stared at him. Her face was not suffused with the joy he'd hoped for. In fact, she looked a little pissed.

"More bad word choices?" he asked.

"Please don't joke about getting married. I said we'd keep seeing each other. Let's just leave it at that."

"Well, I'd leave it at that, I really would, except marriage is all I've been thinking about all day."

"That's natural. We've been at a *wedding.*"

He shrugged. "So? It put things in perspective. It showed me how good it could be. How if I had it with anyone, it would be with you."

"*If* you had it?"

"Stop nit-picking my words! I'm proposing here, damn it!"

"Well, don't! I'd just decided you were right and it was best to take it slow!"

They stared at each other, now sitting a couple of feet apart on the bed. Breathing heavily, Lucy spun away from him and grabbed her T-shirt again. This time, Miles also got out of bed to cover up. His armored motorcycle suit would be nice, given how raw his ego felt, but he had to settle for his boxer briefs.

He stood with his back to her, struggling to rally his confidence. She liked having sex with him, obviously; why did he assume she'd want him for anything else? Her thing about marrying Alex always seemed like a smokescreen to him, so why would he be any different?

***

"MILES." She came up behind him, sliding her hands around his waist. He was warm and solid. Real. Too good to risk losing now. "You're a wonderful man."

"Not enough, I guess."

She tried to rotate him, but he was as immovable as Half Dome. Smiling against his skin, she hugged him tighter. "You don't have to propose to me."

"Oh, yes I do."

His belly was warm. She spent a moment enjoying it. "You were right. It's too soon."

"I'm not afraid of commitment. I'm afraid of the opposite."

"I know."

"You've met my father. Who's to say I can do any better than him?"

"I do. You have and you will." She stepped around him and looked up into his face. "But this is exactly why I don't want to rush you into anything."

"You're worse than I am, you know."

"How do you figure?"

"You'd be married by now if you really wanted to be."

She sighed. Rested her cheek against his chest. "I wish that were true."

"You don't think so?"

"It's hard to admit I would've married somebody like Dan instead of waiting for you."

"You did wait for me."

"No, he dumped me. Thank God."

"I don't believe it. He was just a decoy. You stayed with him so you could avoid the real deal. Because you weren't ready."

She gave him a squeeze. "I'm ready. You're not."

"I'm not like you. I don't need Excel to figure out what I want."

"No, just to figure out what I want." Smiling up at him, she pushed him down on the bed. "I'm ready to work through your spreadsheet, by the way. Starting with 'tongue.'"

"Just say you'll marry me. I've already proposed twice and you've turned me down each time." He pulled her into his lap. "I'm not sure I can keep asking."

She put a hand on his cheek. "Tell you what. When I think you're ready, I'll ask *you*."

"How can I be sure you won't string me along for years until I'm too old to make it with someone new?"

"You'll have to trust me."

"It'd be great for a few months, maybe even a couple of years," he continued. "We like each other, we're great in bed, et cetera."

Laughing, she twisted around until she was straddling him. "I can't wait for the et cetera."

"But then I'd start talking about the future and you'd start pointing out all the problems we had together. Why we're not ready to buy a house. Become parents. I'd be a sucker for all these arguments because I'm very practical."

With a push, he was on his back. She flopped on top of him, pinning his hands above his head. "If we're not, we're not. But we'll have each other."

"Next thing you know, I'll be forty and you'll shack up with some young dude who doesn't shoot blanks and I'll have to get a dog—no, fish. For the aquarium. Lots of fish—"

Her mouth shut him up. And her weight on his lungs, knocking the air out of him.

"Since you'll be in Reno," he gasped. "The end."

"I'd follow you anywhere." She kissed her way down his jaw to the pulse in his throat. He smelled good. He felt good. He tasted good.

"Anywhere?"

"Mmm-hmm," she said, trailing kisses on her way back up his neck to his mouth.

He broke free of her grip on his wrists and rolled her onto her back. He kissed her until she was panting for breath. "I don't know." He slid his hand down her stomach. "It sounds kind of stalker-ish to me."

She would've laughed, invited him to breakfast for the next few years, told him she loved him again, but what he did next—

Pushed all of her plans right out of her head.

Author Note

Thank you for reading!

Don't miss the next book—*Diving In*—about a phobia-afflicted teacher who gets over her crush on Miles in the very best way—by having a seriously hot, seriously romantic fling in Hawaii. It's a standalone novel but does have a peek of Miles and Lucy's wedding festivities.

To get an email about new books, sales, and goodies, please sign up at www.gretchengalway.com.

And as always, anyone who leaves an online review has my eternal gratitude!

All the best,
Gretchen Galway

Also by Gretchen Galway

SONOMA WITCHES (Paranormal Mystery)

Dead Witch on a Bridge (Sonoma Witches #1)

Hex at a House Party (Sonoma Witches #2)

A Spell to Die For (Sonoma Witches #3)

OAKLAND HILLS SERIES (Romance)

Love Handles (Oakland Hills #1)

This Time Next Door (Oakland Hills #2)

Not Quite Perfect (Oakland Hills #3)

This Changes Everything (Oakland Hills #4)

Quick Takes (Oakland Hills Stories Boxed Set)

Going For Broke (Oakland Hills #5)

Going Wild (Oakland Hills #6)

Oakland Hills Romantic Comedy Boxed Set (Books 1-3)

RESORT TO LOVE SERIES (Romance)

The Supermodel's Best Friend (Resort to Love #1) - Miles & Lucy

Diving In (Resort to Love #2) - Nicki & Ansel

About the Author

GRETCHEN GALWAY is a *USA Today* bestselling author who writes mystery, fantasy, and romance. Raised in the American Midwest, she now lives in in Sonoma County, California.

Sign up for her newsletter at www.gretchengalway.com and hear about new releases, sales, and goodies.

www.gretchengalway.com